THE INTERN

LAURENT BOULANGER is is the author of the critically acclaimed novel *The Girl From France,* winner of the 2014 Paris Book Festival Award for Best E-book. His 2010 novel *The Research* was made into the feature film *Six Lovers* in 2012, starring Cameron Daddo, Peter Kalos and Maria Fernandez. His crime novel *Better Dead Than Never* was short-listed for the CWAA's Best First Crime Novel and won Bronze at the 2014 eLit Awards. His crime novel *Second Cut* won the 2015 Hollywood Book Festival Award for Best Sequel.

THE INTERN

Other titles by Laurent Boulanger

THE INTERN

Laurent Boulanger

Sniper Books

Lake Ozark Press

Copyright © 2005 Laurent Boulanger

Sniper Books is an imprint of Lake Ozark Press.

Typeset in Garamond

Cover design © 2015 Lake Ozark Press

For Kevin, thank you.

PROLOGUE

Brentwood, Los Angeles: Wednesday, 2.08 a.m.

Senator Trevor Garry woke up in a frenzy.

It was almost dark when he tried to reach for the light switch. The warm blood was choking him. He put one hand to his throat and felt the gash which sprayed the red liquid all over his chest.

Delirious, he gasped for air. He didn't know what was happening. All he knew was something was terribly wrong.

Next to him, he noticed the shape of a man dressed in black. He couldn't make out his face.

The blue moon coming from the bathroom glittered on the twelve-inch stainless steel knife the man was holding.

And then, in a split second, Senator Trevor Garry realized he was being murdered.

In quick flashes, like images from a slide projector played at high speed, he saw the killer standing by his side. The killer watched him die. The Senator blinked quickly as he tried to come to terms with reality. His hands were clammy from the shock of experiencing his own death.

Senator Trevor Garry knew he had little time to live. He hunched his shoulders forward and tried to sit up on the bed.

The killer had slit his throat from ear to ear. The Senator had often wondered what it would be like to die, how it would feel to be butchered in the middle of the night by a blood-thirsty lunatic.

And now he knew.

He tried to reach for his wife Alexandra, but in the darkness, he couldn't see what he was doing. He thought about the S. & W. .38 Chief with the two-inch barrel hiding in the side drawer. He bought it last year in a small gun shop in Santa Monica, just off Wishire Boulevard. Because of his sudden fame, he had felt responsible for his own safety and that of his family. The shopkeeper told him it was the most popular gun bought by the average citizen. He tried to

1

sell Garry a more expensive 9mm on the basis that it was the gun cops preferred. It could get off more shots and was easier to load. But Senator Trevor Garry had no intention of making a living as a shooter, so he settled for the .38.

The blood from the cut in the left jugular continued to run down his chest. The Senator kept one hand to his throat and felt the warm liquid fill his lungs through the windpipe. He coughed convulsively.

Suddenly the room felt cold, as if he were standing naked in the middle of Brentwood Country Club in the early hours of the morning. He realized maybe it was him who was getting cold, not the room.

Trevor Garry tried to scream, but no words came out of his mouth—only the gargling sound of blood causing asphyxia.

He waited for the moment when he was supposed to see his life flash before him.

It never happened.

The Senator took one deep breath and tied in vain to get some oxygen to his brain, but all he took in was his own blood.

He fell back on the bed, his head landing softly on the pillow. In his mind, everything seemed to be happening in slow mention, as if the nightmare would never end.

But it did.

At 2.10 a.m. his heart stopped beating.

CHAPTER 1

Downtown Los Angeles: Same day, 9.08 a.m.

'Sorry, I'm late,' Amanda Ryan said and flicked her blonde fringe behind her ear as she walked into the Globe Network boardroom.

Amanda Ryan had tried to make it on time to this morning's round-up meeting, but the usual Los Angeles bumper-to-bumper traffic on the 110 made it impossible for her to be at the office by nine.

And with the temperature already eighty degrees, it wasn't a pleasant morning. She hated herself for being late. She believed lateness was a sign of weakness, a lack of self-control. Not herself at all. She was determined to show the world she was loyal to her job and the people she worked for. And she knew was being late was not a way to show it. Tomorrow she would set her alarm clock half an hour earlier.

The boardroom of Globe Network was on the ninth floor of a gray building on 1st Street, near The Los Angeles Times Building, half a block away from City Hall. The ceilings were high, and the floor covered in dark wooden panels. The air was filled with cigarette smoke from the five out of ten journalists who never kicked the habit. The boardroom was a designated smoke-free zone, but no-one wanted to impose the rule. The company senior executives happened to be the smokers.

The other twelve journalists, all male, were already seated on the black leather executive chairs, around the dark, polished oak table. Two round plates of fresh cookies lay in the middle of the table untouched. Half-emptied cups of tea and coffee were scattered, at one within the reach of each journalist.

Amanda Ryan glanced at the water urn on the east wall, almost testing the cheap instant coffee. She had become accustomed to the mysterious no-name blend within two weeks. Right now she could have done with a cup. But she knew it was out of the question since she was already ten minutes late.

Steve Thorn, Chief News Producer and Managing Director of Globe Network, looked at her without saying a word. He wore a double chin with a matching Caesar cut. His round green eyes were almost bulging out of their sockets. A third of a cigarette was hanging from the left corner of his mouth and filled the room with a bluish smoke. It had already been six months since Amanda begun working for the company, but she hadn't got used to the way he scrutinized her every morning.

Her hair, the color of winter wheat, was tied in a pony tail. She knew Steve Thorn liked the way she flicked her blond fringe behind her ear every time it fell in front of her face. Her hazel eyes had virtually no black in them, a feature which obviously seemed to intrigue Steve Thorn. She bore a perfect complexion, enhanced by a natural make-over. Amanda knew most men didn't realize how applying a natural looking make-up was more difficult than looking glamorous.

Amanda stood at the door for a few seconds, aware of everyone's stare. Amanda was considered slim in society's term, but not like one of those supermodels in fashion spreads. Three times a week, Amanda toned up with weights. She didn't have time to go to a gym, so she worked-out from home. And it showed. Her stomach was flat, and the rest of her body firm and well-rounded. She could have almost been perfect if it wasn't for the left side of her lip which rose slightly higher than the right one when she smiled. But perfect wasn't what she was after. She was aware than a slight imperfection could give a person character, a personal trade mark.

Almost embarrassed, Amanda noticed Steve Thorn's lustful stare lingered longer than those of the other journalists in the room.

Amanda had learned about Steve Thorn within her first four weeks at Globe Network. An intimate conversation with Steve Thorn's personal assistant, Derrick Rudolph, at Cafe Pinot late one night got the gossip rolling.

She knew Steve Thorn better than he thought she did.

CHAPTER 2

Downtown Los Angeles: five months earlier.

When Derrick had asked Amanda to join him for dinner after work, she didn't object. There was nothing that attracted her to Derrick, but she didn't feel like spending another night at home watching television.

Derrick Rudolph was pleasant looking, but not enough to be described as handsome. He bore a straight nose, cropped gray hair, and an artificial tan that made him look like an Egyptian. He talked fast, like if the world was about to end. But without a trace of an accent, and no speech impairment, he was easy to understand. What stricken Amanda was the fact he always said what was on his mind. He never turned away from a good gossip.

Cafe Pinot was located between Grand and Flower Streets in the gardens of the L.A. Public Library. The restaurant was popular with downtown business people, especially during lunchtime. The menu was Californian/French and moderately priced.

Derrick had had one too many drinks that evening. As a result, his tongue was stuck on fifth gear. Over a tender-mustard crusted roast chicken, he tried to seduce Amanda by confiding in her.

'Steve never got used to how attractive you are,' Derrick said, a broad smile on his face. 'When he interviewed you last month, I knew you would get the job. He didn't care whether you had received good grades for your journalism undergraduate study at UCLA. That's what he tried to make us believe, but I knew it wasn't true. The truth is he wanted to see a beautiful woman around.'

Amanda offered an oblong smile in return, wondering where the conversation was going. She played with her seared peppered tuna, too absorbed by Derrick's loose words to bother eating the fish.

Leaning forward, Derrick continued. 'He told me he employed you because this was the nineties. For years the Equality

Opportunity Board has been harassing him as to why he never employed female journalists. His reason was rather personal. Don't get me wrong. He loves women, but not because of their brains. He comes from the old school of thought where men and women have defined roles. Men in the office. Women in the kitchen. And with his marriage on the rocks, his respect for women is thinning out. He always says women are simple-minded and easy to control. He won't tell a woman to her face, but I know he believes it.'

'And is this how you feel?' Amanda said, wondering if this was Derrick's idea of foreplay.

Derrick leaned back on his chair, fidgeting with his drink. 'Hell, no. I love an intelligent woman. If I didn't, I wouldn't be here with you.' He leaned forward again, swinging his feet back and forth.

'What else do you know about Steve?'

'I hope I'm not being too critical here. Don't get me wrong. Steve is not such a bad guy. He worked hard to get to where he is now. Believe me, he was destined to become a journalist.'

'How's that?'

'Steve was born in New York in the forties. His father owned a mechanical workshop. His mother took care of the accounts. It was a family business. They wanted Steve to become a mechanic, but he knew journalism was his calling. He used to spend hours locked in his room, reading newspapers. He's always been fascinated with the printed word. By the time he turned fifteen, there was nothing else in the world he wanted to do. Journalism was the life he had chosen.'

Amanda smiled. In spite of the differences, she could relate to Steve. Her only goal in life was to become a highly-paid successful journalist.

There was a pause, and then Derrick added, 'I bet you want to talk about something else than Steve.'

'No, no. I'm interested. Do continue.'

'Okay.' Derrick took a sip of his white wine, looking across the panoramic windows. 'Against his parent's wish, Steve enrolled at university to study journalism. The rest is history. After he graduated, he moved to California and began a cadetship with the Los Angeles Times. After his cadetship, he moved to Globe Network. He's been the Chief News Producer for the last fifteen years.'

It's as much as Amanda had learned about Steve Thorn that night.

And that was as much as she wanted to know.

CHAPTER 3

Downtown Los Angeles: Wednesday, 9.10 a.m.

The meeting had already begun.

Amanda wore a cream-colored skirt with matching jacket over a satin blouse, showing even more of her fine curves.

Pouting, Steve Thorn stared without discretion at Amanda's breasts. Amanda had an alluring beauty, and she almost hated herself for it.

This was not the case with Steve Thorn. Although he wore a two-thousand dollar tailored suit, he was no hunk. A large, bald spot took over the top of his cranium. His large suit hung loosely over his overweight body. He wore clothes larger than his size, in a monotone dark color. Amanda knew it was a trick to give an impression of sliminess. Steve Thorn changed from a black suit to a black suit on daily basis. It was always a different brand with a different cut. Just as well, otherwise everyone would have thought he wore the same suit day in, day out.

Amanda didn't like the way Steve looked at her. But because her job as cadet with Globe Network was the first one she had since finishing university, she didn't want to lose it by creating a fuss. Steve Thorn never tried to make a pass at her. He was always polite and never made sexist comments, but he stared at her in a strange way, and knew what he was after.

Amanda Ryan took her seat at the conference table amongst the other Globe Network journalists. She sat between Nathan Collis, a middle-aged, bald sports journalist with yellow sweat patches under his arm pits; and Henry Limar, the overweight, bearded senior video editor at Globe Network.

'Good afternoon,' Steve Thorn finally said and winked at Amanda while licking his upper lip.

Amanda ignored his comment. She removed a yellow legal pad

and 2B pencil from her chocolate brown attaché case.

All eyes were on her for the next thirty seconds. Amanda knew there wasn't one man in the room who didn't entertain the idea of jumping in bed with her.

The air conditioning was turned on too high and caused Amanda's throat to tighten. She wasn't sure if it was because of the temperature, or because she was nervous. Even after six months on the job, she still felt like a stranger. Many times, she tried to let everyone know she was capable of conducting her own research and come up with good stories. But all she was getting was the mundane jobs. Proofreading and following up telephone calls.

Since her childhood in Australia, Amanda Ryan dreamed of becoming a journalist. When she applied for a cadetship with Globe Network, she never thought she would get the job. And when she finally did, she thought all her dreams had come true. The position didn't live up to her expectations. It was boring, and she needed some excitement.

When she got up this morning, she knew her life had to change. She couldn't carry on and pretend to be happy. There was only two things to do. Either quit her job at Globe Network or take a stand and get the respect she craved for from other journalists. But first, she had to be given the opportunity to take on a challenge.

When Amanda first joined the company, Globe Network was the most successful CableNews television station in California. But now the network was in trouble. This morning's meeting was meant to sort things out.

Brian Kempt, a senior executive responsible for digging up news stories, opened the meeting. His lower lip shaking nervously, the thirty-three years old journalist was the most handsome man in the room. He didn't wear a two-thousand dollar suit like Steve Thorn, but his athletic build and chiseled face made him look a million dollars above the rest.

'Good morning, everyone,' Brian Kempt said as he stood erected on his chair. 'Just as we are about to discuss why we keep falling behind CableNews, something else has just turned up,' He picked a yellow manila folder from the conference table. 'Have any of you heard of Senator Trevor Garry's death this morning?'

Derrick Rudolph cleared his throat and read from a printed sheet of paper. 'Senator Trevor Garry and his family were murdered this morning in their home in Brentwood at around 2.00 a.m. As you all know, the elections are only two weeks away. The latest polls showing him favored by sixty-two percent. His death has shocked the public and the political community. If he had won the elections, it would have taken him only eight years in politics to become

Senator of the State of California.'

Amanda knew all that already. She had watched the news this morning on CableNews.

'Can someone explain to me what's going on?' Brian asked, flicking through the content of his manila folder, his lower lip still shaking more from anger than nervousness.

'CableNews got there before us,' Steve Thorn, looking bored.

'Someone rang them just after the Senator got killed,' Amanda said, trying to make her presence felt.

Everyone looked at her. Color rose on her cheeks. Usually, she wouldn't say much during the morning meetings. And when she did speak, it was almost as if she was annoying everyone. Today, she didn't care. She wanted to be part of the team.

Brian Kempt stood from his chair. He made big gestures with his hands. 'Who rang up? I'm working my butt of trying to get—'

'Take it easy,' Steve Thorn interrupted, raising his right hand in the air. 'No one is accusing you of anything. We're only here to talk about the ratings in general.'

'Sure,' Brian said and took his seat back. He opened the yellow manila folder and removed a white typed letter-size paper. He continued while reading from the paper. 'But can someone explain this to me: at 2.50 a.m. CableNews received an anonymous phone call telling them of the murder of Senator Trevor Garry. At 3.01 a.m. LAPD gets a call to tell them about the Senator's death. At 3.25 a.m. the news is released to all other television stations. At 3.30 a.m., before any of the other stations can get a crew down to the Senator's house, CableNews is screening an exclusive footage. In fact, the only exclusive footage. The only footage of the Senator's body before he is whisked away with his wife and kid in an ambulance. Who's been tipping them?'

'My guess is as good as yours,' Steve said and passed one hand over his double chin.

No one else wanted to suggest anything. This was the usual morning war between Brian Kempt and Steve Thorn. Amanda Ryan and the other ten men in the room knew better than to get involved.

'That's just great,' Brian continued. 'We're starting to look like a voluntary community television station. We need to do something.'

Eyes crossed the table.

Brian threw the palm of his hands on the conference table, causing some of the coffees to spill. 'I want to know who's feeding them information, how much they're getting paid and if the whole damn thing is legal in the first place!'

Silence.

Amanda cleared her throat. She hesitated for a few seconds, feeling butterflies in her stomach. 'I know what we can do,' she said, her face red from the neck up.

All eyes turned on her.

Steve Thorn smiled. He stared at her breasts through the white blouse. His stare was patronizing, but she choose to ignore it.

'Why don't we send someone there?' Amanda continued before anyone had the chance to talk her down.

'Someone where?' Brian asked.

'Someone at CableNews. You know, like undercover.'

Brian's eyes met those of Steve.

'Don't talk nonsense,' Steve said, obviously angry Amanda had interrupted the Kempt-Thorn morning debate. 'If we can't get the ratings, then we should get our act together. It's not by sending a spy that the problem is going to be solved.'

'I just thought that maybe—'

'You've only been here six months,' Steve interrupted. 'Is that all you can come up with?'

Amanda wished she hadn't said a thing. The last time someone interrupted the Kempt-Thorn morning debate, he ended up being yelled at and thrown out of the room. Her knees knocking, Amanda was waiting for her turn. Maybe she should have stayed quiet like all the other journalists in the room.

'She might have a point, you know,' Brian said and looked at Steve as if he were considering investing on the stock exchange.

'Oh, come on,' Steve said, 'not you as well? What do you take yourselves for? The FBI?'

'But it's not the first time this has happened,' Brian said. 'They always get the big news before we do. What about the O.J. Simpson case? Do you know how many millions they made out of the O.J. coverage? Thirty million dollars in the first quarter! They're doing something right, and we're not. It wouldn't hurt to send someone to see how they work.'

Steve shook his head. He looked as if he was going to explode.

Amanda felt uncomfortable. God, she wished she could just walk out of the room. Steady yourself, she thought. At least they are fighting over your idea.

'You guys don't have any ethics,' Steve said.

'Screw ethics,' Brian said. 'If we go on like that, there won't be any ethics or broadcasting in six months time.'

Amanda knew Brian was right. Another six months, and Globe Network was finished.

Steve Thorn had been working with Globe Network for twenty-five years. And somehow he didn't seem too concerned the network was going to end on the scrapheap. The way he slouched back in his black leather seat, Globe Network's performance seemed to be the least of his problems.

Amanda couldn't believe his arrogance.

'Why don't we put it to a vote?' Brian suggested. Arguing with Steve Thorn was going to be useless. They would yell at each other for the next two hours. Nothing would be resolved. Brian's idea of a vote seemed like a good idea.

'Look,' Steve said, 'we're not sending anyone to CableNews, and that's final.'

'Is that so?'

'Yes.'

'I think I'm going to look for another job.'

'I can go,' Amanda interrupted.

All eyes turned to her again.

'You can go?' Steve said, knocking his no-name coffee all over the conference table.

'Yes, I can do it. I'm not doing much around here. And the way things are going, Brian is probably right. In a few months we're all going to be out of a job.' Amanda couldn't believe what she had just said. But at the same time, she was glad she had made the first move, even if it meant shaking the male-chauvinistic foundation of Globe Network to the ground.

Steve looked at Brian, obviously hoping Brian would change his mind.

'I'm all for it,' Brian said and smiled across the room.

Steve sighed and walked to the coffee bar to get some paper towel. 'What the hell! do whatever you want,' he said, his back turned.

Amanda was excited.

At last she was going to be do something interesting. She would show Globe Network what an asset she was to the company.

Relentlessly, she would discover CableNews biggest secrets and save Globe Network from bankruptcy.

CHAPTER 4

Globe Network, Downtown L.A.: One week later, 4.32 p.m.

Amanda felt getting an interview at CableNews had been damn easy. She blamed it on her outstanding university results. But still, if she had known it would have been so easy, she would have applied for a job there earlier in her career.

On Monday, Amanda sent her resume to Hugh Gawler, the founder and managing director of CableNews. When she got home from work on Wednesday, there was a message on her answering machine telling her to call back to arrange an interview.

When Amanda called Hugh Gawler's secretary, a job interview was set for Friday, 2.30 p.m.

Thursday afternoon, Amanda packed her belongings at Globe Network. Her spying job at CableNews could take six months or more. She knew she was going to get the job. Nothing was going to stop her now. She had always been good with interviews. And because CableNews had responded promptly, they were obviously interested in her.

Amanda was finishing packing her belongings at the office. Two cardboard boxes full of junk were seated on the floor. That morning, she had dressed casually, a pair of jeans and a white tee-shirt. Moving boxes in office attire wasn't a good idea.

Tired, Amanda looked around one more time and made making sure she hadn't left any of her belongings behind. She sure as hell wasn't going to miss this place. The room was small, the furniture was old and scratched, and her work colleagues did not constitute her ideal of teamwork.

She looked through the tinted bay window and could see a clear blue sky over the Parker Center. It was still warm outside. Maybe she'd go straight home to Santa Monica and lay on the white sand for a while. Later in the evening, she could get a seafood platter from one of the many eateries in the area.

Amanda was lost in her daydreaming when Steve Thorn walked in the room without knocking.

'Can I come in?' Steve said, his armed crossed over his chest. His belly was trying to push its way out of his white shirt. He had two sets of bags under his eyes. He spoke without a hint of a smile, looking as if he was about to conduct some serious business.

'Sure,' Amanda said, swallowing a gulp of air.

As an in-house rule, Steve never came to see his employees. He was a god at Globe Network. If he needed to talk to journalists, he had them called into his office. Although Amanda had only been with the news service for a short time, she had already learned the office politics. And when Steve walked in unannounced, she felt her heart pounding. All those stares he'd been giving her had to mean something. Maybe he was coming to get what he believed belonged to him.

Steve closed the door.

'Is everything all right?' Amanda asked and moved two steps back.

'Look, I'm going to be straight with you,' Steve said and locked his bulging eyes into hers. 'I don't like the idea of you going to spy at CableNews—I think it's a lousy call.'

Amanda snapped, 'Two days ago, you said it was okay.'

'I didn't have a choice. It doesn't mean I like the idea. All I'm asking you is to be careful when you're out there. Don't put your nose into things which are none of your business.'

'It's the reason I'm going there.'

'I know. But I think this is a waste of time. I don't think you're really going to find anything interesting. What were you hoping to find, anyway? You've never done a story in the six months you've been here. How are you going to find out how they work at CableNews if you've never worked?'

Amanda felt uneasy. Steve Thorn was beginning to get on her nerves. Why was he giving her a lecture now, one day before she had her interview? He could have said all that in the open the other day in the conference room.

Filled with anger, but lacking confidence, Amanda coughed nervously. 'I don't know, Mr Thorn. I thought we all agreed on this.'

Steve sighed, as if he was losing patience. Beads of perspiration covered his fat face. He was hiding his hands behind his back. His ankles were locked together. 'Look, Amanda, don't play dumb with me. You're only a woman, so let's stop the charade.' There was a pause, and then he added, 'I don't know who the hell you think you are.'

Amanda didn't understand why he was getting all worked up. Globe Network was his company after all. All she was doing was following orders, helping the company to get its ratings back.

'Did I do something wrong?' Amanda asked.

'Not yet. I'm just warning you to not cause us any more hassles than we are already have. When you start working for CableNews, stay out of trouble.' He reached in his shirt pocket and shook a cigarette out of a pack. He placed the cigarette between his lips and lit it.

Amanda was confused. Her brow furrowed. 'Look, Mr Thorn, I think you're ma—'

'I didn't employ you to think!' Steve yelled, menacing Amanda with his fat index. He removed the cigarette from his mouth, holding it between his thumb and forefinger. 'I don't know why you want to be a journalist, anyway.' He looked at her from head to toe.

She hung her head.

He continued, 'Look at you. You should be modeling or something.'

Amanda was speechless. She couldn't believe the arrogance of Steve Thorn. She felt her temper snapping.

'So, this is what it's all about,' she said.

Steve took one deep breath. 'Yes, this is what it's all about. Women like you think they can just walk into an office, wiggle their bums and get anything they want. Your place is not at the office. I can think of a thousand things you would be better at than flirting with every men in this building.'

Amanda was about to say something, but choose not to instead. Christ, she thought to herself, this is the nineties. She couldn't believe men like Steve still existed. '

You have no right to talk to me like that,' Amanda finally said, her whole body alert.

'You just do what you're told and keep yourself out of trouble. I don't have time for this.' He looked at Amanda's belongings on the desk. 'And why are you packing all your stuff? You haven't got the job yet.'

'I don't know why you're so angry at me,' Amanda said, almost in tears now.

Steve Thorn looked at Amanda one more time. He gave her one of those sleazy stares.

A chill rippled down her back.

She knew he wished he could fuck her.

'Good luck with your assignment,' he said darkly and crossed to the other end of the room. Still angry, he left the office and slammed the door into a thunder.

No longer capable of holding back, Amanda let hot tears roll down her cheeks.

Sonofabitch! What was that all about?

CHAPTER 5

Santa Monica: Thursday, 9.41 p.m.

Amanda sat at her study overlooking Santa Monica Bay.

She lived in a cozy two-bedroom townhouse, just off the Pacific Cost Highway. When she finished her studies the previous year, Amanda took a few days to look around before deciding where she would settle. She fell in love with Santa Monica straight away. The rent was high, but she didn't care.

The coastal town was ripped with an arty atmosphere and wacky residents. Not far from Amanda's home was a long pier where she often walked in the evening to watch the sunset and unwind. On the weekends, she strolled around the hundreds of shops in the pedestrian-only thoroughfare, Third Street Promenade. The only problem was the congested traffic to get to work. But in spite of that, Amanda wouldn't have lived anywhere else in L.A.

She moved in when she began working for Globe Network. Her parents in Australia sent her the money to furnish the place. From the outside, the place looked like a plain wood town-house. But inside, it was filled with imaginative furniture and items. Although the rooms were small, Amanda had made the most of the space.

In the bedroom, the pine-bed-platform was built at cupboard floor level. The mezzanine had been lowered to give enough height for standing. Away from the wall, a flight of stairs created a screen for the bathroom entrance and extra storage space. There was more storage space beside the bed.

Amanda had placed the cardboard boxes from the office on top of one another and stored them not far from the hot water tank, also housed in the storage cupboard. Having the hot water tank in the bedroom cupboard meant the room was always warm, even on odd cold days. People only called the Los Angeles Weather Information to find out when the sun will stop shining.

Only two feet next to the bedroom was a study. Like the bedroom, it was furnished in pine. A large desk sat underneath the bedroom window. The view of the bay was breathtaking. Amanda always found the sight of the ocean peaceful to her soul.

In the middle of the pine desk sat a Notestar NP-925 monochrome notebook. It was five years old but did its job. Attached to the notebook was a Hewlett Packard Deskjet 660C.

Within an arm's length of the desk, a bookshelf was filled with how-to books and popular fiction works by John Grisham, Robin Cook, Patricia D. Cornwell and Sue Grafton. Amanda was an avid reader of fiction, but her heart was in journalism.

When she was in high school, like many teenagers, she dreamed of becoming a writer. But while other students were mesmerized by pop and rock stars, Amanda only had burning passion for the printed page.

Just after she turned sixteen, she sent a short story to a literary magazine. The story came back to her with a short note stating the author should pursue a career in anything but writing. The effect on Amanda had been traumatic. She gave up fiction all together and concentrated on journalism. Maybe one day, after she paid her dues, she would go back to short-story writing.

Life hadn't been harsh to Amanda. She came from a middle-class family where education was encouraged and good manners taught. She never lacked much in her childhood. Her parents always attended to her every wishes. They loved her and supported her in everything she did.

Amanda could have done anything she wanted in life. Getting a scholarship to study journalism at UCLA paved her way. Her dream of becoming a journalist had come true, but she could see better years ahead.

Amanda sat behind the notebook, her thoughts pre-occupied with the next day's interview at CableNews. She was looking forward to it. Globe Network was boring, and she couldn't stand the sight of Steve Thorn any longer. She needed a change. What made her think CableNews was going to be any better? She didn't know, but she knew it would be more interesting than doing what she was doing right now.

The notebook screen stayed blank for a minute or so. Amanda struggled with an opening sentence for an article for Single Life magazine. Freelance articles complemented her income and helped her pay the rent.

Frustrated, Amanda switched off the notebook. She needed to get some sleep for tomorrow's appointment.

Knowing that she wouldn't be able to get to sleep straight away, she decided to take a shower.

While the steaming water cascaded down her twenty-three-year-old, perfectly shaped body, she wondered what was on Steve Thorn's mind the other day. It didn't make sense the way he became angry at her for no reason. Or at least for reasons which she couldn't figure out. Sure, she could see the lust in his eyes, but she was certain there was more to it than that.

Amanda stepped out of the shower and stood in front of the steamy mirror. She didn't turn the fan on in the bathroom. It would make the room too cold. She could barely see her figure in the mirror. Her legs were long and straight. Her breasts were round and identical. Her waist was as tiny as a fourteen-year-old's.

With a brush, Amanda slicked back her long golden hair. She knew she was beautiful, but it hadn't been always that way. When she was young, she grew into an awkward teenager. The beautiful swan syndrome. Other students used to tease her at school about her looks. Amanda used to be tall and skinny. Her ears stuck out from her head, and she wore braces. And although her parents told her she was beautiful, she didn't believe them. Every time she looked in the mirror, she saw the ugly duckling.

One evening her father walked into her room after Amanda had had an argument with a male student. He sat at the edge of the bed, took Amanda's hand in his and said, 'Beauty is found inside the soul. If you want to be beautiful, you have to believe you are. If you don't see yourself as a beautiful person, then no one else will. You must love who you are before you let anyone else love you. Don't try to change the outside. First you must change on the inside, then the outside will follow.'

That night, Amanda never saw physical beauty the same way again. She worked hard to build up her self-confidence. Still, It took her years before she gained the confidence that turned her into a beautiful, self-assured woman. But when someone attacked her, life Steve Thorn had done the previous day, she felt vulnerable like the teenager she once was. She felt like she wasn't worthwhile person. Deep down, she knew these were old feelings re-surfacing. Amanda wasn't going to let people like Steve Thorn destroy the self-confidence she worked so hard to gain. No one was going to make her feel sorry for herself. With determination, she would show them who she really was.

Wrapped in a blue bathrobe, Amanda walked to the kitchen for a glass of filtered water.

The reality of what she was going to do tomorrow began to frighten her.

Spying.

What if she got caught? Could CableNews sue her? Would it be the end of her career? Maybe that was what Steve Thorn had been concerned about. Maybe Steve was scared CableNews took him and the company to court if they caught Amanda spying.

Amanda drank the cold filtered water. She left the glass in the sink and went to bed.

At 1.30 a.m., she was still laying in bed, her eyes open. Suddenly the world seemed like a big and dangerous place. She felt like packing everything and going back home to Australia.

Money wasn't a problem. Her father owned a small chain of clothing shops in Perth, Melbourne and Sydney. Her mother was a self-employed architect working from home. Between the two of them, Amanda would never have to work if she choose to.

Although Amanda's parents had always supported her in everything she did, they never really understood why she choose a career as a journalist. The pay was bad, the hours were long, and now that she was in the USA, they never saw her. After all, she was their only daughter and they longed for her to come back home. Amanda knew that, but she felt it was important to make her own path in life.

With all this confusion turning in her head, Amanda hoped to God everything was going to turn out fine. But deep inside, she knew something was wrong. The whole idea of spying for another company didn't sit well with her. All she wanted was to make her mark at Globe Network. But instead she put into motion a crazy idea. She knew she had reached a point of no-return. It was essential she proved to herself and everyone at Globe Network she was worthy enough to take on an important role. This could prove to be a giant step in her career.

Or the end of it.

But no matter how much she tried to tell herself she was being paranoid, she couldn't shake the fear off. Her instinct told her she was crossing a dangerous path. She knew she was walking a thin line between right and wrong. For a long time she stayed awake, worried sick about what tomorrow would bring.

At 3.27 a.m., she closed her eyes and fell into a deep sleep.

CHAPTER 6

CableNews, Hollywood: Friday, 2.25 p.m.

Hugh Gawler skimmed through Amanda Ryan's resume one more time. She was young, intelligent and single. But what impressed Hugh Gawler was her grades from UCLA and her determination to succeed in journalism. Her application letter explained she was currently employed by Globe Network, but dissatisfied with her position. She was looking for a challenge that matched her talent and eagerness. He knew he wasn't even supposed to get her at an interview stage, but curiosity got the better of him.

His office was on the seventh floor of a cream-colored building, a block away from the famous Capital Record building on Vine St., just around the corner from Sunset Boulevard. Hugh Gawler loved the glamour that came with being in Hollywood. It wasn't an incident he choose the headquarters of CableNews to be located so close to Hollywood's Walk of Fame, Paramount Pictures Studio and the Hollywood Wax Museum.

In post-modern style, the office of the nouveau media giant was sparsely furnished. His work desk was made from two-inch-thick glass with no gimmicks of any kind attached to it.

On the right side of the desk sat a state-of-the-art computer with build-in television, double CD-room, connection to the Internet, modern and voice-activated command system.

One original Picasso took the entire wall facing the desk.

Not far from his desk, on the east wall, a mini-bar filled with an expensive array of alcohol and fruit drinks made his workplace the perfect environment.

On the west wall stood a four-drawer filing cabinet.

When Hugh swirled his brown leather-bound executive chair around, he had an interrupted view of Hollywood's skyline through the panoramic wall window of the office. On that particular day, the sky was clear, and the temperature was a pleasant seventy-six degrees. This was the kind of lifestyle Hugh could have only dreamed about of years ago.

Hugh Gawler always interviewed the people he employed himself. He had founded CableNews, and it was important to him to know was working there. And the best way to know was to conduct the initial interview.

With no family to go home to, Hugh Gawler made CableNews his family. A long-time bachelor, he didn't even have time for a serious relationship. The idea of playing father and husband repulsed him. He had seen many of his work colleagues trapped in the ambush of marriage, frustrated by the lack of freedom, not able to taste all the wonderful women who were still out there. Hugh Gawler knew if he was to marry, he would never make a good husband.

Ironically, Hugh Gawler was irresistible to women. He was unusually handsome with a firm body and a golden smile, one which had often been compared with that of Kirk Douglas. There was something about him which made him likable straight away. His salt-and-pepper hair was cut short, and his straight nose gave him an air of dignity. Twice a week his nails were smartly trimmed by a manicurist. He only wore solid color clothes, giving him a ticket to respect. His wardrobe was filled with designer labels, such as Joseph Abboud, Ralph Lauren and Ermenegildo Zegna. He understood the power of first impressions. At the age of fifty-one, he had to look his best. Hugh Gawler knew how to make his age an asset, not his enemy.

He could have easily been a movie star if all else failed.

But Hugh Gawler was not a patient man. His taste for women was varied and his appetite never satisfied. Relationships lasted only a few weeks, a few months at the most, and then he became bored and unresponsive to his partners. He would begin to look at other women, being turned on by the forbidden, the sin of the flesh.

Hugh Gawler knew himself well. At least, he believed he did. He knew he had a few problems, but he also believed he could make those problems work for him.

Hugh Gawler liked Amanda's letter. Nobody dared to write him an application letter with such openness and self-assurance. That was the kind of people he was looking for in his business. Of course, he knew there was more to why Amanda wanted to work for him than what the letter stated.

As he was scanning Amanda Ryan's resume for the hundredth time, a metallic voice came through the telephone intercom on his desk. 'Mr Gawler, Amanda Ryan has arrived for her 2.30

appointment.'

Hugh Gawler looked at his gold Cartier. The needles said 2.28 p.m. He liked people who were punctual.

So far, so good.

'Send her in,' Hugh Gawler said in a friendly voice.

He closed the Amanda Ryan file and placed it in his OUT tray. Amanda Ryan seemed a good candidate for a cadetship, but he had enough people working for him. And she would be there for the wrong reasons. He couldn't remember when he had decided to see her, but now it was too late. The appointment had been set, and he was a man of integrity. He hated when people canceled appointments, so he avoided canceling his.

Amanda Ryan and he would have a nice talk. He would give her something to drink. Then he would tell her he would get in touch with her if she was needed. There would be no need to lie. The truth was he didn't need someone else right now.

But then, if Amanda Ryan happened to be his kind of woman.

CHAPTER 7

Cable News: 2.30 p.m.

Amanda Ryan walked into the office of Hugh Gawler.

She was wearing a black Alberta Ferretti skirt with matching jacket. Her make-up was light, almost non-existent. Her blond hair was neatly tied into a pony tail. She felt nervous but walked in a straight line with confidence.

Hugh Gawler walked towards Amanda, offering his hand. 'Welcome to CableNews.' He smile broadly. His shoulders were squared, and he stood perfectly erected.

Amanda couldn't help staring at the green eyes of the tanned man standing in front of her. He looked thirty years older than her, but his grin and posture made him irresistible. He wore an expensive black suit, black shoes and a striped yellow tie. He had an arresting and sensitive face. His gray hair made him even sexier. She realized the man was also looking at her with interest, his eyes sparkling like emeralds. She asked herself why in the world this couldn't have been her boss instead of Steve Thorn.

'I've heard so much about you,' Amanda lied, bringing forward one hand from behind her back. 'I'm glad to meet you in person at last.' She returned his handshake with a firm grip.

'The pleasure is all mine. Please take a seat.'

Hugh Gawler moved back behind his desk, always smiling, as if life was nothing more than a joyous experience. There was an aura of power around him. He seemed at peace with himself, but at the same time in possession of a mystical power. It was as if he knew a big secret, and the rest of the world was plunged into darkness.

Speechless, Amanda felt like a sex-craved teenager. Hold on to yourself, she thought. How could a man who could have easily been her grandfather provoked in her such primitive emotions? In the past, she found looks never really mattered. But this man was a match for Venus. Amanda wondered how it was someone so handsome could also be so wealthy. God hadn't divided equally amongst his children.

'I'm happy you could make it,' Hugh Gawler continued. His voice was warm and gentle. When he spoke to Amanda, he locked his green eyes into hers. Even when he said nothing, his lips were slightly parted, indicating some kind of sexual interest. At least, it was what Amanda liked to believe. She wanted to turn her eyes away from him, but felt hypnotized by his presence.

For years she had abhorred men who judged her merely on her looks, and now she was doing the same thing. She could feel her hands going clammy.

'Thank you, Mr Gawler,' Amanda said, taking a seat on the other side of the glass desk. She tried to focus on the situation and disregard her emotions.

'Call me Hugh,' he said. He seemed surprised to hear tension in her voice. Amanda knew he was a man who had dealt with hundreds, maybe even thousands of people in similar situations. She couldn't help feeling helpless, as if she was of no real importance. She felt like apologizing for wasting his time and leave the room.

But then, something strange happened.

Amanda felt electricity passing from her soul to his. A connection had been made. Something which he had never felt with anyone for a very long time. Although she seemed confident and in control, she was on the edge of losing her rationality.

Amanda was embarrassed by her churning emotions. She hoped it wasn't obvious to Hugh Gawler. She smiled back at him, feeling heat on her cheeks. She wondered if he felt the same way about her. Oh, stop it, she thought, he's probably like the same with everyone.

'Can I get you something to drink?' Hugh said, raising one eyebrow.

There was a pause, and then Amanda said, 'No, thank you,'

Get a grip on yourself. This man has every women down on their knees. Why the hell would he be interested in someone like you? I'm not going to let myself be driven by silly emotions. Let's get this over and done with.

'Look, Amanda,' Hugh said, his legs spread under the glass table. 'let's not conduct this like an official interview. I've read your resume, and I know everything about you. I'm impressed. You're the type of person I would love to take on board.'

'I'm flattered. When can I start?'

Hugh laugh gently. 'I like that,' he said, pointing his finger in the air. 'I like a person who knows what she wants from life. I was like the same once. But let's not talk about me. You told me you knew everything about me already.' He raised a finger to his lip. 'Why did you think you were going to work for CableNews?'

Why did you think you were going to work for CableNews? Is the interview over already? He doesn't want me! Where did I go wrong? Why did he bother seeing me?

Amanda knew she was wasting her time. But why all the smile and pretense? Was he only trying to seduce her?

The hell with him!

And then she decided to play his game. She fell back on her seat and relaxed. She didn't want Hugh Gawler to be in control of the situation. If he had already decided not to employ her, then she would have to turn things around to make him change his mind. Surely he must have had something else on his mind. But how could he? He's never met me before.

'Sure, we don't have to conduct this like an interview' Amanda said, infusing her tone with warmth. 'I can adapt to any situation.' She was now almost slouching on the seat as if she was at home watching television. If this man was going to play sexual games with her, she knew she could get the upper hand.

By the look on his face, Hugh Gawler was obviously surprised. He hadn't anticipated Amanda's move.

'Why CableNews?' Hugh repeated, standing from his chair and walking to the bar fridge. 'You know everyone wants to work for me. I receive over five thousand unsolicited job applications a year. What makes you think I want to employ you?' He poured himself a Southern Comfort on ice.

Amanda realized if he was telling the truth, then surely he wouldn't waste time interviewing five thousand people. If she had made it to the interview, it could mean he was considering employing her after all. This whole thing was so confusing. She straightened up. 'I know CableNews is the best. I've seen the ratings. You people know news better than anyone else. I want to be amongst the best. I want to be in your team. I want to work with you, Mr Gawler. I know I belong here.'

Hugh Gawler didn't seemed impressed. Sipping his drink, he walked back to the desk. He probably heard similar speeches a thousand times. God, Amanda felt like such a fool.

'Why didn't you apply for a cadetship with us when you finished university?' he asked flatly.

She hesitated for a few seconds. 'I knew how competitive it was. I didn't think I stood a chance.'

'This certainly doesn't seem to be the way you feel now. And I can deduct you're not happy with Globe Network?'

'Correct.'

'Have you applied to work anywhere else?'

Nervous, Amanda was fidgeting with a button from her jacket. She was getting tired of the probing questions. She knew it was all part of the interview, but she couldn't help feeling Hugh Gawler was playing a game with her. 'If you don't offer me a job with CableNews, I'll go back home to Australia.' Surprising herself, Amanda knew she was telling the truth. She wouldn't want to go back to Globe Network, not after the way Steve Thorn spoke to her when she packed her things.

Hugh Gawler seemed impressed by her answer this time. He nodded approvingly.

There was a pause, and he added, 'Did you know Steve Thorn rang me this morning and asked me not to employ you?' He asked this as if it was a routine question.

Amanda's stomach churned. How dare did Steve Thorn rang Hugh Gawler up and talk behind her back?

'Did he?' Amanda said, baffled.

'And do you know why he didn't want me to employ you?'

Shit! What has he told him? 'I don't have the slightest idea,' Amanda said, visualizing herself running over Steve Thorn with her SUV in the Globe Network car park.

'He told me you were too good. He didn't want to lose you. He said you were an asset to his company.'

Amanda smiled. Hugh Gawler had to be lying. Steve Thorn would have never said such a thing about her. And if he did, it was because he didn't want her to spy for CableNews. He had made it quite clear the day before.

Or maybe Hugh Gawler was trying to seduce her with his sweat talk.

'I'm flattered,' Amanda said. 'I didn't know you knew Steve Thorn.'

'I don't,' Hugh said. 'He rang me up at 8.00 sharp this morning. I heard of his name before. Twenty-five years at CableNews. I checked the opposition before getting into the news business.'

Amanda was confused. If Hugh Gawler asked her for an interview, surely he must have thought he was going to employ her. Or at least consider employing her. And if Steve Thorn did ring to tell him not to employ her, wouldn't it make Hugh Gawler more determined to get take her away from Globe Network? And if it were the case, why all the charade? He couldn't have just said yes or no straight away. Hugh Gawler had really got her mixed-up.

'And what did you tell Steve Thorn?' Amanda asked.

'That is if you're were as good as he said, then I would do myself some great injustice in not meeting you.'

'I don't understand,' Amanda said, straightening on her chair. 'I came to this interview because I thought you were interest in employing me. Why am I really here for?' Amanda sensed something was wrong. There was never any intention of employing here. It hurt her to realize she was only a token in a game between Steve and Hugh. The way Steve Thorn had his eyes all over her, he must have said something to Hugh Gawler about her looks. You've got to check this babe out!

Hugh Gawler sipped his Southern Comfort while looking at Amanda. He smiled. 'You're here because I want you to be here.' There was a heavy pout on his lips.

Amanda blushed. God, he was sexy! For a few seconds, she wondered what it would be like to make love to him. She brushed the thought aside. She was here for the wrong reason. And this man looking at her wanted something more than a conversation. She could see right trough him. The warmth she had felt between them was now making her feel uncomfortable, as if she was losing complete control of the situation. She didn't know if she wanted to run out of the room or tear his clothes off. She found herself caught between a wave of sexual surge and reasoning. She never knew sexual attraction could be so strong. She never believed it. But now she knew it existed.

'You're a very attractive woman, Amanda,' Hugh said, sounding like he meant every word.

'Thank you,' Amanda said. For a few seconds, she just smiled at him, like a young girl who had fallen in love for the fist time. Then she became annoyed. Hugh Gawler was like every other men. She was nothing more than a pretty girl whom he wanted to slip between his sheets. She was also angry at herself for falling so easily in his web.

Amanda stood from her chair. This wasn't going to work out. It was better to put an end to it right now.

'Leaving already?' Hugh asked, his expression souring.

'I thought I had an interview with a television cable station. Obviously I must be in the wrong office. This must be the office of a modeling agency.'

Hugh Gawler laughed. It was a good-spirited laughter. There was no anger or surprise in his laugh. 'Please, take a seat. Don't leave this way. I was going to invite you for an afternoon brunch.'

'Look, Mr Gawler,' Amanda said, her whole body alert, 'you're a really nice person. And I'm very impressed with what you've done with CableNews Corporation. But I came her for a cadetship, not to socialize.'

'Who said anything about socializing? This is strictly business.' Hugh stood from behind his desk. He walked around to where Amanda was standing.

'Is it? You have a strange way of conducting business.'

Amanda was angry. Men were all the same. She wished at times she wasn't so attractive. At least men would give her a chance to show her real worth.

'Look, Amanda, I'm sorry,' Hugh said, looking sincere, both hands on her shoulders. 'I didn't mean to upset you. I was only trying to make you feel at home.'

I bet you were! She moved two steps back.

Hugh continued, 'What are you doing on Monday?'

'Packing my bags for Australia.'

'So, I couldn't interest you in a job with CableNews? How does Monday morning, 7.30 sharp sound?'

Amanda swallowed her saliva. Did he just offer her the job? She took a deep breath. This had to be another one of his games. She glared into his eyes. 'Are you serious?' Amanda asked.

'If you don't mind socializing with your business colleagues.'

'I think I can get used to it.'

Amanda tried to hide her excitement.

She pulled it through.

Monday morning she would become the twenty-second employer at CableNews Corporation, America's leading news network.

CHAPTER 8

CableNews: 2.51 p.m.

When Amanda left the office, Hugh Gawler poured himself another Southern Comfort on ice.

Why did he do it? He wasn't sure. Something different. He hated to admit it, but Amanda Ryan had churned his hormones inside out.

Sipping his drink, Hugh was confused. He didn't want to let another person rule his head, but this was one woman he had to see again. He had no other choice but to employ her. Even if it was just to show Steve Thorn who was the boss.

He sat behind is desk and switched the Amanda Ryan file from the out-tray to the in-tray. She won the little game, but he would have to keep her on a leash.

Spies were not his favorite type of people.

CHAPTER 9

CableNews: Monday, 7.12 a.m.

Amanda Ryan arrived early at the cream-colored CableNews Corporation building. She has set the alarm at 5.30 a.m. to beat the traffic. The temperature was already twenty-two degree Celsius. While traveling on Santa Monica Boulevard, Amanda had her radio switched to KNX, L.A.'s popular news and information station. The announcer said, 'If you're working in an office, sit under the air conditioning today. Better still, take the day off, fill your bathtub with ice and indulge. We're going for a high of forty-two.'

Los Angeles traffic was one of the worse in the world. Bumper to bumper at peak hour.

When Amanda first began working for Globe Network, it took her nearly two hours to get to work. Her home in Santa Monica was less than half an hour away during off-peak. Amanda was angry she had to waste so much time going to and from work everyday. Maybe she was better off staying in Los Angeles during the week and coming home on weekends only. But she never bothered with the idea.

With her new job at CableNews, things would be different. She made sure she got up early enough so as to not get caught in the traffic. There was still a lot of traffic at 7.10 a.m. on Santa Monica Boulevard, but nothing to compare with the 8.30 a.m. havoc.

At the boom gate of the underground car park at CableNews, Amanda gave her name to the security guard. He wore a coffee-colored uniform.

He ticked her name off a list. 'Welcome to CableNews, Ms Ryan,' the blond, blue-eyes security guard said. His face was oval. Although he looked tired, he smile boyishly.

'Thanks, Thomas,' she said, reading from his name tag.

Thomas pressed a button to lift the boom gate

'Do I have to go through this everyday?' Amanda asked.

He shook his head. 'You'll be issued an identification card. You see that box down there?' He pointed to a keypad one meter behind Amanda's car. 'All you'll have to do is insert you ID, punch you PIN number and you're in.'

She waved to the security guard and drove underground.

To Amanda's surprise, most of the parking spaces were already taken. What time do they begin work around her? Five in the morning?   She parked her blue SUV Chevrolet between two BMWs.

After locking the doors of the SUV, Amanda walked towards the elevator at the north end of the car park. She glanced to her left and right. Most cars were new or near-new luxury models. Mercedes Benz, BMW, Volvo and Peugeot. The salaries must be good around here, she thought. She did notice a seventies Ford Falcon hidden between a Mercedes Benz and a concrete slab. She wondered whose it was.

When Amanda arrived in front of the galvanized elevator door, she caught her breath for a few seconds. She swallowed. This is it, she thought, I'm really doing it. Less than a week ago, this whole thing had only been a fantasy of some sort. Now she was at CableNews on a spying mission. The thought made her want to throw up. But she knew she had to be strong. This might just be the most important move in her career. For no reason, she thought about her parents back in Australia. In a flash, she saw her childhood pass by her. It was as if all her life had come to this single moment. She knew she now stood at a crossroad. Everything will change once she steps inside the elevator. For better or worse, she didn't know. She just knew things would change.

Amanda entered the elevator.

She pressed the button for the seventh floor.

The back of the elevator was a full length mirror. From her handbag, Amanda removed a Poppy King mat red lipstick and touched herself up. She choose a dark blue two-piece apparel. Her golden hair was brushed neatly over her shoulders. She couldn't figure out what men saw in her. She couldn't see anything in her reflection but a plain face, with a plain nose and a plain smile.

The inside of the elevator felt stuffy. Her hands were clammy. She wasn't sure if it was because of the lack of oxygen or just her being nervous. The first day at CableNews. She reasoned she had faced harder challenges in life. Then why was it she couldn't remember a single one? As long as everyone else was friendly to her, her task wouldn't be too difficult.

As the elevator reached the third floor, she became acutely aware how no matter how excited she was about her new job, she was only here to spy. And in a way, she was disappointed. She wished she wasn't on a spying mission. Spying seemed like such gross misconduct. For a moment, she wondered what would happen if she forgot everything about Globe Network and carry on as normal. She could always pretend she was really starting a new job at CableNews, that the spying business was just something she made up. Why wouldn't she change her mind? Who was going to stop her? She never signed a spying contract with Globe Network.

The door of the elevator opened.

She pulled her jacket down and stood straight. She blinked rapidly.

Amanda sighed, took her first step on the soft red woven mat and entered her new world.

CHAPTER 10

CableNews: 7.23 a.m.

Hugh Gawler had spent a lonely weekend at home, thinking about Amanda Ryan. He couldn't get himself excited about anything else. Since the young woman had left his office on Friday, she was the only thing he had on his mind. And in a way, it sort of bothered him. He was in the middle of important work at the moment and swore not to get involved with anyone for another few months. But Amanda Ryan had re-opened his sexual appetite. He knew a man of his age and status should have a little more control over his emotions. He also knew the older he became, the more obsessive his passion for young women grew. Why was it that with age his sexual impulses increased? Surely by now, after years of womanizing, he thought he would have settled down. But it wasn't the case. He wondered if other men of his age had the same problem.

When he arrived at the CableNews office that morning, the streets were empty and the sky still dark. Back home in Bel Air, he fell asleep in front of the television. By 3.00 a.m., all he did was toss and turn.

By 4.37 a.m., he was sitting behind the glass desk of his office in Hollywood. His gray hair neatly brushed, he wore a white shirt with a black Valentino suit and red neck wear Anyone would have thought him crazy to start work so early.

But today was special.

Hugh Gawler wanted to be ready for Amanda Ryan. For the last two hours, he has been pondering on how he was going to seduce her. He knew he was extremely handsome, but it could also be a disadvantage. If Amanda felt him to be too confident, maybe she would back away. And he didn't want that. She had to trust him. He had to trust her. It would take time and good planning.

But whatever it would take, Hugh Gawler was willing to make the effort. No women ever said no to him in the past. He knew Amanda would be more of a challenge. His instinct told him although she seemed tamed outside, inside she was a wild one.

He knew about these things.

Women were his specialty.

He had to have Amanda Ryan for himself.

CHAPTER 11

CableNews: 7.55 a.m.

Michael Hall was looking through his diary, planning the forthcoming day.

His office was similar to that of Hugh Gawler, but smaller in size. Unlike Hugh Gawler, Michael enjoyed working in some clutter. There were three beige filling cabinets on the east wall. His wooden desk was drowning in paper work. Michael couldn't tell the difference between his in-tray and out-tray. He just knew where everything was.

On the wall behind his desk, there was a picture of the President. Not that he really admired him, but he thought it looked good. It gave visitors the impression Michael Hall had faith in his country. And if it's what they liked to believe, then Michael Hall was all the more happy.

An entire wall consisted of a huge bay window overlooking Hollywood.

Michael Hall was only twenty-eight years old, but already he was on the board of directors at CableNews Corporation. A pair of gold horn-rimmed glasses sat perfectly on his straight nose, hiding his beautiful gem-polished like green eyes. He wore a blue shirt and a yellow tie with a gold pin halfway down his chest. His thick, black hair was cut short on the sides and brushed neatly at the top of his cranium. The young man was handsome, but never really considered himself to be. He had a strong chin, a long thin nose, and an almost-olive complexion. His parents told him there might be Indian blood in the family. Michael's charm and personality always got him the women he wanted in life. And to date, those were few.

After graduating from UCLA, Michael Hall had been offered a job straight away at CableNews Corporation. Back then, the company had just began to broadcast its news program. No one had ever heard of CableNews. But Michael Hall stayed with the company through the hard times. It paid off. When the ratings of CableNews begin to climb all over the country, Michael Hall was soon appointed on the board of directors. He had dreamed of a fast way to the top, but real life had so far exceeded his expectations.

With his job to keep him busy, he didn't have time for serious relationships.

Every morning, Michael was up at 4.30 and at the office by 5.30. He didn't return home until 6.30 p.m., and sometimes spent the night at the office.

Michael Hall came from a working class family. His father, Tom, worked as a fitter and turner for Gates in Denver, and his mother, Teressa, as textile worker in a garment factory.

Tom and Teressa Hall never saw work as anything more than putting bread on the table. People with good jobs were different. They didn't know what real work was. Working behind a desk as a clerk wasn't really a job. The idea of making a living from something enjoyable never crossed their minds. And when Michael decided to go to university, they thought he was just being silly. The Hall family have always thrived on hard work and keeping their chins up. And it wasn't going to be their son who was going to bring them to shame.

One night Tom Hall took his son aside for a man-to-man talk.

'You see,' Tom said, 'there are two sorts of people in this world. Those who can use their heads, and those who can't. And those who can't have to use their hands. Sometimes son, you have to know your limitations. Because it is better to live simply and have small dreams, then to reach too high and never see the end of the road.'

Michael Hall's decision to go to university had been irrevocably sealed from that day on.

In spite of their different views on life, Tom and Teressa Hall loved their son more than anyone in the world. There had never any bitterness between the two generations, but Michael wished they had been a bit more supportive of his ambitions. He hated himself, however, for judging them when they had lived a harsh life compared to his. And it was probably why he never blamed them for not giving him the support other parents gave their children.

Michael Hall was a self-made man. He carried himself through university on a football scholarship, playing quarter-back. When he landed a job at CableNews, his parents became very proud of him. It was a dream come true. Michael Hall was the first person in his family history to have broken the working-class cycle. And although

Tom Hall had expressed openly in the past his hate for pen-pushers, as long as his son was making good money, it was all right to be one now.

His horned-rim glasses raised to his brows, rubbing the bridge on his nose with his thumb and forefinger, Michael thought about getting a third cup of coffee. He lived on the stuff. If it wasn't for coffee, he would have been asleep most of the time. The pressure of work kept him busy but robbed him of some well-earned sleep.

Two knocks on the door.

Unannounced, Hugh Gawler walked into the office.

Taken by surprise, Michael Hall froze on his chair. It was rare Hugh Gawler came into Michael's office. Usually, Hugh would have him paged to his office.

'Michael,' Hugh Gawler said, broadening his smile 'I'd like to present you to Amanda Ryan. She's our latest recruit.'

Michael stood up from his chair. His lips parted, but no sound came out of his mouth. His jaw dropped when his green eyes locked themselves on Amanda's face.

Amanda Ryan, the Australian!

'Michael!' Amanda said, a look crossing her face.

'Have you two met?' Hugh asked when he saw Michael and Amanda staring at each other like two gold fish.

'Eh...' Michael hesitated, 'at UCLA when I was doing my post-graduate degree.'

'Well, I guess there's no need for a formal introduction,' Hugh Gawler said.

Amanda Ryan and Michael Hall continued to stare at each other.

Hugh looked uncomfortable. 'I give you ten minutes to catch up with the past,' Hugh sighed, as if he was losing patience. He then turned to Amanda. 'Come to my office when you've finished with Michael. I'd like to discuss your salary and bonuses.'

Amanda didn't even look at Hugh. 'Sure,' she said flatly.

Hugh left the room.

Anxious, Amanda froze. Michael knew why. He was the man she had dumped at university for another guy.

Michael had little beads of sweat on his forehead. In all the places in the world. It had to be a miracle. He locked his ankles and swallowed. And they say miracles never happen.

He moved forward. 'Take a seat Amanda,' Michael said. 'It's good to see you. It's been a while, hasn't it?' His tone lacked confidence.

Amanda was more beautiful than he had remembered.

The eyes.

The most beautiful hazel eyes in the world. There was virtually no black in them.

And now that he was standing in front of her, his memory caught up with him. Little flashes of all the times they had spent together were coming all at once in his mind.

He remembered Amanda, all right.

She was the only woman he ever loved.

CHAPTER 12

University of California, Westwood: Four years ago.

Amanda Ryan was excited.

And it wasn't just because she was in another country. Amanda Ryan had been awarded a full-paid scholarship to study journalism at the University of California.

It was the first time she had been overseas since she finished secondary college in Perth, Australia. For years she had dreamed of leaving Australian shores to further her education. She knew studying at UCLA meant a jump-start to her career as a journalist.

Nineteen-year old Amanda was one of the only six hundred and thirteen international students who studied at UCLA that year. The university standard was high, and getting in was rated very difficult in Paterson's handbook for international students.

Amanda loved life on-campus. The UCLA campus buildings were located on over four hundred wooded acres in Westwood Village, east of Santa Monica. The air was fresh, and there was plenty of room to move around. She knew those days were supposed to be the best of her life. And so far, they were.

In the mornings, before class begun, Amanda spent one hour and a half weight training at a gymnasium provided for on-campus residents. Morning exercises always got her fueled for the day. When she skipped weight training, she felt sluggish and tired during the day.

At midday, she usually had lunch with two girlfriends at the Treehouse restaurant. She could have eaten at the Residence Halls' dining room, but she already ate there in the evening. She liked the change of scenery and the variety of food available at the Treehouse.

Amanda Ryan was an on-campus housing resident.

UCLA provided four undergraduate student residence halls, two undergraduate suite complexes, and three residential buildings in Sunset Village.

For reasons she couldn't clearly remember, Amanda had chosen to live in one of the high-rise residence halls in a single-sex floor. She could have chosen to share a floor with male students, but she didn't want the unwarranted attention. Little did she know how with time her decision would become a handicap.

She shared a room with Wendy Diggens, another undergraduate student.

That particular day, Amanda Ryan was having a Chinese chicken salad at the Treehouse restaurant.

The restaurant occupied virtually the entire first level of the Ackerman Union. It consisted of four cafeteria serving sandwiches, entrees, soups, stew, rice, vegetables, pasta, sweets, and a variety of dishes to tempt even the most fussy eaters. The sweet smell of food lashed itself upon anyone who entered the premises.

It was at the Treehouse Amanda met Michael Hall for the first time.

Outside, the sky was clear. The Weather Bureau had predicted warm weather all afternoon with a cool change in the evening.

The Treehouse was buzzing with students and staff members, looking relaxed and cheerful, as if life would go on forever.

Amanda had just finished her Chinese salad. She was sipping an icy-cold 7-Up, chatting with her friends, when Michael approached the table.

'Could you please tell me what the time is?' Michael asked, hiding his hands behind his back.

'Time to get yourself a watch,' said Gyan, one of Amanda's friends. Gyan was attractive, but slightly overweight. She had a grudge against every man she came across. Her attitude had been re-enforced by her foul-mouthed abusing father, and a brother who raped her on her twelfth birthday.

'Come on, guys,' Michael said, shaking his head. He had the most beautiful green eyes. His hair was jet black and neatly clipped behind the ears. He wore stone-washed Levis with a white tee-shirt and a pair of sand-colored Clarks. His body was well-toned and tropically tanned.

Amanda knew how little looks said about a person. She was sick and tired of boys asking her out on dates. They never gave themselves time to find out who she was. Instead they fell in love at first sight.

Aware of how attractive she was, Amanda tried to soften the blow by telling her admirers she was engaged to her long-time boyfriend in Australia.

But it never stopped them from persisting.

Once a young man told her she looked so vulnerable, so naive. What he had meant to say, she realized later, was how Amanda captured a child-like innocence with the sensual awareness of an adult. Although he had meant it to be a compliment, she found his remark offensive and down-right narrow-minded.

'Twelve thirty-seven,' Amanda said, as if cued. She didn't find Michael's opening line very original. If this was part of his flirting routine, he lacked imagination.

But as soon Amanda told Michael the time, he walked straight to Tout De Suite and bought a frozen strawberry yogurt.

Amanda liked his personality immediately. He hadn't intruded longer than necessary, nor had he acted like a love-stricken puppy. She wasn't even sure if he had noticed her.

And in a way she was kind of disappointed.

But somehow she found his indifference even more attractive. A man with a cold heart was interesting. Desirable. Not predictable or pathetic with his compliments and gestures.

And yet, Michael's face expressed warmth and friendliness.

Quickly, Amanda brushed aside the numb-like sensation in her stomach and finished her 7-Up.

Towards the end of the first semester, Amanda Ryan saw Michael Hall outside the College Library. Here again, the numb-like sensation churned her stomach.

Confused, Amanda didn't know why she felt so attracted to the young man. Sure, he was handsome. It was the first thing she noticed about him a few weeks ago. But it didn't explain why she stuttered when she tried to call him.

Michael's carried a stack of books, balanced between his forearms and his chest. All his concentration seemed to be on holding on to the books.

Amanda grabbed him by the elbow, her heart beat quickening.

He nearly dropped his load.

Blushing, Amanda asked him the time, and they both laughed.

'What are you studying?' Amanda asked, her stare locked into his green eyes.

Michael smiled. He seemed perfectly at ease. 'I'm completing a masters in television broadcasting.'

'Very interesting. It's exactly what I want to do. Have you got long to go?'

'I'll be finishing this year,' he said, nearly dropping his pile of books for the second time. 'Hey, do you want to talk somewhere else? I don't have class until later on.'

They decided to go to the Treehouse.

At the Treehouse, Michael talked about his life and his parents. He explained how he came from a working class family and managed to put himself through university against his parents' wish. He didn't speak badly of them, but just stated the facts.

'You've really paved your way,' Amanda said, totally mesmerized by Michael's charm.

'I guess some things were just meant to be. I have a strong belief in destiny. You know, like we're all here for a reason. Things happen for a purpose.'

'Do you hate your parents for not believing in you?'

'Hate? I could never hate my parents. I wish at times they could have been a little more supportive. But hating them, it's not in me. Like many people, they had their own problems and limitations. I understand all that.'

'Their own destiny?'

'They had their own destiny. It's right. Like you and me sitting at this table right now.'

Amanda laughed at his openness. She really liked Michael. Other men were quiet in front of her. They lacked the confidence to express their opinion. But not Michael. She hated the silent type, and Michael was far from being the silent type.

Amanda realized quickly Michael was someone very special. He was a true fighter. A believer in life. Someone who wouldn't just stand there and blame the world for what it was. Someone who had the courage and the faith to chase after his dreams. Michael Hall seemed to share her philosophy of life.

God, she was so happy she had found someone like him.

They laughed and shared jokes together.

'You came all the way from Australia?' Michael asked, obviously captivated by the beautiful nineteen-year old journalism student.

'Perth. It's in the South-West.'

'Is it true there are more yachts per capita in Perth than anywhere else in the world?'

'How did you know?'

'I've read it somewhere.'

Amanda looked into Michael's green eyes, and once again felt the numb-like sensation taking over her.

Is this true love I'm feeling?

Every Thursday afternoon, Amanda saw Michael at the

Treehouse. she never told him how she felt towards him. It was the first time she was so attracted to someone. And although Amanda had always been in control of her emotions, what she felt for Michael seemed to be taking over her.

During the week, Amanda tried so hard not to think about him. But as Thursday got closer, she couldn't concentrate on her studies. At night she stayed eyes open wide, staring at the white ceiling of her room. What if she was wrong about Michael? What if this wasn't really love? She didn't have the answers, but soon she knew she would have to express her feelings openly.

CHAPTER 13

University of California: Two weeks later.

Michael had never felt so in love. He found it hard to be interested in his thesis. Amanda was on his mind all the time. How was he going to find the courage to tell her the way he felt? Couldn't she see it in his eyes? But he knew he had to be patient. If he moved too fast, he might lose her forever. When he was a teenager, he made that mistake too often. Revealing his true self too early made him lose girls who would have otherwise gone out with him.

Michael craved to love and to be loved. In spite of his good looks, Michael felt lacking confidence when it came to courting. He couldn't cope with rejection. The fear of not been wanted paralyzed him.

Destroyed him.

During his final high school year, he managed to go steady with a girl named Joseane for three months. And then she dumped him. It took him nearly two years to recover. During those two years, he became introverted, spending all his time studying. Morbid thoughts came to his mind. He pondered for a while on how he would take revenge on Joseane. He was so angry with everyone. He swore to never go out with another girl again.

But with the years, he changed his mind.

There would be no rush with Amanda Ryan.

He would wait for the perfect time. He didn't want to frighten her.

He knew he could love this woman forever.

CHAPTER 14

One months later.

Three months before final examination week in March, Amanda met Michael for a 7-Up at the Treehouse. It was another hot day in California.

'I'm having problems with Writer & the Law,' Amanda said, sipping her lemonade. 'It's such a hard subject. Actually, the subject is not too bad, but the lecturer is a real pain.'

'Dr Schulman?' Michael asked, his eyes expressing genuine concern.

'Was he one of your lecturers?'

'In first year journalism. He's a hard marker.'

'Do you think you could come to my room tonight and help me with my studies?'

Michael blushed.

Amanda was tired of waiting. She never said anything to Michael about how she felt. She thought she was being obvious. But it seemed Michael only wanted to be friends. He never touched her. Never said anything which showed he was attracted to her.

'Sure,' Michael said. 'I'm be glad to help.'

'Thanks.' Amanda kissed him on the cheek. 'You're a sweetheart.'

Michael looked as if he was going to fall from his chair.

'Are you all right?' Amanda asked, infusing her tone with concern.

'Sure, just the hormones working overtime.'

One hand to his mouth, Michael seemed to realize what he had just said.

Amanda looked at him and laughed.

Still trying to catch his breath, Michael laughed with her.

That same evening, Michael slipped into Amanda's room on the single-sex floor of the high-rise residence hall. If he got caught, he would become subject to the On Campus Student Conduct Procedures and the UCLA Student Conduct Code of Procedures. At the worse, this would mean expulsion from the university.

Amanda was aware of the risk Michael was taking. She wondered why he hadn't suggested to meet in one of the study rooms of the residence hall. When she asked him to help her with her study in her room, he didn't even hesitate. Maybe he had something else in mind.

When Michael came in the room, Amanda pretended to be reading. Her thoughts had been preoccupied with Michael all evening. She tried to study, but she found herself reading the same page over and over.

'Come in,' she whispered, closing the door behind him. 'We don't want to attract any attention.'

The room was small with just enough space for two desks and two single bunks. Unlike other students' rooms, the walls were bare. There was no indication of pop or movie star worshiping A small window was half-open. A breeze from the coast brought in the smell of the ocean.

Amanda shared the room with Wendy Diggens, a philosophy major undergraduate.

Earlier that evening, in the dining room of the residence hall, Amanda told Wendy she would have a boy coming over. At first Wendy opposed the idea, insisting it was too risky and against regulations. Later on, she agreed stay away for the evening with the condition Amanda would return the favor one day.

Dressed in a blue flannel checkered shirt and a new pair of Red Tab Levis 501, Michael blinked rapidly. He looked around the room. 'Isn't your roommate going to say anything?' he asked as if he expected Wendy to jump out from somewhere at any moment.

'She's out for the night. I told her I had someone coming over.'

'Oh,' Michael said, a slight tension in his voice.

Amanda had been looking forward to be alone with him. She hoped he would finally make a move. Or say something. Or tell her he needed her as much as she needed him.

But Michael sat at the desk and said, 'So, what do you need help on?'

CHAPTER 15

Two hours later.

Michael found it hard to concentrate on tutoring Amanda. He wanted so much to hold her in his arms and tell her how he felt. But he was also scared of losing her friendship. What if she didn't want the same from him? All he could think about was whether the moment was right to make a move.

Hours went by.

Michael didn't find the courage to express his love for Amanda.

CHAPTER 16

Forty-seven minutes later.

Everything happened unexpectedly.

Amanda grew tired. And yet she wanted Michael to stay. She felt so at ease with him. It was as if he had always been a part of her.

Michael moved closer to Amanda, trying to explain copyright laws.

Amanda moved forward. She didn't think. It was instinct. She knew it was the right thing to do.

Michael opened his mouth, but no words came out. Amanda's lips crushed into his. She felt the warmth of his kiss. His kiss tasted sweet and erotic.

Michael trembled.

Amanda felt the tension in him. He's so sensitive.

The young couple began to undress each other.

Amanda covered his face with kisses and played with his thick black hair. She felt his warm hands on her breasts. She pushed herself forward.

Her nipples hardened.

She wanted to give all of herself to Michael. Her body, her mind, her soul.

'Make love to me,' she whispered in his ear.

Michael unbuttoned Amanda's dress. She felt his hand running down the back of her thighs. A warm sensation engulfed her mind. Her head was floating in clouds.

Amanda pressed her cheek against Michael's chest. She never realized how much she needed a man until now. She stood up from her chair, looked into his eyes and took him by the hand. She looked at the bed. He acknowledged with a blink.

They made love on Amanda's narrow bed.

When Michael exploded inside her, she began to cry. It was the first time she had experienced something so beautiful.

The melting of two bodies into one.

The grafting of two souls.

Amanda gasped for air and she peaked to a mind-shattering orgasm.

When she lost her virginity that night, she lost part of herself.

But she also found the woman in her.

While Michael held her in his arms during the night, Amanda was sleepless. Never before had she felt so fulfilled, so happy. It was something different. A happiness she had only fantasized about.

Amanda felt Michael's breath at the back of her neck. She wondered what tomorrow would bring. Will he still love me? Will he think I'm cheap because we made love so suddenly?

The only love Amanda had known was that of her parents. She knew they would never stop loving her. But with Michael, she didn't know if it would last. Could she cope with rejection? The thought frightened her. She had never felt so vulnerable and so secured at the same time. The knowledge of having to depend on someone other than herself was frightening.

As she closed her eyes and felt the warmth of Michael's body, she didn't realize all these mixed feelings meant one thing. She had fallen deeply in love.

As the weeks went by, Amanda saw Michael everyday. At university, they became one item. Other students were no longer referring them by their individual names, but as Michael & Amanda.

The Thursday meetings at the Treehouse turned into daily meetings.

Eventually, both Michael and Amanda began to neglect their studies. The boredom of sitting for hours at lectures couldn't compete with the romantic days they enjoyed together.

They spent long mornings strolling in Hollywood.

Michael took Amanda to the Walk of Fame, the Max Factor and Frederick's of Hollywood museums, and the Chinese Theater. For lunch they tried the various eateries in West Hollywood. And if the rest of the day was too nice to go back to UCLA, they spent it hand in hand in Santa Monica or strolling along Venice's Ocean Front Walk.

On the weekends, they often booked a motel along the coast line. Sneaking into the university residence hall was too dangerous.

Michael had to leave early in the morning without getting caught. Amanda's roommate, Wendy, had to be away for the night. And Amanda didn't want to abuse Wendy's generosity.

The two young people were engulfed in the intensity of the relationship. They couldn't see immediately the impact it had on their studies.

It took two months before Amanda realized she was in trouble. She barely scrapped through her International Relations essay. With low marks she would never get a cadetship as a journalist.

Then she feared the worse

Alone in her room, she stared blankly at the wall. Wendy was out for the evening. Michael had to do some research for his thesis.

Amanda thought about what her parents would say when she would go back home to Australia? Sure, they would be understanding. They always were. But deep inside, Amanda knew they would be disappointed. Amanda couldn't afford to be a failure. All her life she had succeeded, always ranked top of her class, always got what she wanted. And now she wasn't going to see all go to waste because of her emotions.

But she loved Michael so much. And for a few days, she became disorientated, not knowing what to do. She didn't want to lose Michael, but she was desperate to get her degree. She knew things had to change. Either she would have to stop studying or slow down her relationship with Michael. Dropping out of her course wasn't really a choice. It wasn't even something she wanted to consider.

That same night, she made up her mind.

Michael had to know.

CHAPTER 17

One months later.

Michael was with Amanda, upstairs in her room at the residence hall, sitting on her bed, looking into each other's eyes.

The window of the bedroom was half open, letting in some fresh air and the smell of seaweed.

Michael was restless but happy. He didn't expect Amanda's roommate, Wendy, to be back until after 11.00 p.m. The clock next to Amanda's bed said 8.32 p.m.

The young couple had spent the day together, visiting downtown L.A. They strolled down Olivra Street and had lunch in Chinatown. The temperature had been in the high seventies, giving them no desire to go to UCLA.

'We have to slow down,' Amanda said, turning to face the wall.

Surprised, Michael gulped air. He had heard that sentence before. The last time a girl said that to him was two weeks before he got dumped. He knew what was going to happen.

Yes, I know, you just want to be friends.

Or we'll see in three months time.

Or I'll call you when I'm ready to continue this relationship. And that would be the end of it.

If Amanda had been another girl, Michael wouldn't have minded so much. But Amanda wasn't just another girl. She was the only woman he had truly loved. And he knew if everything turned sour, with the passing of time, he would probably forget about Amanda. But right now, it didn't feel that way.

With Amanda around, Michael found his place in the world. He didn't have to prove anything to anyone. He knew Amanda loved him for who he was, not who he could be.

He wasn't going to let go of her.

'Don't you love me any more?' he asked skeptically.

She turned back to him, tears in her eyes. 'Of course I love you. But look at us. We're barely scraping through her work. What about you? This is your last year. You can't afford neglect your thesis.'

He knew she was right.

But he was in love.

Nothing mattered but Amanda. He told himself the only reason why he ended up studying was because fate had set him up with Amanda.

'I know,' Michael said, wiping the tears from her face. 'But we don't have to be apart. I'm sure we can work something out.'

Amanda took his hand and looked into his eyes. 'I never said anything about being apart. I don't want to lose you. We'll have to stop seeing each other during weekdays. And if we see each other on weekends, we have to make sure we do our homework.'

There was little point in arguing with Amanda. She made perfect sense. At least she hadn't dumped him. But spending the whole week by himself and only seeing her on the weekends seemed impossible.

'We'll do whatever you think is right,' Michael said, pressing his lips against hers.

Michael had a hard time getting back into his thesis. All he thought about was Amanda. A whole week without her was too long. The fire inside him burned all night, keeping him awake. He longed for Amanda's body and soul. He longed for someone to hold him at night and tell him she loved him.

At times he wished he could go back home to Denver. But Denver wasn't filled with love. And it was far away. There was only one person who really cared about him.

He couldn't let Amanda go, not for anything in the world.

At night, he was sleepless. During the day, he dozed off at lectures. This arrangement with Amanda was no good. There was no way Michael would be able to maintain this lifestyle for the rest of the academic year. He knew it was only a matter of time before he would have to break the agreement he had with Amanda.

Weekends only.

It was like having a part-time girlfriend.

The hell with it!

On Thursday evening, Michael cracked up. He bought a dozen red roses and went straight to the residence hall where Amanda was staying.

As Michael climbed the stairs one at the time, he felt perspiration running down his back. He had never been so scared. And at the same time so happy. What was this girl doing to him? Why couldn't he think, eat or sleep normally any more? Is this what love was all about? Michael wasn't sure.

All he knew was how he wanted to see her every hour of every day.

CHAPTER 18

Amanda was in her room, working on a second submission of her international relations essay.

A knock on the door.

At first she was glad to see Michael. She missed him so much. The smell of his hair. The hardness of his body. She hugged and kissed him all over the face. God, she missed him.

'The flowers are so beautiful,' she said, arranging them in a cheap glass vase she bought at the student market.

They made love on Amanda's narrow steel bed. It was just like the first time.

Amanda cried as Michael entered her. She trembled from head to toe, wondering how she could have waited so long for Michael to make love to her again.

But as their lovemaking began to unwind, Amanda regained her commonsense. She realized she had let her feelings take over her reasoning once more. She had been determined not to let it happen again.

Amanda was confused. Why did it feel so good to be with Michael, and yet so wrong? She loved him and wanted to spend more time with him, but she knew this would mean sacrificing her goals. Everyone always spoke about the power of love, but no one ever told her love could drive you crazy.

Amanda sensed Michael knew something was wrong. Usually when they finished making love, Amanda would hold him in her arms, whispering sweet words in his ear. But this time, she lay on her back and stared at the ceiling, keeping whatever was troubling her bottled up inside.

'Did I do something wrong?' Michael whispered to her

intimately.

'No,' Amanda said, avoiding eye contact.

'Do you want me to go?'

She puzzled over his question for a few seconds. As much as she wanted Michael to stay, she knew it would be the wrong thing to do. Slowly, she turned her eyes away from the ceiling. There was no point hiding her feelings any longer. Michael had to know how she felt. After all, wasn't a relationship about sharing everything with another person? And didn't that mean the bad as well as the good? If Michael really loved her, he would understand.

'I love you, Michael,' she muttered softly. Holding his hand in hers, Amanda locked her eyes in his. 'You know I do. But we made a deal.'

'It was only for one night.'

'I know. And tomorrow will be another exception.'

'But I missed you. It's hard to be without you.'

'I missed you too. We have to be strong. My work is important to me. I can't afford to fall behind my studies. I've still got a lot of work to catch up with.'

He greeted her response with a cold stare, shaking his head back and forth.

'All right,' he said, his voice disembodied. 'I'm sorry I came over. I should have kept to our agreement. I'll wait the weekends.'

When Michael left the room, Amanda cried. She loved him so much. But what choice did she have?

Torn apart between her love for Michael and the desire to succeed, Amanda's mind was filled with confusion.

And she hated herself for it.

CHAPTER 19

Same day: 9.15 p.m.

Michael went to the Treehouse.

He sat by himself, digging a plastic spoon in a frozen strawberry yogurt. He felt a knot in his stomach. *Am I less important than her homework?* He knew he wasn't being reasonable, but he felt trapped. *Why does life have to be so complicated? Always having to compromise one thing for another.*

Scrapping the frozen yogurt from the bottom of the cup, Michael sighted. He was tired of having to make choices. He hated how study had come in the way of their relationship.

But deep down he knew Amanda was right. Study was important, to her anyway.

Her maturity astounded him. Where did she find the strength to fight her emotions? How could she be so strong?

Michael always thought women were weaker than men. He had always been made to believe women were emotionally driven. Men were the stronger sex.

But now he knew he was wrong.

That same night, Michael knew he couldn't wait for the weekend to see Amanda.

He was in love.

And love was impatient.

His love for Amanda was stronger than anything he had ever experienced. No longer had he the desire to become successful at his studies.

Amanda was everything.

CHAPTER 20

Two weeks later.

When Amanda found out Michael failed one of his broadcasting assignments, she was furious. She knew the way the relationship was going, Michael would never get his Masters. She felt guilty because she believed she was the reason for his failure.

One evening Amanda confronted Michael in her room.

'See,' Amanda said, a tad shot of breath. 'I told you it was going to affect our studies!'

'I don't care about my study,' Michael said. 'I only care about you.'

'I care about you too,' she said, feeling her temper snapping. 'But I don't want to go out with a loser.'

For a few seconds, Michael remained speechless . He frowned and said, 'I don't understand you. I thought you loved me for who I was, not for what I did.'

Before Amanda had time to answer, Michael left the room, slamming the door behind him.

A faint nausea rippled through her.

Amanda made herself sick all night. This love affair was all wrong. As much as she loved Michael, she couldn't bare seeing him being defeated by their relationship.

What she had admired about him was gone. He was no longer enthusiastic about his work. He didn't care about anything but her. And even the topic of his conversations became one-dimensional. All he ever talked about was how much he loved her.

Amanda knew things had to change. She had to do something before they ended up destroying each other. She cried for hours, wondering what she was suppose to do.

And then, between two and three in the morning, she came up

with an idea. At first she tossed it aside, but then she thought about it some more. The plan she had conceived in her mind seemed so cruel. But it was the only idea she could come up with.

Michael was going to suffer.

But if it meant he would get back into his studies, then it was worth a try.

CHAPTER 21

The next day: 11.43 a.m.

When Michael first saw Amanda at the Treehouse with Curt Housman, he thought they were just having a chat. After all, Curt Housman was always chatting up girls. But as Michael got closer to the table, he saw them holding hands.

Curt Housman was the university playboy, always strolling around the campus with a new girlfriend. His blond hair was brushed into a flattop, and he wore a white Armani tee-shirt with a pair of black pants. His strong jawline gave him a wholesome American look.

Michael knew Curt Housman had a high opinion of himself. From the variety of girls he went out with, so did half of the university. Curt Housman wasn't the type of person Michael wanted to see around Amanda.

His shoulders hunched, Michael thought he was going to lose his temper. But somehow he appeared calm. 'So, who's the new friend?' he asked, his eyes locked into Amanda's.

Curt Housman looked at Amanda and then at Michael.

Amanda introduced them to each other. 'Why don't you join us for a drink?' Amanda asked, almost quivering with excitement. She picked up her 7-Up as if nothing unusual was happening.

'Yeah, man, join us for a drink,' Curt said, sucking on his ice-cream stick.

'I've got too much homework,' Michael snapped. He glared at Amanda and walked out the restaurant.

He began walking towards the Lot 6 parking. Suddenly he changed his mind. He turned around and went straight to the men's gym, opposite the Plaza Building.

He needed to diffuse his anger.

CHAPTER 22

Same day: 11.55 a.m.

As soon as Michael left the Treehouse, Amanda broke into tears. Hurting Michael was the last thing in the world she wanted to do. But if it was going to get him back into his studies, then it she had done the right thing. She knew what she had done was irreversible. Michael might never come back to her.

But this was a chance she had to take.

'What's the matter,' Curt Housman asked.

'Nothing,' she said, her heart thundering.

She needed some space, and Michael never understood why. Because he was so madly in love with her, she knew reasoning wouldn't have worked. She tried before and got nowhere.

When she woke up that same morning, she knew she would go ahead with the plan. She knew it was wrong to use Curt Housman, but then he used everyone for his own gratification. Now she was wondering if she'd been to harsh on Micheal.

She loved him too much to see him destroy himself.

CHAPTER 23

Los Angeles: Two days later.

Michael bought a Beretta Cougar .32 auto from a loan shark in Downtown Los Angeles.

Michael hated guns. He swore he would never own one.

But things were different now.

The heartache.

Sonofabitch got my girlfriend! Bloody user. Can't she see she's been used? Morons! The world is just filled with morons.

The only woman he really loved.

One evening, alone in his room, he held the gun in his hand, wondering what it would be like to kill someone. He loved the way the piece felt in the palm of his hand. It made him feel powerful In control. Capable of shaping his own destiny.

What would it be like to kill Curt Housman?

He aimed at the bedroom window.

Bang! Bang!

He tried to imagine what the gun would sound like if he pressed the trigger.

Filled with rage, he threw the gun in the drawer.

He couldn't do it.

CHAPTER 24

Los Angeles: The same day.

Amanda broke up with Curt Housman two days after she last saw Michael at the Treehouse.

Amanda knew Curt Housman didn't care. He was a womanizer. Everyone at university knew it. It had been easy for Amanda to set herself up with him.

But now, Amanda wasn't sure if she had done the right thing. Instead of finding her studies easier, she found them harder. And Michael wasn't there to help her any more.

At night, she stayed awake in bed, wondering if love struck only once in a lifetime. If it did, then she already had her turn. She tried to brush thoughts of Michael aside, but deep in her heart, she knew was fooling herself.

She became more recluse as the academic year came to an end. Her first year at UCLA hadn't been perfect *Keep your chin up.*

The past was gone.

There was no need to hang on to it.

During the next two years, Amanda worked hard. She was determined never to fall in love again. Her first year at university had almost destroyed her. She avoided having too many friends, male friends especially. All she had to do was keeping herself busy with studies. She spent her weekends locked in her room, devouring literary works from Homer to Robert Burns to John Cheever.

As her fourth year at UCLA ended, Amanda regained her confidence. All those hours she had spent in her room during studying helped her to get top grades. She was ranked best student at her year level. She was determined to get a cadetship as a journalist.

When Amanda finally graduated from UCLA she knew what she

wanted to do for the rest of her life. She had always known. The desire to become a successful journalist was still there. She believed how after four years of study, the passion might have died. But it never left her. She would get everything she always wanted.

One day maybe.

But as she left UCLA for the last time, she realized she had made the biggest mistake of her life.

She was still in love with Michael Hall.

CHAPTER 25

'What are you saying?' Hugh Gawler said. He shook his head and muttered something Amanda didn't understand. He walked around the glass table, hands behind his back, fidgeting with his watch.

'I've been thinking about the conditions,' Amanda said, a chill rippling down her back. 'Maybe this job is not right for me after all.' She bowed her head and looked at the floor. She felt like such a fool, but she had made up her mind.

Hugh shook his head from left to right, obviously trying to comprehend what was going on. She knew he had every right to be angry. She only begun working for him half an hour ago. And now she wanted to quit. Surely he must have thought it was a joke.

Amanda was seated in front of Hugh's desk. She kept her eyes down. She couldn't believe Michael Hall was working in the building. And right now she couldn't figure out how she felt about him. All she knew was how it would be impossible to work here knowing Michael would be around all the time. She didn't need time think everything over. It was instinct. And rarely did she not follow her instinct.

'Is it the money?' Hugh Gawler asked. His brow furrowed. Did he really believe Amanda could be so greedy? If she wanted a higher salary, she would have just asked him. She knew Hugh thrived on money. After all, he was an entrepreneur.

In business money was everything. The bottom line was profit. Nothing else mattered. If people want it, sell it. If this was Hugh's frame of mind, then he probably believed Amanda was after an extra dollar or two.

He is wrong, Amanda thought.

'What are they offering you at Globe Network?' Hugh continued. 'Whatever it is, I'm prepared to double it. Fifty thousand dollars a year. No cadet gets that kind of money.'

Amanda didn't answer. She was confused and embarrassed. She almost forgot why she had decided not to work for CableNews. *I'm here to spy. And Michael, my God! Can I really go through all this again?* All she knew was Michael was here, she was here, and everything seemed out of place.

Amanda looked at Hugh Gawler. His green eyes expressed pain. He seemed hurt. How could anyone refuse to work for him? Amanda felt his agony. He was the major player in a news network. She was barely out of university. If people outside heard that she resigned after one hour, he would be laughed at. But what could she do?

'I don't understand you Amanda,' Hugh said, infusing his tone with warmth. He walked around the glass table and stood in front of her. 'You're an intelligent and beautiful woman. I'm offering you the chance of a lifetime. And you're saying no.'

Amanda was reminded of how handsome he was. From up-close, his skin texture was perfect. He bore a light tropical tan, and his eyebrows were naturally manicured.

'I'm sorry, Mr Gawler,' Amanda apologized. ' But I think it would be best if I went back home to Perth.'

Passing one hand over his salt-and-pepper hair, Hugh seemed intrigued. Less than an hour ago Amanda came to the office, obviously prepared to work. And now, within ten minutes, she had decided the job wasn't right for her. 'Does this have anything to do with Michael Hall?' He said, his tone suggesting betrayal.

Amanda blushed. She looked up to Hugh, locking her eyes into his. 'Oh, no! It's just that—'

'—You're not making any sense,' Hugh interrupted, losing patience. 'What do you want? A company car?'

'There are other people out there who would love to work for you. Why are you insisting on employing me?'

Hugh puzzled over her question. He didn't answer. Alternatively, he looked at Amanda and at the Hollywood skyline. He appeared shocked, as if he knew something she didn't. But whatever it was, he wasn't telling her.

'Why?' she asked again. 'Why me? There are better qualified people out there. Just give me one good reason why you can't let me go.'

One hand behind his neck, Hugh paced around the desk. 'People like you come once in a lifetime. I know where you come from, and I know what you are worth. This company wants you. And I want you to work for me. You can't tell me no. This is not a choice, Amanda. I want you to work for this company.' His tone had a Military style, as if Amanda had signed a contract for life.

Amanda couldn't understand why he was insisting so much. And then her thoughts drifted to Michael Hall. She couldn't work with him in the building. When she was in his office before, she thought she was going to faint.

All those years waiting, wondering if she would ever see him again. All those years trying to erase him from her mind.

And now he was here.

What would happen if they decided to get back together? She knew there was a possibility. She also knew business and sex don't mix. Someone always ends up losing. If she was to get Michael back in her life, then it couldn't be at CableNews.

She had to turn the job down.

'All right, I'm offering $80,000 a year and a company car,' Hugh said, raising his eyebrows. He seemed determined to get through to her, no matter what. Did he think he could just buy her?

Money means nothing, she thought.

'Mr Gawler-'

'And you even get your own office,' he interrupted.

'But-'

'With a view.'

'I-'

'Don't say another word. Don't say something you might regret. This is my last offer. I don't want to talk to you any more. Go home, take the day off, and come back tomorrow. Your office will be ready. And I won't take no for an answer.'

'Mr Gawler-'

'Just go now, Amanda. You're going to make me very upset.'

Amanda stood from her chair.

Hugh smiled at her and walked her to the door. One hand behind her back, he ushed her out of the office. 'Think about the offer. I'll see you tomorrow.' He slipped his business card in her hand and shut the door behind her.

Amanda stood in front of the door, looking at the business card, not believing what had just happened.

As she took the elevator down to her SUV, she thought about the package. *An $80,000 a year salary. A company car. My own office.* It was an offer hard to refuse. But it also meant she would have to work with Michael Hall every day. And it didn't seem like a good idea.

The elevator reached the underground car park.

Amanda walked to the SUV, her head filled with confusion. She thought about Hugh Gawler, wondering what mysteries lay behind the awesomely handsome man. She couldn't hide her infatuation.

Maybe to the world she could.

But not to herself.

Why she felt so attracted to a man she knew little about was a mystery. There was something different about Hugh Gawler. She couldn't figure out whether it was his arrogance, his perfect look or his success. He seemed to be bathing in a magical aura.

An aura of power.

Whatever it was, Amanda didn't know if it was a good or a bad thing. She didn't feel for Hugh what she had felt years ago with Michael Hall. Although she hated to admit it, she feared Hugh Gawler a little, like a child fears her parents.

She jumped in the SUV and crunched the gears to reverse.

If Hugh Gawler wanted her so badly, there could only be two reasons. Either she was worth more than she thought, or Hugh was letting his dick rule his head.

As the SUV left the underground parking, Amanda felt she had made the biggest mistake of her life by volunteering to spy for Globe Network.

All she ever wanted was to prove her worth at the news station.

And now she would have to come back to Steve Thorn, being humiliated in front of everyone.

She could just imagine how Steve would relish the victory, how he would tell her how he had been right, that she should have never gone to spy at CableNews.

She turned into Santa Monica Boulevard, her mind filled with confusion.

Later that night, alone in her room, Amanda sat on her bed. The clock next to her bed flashed 11.34 p.m. The bedroom windows was open, letting some fresh air in.

She thought about Michael. How was she going to solve the problem? What was she going to do? She felt like a freshman again. All the emotions she had felt for Michael were coming back to her. The numb sensation in her stomach took her by surprise.

Oh, God. This is too much.

Amanda stood from her bed and walked to the bathroom.

She knew she had another sleepless night. Her life had become so complicated in such a short time.

After shedding her blue bathrobe, she stepped in the shower. Her eyes closed, she let the hot steamy water cascade down her body.

She thought about Michael again. She could almost feel him,

smell him, taste him. As the thought of Michael became stronger, Amanda massaged her breasts. They hardened. Her nipples erected. She imagined her hands to be those of Michael. She moved them down her body, between her legs. In her mind's eyes, she saw Michael entering her.

I love you, Michael. I've missed you so much.

When she finished masturbating, she remained seated under the steaming shower.

There was no way out.

She had to have Michael, no matter what.

And if Hugh Gawler had something else in mind for her, then let it be his problem.

Her mind made up, Amanda stepped out of the shower and slipped into her bathrobe.

Trembling with excitement, she walked to the study.

Maybe everything can be like it was when we first met. Now that university is over, it will be easier to have a proper relationship. No homework to sour our relationship.

Amanda knew why she had never gone out with anyone since Michael. He was the only man she ever wanted. The only man she ever loved. The only man who could fulfill her.

Amanda entered the study. She found Hugh's business card in her briefcase. She picked up the phone and dialed Hugh's after hours number.

The phone rang twice.

Hugh answered.

'What's wrong, Amanda?' Hugh asked, his voice expressing deep concern.

'I'm taking up your offer.'

CHAPTER 26

CableNews, Hollywood: Tuesday, 2.33 p.m.

Hugh Gawler placed the receiver back in its cradle.

After lunch, the temperature dropped to sixty degrees. The sky was clear, but the weather bureau predicted rain later in the evening. The view from Hugh's office was magnificent

Hugh Gawler kept his word and gave Amanda her own office the very next morning.

That afternoon, a new green Camaro was waiting in the underground car park of CableNews Corporation.

Hugh Gawler didn't know why Amanda changed her mind so suddenly, but the important thing was she did. Maybe it was the money. Maybe it was the car. Or maybe she fell for his charm. Most women did eventually. Some took longer, but sooner or later, they were drawn to his magnetism.

Hugh invited Amanda in his office to discuss the final details of her appointment with the company.

She looked petite and shy in comparison to the previous day.

'It looks as if you're not going to need the SUV much longer,' Hugh told her as he handed the keys to the green convertible Camaro. He wore a dark three-piece Emporio Armani suit with yellow neck wear His salt-and-pepper hair was smartly brushed.

Amanda smiled broadly.

Hugh handed her two laser-printed sheets of paper. 'This is your job description and requirements.' He smiled back and parted his lips, showing a sexual interest.

Amanda took the paperwork Hugh presented her. 'But I thought I was a cadet?' Amanda muttered softly, staring at the job description. 'This says Senior Investigative Reporter.'

'You are. It's just difficult to justify $80,000 a year for a cadet. So

I changed your job description Your duties are also flexible. And I also know you're capable of doing much more than a first year cadet.' He winked at Amanda.

She looked down at her paper, obviously trying to ignore his over-zealous friendliness.

Hugh Gawler didn't care. He was glad she had decided to join the company. It would take time to work on her.

I have plenty of time.

'Who will I be answering to?' Amanda asked.

'Michael Hall,' Hugh said. 'He's responsible for assigning reporters to various news stories. A lot of reporters are freelancers. As you know with a crew of twenty-two people, a lot of our work is sub-contracted. It keeps our overheads to a minimum and ensures a good coverage of all the news across the country. I also find the quality of the reporting is maintained at a high level.'

'I'm looking forward to be working with Mr Hall,' Amanda said. He tone suggested a lifetime commitment to the company.

'I'm sure you are,' Hugh said. He left his chair and stood in front of Amanda. 'How about dinner tonight? I always celebrate a new team member.'

Amanda hesitated, mulling over the offer. She opened her mouth, but Hugh interrupted before she had time to answer.

'Don't say no. This is a business meeting. And you have to attend.'

'All right,' she said, shifting uncomfortably.

'I'll pick you up at seven o'clock.'

Hugh Gawler removed a cream manila folder from the in-tray. 'Go and see Michael Hall and tell him you've been assigned to him. Come back here in ten minutes. I've got an assignment I would like you to work on. Michael will fill you in on the details later.'

When Amanda left the office, Hugh regained his seat. When Amanda rang him last night to say she would take his offer, he had been taken by surprise. He knew she would eventually come back to him. He never expected it to be so soon.

After she left the office, he found it difficult to get back to work. Images of Amanda in the nude kept him distracted. *I wonder what it would be like to fuck her? I'm going to make this bitch beg me to make love to her.* He could almost taste Amanda's flesh. So young.

So delicious.

He wanted to make her his. Another to add to his collection. But this young woman was rather special. Not like the others. He won't push himself on to her. He will win her love. Not by forcing her. She would have to come to him and beg him to make love to her.

Oh, yes. I'll make the bitch beg for me. She'll come crawling like a dog on her hands and knees.

He punched a few numbers on his telephone.

'She's in,' Hugh said, talking in the receiver.

'What do you mean she's in?' the panicking male voice of Number 2 asked at the end of the line.

'I took her on. I think she'd be good for the company.' Hugh visualized Amanda naked, her legs parted, offering her body for his abuse.

'You're crazy. The girl is not *that* good. Jesus, now that she's working for you, she's going to start snooping around.'

'She won't,' Hugh said with authority.

'How's that?'

'She'll have so much work, she won't have time for anything else. I'll take good care of her. Trust me.'

'Well, I feel better,' Number 2 said sarcastically. 'I suppose since she's only a cadet, she'll do less harm than a senior journalist. For Christ's sake, listen to yourself.'

When Hugh hanged up, he felt anger building up inside. He was getting sick of Number 2. So Number 2 kick-started his career. He gave him the leads to all the major news during the first few months. He helped him to set up a network of reliable freelancers and journalists. But now he was becoming a real pain.

And soon Number 2 would move here to CableNews Corporation. Hugh had promised him that much.

From the bar fridge, Hugh removed some ice cubes and placed them in a short glass. Angry, he poured himself a Southern Comfort.

Damn Number 2!

There was no way they would be able to work together. Already Number 2 had begun to give him orders. Do this, do that. *I've been in the business longer than you have. I know how things get done. Without me, you wouldn't be where you are today. Don't take Amanda Ryan on board. She's going to be nothing but trouble.*

And that was why Hugh took Amanda on board. Just to show Number 2 who was the boss at CableNews Corporation.

Who was Number 1.

And to fulfill his own gratification.

CHAPTER 27

Same day: at the same time.

Michael Hall looked up when Amanda Ryan walked unannounced into his office and shut the door.

Michael walked up to her. Infatuated, he locked his eyes into hers and knew immediately how she felt. It had been a long time since he had seen Amanda. In fact, he had given up on ever seeing her again. When Amanda stopped seeing him at UCLA, he never understood why. Only when he returned to his studies and completed his Masters, he began to see things differently.

Then he spoke to Curt Housman.

'Did you actually sleep with her,' Michael asked Curt.

'None of your business,' he answered darkly.

'Come on. It's not like you're going out with her or anything. You hanged around for two days or something.'

'Look, I'll tell you what I think. I think she only went out with me to make you react.'

Michael shook his head, baffled.'React?'

'She knew you were going to be angry at her. It's like she had this whole thing planned.'

'If she didn't want to go out with me, why couldn't she just tell me to my face?'

'I don't know. Maybe she didn't want to dump you, but she felt she had to. Her parents. Something. Maybe you were a pain in the ass. You figure it out.'

It didn't take long for Michael to work out all the arguments he had had with Amanda were about him falling behind at university. Maybe it was because she loved him so much she dumped him. She didn't want to see him mess up his life. Looking back, it seemed she had made quite clear, but back then he had been too blind to see.

For years, Michael hoped Amanda would one day come back to him. In his heart he had never managed to convince himself Amanda stopped loving him. And now Amanda was standing in front of him, looking into his eyes, he knew he was right.

Michael moved behind Amanda and locked the door of his office. He walked behind his desk, grabbed a remote control and shut closed the shutters of the office. Only a dim light was left on.

Amanda stood in the middle of the room. A lustful stare crossed the room. He knew she had been thinking about him all night. He'd barely got any sleep himself.

Amanda moved close to him, her lips almost touching his.

'Make love to me,' she said, as she began to unbuttoned his white shirt.

Michael felt his pulse racing. His breathing became irregular.

Amanda place one hand on his hard crotch. She removed the shirt and threw it on the red woven carpet.

Sexual tension built up inside Michael. He loved playing the game of seduction. He wanted to rip Amanda's clothes off, but he liked it better when she was in control.

He knew Amanda loved teasing him.

Slowly she pulled off his belt and unzipped his trousers.

Aroused, Michael slipped on hand under her dress and ripped her black stockings. He felt the firmness of her perfectly round buttocks.

Aroused, they slid to the floor.

'So how come you never tried to contact me?' Amanda whispered in his ear.

Michael didn't know why she was asking him such an awkward question now. She was the one who dumped him. What did she expect him to do? Stalk her. Revenge of one sort or another had crossed his mind a few times, but his senses always got the better of him.

'I thought you didn't love me any more,' Michael said softly

'I've never stopped loving you.' Gently she bit his left nipple. 'Couldn't you tell?'

'Then why did you go with another man?'

'It was a lie.' She pulled down his white underpants.

Michael believed her. But at the time, he wasn't too sure. Falling in love with Amanda had almost destroyed his chances of a career in journalism. Only now he began to realize how lucky he had been how Amanda had been much more mature than he had back at UCLA. If it hadn't been for Amanda dumping him, he would probably be back home in Denver, working on factory floor at

Gates with his father.

Michael was too aroused to continue the conversation. All he wanted was to be one with Amanda. He could feel Amanda's wetness his groin. He had longed for this moment for years. Since he had loved Amanda, he had never felt the same with anyone else. He met many women since Amanda. But he never was interested in any of them. When he spent time with another woman, he only had Amanda on his mind. No other women could have ever replaced her.

Michael felt a surge of energy as he entered Amanda. He was one with her.

Groaning with pleasure, Amanda closed her eyes and held on to Michael's body.

Waltzing back and forth, he was losing her mind. The love Amanda was giving him was too much. He hadn't felt so good for a long time. He had forgotten how empty his life was without her.

Lying on his back, Michael held on tight to Amanda's thighs He had never forgotten how perfect Amanda was. Her body was toned and smooth. Her breasts were perfectly round.

Amanda shook like if her body had been subjected to a high voltage. She climaxed to a mind-shattering orgasm at the same time as Michael exploded inside her.

At last, he had found himself again.

CHAPTER 28

Same day: 3.33 p.m.

Hugh Gawler looked at his watch. It had now been more than half an hour since Amanda had been in Michael's office. What were they doing in there? He had given Amanda ten minutes to talk to Michael.

Frustrated, Hugh stood from his leather-bound executive chair and walked to the bar-fridge. His hands were clammy. He was about to pour himself another glass of Southern Comfort but realized the bottle was empty. Just as well. This drinking was becoming a problem. He poured himself a glass of water instead.

Hugh took back his seat, wondering whether he should call Michael on the intercom. He played with the telephone cord, muttering to himself.

Bitch!

Then, he had a better idea.

His whole body alert, he sprung from his chair.

CHAPTER 29

Two minutes later.

Amanda was adjusting Michael's tie when someone knocked on the door.

The door handle jerked.

But because Michael had locked the door earlier on, whoever was trying to get in found himself locked outside.

'Michael, is Amanda with you?' Hugh yelled from behind the closed door.

Michael froze. A look crossed his face.

'Damn! I forgot,' Amanda said, remembering the Hugh had asked her to be back in his office in ten minutes.

'She's here,' Michael said, walking towards the door.

Amanda was straightening her dress when Hugh walked into the office. He smiled his cocky smile.

'I was just on my way,' Amanda said, lying through her teeth.

'You must have had a lot to catch up with,' Hugh said, quickly glancing around the office.

'I guess we did,' Michael said, after the barest hesitancy.

Hugh looked at both of them briefly and then moved on. 'Well, we better get back to work now,' He opened the door widely. 'After you, Miss Ryan.'

Amanda walked in front of him. A faint nausea rippled through her. She felt heat on her cheeks.

In a glance, she saw Hugh turn around, giving Michael a strange stare. Not an cold stare. Not a smile. Just a weird look.

When Michael smiled back thinly, Amanda felt her stomach churning.

CHAPTER 30

One minute later.

'Can I get you a drink?' Hugh said, walking towards the bar-fridge.

'Thanks, but I'd rather wait until later,' Amanda said, tension in her voice.

Hugh grabbed the bottle of Southern Comfort. When he lifted it and felt its weight, he remembered it was empty. He took his seat back. He leaned over and opened a cream manila folder. It was the same folder he had taken removed from the in-tray when Amanda first came to see him.

'Let's discuss your first assignment,' Hugh said, his stare deviating towards Amanda's legs. He wasn't sure why he felt the urge to look at her legs. But he was mesmerized by the whitish flesh. 'You've put on your application letter you love investigation work. Is that right?'

'I do. It's something that comes naturally to me. I love talking to people and doing interviews.'

'Good.' *Such white legs.* 'As you must be aware, Senator Trevor Garry got killed a few days ago. I'd like you to interview his friends and family. We're going to do a special half-hour program on his life and background. This is a very important report, and I'd like you to tackle it.'

'Sounds great,' Amanda said, showing the excitement in her voice. 'You're throwing me in the deep-end.'

'It's the only way to learn. But don't worry. I've told Michael you'd be working on this story. He'll guide you all the way since this is your first assignment. I'm sure you won't have any problems. If you do, don't hesitate to see me. My door is always open for you.' The end of his sentence trailed off as he looked at Amanda's legs.

Such white legs.

Now he remembered.

When Amanda was in his office one hour ago, she was wearing black stockings.

He lifted his head and locked his eyes into hers.

He smiled, but felt the rage building up inside him.

CHAPTER 31

Santa Monica: 6.32 p.m.

Amanda was in the shower.

It had been a long day, and the hot water cascading down her body made her forget for a while the complexity of life.

The bathroom was filled with steam, making it look like a sauna. The smell of soap and lavender shampoo filled the air.

Amanda loved long hot showers. It helped her relax at the end of a hard working day.

She shampooed her long golden hair. She thought about how she made love to Michael that afternoon. It felt so good. While gently rubbing her scalp, she wondered how she had managed to survived so long without making love to him. It had felt so natural.

In the last two years, she thought she had found happiness. She told herself relationships were too troubling. If she wanted to be happy, all she had to do was look inside her and create her own happiness. But now she realized how wrong she had been. There was nothing comparable to the feeling of being needed.

That thought made her happy but scared at the same time. Love seemed so fragile. But she was willing to take a chance.

Amanda wanted to fall in love all over again.

As she stepped out of the shower, she reminded herself no matter how right things felt with Michael, the reason why she was working at CableNews was to spy for Globe Network. It would be all to easy to deny her other responsibilities and simply fall into a romantic vacuum. The reality was she was at CableNews to fulfill her part of a bargain. She couldn't let everyone down.

Amanda dried her body with a large pink bath towel, wondering how in the world she became a spy. All she ever wanted was to become a journalist.

Steve Thorn might have been right. Maybe there was nothing to spy at CableNews. Maybe Globe Network was no match for CableNews.

Half an hour later, Amanda was watching television, waiting for Hugh Gawler to turn up for their outing.

A business meeting.

Amanda didn't like the sound of it. And the way Hugh kept on staring at her legs when she was in his office that afternoon. He obviously noticed she wasn't wearing any stockings. She saw the look that crossed his face when he stared at her legs. Something had clicked in his mind. He must have guessed she had made love to Michael.

The thought of Hugh knowing made her shiver. Hugh has such an intimidating personality. She felt like a little girl who had done wrong next to him. But she was determined to not let her fear control her reasoning. After all, she had had nothing to do with him on a personal level. She didn't owe him anything.

Amanda kept on flicking from one news channel to another.

The police hadn't found the killer of Senator Trevor Garry. LAPD detectives were working around the clock.

Brian Kirkham, LAPD's Press Relations Commander, appeared on several channels, making the same statement:

'We have no suspects at this stage. The Homicide Special Section is currently working with the West Bureau. We are still awaiting the coroner's final autopsies reports and will keep the public informed as soon as information becomes available to us.'

LAPD had no doubts the killer of Senator Trevor Garry and his family would be found shortly. It was only a matter of days now.

As Amanda switched channels for the hundredth time, she heard a car engine outside.

She knew it was Hugh Gawler.

Although she was dressed appropriately for the evening —a light, white cotton dress with matching jacket and Guerlain lipstick — Amanda didn't feel ready. She would have rather stayed home and spend a quiet evening by herself. But if she refused to dinner with Hugh Gawler, he would have asked her out again and again. It was easier to get rid of the problem now.

Not that she really expected the evening to be a problem.

After switching the television off with the remote control, Amanda stood from the sand colored sofa.

The headlights of the car outside beamed through the living room.

Nervous, Amanda grabbed her handbag and raced for the door.

Before Hugh Gawler had a chance to knock, Amanda swung the front door open. His marine blue BMW was parked in the driveway. He was already half way up the stairs, looking absolutely stunning in his black two-piece Hugo Boss suit and a red Givanchi silk tie held to his shirt with a Cartier steel-brushed pin.

Amanda gazed at the twelve red roses he held in his arms like a new born. If Amanda hadn't known who Hugh Gawler was, she would have fallen for him. She knew so because she felt a warm sensation in her stomach and heat on her cheeks. Her eyes shifting from the roses to his face, she wondered why such a handsome, wealthy man was still single. She read once in Forbes magazine how Hugh Gawler was one of the U.S.'s most eligible bachelor. Still, she wasn't to going let this fact empower her rationality.

'I thought you said this was strictly business,' Amanda said, turning cagey.

'It is,' Hugh laughed, giving her his best smile. She knew he was here to have a good time. 'There is a rumor going around of how you don't mind mixing business with pleasure. Not what you told me at the office this afternoon.'

Bastard! He really knows about Michael.

Amanda felt enraged. She thought Hugh wasn't going to play games with her. She didn't know if he was joking or just being a complete asshole.

He's as arrogant as handsome.

Annoyed, Amanda didn't bother answering, but turned her back on Hugh. She locked the front door.

'You're not taking the roses inside?' Hugh said, injecting disappointment in his tone.

She hesitated and said, 'I don't take flowers from business colleagues, especially from my superior.'

'Well, I see we're going to have a lovely evening.' His tone had turned sour. He glanced at her sharply and tossed the roses in her garden.

Let him play his silly games, she thought.

He looked at the roses and then at Amanda.

She thought she heard him say something.

Intrigued, she looked at him, but he smiled back.

She was almost certain she heard him say something. But now, looking at his smile, maybe it had been her imagination. He couldn't have said *that*.

She stepped in the BMW, the word echoing in her skull.

Bitch!

81

CHAPTER 32

Santa Monica, Camelions: 7.50 p.m.

Amanda Ryan's gaze moved past Hugh Gawler to the crackling fireplace. The restaurant was definitely not what she had had in mind. The Provencal setting consisted mostly of tables-for-two. It was far too intimate for people conducting a *business meeting.*

The Camelions restaurant was located on 26th Street. It compromised three 1920s stucco cottages with an ivy-trellised brick patio. The aroma of French-inspired Canadian cuisine filled the room. It was almost too hot to be seating inside.

Amanda wanted to eat outside on the patio, but there were no tables left. She had to compromise for the warm interior setting.

She looked up to the beam ceiling, wondering what the hell she was doing here.

The lights were turned low, and the place was filled with loving couples. Surely, Hugh must have had something else in mind. If he thought he was going to seduce her with the romantic restaurant routine, he was a fool.

Amanda had been approached by many men before him. She knew she was just a good-looking chick to most of them. As a result, she learned to say no, even to the most irresistible of them.

'Do you always take your new employees here?' Amanda said, biting into her swordfish zested with a marinade of paprika, coriander and cumin

'Only the ones I like.' Hugh winked at Amanda, obviously unperturbed by the fact she felt uncomfortable. Gently, he dug his knife into a grilled duck breast in ginger sauce.

'I thought you were married,' Amanda lied.

'I'm not. I haven't found the right person yet,' He injected his voice with a phony tone. 'So what exactly is your connection to

Michael Hall?'

Taken by surprise, Amanda coughed. How dare did Hugh Gawler inquire about her relation with Michael? The man had nerves of steel. Amanda was not going to get defeated by him. She had to change the focus of the conversation.

'Let's talk about your life,' she said, the small of her back damp from tension.

'My life? Now, why would you be interested in my life?'

'Well, you seem to be interested in mine' Amanda answered, rising her manicured highbrows and lifting her chin a bit higher.

'True. I like to know what motivates my employers.'

'But you told me you knew what kind of person I was at the interview. You were so sure I was the right person for CableNews. And now, you want to know what motivates me?'

Hugh sipped his white wine, puzzling over her response for a few seconds. He gave a quick wave and said, 'I've never had a serious long-term relationship. And getting older doesn't make it any easier.'

'And why is that?'

'Well, you know what it's like. Women get older. Men remain young at heart.'

In the groin! Amanda thought, feeling Hugh's stare raping her.

'What about Michael Hall?' Hugh continued. 'How good of a friend is he?'

'Just a friend.'

'Just a friend? How deep is this friendship?'

Amanda felt her heart sink. 'What is this? Part two of my job interview?' She felt her eyes rolling upwards.

'I notice things. You've spent an awful lot of time with Michael at the office this afternoon. You too must have had a lot in common at university.'

Amanda was shocked by Hugh's forwardness. At the same time, she considered herself naive for being surprised by his attitude. She snapped, 'This is really none of your business. If you must know, Michael and I were nothing more than classmates. We did some homework together. He helped me with study. We were good friends. Apart from that, I don't know what you're implying.'

'You don't?' He laughed. His laugh was sour.

Amanda had enough. His questioning was out of line. She stood from her chair. 'You're harassing me. And since I'm not at work, I don't have to stay here and take it.'

Hugh nodded and said, 'Come on, Amanda. Don't be so defensive. I'm only trying to get to know you better.' He stood from his chair and grabbed her arm.

'Why? How much of me do you need to know?' Amanda said, pulling her arm back.

'How much are you willing to share?' There was a glitter in his eye. He wasn't trying to hide his game. His face seemed to darken.

Amanda puzzled over his question.

Spying. Remember that's why you're here for. Don't lose the plot. Calm down.

She was here to seek the truth. The truth of what? She didn't know. But she knew as far as spying was concerned, her attitude to Hugh Gawler wasn't going to simplify things. After all, if she was going to spy from within, wouldn't it make sense to get friendly with the most powerful person in the company?

Amanda took her seat back. The bastard was playing games with her. And she was silly enough to get upset. Maybe it was what he had expected all along. She had to control her temper.

'I don't know how much of myself I would like to share? What did you have in mind?' Amanda whispered, leaning forward.

Hugh laughed. Very smart, he must have thought. He obviously didn't expect her to turn the situation around. 'As much as you're willing to give,' Hugh muttered, as if cued.

'And how much do you think I am willing to give?'

'It would probably depend if you consider me a good friend or not.'

'What do you mean? Of course I consider you a friend,' Amanda said, taking his hand into hers. 'I thought everyone at CableNews was part of a team. We are all friends, aren't we?'

He had a blank look on his face. *I'm really taking him by surprise.*

'Some friends are worth more than others,' he finally said.

'Like who?'

'Michael is a good friend to you. Maybe I can be a good friend too.'

She pulled her hand back. Everything Hugh was saying had double meaning. 'How can I be friend with you when you're not honest with me? Your employment offer yesterday sounded more like a sexual proposition. Do you consider all your employers to be prostitutes?'

A stunted look crossed his face. 'That's not nice, Amanda. I've been honest with you. You're the one who lied to me.'

Amanda felt her stomach churning. She felt he was going to bring up something about her spying. But he couldn't. He didn't know anything. And if he did, why the hell did he employ her?

'Lied to you?' Amanda said, standing up from her chair for the second time. 'Have you finished with me? Because I think I've had enough for one night.'

'Sure, I understand. I'm a difficult man. But you'll like me eventually. Everybody does.' Hugh didn't seem at all embarrassed by her leaving the table.

Amanda heard the babble of voices from the other tables. Furious, she picked up her bag and cross the room.

'One more thing,' Hugh yelled across the crowded room.

Amanda turned around. 'What?' she said, feeling the weight of the stares from other people.

'Do you always leave your stockings behind when catching up with an old friend?'

CHAPTER 33

Cable News: One week later.

Amanda's first week at CableNews had been hectic. She'd spent most of her time chasing family members and friends of Senator Trevor Garry. She worked long and irregular hours. It was the first time she had been under so much pressures to complete her work within the deadlines given. For the first time, she realized working has a journalist was not all she had imagined. Much of her time was spent on the telephone and outdoors in all kinds of weather. At the end of a working, she just got home and went straight to bed.

The Senator's murder was her first big story. She spent endless nights tossing and turning, wondering if she was capable of pulling it off. But the whole thing had been easier than she thought. The fear of actually doing the interviews was worse than the interviews themselves.

She found herself being extremely energetic when under pressure. The lack of free time kept her focus on her task. During the whole process of gathering interviews and information, she was aware this was an important story.

It wasn't until later in the evening, usually on her way back home to Santa Monica, that the significance of the story bothered her. She just begun working for CableNews, but she was already responsible for a major news story. The Senator's death was not something that should have be tackled by a cadet. And although Hugh told her he had faith in her, in her mind something didn't add up. The half hour show from the Senator's death was going to bring CableNews a lot of money. How much, she wasn't sure. But nothing less than six figures. She was certain of that.

The incident the previous week with Hugh Gawler at the restaurant also troubled her. He came on to her strongly. She hoped this had been a one-off incident. Now she wondered how long it would be before he would make a move again. Maybe it was why he gave her the assignment with the Senator. Maybe he thought how doing her a favor by letting tackle a big story. Did he expect her to return his kindness some kind of sexual favor?

As far the Senator's murder was concerned, opinions were the same everywhere. The murder the Senator and his family had come as a shock to everyone in Los Angeles. The general consensus was the murders were politically motivated. Of course there was no hard evidence to support this hypothesis.

The opposition candidate, Senator Terence Maxwell denied any involvement in the killings.

In a televised statement, he shared the anguish and the agony of seeing a political candidate being killed in such a barbaric manner:

'The implication, the mere thought, of how I or any other member of the party had anything to do with the death of Trevor Garry and his family is absolutely ridiculous. My deepest sympathies goes to Senator Garry's family. It is a sad thing when a member of our profession, being a member of the opposition or not, dies at the hands of evil. If I win the electoral seat in two weeks, I will do my utmost to ensure the killer of Senator Garry and his family is found and given a sentence appropriate to the atrocity he has committed.'

The parents of Trevor Garry were reluctant to do a camera interview. But Amanda managed to sweet talk them into it. If they spoke on television, there might be a chance a witness would come forward.

The Senator's mother busted into tears half through the taping. 'How could anyone do such a thing?' she sobbed into a white handkerchief. 'The police must find the person responsible for the death of my son. This monster should be killed for what he did!'

By Friday Amanda accumulated more than twenty-three hours of interviews on videocassettes The final half-hour special on Senator Trevor Garry would be screened on the weekend. She knew she had too much material, but it was her first story. It was better, she felt, to have more material than not enough. And the story fascinated her anyway. The more she found out, the more she wanted to know.

LAPD believed the killings were done by a professional. The way the throat of the Senator had been cut supported the assumption. There was only one cut of four inches in depth and eight in length. The killer had cut the left jugular and windpipe to the neck-bone. If there had been more than one cut on the Senator's throat, it could have been assumed it was the work of an amateur. An amateur would have gone through several attempts before succeeding. The fact than both the Senator's wife and his child also died from a one-cut wound supported the theory.

And if the killer was a professional, then it was a premeditated murder. Nothing had been stolen in the house. The motive was not burglary. Evidence found in the house also suggested the killings had been carried out by more than one person.

There seemed to be only two reasons why the Senator got killed: revenge of some sort or a random victim of a ruthless psychopath.

When Amanda finished the interviews, the truth to the Senator's death was still a mystery.

A box full of videocassettes in her arms, Amanda made her way to the editing room at CableNews. The room was at the end of the corridor which was adjoined to Michael's office.

Henry Limar, the senior video editor at CableNews, was busy sorting out the many video cassettes for tonight's news show. Amanda learned how with over twenty years experience, Henry Limar was a veteran in the business. He began editing on 35mm film, but when the video cassette took over, he turned his back on celluloid film.

CableNews Corporation had the latest digital recording video equipment. Henry Limar was a master at his game. The equipment also compromised state-of-the art computer image video digital technology. Nothing was impossible. Moving images could be enhanced, trimmed, cut to size or blown-up to perfection. Sometimes a final cut didn't look like anything like the original footage. It was up to Henry Limar to leave some things behind and only show the public what he wanted.

Or rather what he was told.

Henry Limar was playing nervously with his beard when Amanda walked in.

Slumped on a backless chair, his body was piled like a sack of potatoes. Henry Limar was overweight and wore a bushy beard. His eyes were almost hidden inside his head. His hair was combed to one side to hide a rather large bald spot. He wore a chocolate brown wrinkle-free slack and a stripped blue shirt. He had the look of a nerdy scientist.

'Let me help you with these,' Henry said, his voice disembodied. He stood from his chair. Effortlessly, he managed to catch Amanda's box of videocassettes before she dropped them to the floor.

'Thank you,' Amanda said, her knees still shaking.

'Are these the videocassettes on the Senator's death?' Henry Limar asked, avoiding eye contact.

'Yes.'

'You're late,' he snapped.

Amanda heard Henry Limar hated people who didn't adhere to his timetable. His job took a lot of hours and every minute counted.

'I was expecting those videocassettes yesterday afternoon,' he went on.

'I know,' Amanda said, feeling like a school kid being reprimanded. 'You know what it's like. I had this last minute interview to-'

'Spare me the details,' Henry interrupted. 'I run on schedule. And if you're late, I'm late. And at the end of the day it's my ass on the line. Do me a favor and get your videocassettes in on time.'

'I'm sorry,' Amanda muttered, her heart thundering.

Henry Limar didn't seem friendly. Maybe it was because he worked so hard. Maybe he was right. It was her fault if she was late. She didn't need twenty-three hours of recordings for a half hour show.

She tried to make eye contact, but Henry Limar was avoiding her. He was blinking rapidly, his ankles locked together.

Listening to him clatter, Amanda wanted to ask him if there was anything wrong. But she knew better. She had already made a nuisance of herself. She turned around and left the room.

At the last second, she glanced behind her back.

Henry Limar looked at her sharply.

It was a cold stare.

CHAPTER 34

Two minutes later.

Henry Limar re winded a videocassette on Recorder A. He fast-forwarded the videocassette He froze the frame, then re winded it at slow speed. He played back at normal speed. He stared at the video display terminal.

Hell! They're up to it again.

His body bathed in sweat. His complexion turned gray

Nervously, he pressed the STOP button on Recorder A.

How much longer could Henry Limar keep his mouth shut?

At night he lay awake wondering who to talk to. And now he knew it was only a matter of time before he would crack under pressure.

This had been going on for too long. But he knew there was nothing he could do.

Hugh Gawler's instructions had been clear.

Anxious, Henry Limar shook his head nervously, chewing on his pen. He appeared shocked. He sighed heavily as if he was losing patience.

Quickly, He glanced towards the door before pulling the duplicate videocassette from Recorder B and throwing it in a plastic box filled with other videocassettes

With one hand, he wiped the beads of sweat from his forehead.

He stood silent for a full minute, staring at the snow on Monitor One.

Then suddenly, as if he had been clubbed at the back of the neck, he leaned over and opened the top drawer next to Recorder A.

His look was blank.

He locked his eyes on the colt .45 sitting at the bottom of the drawer.

CHAPTER 35

Texas, USA; 5.32 a.m.

Tom Davidson was asleep when someone thumped him on the shoulder.

'Hey! You're not dozing off, are you?' Sam Willicon yelled, re-adjusting his Texan Militia cap tightly on his head. His voice was coarse as if he had smoked five packs a day for the last thirty years. 'You wouldn't wanna sleep and lose control of your thoughts now, would ya?'

Tom Davidson felt the cold wind from outside. The smell of wet dirt filled the room. It wasn't quite daylight yet.

Sam Willicon took two steps back. His face was tanned like leather. He wore a wool-padded Wrangler's jeans jacket and a pair of 501s. His hair was tied into a pony tail, hanging from the gap at the back of his red cap. He looked all of his fifty-two years of age, maybe even a couple of years older.

His shaved head throbbing with a migraine, Tom Davidson wanted to tell the leader of the right-wing neo-Nazi extremists militia where to stick it. But he knew it was all part of the test. To achieve enlightenment, to prove himself to be a worthwhile member of the ultra-right, Tom Davidson had to fight against sleep. Sam Willicon had made it very clear when he enlisted Tom Davidson in the Texan Militia.

Tom Davidson, a twenty-seven year old redneck, has had his share of running around. He bore a wholesome American look with a straight nose, thin lips and a head shaped like an egg. His shaved cranium suited his physique. Some would say he was a rather handsome man. But his small dark eyes showed years of anger and frustration.

Tom Davidson left home in Philadelphia at the age of sixteen after a heated argument with his father. Tom wanted to become a professional football player. His father wanted him to get his head into study. The young man had always been a rebel, the one person who didn't fit anywhere.

Back at school, young Tom Davidson provoked fights all the time. He couldn't settle into school life. Bored by classes, Tom Davidson made a nuisance of himself and spent hours in detention. The only thing he loved was football. His dream was to make the state league.

But one day, for reasons unknown to him, he enlisted in the Defense Force. Nine months after he joined the army, Tom was dishonorably discharged for intentionally shooting another soldier in the foot. A court martial found him mentally imbalanced.

For a while Tom Davidson traveled from one state to another, trying to find some meaning in his life. In less than a year, he had been to Alabama, New Mexico, north to Wyoming, Montana and North Dakota, and finally south again to Texas. He began to hate everything. Everywhere he went, people were prisoners of their own existence. No one seemed to believe anymore.

And then one evening, at the Blue Club in Houston, Texas, drinking himself to the grave, Tom Davidson met Sam Willicon.

Sam Willicon took the broken lad under his wing, gave him a shelter, some food, and the belief there were other people just like him. People dissatisfied with the system, with the government, with all the Asians, the blacks and the greasers. He told Tom Davidson he wasn't alone. His brothers were here to help each other, to help fellow Americans, to bring down the Zionist Occupational Government, otherwise known as the US Federal Government.

The ultra-right hated Washington and everything it stood for. Washington was part of the New World Order, an international conspiracy of politicians, media big shots and bankers.

And Tom Davidson had learned everything quickly.

The Texan Militia's training was second to none.

When Tom Davidson enlisted in the Militia, he was brainwashed through isolation. He spent days alone in a closet to test his strength of character.

It was all part of the training.

Sam Willicon told Tom Davidson only a handful of men could make it through the training. Only real men. The rest were just yellow-belly scums, not any better than those dumb black arses.

But Tom Davidson was determined to win this time. He'd been trained in the army. He knew what discipline was all about. The Department of Defense had had a good man working for them, and it discharged him. Tom would show them now. He would show the whole world what a real man was.

Tom Davidson would soon be a full-pledged member of the Texan Militia. Like all the soldiers of the right-wing fascist group, Tom Davidson was dangerous because he truly believed what he was doing was right.

Together with his American brothers, Tom Davidson was going to overthrow the United States government, the Military and the common people.

The Texan Militia was strong enough to start a revolution. People would open their eyes and join the militia's cause. Just like their forefathers had declared their independence, the Texan Militia would begin a revolutionary war.

The Texan Militia was well equipped. Weapons, ammunition and shelters were funded by armored cars robbery.

Each soldier wore Military clothes and carried Military weapons. Political propaganda was recited over and over during training and general meetings. The cause was everything. Even if it meant sacrificing oneself or a comrade.

It was a war the Texan Militia was going to win.

Sam Willicon helped Tom Davidson to his feet.

'Come on, buddy,' he said, 'not long to go now. Tomorrow mornin', you'll be ranked as a full member.'

Tom Davidson tried to keep his eyes open.

He did it.

He was nearly there.

Three months of hard training, but hell, he did it.

Together Sam Willicon and Tom Davidson walked out of the badly lit cabin, and into the morning sunrise.

Tom Davidson could hardly stand on his feet. He grimaced as the morning sun blinded him.

'You know what we gonna call ya?' Sam asked.

'What?' Tom forced a smile.

'The Mad Bomber.'

'Why is that?'

'Ten points if you guess.'

'You want me to blow something up?'

Sam imitated the noise of a quiz-show buzzer. 'Ten points. You win.' He placed his arm around Tom. 'You see, if we're going to win this damn war, we have to hit at the source.'

'At the source, yes,' Tom said, agreeing to everything he was told. For the past three months, he had been told when to eat, when to shower, when to sleep, when to shit. And now, he couldn't do anything without being told when, how and where.

'I'm talking where it really hurts,' Sam continued. 'FBI, Drug Enforcement agency, Marine Corps, Army Recruiting Department... the whole bloody lot.'

'I'm going to be a hero, eh?'

'The Mad Bomber, my friend. Your name will echo in all the newspapers around the world.'

Tom Davidson's migraine was still in full force, but the fresh air outside gave him some strength to carry on.

He dreamed of becoming a national hero for years.

And soon he would become one.

Sooner than he ever imagined.

CHAPTER 36

Santa Monica: Thursday, 9.37 p.m.

Amanda and Michael had just finished dinner. The windows of Amanda's townhouse were open, letting a cool wind enter every room. The smell and sound of the ocean filled the air with tranquility.

It was the first time Michael got invited to Amanda's home. He fell in love with the place immediately It was small, but Amanda had done a good job with storage space. Michael remembered Amanda to be tidy, even back at university.

'I'm going to have a shower,' Amanda said, already half way down the hallway.

'You go ahead,' Michael said, his gaze following her. 'I'll finish cleaning up.'

Michael and Amanda had been the only two to have dinner, and yet the kitchen was filled with dirty dishes. Michael had watched Amanda cooked. She used as many pots and pans as she required, obviously not thinking ahead at the mountain of cleaning to be done afterward But since she had cooked, then Michael was on dishes duty. It hadn't been said. It was just a normal progression for the evening.

It wasn't common for Michael to do the dishes. Most of the time, he ate out. His apartment in Downtown Los Angeles was just somewhere to sleep.

Since Michael graduated from university, his eating habits hadn't changed much. Like many male bachelors, he lived on take-away, canned food and frozen dinners. He never got to do many dishes. But he once read in *Men's Health* how real nineties men were expected to help with the chores. In tune with the latest trend, he volunteered to clean up.

His forearms up to his elbows in dishwater, he tried to come to terms with his relationship with Amanda. Everything had happened so fast. It was hard to believe she was back in his life. Somehow he had thought she had disappeared forever. And suddenly she came out of nowhere, sweeping him away for the second time.

While drying the glassware, he realized he never stopped loving Amanda. All those years without her hadn't been easy. He tried to forget about the intense relationship he had at university by becoming a workaholic But she never vanished from the back of his mind. Did he let go of her too easily when she dumped him?

Sure, he could have nagged her, turning the whole thing into a sexual harassment case. But that wasn't Michael. He knew he would have been incapable of hurting Amanda.

He placed the cutlery in the top drawer of the pine kitchen bench.

Back at university, his whole life had been molded around Amanda. When she left him, he had almost gone insane. And now that she was back in his life, he feared how his sanity depended on her. He wouldn't be able to endure another heartache. If he was to lose her again, this time he wouldn't find the strength to carry on.

There was only one problem.

Things were different since he was at university. The heartache and passing of time changed him. Amanda hadn't realized that yet, but Michael knew he wasn't the same person she fell in love with. His ideals have changed since. His beliefs were different, maybe not even agreeable with hers.

He shrugged as he placed the drying cloth at the back of a kitchen chair.

In the distance, he could hear the ocean. He also heard the shower running upstairs.

A boyish smile lightened up his expression.

The bathroom was filled with steam in spite of the open window. Amanda's clothes were carefully placed on a chair next to the hand-sink

Michael took pants and shirt off and threw them on the tiled floor.

Amanda didn't say a word. She probably didn't hear him coming in.

Completely naked, Michael pulled the yellow shower curtain.

Her eyes closed and her head tilted backwards, Amanda was enjoying the cascade of steamy water on her body.

For a few seconds, Michael just stared at her. He was captivated by her long legs, tiny waist and perfectly round breasts. When he finally placed one hand on her stomach, she jumped up.

'God, you scared me,' Amanda said. Her surprise turned into a smile as he joined her under the hot water.

Michael lowered himself until he was on his knees. He leaned forward. Gently he licked the water running down Amanda's body.

Sex was the best thing in the world, and he just couldn't get enough of it.

'Oh, Michael, you feel so good,' Amanda whispered softly. She clutched Michael's shoulders.

Michael was too busy exploring her body to hear what saying.

Gently, Michael passed one hand across her buttocks. His head resting against her chest, he felt her erected nipples hardening.

'Why don't we finish this in bed,' Michael said, his erection fully grown.

Amanda looked down and approved with a smile.

A lustful fever took over him. He wanted to please Amanda like no one had ever pleased her before. He wanted to resign himself to her every wishes. He wanted to be one with her.

As Michael stood up, Amanda let herself fall to her knees.

Gently, she took Michael's hard organ in her mouth.

CHAPTER 37

CableNews: The following day, 5.32 p.m.

The day had been a hectic one. Amanda should have been exhausted. But instead, she felt restless.

Alone in her office, she kept fidgeting with a blue Biro Someone had turned the central heating on too high. The small of her back was damp with perspiration.

She shifted uncomfortably in her seat, chewing nervously on the Biro She knew it was time to do what she had set out to do. Find something to bring back to Globe Network, some information disclosing how CableNews managed constant high ratings.

A week had gone past, and so far Amanda had come up nothing. She feared been treated like a fool on her return to Globe Network. She could just imagine the scenario between Steve Thorn and herself.

'So what have you found out about CableNews?'

'I tried, but-'

'But you've found nothing! Why? Because there was nothing to be found. And don't say I haven't told you.'

'But-'

And then he would jab out his fat finger in the air, his lower lip shaking with anger.

'Christ, you're as useless as the rest of them! What do you want me to do with you now?

And then he would give her a lustful stare.

Amanda almost stood from her chair, a faint nausea rippling through her. There was no way she would go back to Globe Network defeated. The sonofabitch wasn't going to make her feel useless. He wasn't going to prove there was nothing more to Amanda Ryan than her good looks.

She had to take a risk.

CHAPTER 38

Same day: 9.29 p.m.

By 8.00 p.m. most of the CableNews staff had gone home.

At 9.29 p.m., Hugh Gawler decided to call it a night. He knew Amanda was still in the building. He had seen the light from under her door. But he was tired of waiting and wanted to go home.

Standing from his leather executive chair, Hugh Gawler thought for a moment about leaving Amanda by herself.

His face was lined with soft creases.

Amanda wouldn't find anything in the building, he told himself. His office door would be locked anyway. And so would all the other doors in the building.

Hugh cleaned up his desk, turned the computer off, and packed his briefcase. He locked the door of his office, walked down the hallway, and stopped in front of Amanda's office.

He knocked twice.

'Come in,' Amanda said.

'How come you're working so late?,' Hugh said as he walked into the office, a grin on his face. God, Amanda seemed even more gorgeous at the end of a working day. She was wearing the same black stockings she wore when she began working in the office.

'This story with Senator Trevor Garry,' Amanda said, raising a yellow manila folder in the air.

Hugh frowned. 'What about it? You've finished the Senator's story last week.'

'I know. But no one knows who the killer is...I just thought-'

'You thought you could find who the killer was?' Hugh interrupted.

'Not really, but after interviewing so many of the Senator's friends and relatives, I feel so close to them. I need to work on this a bit more.'

Hugh didn't want to sound suspicious. If he told her to stop and go home, it wouldn't look right. After all, any company director thrived on the idea some workers didn't go home until ten or eleven o'clock at night. Fixed salary and maximum output. But with Amanda, he had to be careful. She wasn't really here to work. He knew the truth.

But she didn't know he knew.

'Look, Amanda,' Hugh said, locking his eyes into hers. 'You're a hard worker. I knew you would be good for the company. Keep up it up, but don't kill yourself.'

'Thank you, Mr Gawler.' She injected her tone with warmth.

'And don't work late all week. I'd love to take you out to dinner again.' He stared at her legs, remembering the whitish flesh that lay below them.

She looked down, ignoring his last comment.

CHAPTER 39

Amanda stared the blank computer screen on her desk, pretending to be getting on with whatever she was supposed to be doing.

When Hugh left the office, she turned the computer off.

At last she was alone.

She thought for a moment about where she would start. Hugh's office would be the most obvious place to begin prying around. But it was unlikely he would have left the door unlocked. And she didn't know anything about picking locks. Where in the world would she find such information anyway?

At 9.51 p.m. Amanda stood from her chair. After a few seconds of reflection, she regained her seat. Too early, she decided. If Hugh Gawler had forgotten something, he would be back any second.

Amanda gave herself until 11.00 p.m. before making her move.

She flicked the computer back on. Out of her briefcase, she removed a computer diskette and inserted it into the 3.5 inch A drive. She clicked the Microsoft Word icon and retrieved the file ARTICLE.DOC from the A drive. She decided to work on her *Single Life* article. There was nothing else to do anyway.

Although she had been genuinely interested in Senator Garry's story, there was nothing more than she could research on. It was now up to the LAPD's Homicide Bureau to come up with the answers.

Amanda re-read the last two pages of her article. This was useless. No matter how many times she tried to convince herself her writing was good, she didn't believe it. *Even a cat can write better than me.* Hell, she knew if she didn't finish at least the first draft, there would be no chance of getting it published.

Unable to concentrate, Amanda stared at the screen for a while. Her mind wandered to Michael and her spying job at CableNews.

Maybe it would have been easier if she had not accepted the job after all. Caught in a tangled situation, she feared how it would all end.

By the time she was ready to type another paragraph of her article, she noticed the time: 10.47 p.m. There was no need to even begin typing. Hugh Gawler hadn't come back. And it was unlikely there would be anyone else left in the building.

Amanda was anxious, but the more she thought about it, the more she realized there was nothing to it. If no one was in the building, it would be no problem. If there was still someone there, she could always make up some story about leaving a file of some sort somewhere and looking for it.

Amanda flicked the computer off. She stared at her briefcase for a few seconds. She decided to leave it in the office for the time being.

She opened the door of the office.

The hallway was empty.

As she closed the door behind her, she swallowed

Psychologically, she had reached a point of no return.

CHAPTER 40

At the same time.

Henry Limar sat alone in the dark. The only light in the room came from the two video display units connected to two video recorders.

The video display units were playing nothing but snow.

Henry Limar locked his eyes into the blue tube of video display unit ONE.

In his right hand, Henry held a Colt .45 semiautomatic. The flesh of his fingers was ghost-white. The gun was now at body temperature because he held it for a while. He blinked rapidly, tears running down his face. His breathing was unusually slow for someone who knew he was going to die.

Henry looked down to the gun.

It was loaded with two rounds. The Colt .45 was capable of holding seven rounds in its magazine, but Henry thought two were enough. One to do the job. The other in case he missed or injured himself badly.

As Henry gazed back at the snow of video display unit ONE, tears continued to cascade down his face, trapping themselves in his bushy dark beard. In the night, drowned in the glowing bluish light of the monitors, the tears looked like little crystal droplets.

Henry began to shake his head nervously.

He had seen too much.

Knew too much.

And now, he wanted out.

But he also knew there was no way out. Hugh Gawler was a mean sonofabitch. He wouldn't let him just walk away. There would be a price to pay.

There was always a price to pay.

Henry couldn't remember when he first began to feel uneasy

about the whole business. Which of the incidents triggered his mind? When did he make the connection?

The tears were now staining his white business shirt.

His hand shaking uncontrollably, Henry lifted the gun.

His mouth wide open, he inserted the side of the barrel inside his mouth. It was a large piece. The Colt .45 didn't fit easily or comfortably between his lips. He should have picked a smaller gun. But at the time, he was scared a small piece would not actually kill him, but leave him in a vegetable state.

And it would have been too great of a burden on his wife.

His wife.

Slowly, he counted backwards from ten.

Ten.

His tongue felt like a piece of cardboard.

Nine.

The tears forced him to keep his eyes shut.

Eight...Seven.

He thought about his wife.

Six.

He thought about his life. Not much of a life.

Five.

His hand began to shake nervously. He nearly dropped the gun.

Four...three.

He applied a light pressure on the trigger.

Two.

He opened his eyes.

Suddenly he was blinded by a bright light.

Surprised, he loosened his grip on the Colt .45.

The gun went off.

Someone screamed.

A female voice.

God, damn it! What the fuck is going on?

CHAPTER 41

Amanda tried to open Hugh's office door. As she had anticipated, it was locked.

She moved on to Michael's office, but it was locked as well. She actually felt relieved. She wasn't if she would have been able to go through Michael's belongings without feeling lousy.

She tried entering other offices, but all of them were locked. Feeling cheated, Amanda realized she had been naive to believe her co-workers would leave their office doors open. After all, she had locked her own door.

Disappointed, Amanda walked back to her office. And then she spotted the blue light coming from under the editing room.

Maybe Henry Limar had forgotten to switch off one of the video display units. Maybe he was still in the editing room. No, he couldn't have been. Henry Limar usually finished at 9.30 p.m. She seen him leave his office a few times. And even if he was still in the editing room, he always worked with the light on.

Nervous, Amanda slowed to a creeping pace down the hallway. The blue light from one of the video display units was dancing from under the door.

She stopped in front of the door.

Slowly, she turned the handset.

The door wasn't locked.

Amanda pushed it and peered inside. The blue light was coming from the two video display units, just like she had anticipated.

Then she saw the shadow of a head next to the video display units. She couldn't make up exactly who it was, but she guessed.

'Henry?' she whispered, realizing no-one could have heard her whispering except herself.

As she moved closer, she could see Henry Limar clearly.

He pulled up a gun from his laps on placed the barrel in his mouth.

Hell!

Amanda froze.

She took two steps back.

Her forehead was covered in perspiration. She locked her knees. She didn't know what to do. If she tried to stop him, he might get frightened and shot. She realized she had little time to think.

Amanda never really liked Henry Limar, but watching him blow his brains wasn't exactly what she had in mind.

She was back at the door now, surprised how far back she had moved.

Her hands were clammy.

She reached for the light switch.

Her eyes closed, she held her breath.

She flicked the light on.

Bright light.

A shoot.

Amanda shrieked as she moved towards Henry.

The gun was on the floor.

Silence.

A nausea rippled through her body.

Amanda circled the room to where Henry was seated. She looked into his face, expecting to see his brain resting on his white shirt.

Instead, she saw Henry staring back at her with blood-shot eyes.

CHAPTER 42

One minute later.

Henry looked furious.

'Do you want me to call a doctor?' Amanda said, applying a soaked handkerchief against Henry's forehead.

'Why the fuck did you come in the room?' Henry asked in a dead pan voice.

'I thought you left the video monitors on. I saw the light from under the door. I was on my way out.'

He shook his head. 'I nearly did it. It was close. And then you came. Hell, why did you have to come now?'

Amanda took one step back. 'I think I better ring an ambulance.'

'No.' Henry's look was startled.

'Then you better tell me what's going on.'

'You don't want to know. The least you know, the better. Anyway, why don't you go home? I'll be fine.'

Amanda titled her head. If she went home, and Henry shot himself, she would blame herself.

'Does this have something to do with work?'

'What are you? A shrink?' He tried to stand from his chair, but the effort seemed too great. He remained seated.

Amanda continued to wipe the sweat and tears from his face. 'Maybe I can help,' she said, injecting concern in her tone.

Henry opened his eyes and looked at her. There was fear in them. A fear like she had never seen before. A fear which told her he would have killed himself if she hadn't walked in on him. She had to know why if she was going to help him. Sometimes things seemed worse then they were. If Henry shared a little bit of himself, maybe they could work out something. Just maybe, he would realize his problem wasn't really a big problem. Not to the point of ending his life.

'You have to tell me what's troubling you,' Amanda said, holding on to Henry's hand.

'You don't want to know.'

'If you don't tell me, I'm going to have to tell someone else. You're not going to leave me any choice. I won't be able to handle this by myself.'

Henry seemed thoughtful. He was staring straight past Amanda. 'You did the Senator's program, didn't you?' Henry asked.

'You know I did. I was even late with the videocassettes'

'Sure. I remember. Well, you want to know something?'

'What?'

He locked his blood-shot eyes into hers. 'I'll tell you something. The Senator's killer. I know who he is.'

Amanda swallowed. 'Who?'

'Tomorrow, the killer will be all over the papers. Late edition.'

'How do you know?'

'Trust me. I know who he is.'

'Tell me?'

'Yeah, sure. I'll tell you. But once I tell you, you get the fuck out of here.'

'Who?'

'Gavin White.'

'Who's Gavin White?'

'Some junkie who's been out of work for two years.'

'And how do you know?'

He shifted uncomfortably on his chair. 'Do me a favor and go home,' Henry said. He grabbed the soaked handkerchief from Amanda's hand.

Amanda looked at him and then at the floor. She went down on her knees and grabbed the Colt .45.

'And what are you doing with my gun?' Henry yelled frantically.

'It's going home with me.' Amanda walked towards the door.

'Hey,' Henry screamed. 'Come back here. Give me my gun back.'

Amanda played deaf and walked out the room.

She ran to the washroom, holding the .45 magnum tightly in her hand. *God, it's a large piece.*

She went straight to the ladies' room at the end of the hallway.

As soon as she stood in front of the large mirror above the sink, she placed the gun on the bench. She stared at the gun, realizing the damage it could have caused.

Trembling, she looked in the mirror. Her complexion had turned white. He lower lip was quivering.

With both hands, she grabbed the sink and moved her head down.

Convulsively, she let the sickness out of her stomach.

CHAPTER 43

Santa Monica: two hours later.

Amanda looked at the red fluorescent alarm clock.

1.26 a.m.

Every minute felt like an hour. She kept thinking about Henry Limar. Maybe she had done the wrong thing. She should have never left Henry by himself in the editing room. It was an irresponsible thing to do, and she knew it. If Henry killed himself after she left, she would regret it for the rest of her life. It was just as well she took his gun away.

Amanda looked around the bedroom. She knew it would be hard for her to get to sleep. The room was dark, but she saw light from the lamp post just outside her home.

Wrapped in her blanket, Amanda couldn't get Henry's terrified face off her mind. What could have frightened so much that he wanted to die?

1.27 a.m.

She turned around, avoiding the numbers on the alarm clock. What if Henry had another gun and shot himself overnight? What about Gavin White? Was Henry telling the truth or was he out of his mind? And who was Gavin White? How did Henry know about him?

Amanda turned around again.

1.28 a.m.

Damn it! She reached for the switch light. It was wrong to keep everything to herself. If Henry killed himself, she would always feel responsible for not having done her utmost to save him.

Nervously, Amanda picked up the phone and dialed. She had to talk to someone.

The phone rang six times before it was answered

'Yeah, who's this,' the drowsy voice said at the end of the line.

'It's me, Amanda.'

A few seconds of silence. 'Do you know what time it is?'

Amanda looked at her alarm clock: 1.30 a.m. 'I know. But I had to talk to someone.'

She wasn't sure why she called Hugh Gawler, but at the time it seemed to be the natural thing to do. Hugh was Henry's boss. And if Henry killed himself it would have been at work. So it seemed only normal to call Hugh.

Amanda told Hugh everything about Henry. Everything but the name Gavin White.

'Has he said anything else to you?' Hugh said.

'He didn't want to talk about what was bothering him. I didn't know what to do. I took his gun and left.'

'And he didn't say anything?'

'Nothing. Look, I think we shall call a doctor.'

Silence.

The silence made Amanda feel uncomfortable. What was there to think about? If Henry had a problem, and he was ready to kill himself, then taking him to a doctor seemed the right thing to do.

'Are you there?' Amanda asked, thinking maybe Hugh had gone back to sleep.

'Leave it to me, Amanda. You've done the right thing calling me first. I'll take care of everything. You get some rest. There's no need to be alarmed. I'm sure Henry was just going through a phase.'

'A phase?' Amanda stood straight on her bed. Didn't he listen to her? Henry nearly killed himself. 'He had the gun in his mouth when I opened the door.' She spoke slowly, pronouncing every word as if Hugh was an idiot.

'I know you're feeling a bit stressed, Amanda. But trust me. Things will look different in the morning.'

Amanda hung up.

Staring at the ceiling, she wondered why Hugh acted so casual about Henry's suicide attempt.

As she sank into the sheets, she knew she should have called Michael instead.

CHAPTER 44

Cable News: Same day, 7.36 a.m.

Amanda arrived at the office of CableNews flushed out. She hadn't slept much, and it was showing. Her eyes had dark circles around them. Her complexion was cadaverous. Somewhere at the back of her skull, a migraine was developing.

She crossed the hallway and rushed straight to the editing room where Henry tried the kill himself.

The door was locked.

Feeling blood rushing to her head, Amanda raced to Hugh's office. She thought the worse had happened. Maybe Henry killed himself after she left him by himself.

Amanda stopped at the desk of Tracy Hamilton, Hugh's secretary.

Tracy Hamilton was in her mid-forties. She had head full of red hair and two little eyes shinning like emeralds. She looked up when Amanda approached the desk.

'Can I see Mr Gawler?' Amanda asked, a strain in her tone. She could feel her temper snapping.

Tracy Hamilton didn't seemed alarmed in any way. Obviously she was not aware Henry attempted suicide.

'He's with Mr Limar,' she said with a smile. 'I'll get him to call you as soon as he's finished.'

'Thank you,' Amanda said. The worried frown on her face vanished. Henry Limar wasn't dead.

She stopped in front of her office door and took a deep breath. Reaching for her keys, she noticed the door had been left ajar. *Funny. I'm sure I locked it last night.*

She walked in, placed her briefcase on the desk and circled the room with her eyes. Everything looked in place. *Maybe I did forget to lock the door after all.*

When she sat behind her desk, she sensed something was wrong. She couldn't figure out what it was. It was as if the furniture in the room had been rearranged. She looked around and shrugged. Everything was in its place. She hung her head. This spying business was driving her imagination wild.

But when she lifted her head again, she knew it wasn't her imagination. The keyboard of the computer had been moved. It might have been a small detail, but she always lined it up with the computer monitor.

Anxious, she looked around the desk for something more substantial.

The desk calendar was at the wrong date.

What the hell is going on?

Amanda felt the heat on her cheeks. She was the spy, but someone else was spying on her.

She stood from her chair and raced to Michael's office.

Without knocking, she walked straight in, slamming the door behind her.

Michael looked up and smiled.

'Couldn't wait another minute,' he said, his eyes gleaming with content. He was obviously misinterpreting the reason for her visit. He went on, 'Well, if it makes you feel any better, I missed you too.'

But Amanda's expression remained serious. She stood still, arms folded over her chest.

Michael stood up from behind his desk. 'What's the matter?'

'Someone's been through my office,' Amanda said, keeping her voice down.

'Why are you whispering?'

She injected her tone with anger: 'I'm telling you, someone's been going through my office.'

'Well, what happened? Did they take anything?'

'No, no. Someone moved all the things on my desk.'

Michael smiled. 'The cleaners. They start early in the morning.'

'What cleaners?'

'Hugh hasn't told you?'

A blank look crossed her face.

Michael continued, 'Once a week, at five o'clock in the morning, two contractors clean up the office.'

Amanda puzzled over his response for a few seconds. Sure, she knew about the cleaners, but it didn't explain everything. 'What about my desk calendar?'

'What about your desk calendar?'

'It was flipped to the wrong date.'

Michael moved closer to Amanda, locking his eyes into hers. 'Come on, Amanda, what's the big deal? So, someone accidentally dropped your desk calendar while dusting. You're overreacting. And why would anyone go through your desk?'

Maybe Michael was right. It could have been this whole thing with Henry Limar. She hadn't slept much the previous night. The stress was obviously getting to her.

Amanda moved forward. She crushed her lips against his. 'I'm sorry,' she whispered. 'Maybe you're right. I'm still shocked from last night.'

Michael took one step back and said, 'Last night?'

Amanda told him about Henry Limar.

'Jesus, Amanda,' Michael said. His face seemed to darken. 'Why didn't you call me? No wonders you're in such a state!'

Amanda sighed, almost bringing tears to her eyes. Michael's reaction made her realize how much she had gone through. It was the first time she had seen someone attempting suicide. Maybe after many years of working as a journalist, she would get used to the fact many people were being murdered. Or committed suicide. But for now, the thought of death sent a chill rippling down her spine.

'I don't know how much more of this I can take,' Amanda said, a gloom in her voice.

'Can I make you a coffee?' Michael said. He passed a hand through his hair. His eyes creased with concern. He stared at her as if he was trying to understand what she was going through.

A frown on her face, Amanda was lost in her thoughts.

'Can I make you a coffee?' Michael repeated.

'No, thanks,' Amanda answered, waking up from her daydreaming. 'There's something else I forgot to mention.'

Amanda remembered about Gavin White. But what if Henry was wrong? She would end up looking like a fool.

'What is it,' Michael asked.

Hesitating, she didn't answer immediately She decided it would be better to wait for the evening papers to break the news.

'Never mind,' she said.

As she kissed Michael, she didn't know who to trust anymore.

CHAPTER 45

At the same time.

'What's the matter?' Hugh Gawler asked, redness getting to the root of his salt-and-pepper hair. 'We're not paying you enough?'

Sitting in front of Hugh's desk, Henry Limar was fidgeting with his beard. All he could think about was getting out. Getting a normal life. A normal job. But he knew it was never going to happen. He didn't bother answering Hugh.

There was a pause, and then Hugh added, 'What did you tell Amanda?'

'Nothing,' Henry muttered He had a blank look on his face.

'You better not be lying to me. If she knows anything, I'll find out sooner or later.'

Henry jumped from his chair. His temper snapped. 'I don't want to work here any more. I'm through.'

Henry wished he told Hugh what to do with his job a long time ago. But he never had the courage. And even now, it wasn't courage, but despair which gave him the strength to speak his mind.

Somehow, Henry still hoped Hugh would let him go. But his reasoning told him it was impossible.

Hugh puzzled over Henry's outburst. He shook his head like a pendulum and said, 'Henry, Henry, Henry. What I am going to do with you? We've been friends for a long time. We've seen this company grow from nothing to become the largest cable news provider in the country.'

Henry tried to disguise his lack of interest by locking his eyes into Hugh's. He didn't need a sermon right now.

Hugh went on, 'I know at times things seemed a little unfair, but to run a successful company, we have to break some rules.'

Break some rules! Henry was stunned at the way Hugh took

everything casually. His heart sank. At that second, he wanted to break Hugh's neck.

'You're an important member of our team,' Hugh continued. 'Whatever problem you have, we can solve it here. If you're stressed, take a vacation. Have a week off with full pay. You know I value my employees. If there's anything I can do for you, let me know. I have faith in you, Henry. Have a little faith in me.'

Henry's look was confused. The rage was building up inside him. Hugh was always playing little mind games, making it sound as if Henry was the one losing his marbles. But the worst was how Hugh sounded convincing, so convincing in fact, Henry was losing losing grip with reality.

'I've had enough,' Henry said. 'I want out. I can't cope with this any longer.'

Hugh raised one hand. 'Listen to me, Henry—'

'Out! I went out,' Henry screamed, his face two inches away from Hugh's.

Hugh stood from his desk. He was smiling thinly. 'So what are you going to do? Blow your brains out?' he said, obviously controlling his temper.

Calmly, Hugh opened the top drawer of his desk and removed a Beretta Model 92 9mm Parabellum. He presented the semiautomatic pistol to Henry. 'Be my guest. It's loaded. It's fast. It won't leave a mess.'

Henry's eyes opened widely. Henry glanced at Hugh and at the pistol. *Bastard!* He stood there, tears cascading down his cheeks.

'Oh, for Christ's sake,' Hugh said, putting the gun back in the drawer, 'act your age.'

Henry sniffed and wiped his nose with his sleeve. 'You know I can't take this any more. Why don't you let me go?' His voice was disembodied. He was beaten. His rage turned into whimpering. There was nothing he could do. He knew Hugh wouldn't let him go. If he didn't keep his chin up and changed his tune, Hugh would make his life hell. But he couldn't change his attitude. It was stronger than him. His sense of righteousness was destroying him. Why couldn't he be ruthless like everyone else?

Losing patience, Hugh circled the room. 'Why am I going to let you go? Look at yourself. I let you go, and the next thing I've got is the entire LAPD bursting in my office.'

'But, it's not true. I promise I won't say anything to anyone.' Henry was telling the truth. But he knew Hugh wouldn't take the bite.

Hugh glanced sharply at Henry. 'Look at yourself, Henry. You're a mess. You don't even know the difference between night and day.

Why should I believe you will keep your mouth shut? You can't even stay level-headed with your job.'

Henry began to sob again. 'I just want...' He couldn't finish his sentence at the thought of what Hugh could do to him. He had seen it many times before. Fighting would be useless.

Hugh paced around Henry, his hands behind his back. He stopped behind Henry and rested one hand on his shoulder. 'My friend, there's not need to despair. I'm sure together we'll be able to work something out.'

'But-'

'You think I'm going to waste you. After all the good work you've put into this company. Come on, Henry, you should know me better. I'm a man of integrity. I always look after my own people. I promise you, Henry. together we will find a solution. And before you know it, everything will be back to the way it was.' Hugh massaged Henry's shoulders. 'I promise, Henry. I promise.'

Henry realized the mistake he had made. He should have walked away on day one. He shouldn't have agreed to anything Hugh told him. He shouldn't have taken the money.

And now the secret deal with number 2. If Hugh found out about the deal, he wouldn't just kill Henry, he would have him tortured. If only he could turn back time.

But it was too late.

There would be no way out.

Hugh was never going to let him go.

If Amanda Ryan hadn't walked on him the previous night, it would have been all over by now.

Henry wanted to ask Hugh for the 9mm semiautomatic and blow his own brains right now. Make a mess on Hugh's desk. At least it would be over and done with quickly.

But he knew Hugh had other plans for him.

CHAPTER 46

CableNews: Same day, 10.21 a.m.

Michael Hall called Amanda on the telephone intercom.

Amanda was in her office, organizing her files for story of a break-in at a television celebrity's home.

'They've found the killer of Senator Garry E,' Michael said.

Amanda gulped air. She was sure Henry said it would be in the evening papers. She picked up the handset. 'Who did?'

'Just got a call from LAPD. I've already sent a news crew to the scene.'

'Who was it?'

'Some guy called Gavin White.'

Amanda felt her head burning. Suddenly the room seemed to cave in. Henry had told the truth. But how did he know Gavin White had been the killer? And what else did he know? Was there a link between Senator Garry's death and Henry's suicide attempt?

'When did the police find out?' Amanda continued, startled.

'This morning. An anonymous tip-off.'

Amanda swallowed without saying a word.

'Are you all okay?'

'I'm fine,' Amanda said, a tad short of breath.

Trembling, Amanda hung up the phone. What the hell was it that made Henry so scared? She had to ask him. She had to find out how he knew about Gavin White. But most of all, she had to know why he tried to kill himself.

As she stood from her chair, Tracy Hamilton's voice came through the intercom. 'Amanda, Mr Gawler would like to see you in his office now.'

Henry was just coming out of Hugh's office when Amanda

stopped in front of Tracy Hamilton's desk.

'Henry,' Amanda muttered, a worried look on her face. She reached for him, but he was unresponsive.

Staring at the empty space, Henry moved on to the hallway.

Amanda followed him. She stood in his path. She tried desperately to get his attention. 'Henry, are you all right?' she asked, holding eye contact with him. Just when his eyes locked themselves into hers, Hugh came out of his office.

'He's fine,' Hugh said. 'In my office, Miss Ryan. I'd like to see you *now*.'

Hesitating, Amanda moved away from Henry.

Hugh was looking at them with a cocky smile. 'Come on, Miss Ryan. I haven't got all day.'

Amanda moved away from Henry.

Henry stood still in the middle of the hallway.

Glancing behind her shoulder, Amanda walked into Hugh's office.

'Is he going to be okay?' Amanda asked, injecting her tone with concern.

'He'll be fine,' Hugh said. He sat behind his desk, gesturing impatiently.

'Is he going to get some help?' Amanda took a seat.

'I've given him time off. I've made an appointment with his GP.' Hugh looked up to Amanda, his fingers crossed. 'Now, about last night. Was there anything Henry told you you'd like to share with me?'

Amanda puzzled over his question. 'I've told you everything.'

Hugh stood erected on his chair. 'Perhaps you forgot a detail of some sort.' His tone was serious.

There was a pause. Maybe Hugh knew something about Gavin White too. If Henry did, then there was a good chance Hugh did. Or maybe it was Henry who told him. Now Hugh was waiting to see if she would tell him as well. And if she didn't say anything, then Hugh would probably wonder what she's got to hide.

Of course, Amanda realized there was also the possibility she had an over-zealous imagination. But the name Gavin White was no imagination. She knew what Henry had told her.

'He didn't say anything about work?' Hugh insisted.

'Nothing. Look, you probably know more than I do by now.'

Amanda hoped she was coming across as sincere. Hugh had no way of knowing what really happened the night Henry tried to commit suicide. If he did, he wouldn't bother with the inquisitive interrogation. But still, Amanda couldn't be certain. What if Henry

119

had already told Hugh what he told Amanda? Or maybe Henry didn't confine the whole truth to her, but Hugh thought he did. And now Hugh wanted her to admit it, just in case she knew more than she was telling.

Hugh continued, raising one finger. 'You understand Henry has been under a lot of stress lately. He's a sick man. And whatever he might have told you, he probably made it up.'

Amanda became impatient. She elevated her voice. 'I don't understand, Mr Gawler. What kind of things are you talking about?'

'Things you don't understand, Amanda. Or things you understand, but you choose to forget right now. But just in case your memory begins to catch up with you, I'd like you to remember you're working for me. You're part of a team. As a team member, I expect you to be a good player. The only reason why CableNews is so successful is because we all have faith in one another. There are no secrets in this company. You have a bright future with us, Amanda. Keep that in mind. If you remember anything Henry told you, let me now.'

'Sure. I'd let you know. But I believe I've told you everything I know.'

His smile told her he knew she was lying.

He stood from his desk. He circled the room and stopped behind her. He placed on hand on her shoulder.

Amanda gulped air.

Hugh infused his tone with warmth. 'I like trustworthy employees. How about dinner tonight?'

A chill rippled down Amanda's back. She thought he had given up on seducing her. She leaned forward on her chair. 'I'm feeling a bit tired. You know, all this thing with Henry. I think I'll have an early night.'

'As you wish,' Hugh said, tracing Amanda's jaw line with his finger. 'But don't make me wait too long.'

Amanda shivered. This time she wasn't imagining things. She had been right all the time. At first it could have almost been an innocent flirt. But now, Hugh was moving at high speed.

'I don't think dinner is a good idea,' Amanda snapped. She stood from her chair and glanced at Hugh.

'Come on, Amanda,' he said, 'why did you think I gave you a job at CableNews. Because you qualified first at university? Because Steve Thorn told me not to employ you? You can be so naive.' He reached out and played with her blond hair.

'I wish you wouldn't touch me, *sir*. Your conduct is unsolicited.'

Hugh removed his hands immediately. 'Obviously they've taught you big words at university.'

Amanda felt her stomach turn. She didn't know what it was about Hugh, but he had a way of staying on top of any situation. She crossed the room to the door. 'Is this all you wanted to see me about?'

'I guess it's a definite no for dinner. Unfortunate. I had already made reservations.'

'You'll just have to go ahead and cancel them.'

Amanda knew women never said no to Hugh. He had money. He had charisma. He had power. She could have easily been one of them. But no matter how forward Hugh was, she wouldn't take the bait.

Looking perfectly calm, Hugh regained his chair. 'I'm disappointed in you, Amanda. I thought you were clever. When you took this job, you said you could get used to becoming sociable. So far, you haven't been. If I had known this, I wouldn't have employed you.'

Angry, Amanda turned around and approached Hugh. She slammed her hands on his desk. Her cheeks reddened. She yelled, 'When I said socialize, I didn't mean sucking your cock!'

Hugh gestured for her to keep her voice down. 'I should have known. Maybe I better ask Michael what degree of socialization he has encountered with you. You must be a selective cock sucker then.'

'Do you realize this is sexual harassment?' Amanda said as she began to walk towards the door.

'Sure. But if you'd like to come to dinner with me, the offer still stands.'

Bastard! He won't get away with this!

CHAPTER 47

When Amanda closed the door of the office, Hugh smiled to himself. He poured a Southern Comfort on ice from the office bar.

Amanda was losing her head. All he had to do was keep on pushing. After all she rang him up when Henry tried to kill himself.

Not Michael Hall.

Not anyone else.

Amanda trusted him only. It was a good sign. It showed she had faith in him.

Blind faith maybe, but faith.

In fact she was probably attracted to him. She just didn't know it yet. But Hugh didn't mind waiting. He was used to waiting. But not forever. If Amanda wouldn't come to him, he would find a way to get to her. She was no different from the women he seduced before. Before she'd know, she would come crawling on her hands and knees.

Looking over the panoramic Hollywood scenery from his office, Hugh sipped the Southern Comfort. He wore a smug expression.

Whether Amanda realized it or now, he knew soon she would find herself in bed with him.

Very soon.

CHAPTER 48

East L.A.: The previous day, 11.28 p.m.

The black Ford pick-up stopped in front of Gavin White's apartment. The brick veneer building was in a lot of nine over three levels. Gavin White lived at number eight on the third floor.

Two men dressed in full army camouflage attire came out of the black pick-up. The first man carried a backpack. The second man a Heckler & Koch sub-machine gun chambered in 9mm Parabellum with a built-on silencer. The Heckler & Koch MP5 SD1 was capable of firing at a cyclic rate of 800 rounds per minute from fifteen or thirty-round box magazines.

A third man stayed at the wheel of the Ford pick-up.

None of the men said a word. They had gone over the plan a thousand times. They had to make sure no-one would see them enter the apartment. At such time of the night, it wasn't a challenging task. In and out of the building in a whisk.

The driver would stay in the car during the operation. If anyone approached the apartment, he would honk twice. The other two men would leave through the emergency exist.

But no-one was in the street when the two men made it through the lobby door of the apartment.

So far so good.

They didn't expect any trouble. The area was quiet and most people minded their own business. Even if someone saw something, this was a neighborhood where everyone had something to hide. No one was going to call the police to check out anything suspicious. But like everything else in life, there were no guarantees.

The apartment, built in the sixties, had a single flight of stairs joining the three levels. Quietly, the two men climbed up to the third floor. The staircase was dark. No one had bothered changing the blown-up light bulbs.

The first man took very little time to open the door of the

apartment. He had practiced on many different type of locks during his induction training period. Now he was capable of opening virtually any type of locks within seven seconds. He had been chosen as a lock picker because of his high level of dexterity.

After inserting the pick into the keyhole to raise the pins to their opening point, the lock picker used a tension tool to keep pressure on the pins while rotating. Feeling the vibration of the pins in his fingers, he waited for the distinctive click of the lock before pushing the door in.

Before entering the apartment, he inserted a toothpick inside the lock. If the owner happen to come home early, he wouldn't be able to insert the key in the lock. While the owner would try to figure out what was wrong with the lock, the two men would have enough time to leave by the bathroom window.

Of course, they didn't really expect anyone to come. But they couldn't take a chance, even if the third man seating in the van had the task of raising the alarm if anyone approached the apartment.

The second man flicked on a pen light. They couldn't take the risk of turning the lights of the apartment on. Someone could have seen it from the outside. Although the street was quiet at such time of the night, a neighbor might be suspicious of seeing a light in Gavin's apartment. And if the neighbor was a curious one, she would have noticed Gavin was never home on Thursday evenings. A light in his apartment would have appeared highly suspicious.

The men of the Texan Militia had watched Gavin White closely in the past few months. They knew when he woke up, when he went to bed, how many times he showered -twice a day-, how many different girls he slept with in a month -two brunettes and a blond-, and even the brand of the cereals -Post Raisin Bran and Natural Valley Lowfat Fruit Granola- he had for breakfast.

Tonight was Thursday, and Gavin White was in town having a drink with two friends from the local gym. It was weekly routine. Gavin White had been doing it since the Texan Militia had their eyes on him. He wouldn't get home until 1.00 a.m. on Friday. The men had plenty of time to do what had to be done.

The apartment was small and poorly furnished. The living room consisted of a ten-inch black and white television, a chocolate-brown bean bag, and a plywood home-made coffee table. A single mattress without sheets was thrown in the middle of the bedroom. The apartment had obviously being furnished by someone who was constantly on the move. When the militia checked Gavin White's electricity record, they knew he had only moved in three months ago.

Gavin White was a drifter. He never held a steady job. With a stream of minor drug convictions and assaults, Gavin White was the perfect candidate for the set-up. Single, colored, foul-mouthed, chauvinist and a compulsive liar. There was no way in the world he was going to get out of this one.

In the bedroom, the first man opened the backpack and emptied its content on the mattress. Guns, newspaper clippings of Senator Trevor Garry before and after his death, knifes, hard-core violent erotica, b-grade torture and murder videos, Military equipment.

The first man unzipped the side pocket of the backpack and removed two small 150 ml jars. One of them contained a blood sample of Senator Trevor Garry, the other soil from the Senator's garden.

The first man gave the jars to the second man.

The second man went to the closet of the bedroom and removed a dirty pair of Nike's. With Military precision, he opened the soil jar and spread the sole of the shoes with the dirt. He sprinkled blood from the other jar on top of the shoes. Confident and proud of his work, he placed the shoes back inside the wardrobe.

Meanwhile, the first man was busy spreading evenly the contents of the backpack in the living room.

The second man took a tee-shirt from a drawer in the build-in wardrobe, stepped on it to give it a ragged look, and sprinkled it with the Senator's blood. Satisfied he had done a good job, he found the laundry basket just behind the galvanized fifty-liter washing sink. The second man crumbled the tee-shirt and threw it in the washing basket with the rest of Gavin White's dirty laundry.

The operation was carried out like clockwork. No one said a word. They knew exactly what they had to do and how long it would take to do it.

The first man was still busy arranging the content of the briefcase everywhere in the apartment when the second man finished his task. Everything had to look natural.

No one had ever been at Gavin White's apartment. They knew it. A surveillance team had watched Gavin day and night. Gavin was a loser and a loner.

When both men had finished the job, the apartment looked like the home of a lunatic, a psychopath, gun-crazed sonofabitch.

Soon Gavin White's life would take a new turn. There was enough evidence in his apartment to send him to jail for at least five lifetimes. And if his numbers came up, to the death chamber.

Gavin White's conviction would be big news. Coast to coast prime time nail-biting television real-life drama. It would make the O.J. Simpson trial look like bad acting.

The two men looked at the room one more time, checking they hadn't left any of their tools behind. One slip up ,and the whole plan would crumble. On their way out, the first man removed the toothpick from the keyhole with a pair of tweezers.

Everything was perfect.

A professional job by any standard.

CHAPTER 49

CableNews: Three days later, 4.17 p.m.

Two days after the incident in Hugh's office, Amanda found it hard to concentrate on her work.

The door of her office was closed. Her computer was turned off. She sat gazing at the white wall in front of her. Her thoughts were confused.

Hugh had made it clear how the only reason he employed her was for own gratification. And even though, she spent a lot of time away from Hugh, his presence was felt everywhere in the building. Even when she was locked alone in her office, it was as if Hugh was looking over her shoulder. When she closed her eyes, she could feel his breath down her neck, the smell of his after-shave, the flicker of his hand on her hair.

Amanda experienced an uncomfortable mixture of fear and attraction to Hugh Gawler. As much as his manners repulsed her, his aura had strong magnetic power. He could talk himself in and out of anything. Amanda wasn't surprised by his success.

But now she feared she was in the wrong place at the wrong time. She had to figure out whether she would continue to stay at CableNews. Sure, she still had the spying assignment to complete, but now the whole idea seemed silly.

And the incident with Gavin White drove her insane. She found it hard to sleep at night. During the day, she struggled to focus on her work. How did Gavin White really fit into all this?

It was clear Henry Limar knew about Gavin White before anyone else. And since he did, then something strange was going on. Amanda wasn't sure she wanted to find out what. If she tried too hard, maybe she would end up suicidal like Henry Limar.

She kept on turning the story in her head, but couldn't find an answer.

Maybe there was no answer.

Nothing made much sense.

If Henry Limar knew about Gavin White, then why didn't he tell the police? Or was there an informant at the police who rang him up and told him? If this was the case, what was Henry so afraid of? What was the big deal? In the cut-throat business of journalism, it was important to have good contacts. If Henry Limar had better contacts than others, then it was no sin.

But still, there were too many lose ends.

Henry never told Amanda what he was so afraid of. And now Amanda's curiosity was playing with her emotions. On the one hand, she wanted to know the truth. On the other, she felt her life might be in danger if she got too involved. If there was some sort of conspiracy going on at CableNews, and if Henry Limar's suicide attempt was tied to this conspiracy, then she had all reasons to fear for her life.

By Wednesday, Amanda no longer wanted to stay at CableNews. She reasoned how the whole idea of spying was silly, not to mention dangerous.

Henry Limar was on leave because of stress.

Hugh Gawler was attending a conference in New York with some broadcasting big-shots.

Amanda felt she was being unfair to Michael. Her relationship would never be an honest one if she couldn't tell him what was on her mind. And as long as she worked as a spy, she had to lie to him. It wasn't an ideal relationship. She wanted to devote more time to Michael. The relationship had to be an honest one. But as long as she continued working for CableNews, she knew this would be impossible.

At 5.00 p.m. exactly, Amanda decided to call at the office of CableNews to see Steve Thorn. She had to convince him to let her leave CableNews. Since Steve didn't want her to be there initially, it wouldn't take much to persuade him.

Besides, she needed to talk to someone. Keeping everything in her head was driving her insane. The pressure was too much. It felt wrong not to share the truth with Michael. Would Michael ever accept her spying at CableNews? Amanda realized how naive she had been by deciding to spy for Globe Network.

Caught in L.A. peak-hour traffic, she realized Steve was probably not the best person to talk to. But she didn't have any choice. She would explain everything carefully, leaving some of the details out. Hopefully Steve would tell her to pack her bags and come back home to Globe Network.

But even now, she wasn't sure it really was she wanted. Maybe it was better if she just packed her bags and went home to Australia instead.

She promised herself if she got her job back at Globe Network, she would never be bored again. This time she would make it work. And if no one would give her enough work to get on with, she could always lock herself in the office and write freelance articles.

Amanda parked the green Camaro outside the gray Globe Network building on 1st Street, near the Los Angeles Times Building. She began to feel nervous, the small of her back damp from tension. She slammed the door of the Camaro and took a deep breath. All she had to do was to be patient and diplomatic with Steve Thorn.

Everyone on the ninth floor of the building was running like crazy. They acknowledged Amanda's presence in a flash with a smile or hand gesture.

When Amanda stepped into Steve's office, he seemed busy and annoyed. He saw her coming through the glass partition of his office, but ignored her.

Amanda walked straight in, not bothering to knock. 'I've had enough,' she said. She spoke as if her life was about to come to an end. Her cheeks were flushed and her hands clammy.

'Knock, knock, knock,' Steve said. 'Hasn't anyone taught you to knock before walking into someone else's office.'

She placed the palms of her hands on his desk, locking her eyes into his. 'I'm quitting CableNews. I'm coming back to work for you.'

Steve stretched on his chair, a smug smile on his face. He placed his hands behind his head. 'You've only been there a month,' he said, blandly. 'After all the trouble you've caused me, you think I'm going to take you back after a month?'

'Okay, so you were right. I admit it. Can't I just get my job back?'

He rolled his eyes. 'Be patient. You haven't learned a thing in a month. What have you done? Senator Garry's story. I saw the program. It was good. But what have you learned?'

'No big secrets. Everyone just works hard. I don't know.' She stood back form the desk, her hands behind her back.

Steve leaned forward. 'Look, Amanda. I don't think it's the right time for you to give in right now. Give it another two months or so. Then we'll review the situation.'

Amanda shook her head. She didn't want another two months. She didn't want another day. How could she ever work with Hugh again? How could she ever look at him in the eyes? But Steve Thorn didn't understand. She didn't tell him everything. And it was probably why he wasn't willing to let her go.

'I don't get it,' Amanda said. 'I thought you didn't want me to do this investigation. Why do you suddenly insist on keeping me at CableNews?'

Steve puzzled over the question. She asked for trouble and now she got it. 'I've done all I could for you, Amanda. What is it you want from me? My support? I don't really care. Just stay there for a few more months, and then I'll review your situation.'

Amanda had to tell him about Hugh Gawler. She abhorred the man. And with Michael working there, everything was such a mess. Hugh already knew Michael and her were lovers. It wouldn't take long before Michael would lose his job. This was not something Amanda wanted to be held responsible for.

'There something important I haven't told you,' Amanda muttered

'What?' Steve really seemed annoyed. He grabbed paper work from his desk. 'Make it fast. I haven't got all day.'

Amanda told Steve about Hugh's advances. 'I don't know how to handle him any more,' she added.

Steve stood from behind his desk, unmoved. 'I understand this is a difficult situation for you, Amanda. But try to look at it as a challenge to your assignment.'

Amanda opened her eyes widely. 'What kind of a challenge is that? The guy is sexually harassing me. Should I wait until he rapes me? Jesus, what the hell is wrong with all you guys?'

'Look, Hugh flirting with you is not as bad as you think. This will help you to get closer to him. You know, win his trust.'

'Why would I want to win his trust? I'm not interested in Hugh Gawler.' She blushed, remembering how she felt Hugh's sexual magnetism when she first met him. 'I don't give a damn about him. Not now, anyway.'

Steve pointed his index at her face. 'Ah, but you see. You are interested in him. Maybe not as someone to screw around with, but you are interested in him. This is where you are wrong. You're young and inexperienced. It's why I didn't what you to go and spy there in the first place. You have to focus on your work and not worry about all the charade going on around you.'

Amanda frowned.

'You're spying for us. Therefore, you must find information that would explain why CableNews is always one step ahead of us. And to find such information, you have to get close to the person who knows everything. You can't just give up when your personal space is been stepped on.'

'Are you suggesting I use Hugh Gawler?'

'What I'm saying is Hugh is using you for his own purpose. Why don't you take advantage of the situation instead of running away from it? Use the sonofabitch. He's using you, isn't he? You just told me yourself.'

Amanda knew Steve was right. Maybe she had shown signs of weakness. Would she just let everything go because she felt a little insecure around Hugh Gawler. 'Okay, say I decide to go ahead with your advice. What do you suggest I do to get this so called information you're after?'

'You're an attractive woman, Amanda. Use it to your advantage. Play his game. Pretend you're interested in his advance. Lead him on for a while. See how much is willing to share if you give him the promise of more things to come. Don't be a victim. Use the situation to your advantage.'

Amanda reflected on the idea. If Hugh wanted her so badly, instead of playing hard to get, she could manipulate him. Reversing roles would be interesting. But still, the idea frightened her. What would happen if Hugh touched her again. Would she just go along and play the game? How far would she go? She knew Hugh wanted to make love to her, but she wasn't willing to go all the way just to get some answers.

'This sounds like a good idea,' Amanda said, 'but I don't know if I can use someone in such a way.'

'He is using you. What's the difference,' Steve said, his voice now filled with excitement. 'He never employed you because he wanted you to work for him. You told me so. You only got in the hot seat because he wants to fuck you. Was it fair? And what about your assignment? Did you think it was going to be easy? Come on, Amanda. If you're going to become a good journalist, you can't give up as soon as you feel uncomfortable. You're a woman, for Christ's sake. And a damn good looking one too, I might add. Some guys out there are waiting to jump in your pants. Journalism is a tough business, and as a woman you have to play it tough. You can't just give up because some moron's testosterone is shooting through the roof.'

Giving up now meant she had wasted precious time for nothing. Since Globe Network was going to be out of business soon, then it would get her nowhere to come back and work here.

'Maybe you're right,' Amanda said, half convinced Steve's logic was the right path to follow.

'Of course I am. I tell you what. If you have any problems, just give me a call. I'm here if you need to talk to someone.'

Amanda found it strange how suddenly Steve became friendly to her. Maybe he wasn't such a bad person after all. Sometimes people were not what they first seemed to be. And since there was no one else she could really talk to, then Steve's offer was hardly an offer to refuse. At least she wouldn't be fighting the battle by herself. She had a shoulder to cry on.

More or less satisfied with what Steve had told her, Amanda stood from her chair. 'Thanks for you help, Mr Thorn. I'll keep my eyes open. I won't let Hugh Gawler underestimate me.'

'You're welcome,' he said and gave her a firm handshake.

Amanda was determined to get back at Hugh Gawler.

CHAPTER 50

When Amanda left the office, Steve Thorn picked up the phone. 'She's just left'.

'And?'

'Nothing. She telling me she was wasting time working for you. But I told her to hang on a bit longer.'

'Good. If she finds out anything, let me know.'

'Sure.'

Steve wasn't going to tell Hugh Gawler he knew about the flirting. It would make everything much more interesting. Maybe later, after Hugh had pushed himself on Amanda, Steve would counsel Amanda into finding an attorney and suing for sexual harassment.

Steve Thorn smiled to himself at the idea.

This would be another perfect way to get even with Hugh.

And if Amanda was having a hard time dealing with Hugh Gawler, it served her right.

Steve had to admit the girl was unbelievably attractive. Many times he fantasized about making love to her. But he never took his fantasies seriously. Not like Hugh Gawler.

Hugh could get anyone he wanted. He was a greedy bastard. If he wanted Amanda in his bed, he would do everything in his power to get her.

Steve Thorn knew Hugh Gawler didn't just have fantasies.

He acted on them.

Satisfied with his little act, Steve smiled to himself. Amanda Ryan was so naive. She believed everything she was told. Her attitude made him laugh. She truly believed she was important in all of this. In spite of his critical attitude, Steve couldn't help admiring her. She was so determined to succeed as a journalist, she took risks no one else would bother taking. She obviously didn't realize she was wasting her time. She thought herself of great importance, but she was nothing.

A dispensable token in a power game.

CHAPTER 51

Santa Monica: Same day, 6.47 p.m.

When Amanda got home, she didn't want to stay by herself.

She had opened all the windows of the townhouse. Outside, she could hear some kids playing. The temperature was mild but inviting. The sweet smell of the ocean circled the house.

Tired, Amanda lay on her bed, watching the white curtains of her room play gently with the outside breeze. Although the talk with Steve Thorn had released some tension, her thoughts were still confused.

The incident with Henry Limar was fresh in her mind. She knew if she had come into the editing room seconds later, she would have found Henry's brain all over the floor. Such realization made her nauseous. She knew she was heading for another sleepless night.

Tired of listening to her own thoughts, Amanda rang up Michael and told him she was anxious to see him. She had had a long day, and she could really do with some loving and cuddling.

But as his car pulled up in the driveway, she wanted to be alone.

Since she begun working for CableNews, her moods shifted from one minute to the next. The only thing she wanted to do right now was to run herself a warm bath. Afterwards, she would curl back up in bed and read herself to sleep with a Sydney Sheldon.

She was lost in thoughts when two knocks on the door made her jump from the bed. She had heard Michael's car parking in the driveway less than a minute ago, but already she had forgotten he was there.

Amanda stood from the floral couch, surprised at how jumpy she was. She walked down the hallway, wondering why she had bothered inviting Michael. Half an hour ago she wanted some company. Now she felt like being alone again.

When she opened the front door, he smiled at her tenderly.

She was glad he came after all. An evening all by herself would have been such a bad idea. She would have drowned in her thoughts, running all those stories in her head, trying to make sense of everything happening around her.

Half way through a dinner of cold pork and three veggies, Amanda locked her eyes into Michael's. 'I've got to tell you something,' she said, her tone dead-serious.

She knew there was no point in keeping dark secrets from Michael. She loved him and wanted their relationship to be the best. But she knew unless she was honest with him, the perfect relationship would only be a perfect illusion.

And perhaps it wasn't because she wanted a perfect relationship. Perhaps it was because she cared too much about Michael to lie to him.

'Shoot up,' Michael said, gazing back at his plate.

'It's serious.'

Michael looked up, as if expecting some romantic revelation about wanting to marry him, or something similar.

'You know how the police found the killer of Senator Trevor Garry?'.

'I'm the one who told you.'

'Henry Limar knew about it.'

'Of course he knew. Everybody knew.' Michael picked a carrot with his fork.

'No, he knew before you told me.'

Michael didn't look surprised. 'So he did. Maybe Hugh told him. I didn't find out until around ten in the morning, but the cops knew since eight.'

'Henry told me about Gavin White the night before.'

Michael dropped his fork on the plate. 'What do you mean he told you the night before?' He had a blank look on his face.

Half-hesitating, Amanda told him how she found Henry with a colt .45 in his month the day before the police arrested Gavin White. She also told him Henry knew Gavin White was the killer before they found out the next morning.

Michael puzzled over the news for a few seconds. 'Who else knows about it?'

'About what?'

'What you've just told me.'

'Hugh knows about Henry trying to commit suicide. I haven't told anyone Henry knew about Gavin White.'

'So, I'm the first person you talk to?'

'Yes.'

Michael's expression relaxed. He picked up his fork and played with a piece of cauliflower. 'Maybe Henry had contacts at LAPD.'

'It's possible. It crossed my mind. But something still doesn't make sense.'

'What? The cops must have had Gavin White as a suspect for a while. It's not like they just jumped on him overnight.'

'Yes, but how come Henry didn't say anything?'

'To who?'

'To us. Don't you think Hugh would have liked to know who the killer was? Don't you watch television? You work for a news channel, remember?'

Amanda knew she was right. Even if Henry had known just the night before, he would have told someone at the office. It would have meant getting the story much easier. And if Henry had known for a while, then why did he keep quiet? And why did he try to kill himself? It was obvious he was afraid of something, something so frightening, he was ready to die rather than facing it.

'I'm sure there is good explanation to all this,' Michael said, gently applying the palm of his hand on Amanda's cheek. 'You're overworked. Why don't we go to bed early?'

Amanda would have loved to believe Michael, but to her it seemed more complex. She had gone over the story in her head a thousand times. Her instinct told her something was very wrong, far worse than they could imagine.

Amanda went on, 'The problem is you weren't there the night Henry tried to commit suicide. You haven't seen his face the way I have. Believe me, this was not a phase he was going through. I've seen death in his eyes. The man was frightened to the point of taking his life.'

'It happens all the time. Marital problems, money problems.'

'If it was a marital problem, he would have mentioned it. Henry was in mental agony over something, and he could no longer take it. You want me to believe he suffered from some kind of depression. If you had been there that night, you would have seen the fear in his eyes. He wanted to kill himself because he feared something. Something or someone is after him, Michael. It's what I reckon.'

Michael chewed over her hypothesis His face expressed boredom Suddenly, he stood straight on his chair. 'Okay, so what do you want to do? Henry is on leave. Do you want to knock at his door and ask him to elaborate?'

'Why not?'

'Did it ever occur to you the reason why he hasn't told you anything is because he didn't want to?'He looked as if he wanted to say something when he left Hugh's office the other day. We made

137

eye contact, and he looked desperate. He was crying for help. But Hugh rushed me into the office. And then Hugh began questioning me about Henry?'

'Of course. He was concerned about him.'

'No, I said *questioning* me. He insisted I tell him whatever Henry had told me. And when I said I didn't know anything, then...' Amanda stopped mid-sentence. She didn't want to tell Michael about Hugh's advances. She pictured in her mind Michael storming into Hugh's office the very next day and losing his job over an argument.

And all that because of her.

'Then what?' Michael asked, now somehow interested.

'Then...he insisted, saying how he must have told me something.'

Michael stood from his chair. He talked while clearing the table. 'Why don't you go and run yourself that bath you've been talking about? I'll do the dishes.'

Amanda rolled her eyes.

Damn! I wish someone would take me seriously!

As Amanda knelt into the steaming hot bath, her eyelids grew heavy. She was more exhausted than she had first realized. Working for CableNews didn't seem glamorous any more. She should have settled for a daily newspaper. Or if she really wanted peace and quiet, for a small country bi-weekly.

But now she was deep down in this spying business.

And she wasn't sure what it really meant.

All she knew was her career as a journalist was not going to take off. This acknowledgment seeded a deep frustration in her. If all came to worse, all this mess with Hugh Gawler could become a source of inspiration for some creative writing.

The scent of lavender shower gel filled the room.

Amanda closed her eyes and let her body absorb the heat of the hot bath. Even with her eyes closed, she could see it was still daylight outside.

She thought about Michael downstairs. Why was it he didn't really believe her? She felt disappointed in a way. She had hoped Michael would be the one to believe in her. But he seemed just as aloof as everyone else.

And then her mind wondered into a dream-like state.

She didn't hear Michael coming in the room.

She felt his presence instead.

'Decided to join me?' she said, letting her brown aureoles peak out of the water. She opened her eyes and saw him smiling at her.

'If there's room for two,' he said, shedding his clothes.

In less than ten seconds, Michael was in the bath, rubbing himself against Amanda. He slid his hands along her body, slowly moving them towards her breasts. With his fingers, he felt her brown nipples hardening.

Inside, Amanda felt a warm sensation taking over her. She hadn't felt so good for a while. Michael's hands were gentle. Slowly she felt his caresses working up her body. Her mind was floating gently in a mist of sensuous desires and lust. She opened her mouth and gasped for air. Instead she found Michael's lips crashing against hers.

They made love in the bathroom, bodies hot, wet and sweaty.

For a moment, Amanda forgot her problems. Michael made her feel protected. There seemed to be nothing which could harm her.

If only things could remain this way forever.

She guided Michael's hard organ inside her.

Later that night, while lying in Michael's arm, she realized the peace she had found was only temporary.

Tomorrow would come.

And all her problems with it.

CHAPTER 52

Longbeach: The next morning, 8.02 a.m.

When Hugh Gawler arrived at the reception and was escorted to the conference room on the second floor. The sky was perfect blue. He could hear the ocean in the distance.

The hotel was situated in a secluded street of Second Avenue. Hugh had chosen this particular hotel for the meeting because of its location. The street was almost invisible from the many shops and restaurants on Second Avenue. So early in the morning, he knew little could go wrong.

The room attendant took him to a small conference room.

Hugh was the first one there.

The conference table was large enough to accommodate twenty-five people. Near the bay window was an eighteen inch television screen with an Amstrad double-decker video recorder. Next to it stood a clean white board with three color markers resting on its silver metallic edge.

Hugh's feet sank inside the one-hundred-percent burgundy wool carpet. He took a seat at the large table.

'Can I bring you something to drink, Mr Johnson?' the room attendant asked, his hands behind his back.

'No, thanks.'

Hugh had given the clerk at the reception a fake name when he booked the conference room. It was important the meeting be held in total secrecy. He could have chosen someone else to make his transactions, but Hugh didn't trust anyone else. He had learned after spending years in the trade how no one could be trusted, no matter how close you were to them. Greed was an essential part of success in any business which dealt in corruption.

Hugh looked at his gold Must de Cartier watch.

8.05 a.m.

Another five minutes and he would leave the building. He hated people who were not punctual. It showed lack of respect for others. It also meant something could have gone wrong. And Hugh wasn't going to hang around until LAPD or the FBI busted in the room.

To Hugh's relief, the other man arrived less than thirty seconds later.

Senator Terence Maxwell shook hands with Hugh Gawler. He sat at the conference table, a blank look on his face.

Both men hated each other. But this was business and nothing else. Each would get what they wanted and walk away a winner.

'Have you got the money?' Hugh asked, not feeling the need nor the time to greet his partner in crime.

Senator Terence Maxwell placed his briefcase on the conference table. He turned the combination lock to 2934 and opened the briefcase. It was filled with one hundred dollar notes. 'One hundred thousand. It's all in there.'

Hugh opened his briefcase and began to switch the money over.

'Are you sure it's safe in here,' Senator Terence Maxwell asked, blinking rapidly. His eyes circled the room nervously. If this transaction came to the intention of the police, it would be the end of his career and his life. Hugh Gawler knew the Senator had a morbid fear of spending the rest of his life in jail with murderers and rapists. He wouldn't survive a week.

Senator Terence Maxwell was a pen pusher. Slim, red lips and white skin, he was the perfect representation of a nerd. His thick glasses sat awkwardly on his nose, making his eye balls look twice as big as normal. For a politician, his physic was a huge disadvantage. But it never stopped the man to get things done his way.

'I've asked not to be disturbed,' Hugh said, injecting some authority in his tone. 'You don't have to worry about a thing. Let's just get this over and done with.'

'What if someone finds out we killed Trevor Garry?'

'No one's going to find out as long as you keep your mouth shut.'

Hugh Gawler had asked a deposit of $100,000 dollars for the death of Senator Trevor Garry and another $100,000 on completion of the job. The fees also included favorable news reports on Senator Trence Maxwell.

Two hundred thousand dollars was pigeon feed. He could have asked Senator Terence Maxwell for five times that amount.

But money wasn't the issue.

The money would be re-directed to the Texan Militia. The

Militia had done a good job with the murder of Senator Trevor Garry.

The real money was in the distribution the exclusive footage of the Senator's death. So far, distribution of Senator Garry's footage has made CableNews twelve million dollars. And now the follow-up story with Gavin White would make even more money.

Hugh Gawler finished switching over the money and closed the briefcase. 'I'll get in touch with you regarding the talk show,' he said in a matter-of-fact tone.

An exclusive face to face interview had been arranged with Senator Terence Maxwell. The show would highlight the politician's qualities. It would ensure the fresh-faced replacement of Senator Garry wouldn't stand a chance at the forthcoming election.

'It's nice doing business with you,' Senator Terence Maxwell said, obviously relieved nothing had gone wrong.

'You're welcome.'

Hugh Gawler shook the senator's clammy hand and watched him step out of the room.

As he grabbed his briefcase, his thoughts drifted back to Amanda Ryan. She had been on his mind for the last few days. She was playing hard to get. Didn't she know this made Hugh Gawler even more determined to get her? The longer she made him wait, the stronger the desire.

And the tougher he would get.

When Hugh Gawler left the conference room, he had no idea he was being watched.

CHAPTER 53

East Los Angeles: The next day, 1.59 a.m.

Henry Limar was drunk when he left the Blue Turtle bar. The air was cold, but he couldn't feel it. He stumbled along the footpath, trying to figure out which foot had to go in front of the other. His hair and beard were messy, and his tie loosened down to his torso. No one in the street could have imagined Henry Limar was a man earning in excess of $60,000 a year.

Not that they would really care anyway.

The street was filled with losers, drug dealers, psychopaths and other misfits of a highly civilized society. And tonight, Henry looked no different from them. He fitted nicely with the environment. Even at 2.01 a.m., East Los Angeles was very much alive.

A few people looked at him, but no one gave a damn. Cheap suit and an over-zealous tie. There was stain of vomit on his yellow-would-be-white shirt. Henry looked twenty years older than his forty-two. He could have never imagined he would end up like this. No friends, no hope, no one to turn to.

Defeated by fate, Henry wanted to walk the street until the end of time. He knew nothing could rescue him now. His choice of career had been a big mistake. Nothing could have prepared him for all the deceptions he had faced in the last few years.

The sickness was taking over Henry. He couldn't see straight. The only thing he could think of to ease the pain was his gun. *Damn Amanda Ryan!* Taking his Colt .45 away from him. Why did she have to walk in the editing room that night? It would have been all over by now if she had minded her own business.

As Henry continued to zigzag the footpath, he thought about

143

drowning himself.

Too dramatic.

What if he got rescued on time and became brain damaged instead?

No.

It had to be a clean death. Something fast and certain.

His brain felt like a war zone. He didn't want to think any more. The whole scheme had run over his mind hundreds of times. There was no way out of this.

During the past six months, he had slowly built himself up to an acute depression. No matter how hard he tried, he couldn't think optimistically for even half a second. His life stunk and he wanted out.

Only twenty feet behind him, a black Mercedes 420SE slowed along the footpath. Its black tinted windows made it impossible for anyone to see the occupants.

Too pre-occupied with his gloomy thoughts, Henry didn't notice the black 420SE.

No one else in the street cared about the Mercedes. There was a lot of dealing going on late at night, and no one was surprised if a Mercedes pulled up on the curb.

Slowly, the black Mercedes moved closer to Henry.

As Henry continued to stumble his way across the footpath, the back window of the Mercedes opened slowly.

'Hey, Henry,' a voice shouted inside the vehicle.

Henry hardly heard the voice. The buzzing in his ears took over his mind. Everything around him was blurry. His eyesight was locked into tunnel vision. The familiar voice didn't register in his memory bank.

The Mercedes stopped to a halt. The back door swung open. Hugh Gawler stepped out of the car. He wore a black shirt, a black wrinkle-free slack and a matching blazer. With his hair slicked back, he no longer looked like the owner of a multi-million dollars news network, but like a drug lord.

Nausea taking over him, Henry vaguely heard word which sounded like his name. But he couldn't tell whether it was coming from inside or outside his head.

In a very casual manner, Hugh Gawler stepped behind Henry and grabbed him by the right arm. 'How're you doing Henry? You don't look too good.'

Not surprised, Henry turned around to see the face of Hugh smiling with all its teeth. It was like meeting the devil in the streets. Maybe Henry was dead already. He didn't know. Confused, he mumbled something incomprehensible.

'You should be at home,' Hugh said. 'What do you think sick leaves are for? I've been looking all over town for you.'

Despite being drunk and out of his mind, Henry knew something was wrong. Why did Hugh track him down in the middle of the night in a street full of drug pushers and teenage prostitutes? Henry knew very well Hugh didn't care about his welfare. Hugh was obviously here to destroy him. Henry wished he had the strength to tell Hugh to get stuffed, but he couldn't get his mouth to form one syllable.

'Let's take a little walk,' Hugh said darkly. 'I need to know something.' Hugh grabbed Henry firmly by the arm and dragged him to a badly lit side-street. 'Something I need to clear up in my mind.'

Henry mumbled. 'What d'you want. I'f told ya all I know.'

'I know you have, Henry. But, it's just sometimes the mind plays tricks. One minute you don't remember a thing, and the next you've got enough material in your head to write a book.'

'Fuck off.' He yawed and turned away.

'Ah, come, Henry. It's not nice. I'm the guy who gave you a job. Look, I'm going to be straight with you. I only want to know what you've told Amanda Ryan.'

'Nofin.'

'It's what you said the last time. But we know it's not true. What did you tell her?'

Henry was not a happy man. Why couldn't Hugh just leave him in peace? 'She took my gun,' Henry said.

'I know she did.' Hugh reached inside his blazer and removed the Colt .45. 'Here it is. I got it back for you. Thought you might need it. You know, self-defense. Walking the streets at night can be dangerous.' Hugh gazed around as if he had never been in East Los Angeles.

Shaking with fear and drunkenness, Henry gazed at the Colt .45. He lifted his eyes to Hugh.

Hugh was still smiling at him as if he was his best friend.

Henry tried to snatch the gun, but lost balance and nearly fell over.

Hugh caught Henry on time. 'I'll make a deal. You tell me what you told Amanda, and you can get your gun back.' The magazine of the Colt .45 was fully loaded with seven rounds. Henry reached for the gun, but Hugh held it away from him. 'What did you tell her, Henry?'

Henry wanted the gun badly. Amanda Ryan came back to mind.

He remembered the night she walked in on him. But the memory was shaky. She came behind him. Not, it wasn't like that. She turned the light on first. It was minutes after he copied the videocassette He hadn't even turned off the video display units.

Hugh kept smiling. 'Is it coming back, Henry? Just give me one thing, and the gun is yours.'

Henry puzzled over what he remembered.

The videocassette

Amanda Ryan.

'The videocassette,' He mumbled.

'What videocassette?'

Did Henry tell Amanda Ryan about the videocassette? He couldn't remember for sure.

But then he saw the gun.

The pain.

He had to get rid of the pain.

The gun was there was within his reach.

His gun.

Henry wanted the gun now.

Amanda Ryan.

The videocassette

Maybe he did tell her about the videocassette after all.

'The videocassette,' Henry mumbled again as he reached for the gun.

'What videocassette?' Hugh said, his eyes widening.

'I told her about the videocassette'

'What videocassette are you talking about?'

'The videocassette,' Henry said, a mouthful of vomit rising from his stomach.

Hugh moved to the side just on time. Henry opened his mouth and vomited all over his beard and shirt.

'Oh, Jesus, Henry,' Hugh said. 'You don't look good man.' He pushes the gun into Henry's ribs. 'Why don't you take this?'

Wiping his mouth with his sleeve, Henry felt the barrel of the Cold .45 digging into his abdomen.

Hugh had his finger on the trigger. 'Take the fuckin' gun, Henry.'

Sweating profusely, Henry grabbed the barrel of the .45.

'I gotta run now,' Hugh said, as he began to walk away.

Then suddenly, Hugh turned back as if he had forgotten something.

Henry was standing against the wall with the gun in his hand.

146

Hugh walked back to him. 'And Henry. You life sucks. Why don't you do something about it.' Hugh raised Henry's hand until the gun was parallel to his temple. 'Come on you sonofabitch. Just press the god-damn trigger.'

Hot tears came rolling down Henry's face.

The pain.

He held the gun tightly, his knuckles turning white.

'I'll see you at your funeral, Henry,' Hugh said as he walked out of the side-street.

Henry was alone now.

The gun was still aiming at his temple.

His arm was locked into position.

The pain.

He could now feel the cold of the night.

Amanda Ryan.

Hugh Gawler.

Bastard!

He pressed the trigger.

CHAPTER 54

Santa Monica: same day, 6.32 a.m.

A blank look on her face, Amanda sat cross-legged on the living-room couch, a bowl of cereals on her laps. She switched from one news channel to another with the remote control.

The body of Henry Limar had been found at around 3.00 a.m. by two teenagers. The bullet from the Colt .45 had blown off half of Henry's face. He was identified by his driver's license.

Still shocked, Amanda picked up the phone and dialed Michael's home number.

'Yeah.' His voice was disembodied.

'It's me,' Amanda said. 'Did you see the news this morning?'

'I'm still in bed.'

Amanda told him about Henry's suicide.

Suddenly Michael seemed fully awake. 'When did it happen?'

'Early this morning. Between midnight and three.'

'I'm stepping in the shower now. I'm coming over.'

Flicking the television off with the remote control, Amanda jumped from the couch. Confused, she let the bowl of cereal slip from her hands. She felt she was the one to blame. Maybe there was something she could have done. She didn't know what, but somehow she felt shamefully responsible for Henry's death.

While sponging off the cereal and milk from the carpet, Amanda wondered how it could have happened. Henry should have been at the care of his doctor. Circling the living room, she remembered Hugh telling her he had arranged an appointment with Henry's GP. So why was it Henry shot himself in the early hours of the morning in the middle of nowhere?

While she was showering, Amanda's mind became numb with guilt. One thing seemed now certain: she was not going to give up

148

her work at CableNews. Something was wrong, and what it was, it got to Henry. She didn't want to jump to any conclusion, but she felt Henry's death was somehow tied to Hugh Gawler. Why did Hugh insist so much to make her talk? Talk about what? What was it Henry should have told her? Did Hugh know whatever it was Henry knew? Was this the reason why Henry killed himself? There was no doubt in her mind foul play had taken part.

Bitter, she stepped out of the shower and dried herself with a white cotton towel. Since she started spying at CableNews, she had achieved nothing. The only thing she had done was running around and getting told off.

And now she couldn't rid of the guilt she was responsible for Henry's death. Something had to be done.

It was time to move on. No more sitting around and feeling sorry for herself. Steve Thorn was right. If Hugh wanted her badly, then she should play the game his way.

Amanda was just coming down the stairs when Michael parked his car behind hers in the driveway.

Michael knocked once at the front door.

Amanda rushed down the hallway. She opened the front and kissed him hello. He wore a three two-piece dark suit, white shirt and a red tie secured with a golden pin in the shape of an airplane

Michael followed her to the kitchen.

'I can't believe this has happened,' Amanda said, pouring water into two cups of instant decaf. Like Michael, she was already dressed to tackle the day. But unlike her appearance, her mind was a shamble.

'What did you expect? Of course he was going to kill himself!'

'But I thought he went to see his GP,' Amanda said. 'It's what Hugh told me.'

'And maybe he did.'

'So what was he doing in the streets at 2.00 p.m.?'

'The guy was depressed.'

Amanda gave Michael his cup of decaf. 'Something's not right.' There was a blank look on her face.

'Come on, Amanda, you're obviously upset. What do you think happened? Someone killed him?'

Amanda placed her cup of decaf on the kitchen table. 'Who gave him the gun?'

'Didn't you tell me he had one?' He sipped his decaf.

'I gave it to Hugh.'

'Maybe he had another one.'

'The news report said he was shot with a Colt .45. There showed a picture of the gun on television. It sure did look like the gun I grabbed from him the other night.'

'Okay, let's assume you're right. Let's say Henry is involved in something unethical and very dangerous. Maybe he was selling drugs or something. Maybe he owned a lot of money to a lot of people. Is this really any of your concern?'

Amanda gave Michael an angry glance and rolled her eyes.

Michael went on, 'Well, not if you're insisting on pinning it on Hugh. I mean, there's nothing you can do about it anyway.'

Amanda couldn't believe Michael's arrogance. 'You worked with him,' she yelled. 'How can you talk about Henry as if he was nothing. Don't you care?'

Michael sighted. 'Of course I care. Making blind accusations is no sign of compassion. And what do you want me to do anyway? I'll send flowers to his family. I'll go to his funeral. I'm not a private investigator. I don't work for the cops. If there's something fishy about Henry's death, it up to the police to work it out. We're only here to report the news, not to investigate a homicide.'

'So you'd rather close your eyes to the truth?' Amanda tipped the rest of her decaf in the sink. She shook her head. 'You're all the same. As long as you're comfortable in your padded executive job, the world can go to hell.'

Michael jumped from his chair. 'Jesus, Amanda? What the hell is wrong with you? People commit suicide everyday. Just because it was someone you worked with this time, it doesn't make it a murder. And to begin with, you know little about Henry. Just because he was working in the same building as you, it doesn't mean you knew him intimately.'

Amanda sulked. 'Was he always depressed?'

'Henry? Nope. Not that I really noticed. You know, he spent most of his time in the editing room. The little time I saw him, he seemed fine.'

'Did he joke or anything?'

'He took his job seriously.' Michael looked at his watch. 'It's almost seven thirty. I better get to the office. I've got plenty of work to do.' He finished the content of his cup.

'I'm coming with you,' Amanda said.

She rushed upstairs to get her coat and briefcase. She knew work was going to be hell with Henry's death on her mind. Hugh would have to find a quick replacement for the video editing job. Everyone would be running around like crazy. But it wasn't what Amanda was the most worried about.

As she run downstairs, the name Gavin White was still ringing in her head. Henry's suicide and Senator Trevor Garry's murder have been treated by the media as separate incidents. Amanda was certain the two deaths were connected to one another. How exactly, she didn't know, but she was dying to find out. Maybe Hugh Gawler knew more than he appeared to.

It was time to find the truth behind the deaths.

Time to take some calculated risks.

At whatever the cost.

CHAPTER 55

Cable News: meanwhile.

Hugh Gawler had been at the office since 6.00 a.m.

LAPD had already been in and out of the building, asking all kind of questions about Henry. Hugh told them Henry had been depressed for the last few weeks. After talking to him a few days ago, he let him off on sick leave.

LAPD didn't think there was any suspicious circumstances. Hugh seemed honest. The questioning was just routine. Hugh understood. He told the police to call anytime if they needed his cooperation.

But for now, Hugh would have to employ someone else in the editing room. Advertising in a newspaper would take too long. A phone call to a temp agency would fix the problem in the meantime. But what troubled him the most was Amanda Ryan.

The videocassette

What exactly did Henry meant? Did he actually give Amanda a videocassette? A videocassette of what? It could have been a videocassette from the editing room. But what did it reveal? Hugh had to find out before the mysterious videocassette got into the wrong hands.

From his briefcase, He removed a bottle wrapped in a brown paper bag. Walking to the bar-fridge, he took the bottle of Southern Comfort out of the paper bag. He poured the brown liquid into a short glass filled with crushed ice.

This drinking was really becoming a problem.

Usually Hugh would never drink in the morning, but with the stress of the past week, he needed a lift to get the day on the way.

He knew he would stop drinking one day. It's never been a problem in the past. He had faced worse challenges than the bottle.

But as he became older, it became harder to stop drinking. The fact was he enjoyed having a drink now and then.

And he didn't really want to give it up.

All night Hugh had been tossing in bed. His mind with filled with images of Amanda Ryan. How was he going to fry her? So far, she had been defensive. And he liked that. A woman of character. So rare these days, especially when faced with a man of his status. Women went down on their knees, begging him to make love to them, to marry them, to give them a child.

But Hugh abhorred this kind of women.

He liked a challenging relationship.

Amanda Ryan was strong, sexy and assertive. She was a woman he could share the rest of his life with. But being who she was, she liked to tease him, to play games, to make him beg for her love. He knew the routine. He played it all the time with other women. He knew Amanda was priceless. The more he would lay at her feet, the further he was from getting her. It made the challenge even more exciting.

He would win her instead.

Hugh checked his watch. It was 9.30 a.m. in Texas. Time to call Sam Willicon, the leader of the Texan Militia. The Militia had done a good job with Senator Garry and Gavin White.

Now Hugh had a bigger challenge for them. Something which would make news from coast to coast around the world.

The news industry was going to be a exciting venture this year.

And a very profitable one.

CHAPTER 56

At 10.32 a.m., Amanda was on the phone to Dr Frank Brook, Henry Limar's GP. Sitting behind her desk at CableNews, she scribbled on a yellow legal pad.

'I've heard the news this morning,' Dr Frank Brook said.

'Did he ever come and see you about this suicide thing?' Amanda said.

'Who did you say you were?'

'I worked with Henry just before he killed himself.'

'You know what Henry discusses with me is confidential. I can't tell you anything.'

'I don't want to know what he said. I just want to know if he's been seeing you in the past two weeks about any suicide attempt.'

'I haven't seen Henry Limar for over six months.'

There was a pause.

'In your opinion,' Amanda continued, 'why would he kill himself?'

'As I've said, I haven't seen Mr Limar for more than six months. In order for me to properly diagnose Mr Limar's problem, I would have had to conduct a full investigation on his background. Anything could be a triggering factor. His work might have caused him to much stress. He might have had problems at home. Or maybe he was carrying a suicidal tendency with him for a very long time. My guess is as good as yours at this stage. All I can say is if Mr Limar suffered from suicidal bouts even for a short while, he should have been attended to. I was never given a chance to look into the problem.'

This did not surprise Amanda. The way Henry Limar had behaved that night, she realized he had never asked for outside help.

As soon as she got to the office at 8.31 a.m. that morning, she rung up Mrs Limar. According to Mrs Limar's tone, she was still in shock from her husband's death. She gave Amanda's Dr Frank Brook's telephone number. Hugh had told her he had called Henry's GP when she saw him in the office the day he made an advance on her. She remembered it quite clearly. And now she knew Hugh lied. But why?

'Thank you, Dr Brook,' Amanda said, ending the conversation.

She spun her chair around, thinking of all the reasons why Hugh Gawler would lie about Henry's GP. If Hugh wanted Henry dead, then Henry must have known something which placed Hugh in a difficult situation. This would explain why Hugh tried to drill her the other day for some information Henry might have told her. So, if Hugh wanted to get rid of Henry without any suspicion, the best thing to do was not to call a GP, but to let him kill himself. And this seemed even more conclusive when she considered Hugh gave Henry back his gun.

As she stood from her chair, she knew the gun was the same one Henry had used when she walked in on him. Everyone assumed Henry committed suicide. But no one really knew for sure. Did Henry actually pull the trigger? Did someone help him? And this business with Gavin White? Was there a connection with Henry's death?

Enraged, Amanda raced out of the office.

She was ready to confront Hugh Gawler.

CHAPTER 57

10.45 a.m.

'Amanda wants to see you now,' Tracy Hamilton, Hugh's secretary, said through the telephone intercom.

Not really surprised, Hugh told her to send her in. He wore a dark suit with a white shirt and yellow tie. All morning, he had been expecting Amanda to come and see him. They were the only two who knew about Henry Limar's suicide attempt less than a week ago. He expected Amanda to have difficulties coping with Henry's death.

A company meeting had been set at 3.00 p.m. Although everyone knew about Henry's suicide, it was Hugh's responsibility to make an official announcement. He would have felt awkward if Amanda had not discussed anything with him before the three o'clock meeting. At one stage, he thought about paging her to his office but reasoned it was better if she came to him instead. This way he would be able to comfort her. It was important she learned to trust him. She was an intelligent woman. Seducing her had proven to be a difficult process. But if she let herself off-guard, he might get close to her and break through.

Of course, he didn't forget about the damn videocassette What did Henry actually say to Amanda? And did he give her a videocassette like he claimed he did? If so, Hugh would have to get the videocassette back at any cost.

Hugh Gawler was unhappy with the situation. He wanted Amanda to be his lover, and yet he knew she was also the enemy. She had to be convinced of his good attentions. He wanted so much to get her involved in his plans. Maybe she would like what he did. Sure, at first she would be shocked, but eventually, captivated by his charm and superiority, she would let herself fall in love

Hugh was certain he could make her fall in love with him.

Suddenly, Amanda walked into the office without knocking on the door. Her lips were tight, and her eyes burning with rage.

'Why did you give him his gun back?' Amanda snapped, jabbing her finger in the air.

Hugh felt his blood pumping. He didn't expect this. Puzzled, he didn't answer immediately His face turned chalk white. Suddenly he no longer felt like the god corporate executive who had it all under control. He had anticipated Amanda was going to ask questions, but not in that tone of voice. 'A beg your pardon?' Hugh finally answered, his body fully erected.

'You gave him his gun back,' Amanda said, obviously unable to control her anger. 'You knew he was going to use it. So why did you give it back to him? You might as well have shot him.'

Shocked, Hugh stared at Amanda's index pointing directly between his two eyes. 'Of course I gave him back his gun. It was his gun,' Hugh mumbled, trying to think of a good defense tactic.

He stood from his chair to make sure he wasn't being talked down to. 'What else was I supposed to do?'

'You murdered this man. You gave him the weapon which killed him.' Amanda was losing control. She began to shake nervously as tears rolled down her face.

Speaking softly, Hugh circled the desk. Now was the time. 'Come on, Amanda. I know you're upset. Right now it's easy to accuse someone else. But Henry killed himself.' Strategically, he stopped in front of Amanda and placed one hand on her shoulder.

Amanda shrugged back. 'Why didn't you tell his doctor?'

Hugh's lips parted, but no sound came out.

Amanda pressed on, 'You never called him, did you?'

Hugh was confused. What was she on about? 'Why would I call Henry's doctor? What on earth are you talking about?'

'You told me you rang up his GP the day when he left your office. You said he had an appointment in the afternoon.'

'And so he did.' Hugh didn't remember what he said. Amanda seemed to have a better memory than he did. 'What in the world does this have to do with me?'

Amanda wiped the tears from her face. 'You lied. I rang up his doctor, and he hasn't seen Henry in six months.'

Hell! Hugh couldn't believe it. Amanda actually went behind his back and rang Henry's doctor. Maybe Steve Thorn was right. She was going to cause him more trouble than she was worth. How could he have been so naive?

'Did I say I'd call his GP?' Hugh whispered to her intimately

'Like hell you did.'

'I don't remember. I must have said it like without thinking. I must have forgotten to call him.' He applied pressure on her shoulders.

Amanda moved two steps back. 'You didn't say you would call him, you said you had called him. You're a god-damn liar, Mr Gawler!'

Shaking his head in disbelief, Hugh tried to remain calm. Who the hell did Amanda Ryan thing she was? Had she suddenly forgotten who she was addressing? If she went to the police with the gun story, she would mess up everything. Sure, there was no way Hugh would get convicted. The evidence was lacking. But it would look nasty on his record. And if the FBI got involved, his life would be hell. His file was probably still stored in Washington D.C. The FBI was waiting for him to make one slip-up. They wanted to get even for 1972.

When LAPD questioned him about Henry that morning, he didn't tell them anything about the Colt .45. He never mentioned Amanda finding Henry with the piece in his mouth a few days before he shot himself.

And now Amanda was going to blow everything. Hugh didn't need this. He raised his voice. 'This is not fair, Amanda. Just because I said I was going to call his GP and forgot doesn't make me a criminal. Why don't you look at the facts. Henry came to my office, we had a talk, and he asked me for his gun back. I said no, but he insisted. He said he would see his GP in the afternoon. I didn't know what to do. I removed the rounds from the magazine and gave him his gun. What was I supposed to do? I'm not a shrink. Haven't I enough responsibilities running this company without having to worry about the mental state of every employee?'

'You should have followed up on him,' Amanda said, her tone losing authority.

'Followed up on what? I gave him time off. Is it my job to go and chase up his doctor to see how he's going? I'm not a damn social worker!'

Speechless, Amanda locked her eyes into his.

CHAPTER 58

Amanda looked into his eyes, trying to see if he was telling the truth. But his eyes didn't tell her anything. They were warm like his smile.

Like his face.

Amanda had forgotten how handsome Hugh was. But now she clearly recalled the first time she met him. His features had impressed her.

Mesmerized by her memories, Amanda began to have self-doubts. What if Hugh was telling the truth? What if he had nothing to do with Henry's death? How much more was she supposed to push her weight around? Was she just making a fool of herself?

The anger in her began to dissipate. This whole thing might be nothing more than a misunderstanding. Did Hugh really said he called a GP? Now she wasn't certain. The shock of Henry's death got her in a state of confusion.

'And beside,' Hugh continued, 'why on earth would I want Henry dead? You're not making any sense Amanda. Do you need some time off as well?' He smiled his seducing smile.

Amanda's eyes were still locked in his. She didn't know whether to trust him or not. But she knew her forward accusations would only complicate things. She smiled back at him.

'I'm sorry,' she said, injecting her voice with warmth. 'Maybe I'm wrong. I'm so worked up.' She let her head fall on his shoulder and cried. She couldn't help it. Her mind was shattered from the stress and confusion.

Hugh placed the palm of his hand on the small of her back.

She didn't object. As weak as she was, she remembered the promise she made to herself. She remembered what Steve Thorn told her. If she could get closer to Hugh, maybe he would share his secrets. She forced herself to relax. She clung to Hugh's body and closed her eyes.

With his right hand, Hugh rubbed the back of her cranium, just above her neck. 'Does this feel good?' Hugh asked.

She hated to admit it, but Hugh was good at what he was doing. The tension seemed to dissipate into thin air. She kept her eyes closed. 'It feels great,' she whispered against the side of his skull.

Hugh's left hand fell on Amanda's buttock.

Intrigued, Amanda wondered how far she was willing to go. She felt a warm sensation in her stomach. Hugh smelled good. His aura made her feel secure. She couldn't work out how she could fall so easily for a man she feared so much. Then suddenly she opened her eyes and said, 'Not now, Hugh. This is not the right time or the right place.'

'Fine,' Hugh said, his eyes sparkling with excitement. 'How about dinner tonight then?'

Amanda didn't hesitate. 'Sure, why not?' She knew his game, and she was going to play it his way. The idea of sleeping with Hugh Gawler frightened her. She wasn't repulsed by him. Hugh was unbelievably attractive. A sculptured chisel face and perfect body. And his golden smile. Under other circumstances, maybe she would have been interested in him. Maybe she would have even made love to him. Used him for her own gratification. But things were different. She was in love with Michael and couldn't see herself making love to anyone else.

The voice of Tracy Hamilton interrupted the romantic interlude. 'Mr Gawler, there's a detective here to see you.'

Hugh had a blank look on his face. 'I'm coming,' he said and turned to Amanda. 'You better go now.'

She circled the room with eyes and stopped at the bar fridge. 'You don't mind if I get a drink?'

'Go ahead,' Hugh said. 'I'll be back in a minute.'

Hugh left the room, closing the door gently.

Amanda was alone in the office.

It was now or never.

CHAPTER 59

The detective stood in front of Hugh's desk. He was at least six foot tall. He passed one hand over his cropped hair, his face expressing no emotion. The pockets under his eyes indicated a clear lack of sleep. He wore a lose sports jacket, an older style with brown saw-on patches at the elbows.

Hugh forwarded his hand. He never dealt with a black detective before.

The black man introduced himself as Stan Moore, an LAPD detective from the Homicide Special Section.

'Is Henry's death being suspected as homicide?' Hugh asked. He knew the Homicide Special Section only dealt with cases pertaining to foul play.

'At this stage, it's just routine. Mr Limar's death is being treated like a suicide. I'd just like to tie up loose ends before closing the case. I need to file a conclusive report for the Office Of Operations.' The detective smiled nervously.

'Sure, I understand.'

Stan Moore shifted to the side. 'I was wondering if we could look around Henry Limar's work area and talk to some of his colleagues.'

'Have you got a warrant?'

'No one is being suspected. I understand you've already spoken to two officers this morning. They assured me you would give us your full cooperation Based on such arrangement, I don't see the point of a warrant.'

Hugh smiled his crooked smile. Earlier in the day, Hugh did make a promise to the two police officers the detective was referring to.

But it wasn't really why he was smiling.

He was smiling because Amanda was in his office. She was just the person he didn't want the detective to talk to. It could

161

complicate things.

Hugh shifted authoritatively and said, 'Sure, not a problem. I'll show you around.' He turned to Tracy Hamilton.'Make sure Amanda doesn't leave my office.'

Hugh escorted the detective down the hallway, past the other offices and straight down to the editing room. He pushed the door open and flicked the light on. 'This is where he worked,' he said. 'If you need anything, just let me know.'

Hugh took two steps back towards the exit.

'What exactly did Henry Limar do around here,' Detective Stan Moore asked, removing a notebook and pencil from his pocket.

Hugh hesitated for a few seconds and turned around. 'He worked as a video editor. His job consisted of editing new stories for television viewing. He also did titles, cropping and so on.'

Stan Moore circled the small room searching for god-knows-what. He sketched something on his notepad.

'Did he drink?' Stan asked, half concentrating on his sketch.

'Why?'

'He was intoxicated when we found him last night. Vomited all over himself.'

'Never drank at work. Henry was a conscientious worker. A loner, though. Never said what was on his mind.'

The detective was still looking around the room. 'What's with all the videocassettes?' he asked, pointing to cardboard boxes filled with hundreds them.

'I told you, he was a news editor. To put a half hour program together, we run through hours of recorded material.'

'What does he do with the videocassettes when the editing is over?'

'They get stored down the basement. We keep everything. Never know when there is a need to dig some of old stuff out.'

As Stan Moore approached the east wall, something seemed to have caught his eye. He knelled down and looked closely at the wall.

'Did you find something?' Hugh asked, more than slightly concerned.

Stan Moore didn't answer. He seemed to be jabbing at something on the wall. 'What's this?' he asked without turning around.

'What's what?'

'Looks like a bullet hole to me.'

'A what?'

'A bullet hole. You know, like a gun shot.'

Hugh puzzled over the statement for a few seconds. 'Must have been there when we moved in the building.'

The detective swiped the palm of his hand on the floor, just under the hole. He lifted his hand and showed it to Hugh. It was covered in a thin white powder. 'How often does this place gets cleaned?'

'On daily basis.'

'Tell them to do the corners properly. They left some plaster on the floor. Must have been from the shot in the wall.'

Hugh's stomach churned.

Stan Moore went on, 'You see, if the hole had been there before you moved in the building, there wouldn't have been any plaster on the floor. Someone used a gun recently in this room. The plaster on the floor is still fresh.'

Hugh tried to keep a smile on his face, but his hands were clammy. The detective had only be here ten minutes, and already he was giving Hugh a headache. 'I'm sorry, but I don't follow.'

'Any idea why there would be a hole in the wall?'

'My guess is as good as yours.'

The detective stood back on his feet. He scribed a few things on his notebook. 'I'll have someone coming in early this afternoon to extract the bullet. Looks like it's still stuck in there.'

'Not a problem, detective. Just tell them to go right in there and do their job.'

'I think I'm done with this room,' Stan said. 'Let's go and chat to some of the staff.'

'Just follow me, Detective.' Hugh answered, feeling the rage building up inside him.

Bastard! He should have asked him for a search warrant. But it would have only been a waste of time. It would have also made Hugh look unwilling to cooperate.

And it's the last thing he wanted.

CHAPTER 60

Amanda scanned quickly the surface of Hugh's glass desk. The desk was clear of clutter.

Feeling somewhat nervous, she opened the first drawer. Pens, paper clips, a hole punch, calculator, 3M yellow stick-on pads, six yellow coated HB pencils, two rubbers and a box of elastic bands.

Just as she was about to open the second drawer, a voice interrupted her.

'Amanda, are you in here?' Tracy Hamilton said through the telephone intercom.

Amanda placed on hand on her chest. Blood rushed to her head. She thought she was going to get a heart attack. She stepped back from the desk. 'Yes, I'm here.'

'Mr Gawler asked me to tell you not to leave the office until he comes back.'

'Sure.'

Amanda sat behind Hugh's desk, catching her breath. Maybe she wasn't cut out for this spying business. *Okay, get a grip on yourself. Let's get it over and done with.*

Quickly, she opened the second drawer. Blank yellow legal pads stuck on top of one another. Nothing else in the drawer. The third and fourth drawer were locked.

She turned around to the four-drawer filing cabinet on the west wall. She stood from her chair and walked to the filing cabinet. All the drawers were locked.

God, damn it! Why in the world would he lock his filing cabinet when he was in the office? What was she going to do now?

Disappointed, Amanda sat back at the desk, a blank look on her face. She stared at the blank computer screen.

And then something lit up inside her.

The computer!

She turned it on. After a few seconds booting up, the main menu came up on the screen. She clicked the DIARY icon. The Windows program opened up like a flower in front of her.

There, she was faced with Hugh's daily activities, including all his meeting schedules, deadlines, contacts and tasks.

With the mouse, she scrolled the diary pages to the last entries. The name *Gavin White* caught her eye. Below it was his address and telephone number.

Amanda jaw dropped. She puzzled over the significance of what she had just seen.

She scrolled further down the entries. There is was again, the name *Gavin White*. But this time the words ARRESTED and SAN QUENTIN STATE PRISON was entered alongside it.

Amanda opened the second drawer and took one of the yellow legal pads. She grabbed a HB pencil from the first drawer. She wrote the address of Gavin White and the name of the detention Center

Just then, the door of the office was swung open.

Amanda looked up. A faint nausea rippled through her. The yellow legal pad slipped from her hands and landed on the floor.

In came Tracy Hamilton. She didn't seem particularly intrigued to see Amanda behind Hugh's desk.

'God, you scared me,' Amanda said. As she spoke these words, she realized she would have been better off not saying a thing. Her reaction probably drew more attention to herself than if she had acted calmly.

But Tracy Hamilton didn't seem concerned. She placed two large sealed envelopes in the in-tray.

And then she noticed the computer switched on.

'He's keeping you busy,' she commented, a sour expression on her face.

Amanda shifted uncomfortably. 'You could say that,' she said, feeling like a child caught with one hand in the cookie jar.

When Tracy Hamilton left the room, Amanda turned the computer off and went to the bar-fridge. She poured herself a short glass of Southern Comfort. She hoped Tracy Hamilton wouldn't say anything to Hugh.

As she swallowed the content of the short glass, her mind raced frantically. She wondered why Gavin White's name was in Hugh's diary. Because he was an important news event? Or because Hugh Gawler had a special interest in the man? Sure, the senator's death was a big story, but so were hundreds of other stories? None of them were featured in the diary, so why this story in particular?

Why this name?

Amanda rinsed the empty glass.

She feared she was getting too close to something dangerous.

CHAPTER 61

Michael Hall was somewhat nervous when detective Stan Moore and Hugh Gawler walked into his office.

Stan Moore explained how all he wanted was some information about Henry Limar which would help him to understand why the news editor committed suicide.

Michael understood immediately if a detective was investigating a suicide, there had to be suspicion of homicide.

Hugh Gawler was standing in one corner of the office, behind detective Stan Moore. His body fully erected, he had a nervous look on his face. His knees were locked together, and he blinked rapidly.

Detective Stan Moore, now setting in front of Michael Hall, turned around to face Hugh. 'I don't mean to be rude, Mr Gawler, but I'd like to conduct the rest of these interviews in private.' His tone was matter-of-fact.

Hugh Gawler didn't react to the request. He stood there, lost in his own world.

'Mr Gawler?' Stan Moore said when he noticed Hugh staring at the empty space.

'Oh, I'm sorry,' Hugh said, 'I was just...'

When Hugh left the room, Stan Moore turned to Michael. 'Strange man.'

'He has his days,' Michael said.

The detective removed a flip-on notebook and blue Biro from his sports-jacket 'How long have you been working with CableNews?'

'Since it was formed. I was one of the people who help get it off the ground.'

'And during this time, have you noticed anything suspicious your colleagues?'

'You mean Henry Limar?'

'No, I mean anyone.'

Michael gulped air. 'Everyone. God, you know, no one is really perfectly normal these days. Where do you want me to start?'

'You tell-'

The telephone intercom interrupted the conversation. 'Michael?' The metallic voice of Tracy Hamilton surprised both men.

Michael looked at the detective and then at the telephone. 'Yes?' he said, his voice lacking authority.

'Please pick up the phone?'

'Not now, I'm busy.'

'This is important. Could you please pick up the receiver?'

Stan Moore looked at Michael intrigued. He raised his brows to tell Michael he didn't mind if he picked up the phone.

Michael grabbed the handset. 'What is it?'

'Just hold the line.'

There was a pause.

'Michael?' Hugh said.

'Yes?'

'Don't mention my name. Has the detective said anything about Amanda?'

'No.' Michael glanced at the detective. Stan Moore was preoccupied with his note taking.

'Don't talk to him about Amanda. I think she's in trouble. If he asks you anything about Henry's other suicide attempt, tell him you don't know anything.'

'Why?' Michael features creased. He didn't like the idea of lying to the police.

'Let's just say Amanda gave him a different story. I'm not sure exactly what she told him. But, if you claim complete ignorance, then she would be safe.'

Michael felt dampness at the small of his back. This was not a good idea. But what if Hugh was telling the truth? What if Amanda did give the detective a different story? Michael glanced at Stan Moore. The black detective was still scribbling something in his notebook.

'Okay, it's fine.' Michael said.

There was a pause.

'Thanks,' Hugh finally said.

'It's all right.' Michael looked back at the detective who had now resumed his note taking.

Stan Moore locked his eyes into Michael's.

Michael went on, 'I'll change the appointment to 9.00 a.m., Thursday morning.' He swallowed Surely the detective would know he was just making up the whole thing. He'd be trained to detect when someone was lying.

Michael placed the handset in its cradle and picked up his black leather-bound diary. He pretended to be writing a new entry. 'People can never make up their minds,' Michael said, avoiding the detective's stare. 'First they pin you down for an meeting at an awkward time. The next thing you know, they shuffle you around to reschedule the appointment.'

'Tell me about it,' Stan Moore said, still chewing on his Biro

'So where were we up to?' Smiling broadly, Michael looked up to the detective. His insides were churning. He couldn't wait for the detective to leave the room.

'You were going to tell me about any strange behaviors you have noticed since you've worked here.'

'Like I said, this is going to take a long time.'

'It's fine. I've got time.'

Michael began a long series of characterizations of everyone he had known since CableNews was formed. Everyone except Amanda Ryan. He was hoping by the time he got to her, the black detective would be bored to death.

And he was.

Stan Moore looked at his watch. It had been half an hour since he begun listening to Michael's monologue. He chewed the cap of his pen impatiently. 'This will do, Mr Hall. I think I've got enough for today.'

Michael tried to remain composed but was feeling rather agitated. So far, he hadn't had to lie. He just withheld information. He was glad it was all over. Relieved, he stood from his chair and was about to offer his hand to the detective.

Already on his feet, Stan Moore accepted the handshake. He turned towards the door, changed his mind, and said, 'Ah, one more thing. I almost forgot. Do you know anything about a bullet hole in Henry Limar's room?'

'A what?'

'A bullet hole.'

'A bullet hole?'

'Yes, you know, as if someone shot, but missed, and the bullet landed in the wall.'

Michael puzzled over Stan's inquiry No, he couldn't remember anything about a bullet hole in Henry's room. It must have been the night when Amanda caught Henry with a gun in his mouth. But Amanda never mentioned anything about a shooting.

'I'm sorry, but I wouldn't have a clue. I haven't seen the hole you're talking about.'

'And you've never heard anything which sounded like a gun firing?'

'No.'

'Anyone mentioning anything about a shooting?'

'No.'

'Thanks for you time,' Stan Moore said, removing a business card from his jacket. 'If you do happen to remember anything, give me a call, will you?' He handed the card to Michael.

'Sure will,' Michael said, lying through his teeth.

When the detective left the office, Michael slouched back on his black leather executive chair. He stretched his legs, feeling the tension evaporating into thin air.

Michael hoped the little he had said to the detective saved Amanda from trouble. Either way, he felt uncomfortable with the whole thing. Later he would have to have a talk with Hugh and Amanda to sort out what was going on. His job was important to him, and he didn't have time for lies. If anything went wrong, his own *plans* might be jeopardized. The last thing he needed at present was the attention of the police. Timing was critical if he was to achieve what he had set out to do.

It had taken Michael a lot of hard work to get where he was. He didn't want to see his own life crumble because of some careless calculation by Hugh Gawler or Amanda Ryan.

Nothing would stand in his way.

Not even his love for Amanda.

CHAPTER 62

San Quentin State Prison, California: Tuesday, 2.32 p.m.

Gavin White had been in and out of jail a few times. Drug trafficking, shoplifting, assault and carrying a concealed weapon.

And now for first degree murder. It was the first time Gavin White had been held at a Security Level IV, the maximum level in the state of California.

San Quentin State Prison was the first and most renowned penal institution in the state. Located in the small town of San Quentin, on the north shores of San Francisco Bay in Marin County, the prison handled California's roughest inmates for the last 135 years. It also catered for minimum and medium custody prisoners, level I and levels II & III respectively.

The cell in which Gavin White resided was two by three feet. He lay on a single metal-framed bunk, his eyes staring blankly into the empty space.

Currently, Gavin White was awaiting trial for the murder of Senator Trevor Garry and his family. The district attorney's office would prosecute for the death penalty. Aware San Quentin State Prison held California's only gas chamber, Gavin White feared he might never leave the prison.

The worst was he knew he didn't commit any murder. He was sure his arrest had something to do with him being black. No matter what the media said out about racism thinning out in California, Gavin White knew it was a damn lie. When he stared into the eyes of white people in the streets, on the trains, the buses, the shopping centers, white people gave him the hatred look. That look which is so familiar to all blacks. A hatred look not because of who he was, but because of the pigmentation of his skin.

Senator Trevor Garry was a white man.

He was a black man.

Gavin White knew he didn't stand a chance. He'd been framed, and he would get convicted.

And he would be sent to the gas chamber.

No doubts.

No chance.

No fair trial.

He was a black man.

Senator Trevor Garry was a white man.

Lying alone in his cell, Gavin wondered what the hell he was doing in here. He couldn't even afford a lawyer, so the city appointed one to him. Justin Smith *white* asshole. What a joke!

Gavin recalled clearly the conversation with his lawyer in his head.

'I'm telling you, I didn't do it.'

'Look, Gavin, I don't mean to call you a liar or anything, but if you plead guilty, then maybe we can get you off the gas chamber.'

'For fuck sake, you're not listening. This is a set up. I didn't kill the Senator!'

'What about all the evidence? How do you explain them? Your apartment was filled with clippings of the Senator. You had enough weapons in there to start your own little war. And there's even blood and mud stains on your shoes and clothes. How am I supposed to convince a jury you didn't do anything?'

'Fuck you, man. It's you're job. All you have to know is I didn't do shit and someone's framed me.'

'I can't work with you unless you're going to be honest with me. This is not good. The DA has already prepared a Request for a Grand Jury Hearing Memorandum. You have to get your story straight. When we get in the courtroom, the shit is going to hit the fan if you don't plead guilty. You can still change your story. I can work a deal with the DA and avoid the death penalty. It's your choice. I'll be back tomorrow, and for Christ's sake, I hope you'll change your story.'

And now Gavin White was alone in this cell uncertain about his future. How did this all thing happen? Who set him up? Why him? And this god-damn lawyer who didn't believe he was innocent. What was the good of having a lawyer if all he wanted was to see you canned for life? *What kind of a fuckin' legal system do we have in this country?*

Enraged, Gavin stood on his bed and banged the back of his head against the concrete wall. It shook him out of his skin, but he didn't know what else to do to get the frustration out. He's been clean for nearly a year now. His parole agent had recorded no criminal conduct during that time. Gavin White was almost a brand new man.

And then he got framed for a crime he didn't commit.

Who set him up?

Who the fuck set me up?

Gavin White knew he might never live to find out.

CHAPTER 63

Amanda Ryan arrived at San Quentin State Prison just after three. The sky was cloudless, and the temperature seventy-two degrees. The flight from Los Angeles to San Francisco had been pleasant. She had managed to catch up on some sleep. When she woke up, her mind was clear and her body fully alert. She realized how a good sleep could make life more bearable.

But this was not a leisure trip she was taking.

Amanda passed the security gates at the prison. She parked her rented white Dodge in a space marked *visitors only*.

The previous day, she rang the prison to make an appointment with Gavin White. She told them she was from CableNews doing the story on Senator Trevor Garry. She was informed visits from non-family members had to be made in writing four weeks prior to the visit and approved by the inmate assigned unit staff.

Amanda insisted it was not possible since she was part of the media, and surely there had to be exceptions in these cases.

The person who took the booking remembered seeing Amanda's name at the end of the television documentary on Senator Garry. He admired her show the person said, and he would see what he could do. He rang her back half an hour later to confirm. Amanda could have an interview at 3.15 p.m. the following day.

Amanda stepped out of the white Dodge, her hand clammy from nervousness. No one from CableNews told her to do an interview with Gavin White. But since she did the story on the Senator, then she thought it gave her the right to push even further. Of course, it would be the excuse she would used if Hugh Gawler asked her what she was doing with Gavin White. I was just doing my job, she would say.

Yesterday when she saw Gavin White's name in Hugh's

computer, she knew she had to go and visit Gavin. Maybe he would be able to shed some light on Henry's death.

Amanda knew she had little to go on with, but her instinct told her she was moving in the right direction.

After going through the normal security check, Amanda was escorted to a room separated by a security grill. One side of the room was for visitors, the other for inmates.

Gavin White came in handcuffed with two prison guards by his side. She took one look at him and couldn't decide whether he was guilty or not. To begin with, she didn't expect him to be black. It did not matter much to her, but somehow her perspective on the murder of Senator Garry changed by a couple of degrees. Why in the world would a black person kill a family of white people? She could think of a million reasons, but she knew it was a uncommon thing. Interracial murders were not uncommon, especially in the style the Senator and his family had been butchered.

One of the prison guards sat Gavin on the chair opposite Amanda.

'You've got fifteen minutes,' the guard said as he took a step back.

Both guards stayed in the room in front of the door.

'Do you guys have to hang around?' Amanda asked.

'Yes, mam,' the first guard said. 'Maximum security watch.'

'Great.' Amanda shook her head. How as she supposes to ask straight forward questions to Gavin White with these two stooges standing behind him, listening to every word they said? They'd probably make him feel uncomfortable and unable to trust her.

Gavin White scrutinized Amanda's face. He didn't say a word, just stared as if he was trying to figure out who the hell this person was.

'What do you want?' he finally said. His voice was thick and guttural. 'You're another one of those fuckin' government officials, are you?'

'I'm a journalist working for CableNews,' Amanda said, knowing it would come out sounding worse than it really was. After lawyers, journalists were the least trusted profession in the United States.

Amanda Ryan didn't expect Gavin White to stand from behind the table, jump the security grill and give her a bear hug.

'Oh, shit,' Gavin said, slamming one hand on the wooden table. 'They should've told me your were a god-damned journalist! I would have stayed in my cell.' The white of his eyes contrasted with the darkness of his skin. He stood from his chair. 'I got nothing to say.' Enraged, Gavin White turned to the guards. 'Take me back to my cell.'

175

One of the guards moved forward. He reached for Gavin White.

'Wait, wait,' Amanda said, standing from her chair. 'Henry Limar shot himself a couple of days ago.'

Gavin slowly turned around and stared into Amanda's eyes. What on earth is the white bitch on about, he seemed to be thinking.

The guard continued to move forward.

Gavin held the guard with his hand. 'It's all right. I'll talk to her.'

The guard shook his head and moved back to his corner. He whispered something to the other guard. Amanda thought she heard foul language.

Gavin White took back his seat. He locked his eyes into Amanda's. 'What do you know about Henry Limar?'

'Not much,' Amanda said, 'but he seemed to know about you.'

Gavin twitched. Inquiring thoughts probably crossed his mind. Was she here to set him up? Dig out of him some kind of confession? 'What do you mean he knows about me? I don't even know the man. Never met him.'

'He told me you were going to get arrested before you did. And he's not a cop. Did you know Henry Limar?'

'I told you I never met the man,' Gavin said. 'You sure you're not some kind of fuckin cop, FBI shit, or somethin' like that?'

'I'm doing this research for CableNews. I'm a journalist Gavin. You have to trust me.'

'God-damns television. Trust you?' He rolled his eyes. 'Fuck, man. Is this some kind of fuckin' joke?' Then he leaned forward, looking somehow interested. 'So what exactly do you want?'

Amanda looked at her watch. Time was ticking away, and they were wasting it talking shop. It was better to be upfront with alleged murderer.

She lowered her head and whispered so the prison guards wouldn't hear. 'No one sent me. I came here by myself. Something is fishy. I've got a feeling you've been framed.'

'No shit,' Gavin whispered back, his face creasing into an ingratiating smile. 'And how did you figure this out?'

'I caught Henry Limar with a gun in his mouth one night. He mentioned your name. He said you were going to be arrested for the murder of the Senator. No one else knew, but him.'

'Look lady, I don't know who the fuck you are, but you got one thing right: I didn't kill the Senator. And Henry Limar knows I didn't. Well, at least he knew.'

'Did you talk to him?'

'Yeah. He called me a few days ago here at the prison. Must have been not long after he shot himself. He told me he knew I didn't do it, and he said he could prove it. I asked him who the fuck he worked for, and he said never mind that.'

'And that's all.'

'Basically, yeah. Then he said something about how he felt it was all wrong, but he couldn't do shit. His ass was on the line. He went on about some crap about a videocassette and said he would send me a copy. Never got shit.'

'Did he say where he was going to send the videocassette?'

'All he-'

A loud bang on the door cut Gavin off mid-sentence.

One of the guards opened the door.

Justin Smith, Gavin White's government appointed lawyer stormed in. 'What the hell is going on here?' he yelled.

'I-' Amanda said.

'Who the hell is she? He turned to the prison guards. 'Get this woman away from my client.'

The guards hesitated.

Gavin White had a blank look on his face.

Amanda stood up. 'Excuse me, sir, but I've made arrangements to talk with Mr White.'

'Arrangements, my arse,' Justin Smith said, getting redder by the second. 'This man is held in custody. He cannot see or talk to anyone without my consent.' He then turned to the guards again. 'Who authorized this?'

Amanda stood in front of Justin Smith. 'And who the hell are you, sir?'

'Who the hell am I? I'm Mr White's attorney. And who the hell are you?'

'Amanda Ryan, CableNews Corporation.'

'Well, I don't give a damn what corporation you work for. I want you out of this room now.'

Gavin White stood from his chair.

The guards moved in fast on him.

'It's okay,' Gavin White said, turning to the lawyer. 'I wanted to talk to her. I called her up.'

Justin Smith looked puzzled for a few seconds. 'You did what?'

'I asked her to come and meet me.'

Justin Smith looked at Gavin and then at Amanda. He turned to the guards. 'Get this man back to his cell. I'm his lawyer, and I don't want this man to talk to anyone but me.'

The guards dragged a foul-mouthed Gavin White out of the

room.

Still in a fury, Justin Smith pointed his finger at Amanda. 'And you, I'm going to find out who the hell sent you. And when I do, it's going to be the end of your career.'

He walked out the door before Amanda had time to say a word. She stood by herself in the room, staring at Gavin's wooden chair which was now laying on the floor.

She wanted to go after the lawyer, but she knew better. Gavin White lied to save her ass.

At least she was one step closer.

She knew now Henry Limar had been in touch with Gavin White.

CHAPTER 64

Oklahoma City: Wednesday 19 April 1995, 9.00 a.m.

The bomb ripped through the eight floors of the Alfred P. Murray federal building. It left a crater ten feet wide and two feet deep in the underground car park where the Rydel Rentals truck loaded with 1200 pounds of fertilizer and diesel had parked.

For the next half hour, no one really knew what was going on. Dust clouds covered the building. Those who managed to survive the blast could have been forgiven for believing this was the beginning of World War III.

Public servants occupied most of the building. On the first floor was the Social Security offices; on the second, the General Accounting Office, the Army, Health and Finance departments, a day care center for employees' children; on the third floor, Army recruiting, Federal Highway Administration; on the fourth floor, agriculture, labor, Food and Administration departments, housing, customs, and war veterans; on the fifth floor, Marine Corps; on the sixth floor, Drug Enforcement Administration, housing; on the seventh floor, housing; on the eighth floor, FBI's alcohol, tobacco and firearms bureau, Drug Enforcement Administration, secret service.

Now the departments had been turned into a mixture of rumble, steel and pulped flesh.

It only took a couple of hours for the death toll to reach two hundred and fifty. Eerie cries from victims still trapped inside the bombed building made the rescuers' job unbearable. There was little time to save the people trapped between the tons of cement and steel. At minute intervals, another part of the building crumbled, and with it the life of another innocent person would end.

That same evening the President of the United States of America made an announcement around the globe: 'It was an act of

179

cowardice and it was evil. Let there be no room for doubt. We will find the people who did this... justice will be swift, certain and severe.'

America had taken a blow at the heart of everything it stood for.

Immediately, the bombing was thought to be the work of Arab terrorists. Terrorism experts detailed in the media why middle eastern countries had to be responsible for the carnage. They believed it was only a matter of time before some anti-American Arabic liberation group would claim responsibility.

Across the East Side River, in Brooklyn, police officers invaded Middle Eastern and Muslim communities to avoid an Arab-hatred mob destroying everything in sight. Talk-back radio shows indicated the majority of callers wanted all Arabs deported.

But Americans were wrong.

Arabs had played no part in the biggest act of terrorism this country had even seen.

It was Americans who did it to themselves.

CHAPTER 65

Arkansas: same day, 8.03 p.m.

Tom Davidson smiled as he drove away into the sunset. His red Ford pick-up truck left a trail of orange dust behind.

It was the greatest day of his life. No longer he felt like a nobody. For the first time, he felt like he belonged somewhere He had served his country.

When Sam Willicon, leader of the Texan Militia, told Tom Davidson he would become the mad bomber, Sam knew for months what was going to happen.

Tom Davidson had been the perfect person to do the job. He had been willing to obey. He was young, rootless, and looking for a place to stay. The militia gave him a home, faith in himself, and a reason to go on living.

And now that the bombing was finally over, Tom Davidson was someone important. The Texan Militia had delivered its promise. It had showed the world it would win the war against the New World Order. It would restore faith in the American system, in the constitution, in freedom and liberty.

What Tom Davidson didn't know was soon the Texan Militia would deny any involvement with him. If Sam Willicon confirmed Tom Davidson was one of them, the FBI and possibly the army would raid every Texan Militia property, like they had raided David Koresh's Waco cult. The bombing happening exactly a year to the day of the Waco attack was no coincidence.

But the world hadn't woken up to the truth yet. Everybody was too busy pointing the finger at the Arabs.

Tom Davidson looked in the rear mirror. The road behind him laid out for miles without a single vehicle in sight.

181

He opened the driver's window fully. The cool wind was whipping through the car. He passed one hand over his bristled cranium.

Tom Davidson was a happy man.

He had found freedom at last.

CHAPTER 66

Hollywood: the following day, 7.15 p.m.

Some thirteen thousand miles east of Oklahoma, Hugh Gawler was already counting the dollars. Alone in his office at CableNews headquarters, he admired the panoramic evening Hollywood skyline. He cupped his hands behind his head and smiled.

He knew in Oklahoma a CableNews team had been first at the scene taking exclusive footage of the bombing, the victims and the rescuers. They managed the best pictures and the best interviews. CableNews had sealed exclusive stories with some of the survivors, witnesses and emergency services officials.

Television stations around the world wanted access to the footage. Within twenty four hours hundreds of thousands of dollars began to pour into CableNews accounts across the country for season serial rights to news footage from CableNews.

While America was counting the cost of the bombing, Hugh Gawler was reaping the benefits.

Although Hugh Gawler didn't exactly approve of the Texan Militia's cause, he had used it to his advantage. Instead of having to seek his own little army, all he did was secretly finance the Militia to carry out his dirty deals.

And those dirty deals became news worthy stories.

Stories which CableNews would be guaranteed exclusive footage.

The death of Senator Garry had also been a perfect set up. The Texan Militia had carried out the job in a very satisfactory manner. Everyone thought the murders had been committed by a crazed, angry young black man on parole, Gavin White.

The Militia had been careful when choosing a victim to pin the murders on. Twenty to thirty year-old young men had the highest rate of violent crime in U.S.A. Black people were known to be

183

discriminated against in Los Angeles and probably the rest of the country. They were subjected to racial abuse, unfair recrimination and social injustice. By choosing Gavin White as the murderer, the Texan Militia knew it would fool everyone. Gavin White had to be the most likely suspect. Because of his prior criminal activities and convictions, the Militia knew Gavin White had a grudge against society, and probably a hatred of white people.

But when the death of Senator Garry had finally been carried out like clockwork, Hugh Gawler didn't want to rest on his laurels.

The next story would be bigger.

When Sam Willicon suggested the Alfred P. Murray building in Oklahoma, Hugh knew it would be the international news event of the year.

And this was only the beginning.

Hugh Gawler had a new plan which would eclipse the Oklahoma bombing for generations to come.

No one had ever dared to attempt what he was about to.

Soon, America would suffer its greatest act of terrorism in history. Maybe the greatest act of terrorism in the world.

And in the process, Hugh Gawler would become rich beyond anyone's dreams.

Very rich.

CHAPTER 67

LAPD: Tuesday, 4.02 p.m.

Detective Stan Moore picked up the phone on the second ring.

'Stan?'

'Yeah.'

'It's Gordon from the lab. The bullet you wanted analyzed from the wall at CableNews Corporation. It's from a Colt .45, like the one the Limar guy did himself with.'

'And?'

'Identical. The bullet is from the same gun. You can tell by the gun barrel's riffling. We've looked at them both through the comparison microscope. We then examined the gun's lands and grooves. The bullet in Limar's head and the one in the wall both come from the .45 Limar used to kill himself.'

'Thanks, Gordon.' Stan Moore hanged up the phone.

One hand behind his neck, the detective remained at his desk, chewing up the evidence. Henry Limar shot himself with a Colt .45 in a dark street while he was drunk. The same gun he used was used to shoot at CableNews Corporation probably a few days earlier. A week at the most. Who did the shooting? The gun was unregistered and untraceable. No one knows where it came from or how Limar got it. Hugh Gawler didn't seem surprised how there was a hole in the wall of the editing room. In fact, when he said the hole must have been there before the company moved inside the building, he lied.

Stan Moore picked up a file from the side of his desk. The file had been sent to him by the FBI when he requested it after talking to Hugh Galwer.

Hugh Gawler had been wanted by the Feds for years. He was still on the FBI's list for international drug trafficking. The FBI had waited for a slip-up for years. But Hugh's interest in drug trafficking seemed to have vanished overnight. His file was currently on the

185

back burner.

In the seventies, Hugh Gawler enjoyed a high profile lifestyle in the Big Apple as a drug lord. When he was finally brought to trial, the DA's office had been made into a laughing stock. Hugh Gawler had money and contacts. His appointed lawyers were experts in helping criminals evading the law and escaping detection and prosecution, despite the attempts of law enforcement officers to prosecute them.

Hugh Gawler's trial fell through on a technical cock-up. Even thought Hugh Gawler had confessed to his criminal activities in writing, his confession became inadmissible in a court of law. Hugh's defense managed to prove how at the time of the confession, Hugh Gawler was intoxicated. Medical evidence by so-called-experts was presented. The defense successfully argued any condition rendering a person temporarily incompetent makes his statement valueless. Hugh Gawler's written confession was thrown out of court.

And to add to the difficulty, witnesses who had promised the DA's office to come forwards mysteriously vanished into thin air.

Stan Moore read for hours the five inch file send to him compliments of the FBI's Headquarters in Washington D.C.

It looked as if Hugh Gawler had given up his criminal activities a long time ago. Since his last brush with the law in 1979, not one single complaint had been filed against him. FBI agents who monitored his moves for years came up with nothing.

Hugh Gawler had turned into a saint.

But detective Stan Moore didn't believe any of it. Criminals don't become good citizens overnight. Especially someone like Hugh Gawler who had taken years to build up a perfect criminal network. It was in his blood to do what he had done. It was in his blood to defy authorities, to show them who was the boss. People like Hugh Gawler didn't go down on their knees to apologise The reason why he had maintained a clear record for the last twenty years was because he was more clever than the authorities. Stan Moore was damn sure of it was the case.

Stan Moore yawned and continued to read through the file.

The detective was convinced Hugh Gawler was a cunning sonofabitch who was still getting away with murder. The problem was no one knew how or what he was getting away with.

CableNews made Hugh Gawler a wealthy man, but Stan Moore wasn't convinced it was all black and white. Hugh Gawler wasn't a business man. He was part of a new generation of mobsters. These guys were better educated and more businesslike than their predecessors. The well-known anti-social behavior of past mobsters was no longer the norms. Sociopaths like Hugh Gawler were friendly, charming, and on the surface, pillars of society. They blended legal and illegal activities in such a way, it was almost impossible for law-enforcement agencies to catch them.

But now and then, something went wrong.

Someone knew the truth and was ready to leak it.

And sometimes that someone is the person you trust, the one you work with, the one who's helped you pave your way.

Sometimes that person is a *Henry Limar*.

Stan passed one hand over his cranium while sipping his luke-warm coffee. There was little doubt Henry Limar committed suicide. But why did he do it?

Stan believed the answer to Henry Limar's death would unveil a darker truth. Something which would link everything back to Hugh Gawler. He had absolutely no evidence, but after years in the force, he learned to use his instinct. He knew this was his most reliable weapon when catching criminals.

So, if Gawler knew Limar was going to kill himself, then why didn't he stop him? If he wanted Limar dead, why did he want him dead? Did Henry Limar knew something Hugh didn't want him to know? Had Henry suddenly become a threat to Hugh Gawler's high profile media empire?

This could have been an open and shut suicide case if Stan hadn't found the bullet in the editing room. Who fired the .45 in the room? Was it Henry or someone else? And if Henry Limar's boss didn't hold a place at the FBI's hall of fame, maybe the detective wouldn't have worried too much about the hole in the wall.

But in spite of what Stan believed, there was only one problem.

A big problem.

Stan had very little to go on with.

He had already requested the help of the FBI, but to his surprise, they turned him down. The FBI didn't have time to follow up a certified suicide, nor a suspected criminal with no records or convictions of any kind of illegal activities for the past twenty years. They sent him the file he requested on Hugh Gawler. They told him the subject he requested was nothing more than a historical relic.

Stan Moore was now left on his own with his gut feeling.

There was only one lead to pursue.

Stan picked up the phone and punched a few numbers he read from his desk calendar. He checked his watch: 6.32 p.m.

'Mrs Limar?' he said, his voice was coarse from lack of sleep.
'Yes?'

'Detective Stan Moore from LAPD. Are you busy this evening?'

CHAPTER 68

CableNews: Same day, 5.06 p.m.

Hugh Gawler paced angrily up and down his office. Where was Amanda? He hadn't seen her for two days. With LAPD running up and down his back at the moment, he didn't want to take a chance with Amanda. One slip-up, and things would get out of hands.

Furious, he picked up the phone. 'Michael?'

'Yes?'

'Is Amanda back yet?'

'No, Sir.'

'Make sure she comes to my office straight away when she gets in.'

'I'll tell her.'

Hugh hung up. Shaking, he walked to the bar-fridge and poured himself a Southern Comfort. *Bitch*! He should have known she couldn't be trusted. He only had himself to blame. Just because he was thirsty for some fresh pussy, he took a hell of a chance.

But now it was over.

As soon as she'd walk through the door, she was out.

Hugh didn't want to take another chance.

He drank his Southern Comfort in one go and threw the glass across the room.

The short glass shattered in thousand pieces against the white wall.

CHAPTER 69

Downtown Los Angeles: same day, 5.34 p.m.

Orff's O Fortuna was blaring through the speakers of the green Camaro speeding north-west down highway 101, towards Hollywood.

Amanda's thoughts were confused. She was upset how her conversation with Gavin White had been so abruptly terminated. Just when he was going to tell her something about the videocassette What videocassette was he talking about anyway? A news videocassette Henry was working with? If so, what the hell was on the videocassette?

Amanda just burned a red light, nearly causing death to herself and the driver of a lemon-yellow beaten-up Volkswagen

She wondered what was going to happen if Gavin's lawyer contacted CableNews. Surely what she did wasn't really out of line. No one could really be angry at her.

The Camaro turned right on Sunset Boulevard.

Amanda turned the CD player off. She was convinced Gavin White didn't kill Senator Trevor Garry. The fear in his eyes told her so. But what was Amanda going to do now? And who was going to help her?

Amanda stopped the Camaro in the underground car park of the CableNews Corporation building. She locked the doors and rushed to the elevator.

She could almost hear the beating of her heart as she pushed the first floor button.

If Hugh Gawler had anything to do with the death of Henry, she would have to act quickly. Find some proof or get him to admit it. How was she going to do it, she didn't know. Hugh Gawler was an intelligent man. Amanda wasn't sure if she had the strength and wit to pin down a man like Hugh Gawler.

189

Steve Thorn suggested seducing him. But even if she did, Hugh would probably see through her. Would she be convincing enough for him to trust her and reveal all his secrets? Would he tell her the truth about Henry Limar's suicide?

When the lift stopped on the second floor, Amanda felt dampness at the small of her back.

She sure as hell wanted to find out what was going on.

CHAPTER 70

Brentwood: same day, 8.02 p.m.

Stan Moore found it ironic Henry Limar's house was in the same suburb of the former home of Senator Trevor Garry and the O.J. Simpson melodrama.

Brentwood, located west of I-405, north of Santa Monica and West Los Angeles, was a small but wealthy neighborhood Stan Moore realized Henry Limar had been living on a healthy salary.

The house was a white-stone Victorian with a recent fresh coat of a paint. The hedges in the drive were orderly maintained The wooden porch was generous and housed a great variety of outdoor plants.

The 1992 white Saturn pulled in the driveway.

Detective Stan Moore opened the driver's door and stepped out of the car. He looked as if he didn't get enough sleep. His eyes were heavily bagged and his dark skin dull in texture. No matter how hard he tried to forget about his work when he got home, he couldn't separate his working life from his home life. Being a police officer wasn't just another job. It was a way of life. And unless he was prepared to give it all he got, then there was no point in remaining in the force.

Stan Moore had always understood such commitment since he joined LAPD twenty-five years ago.

As he walked towards the steps, leading to the front door, he realized Mrs Limar was doing him a nice favor. She had been harassed by police officers and journalists since her husband died two days ago. All she probably wanted right now was some peace. She could have told him to go to hell with his questions. After all, her husband was dead and nothing more could be done. It was a suicide, so what was the point of an investigation? But it wasn't how Mrs Limar had reacted on the phone that afternoon. When

Stan Moore asked if he could see her, she gladly obliged.

Stan Moore stopped when the porch planks squeaked under his weight. He glanced to the left and then to the right, feeling slightly paranoid someone might be watching him. Listening carefully, he heard the noise of a car engine in the distance. The evening was warm with a little breeze blowing across the porch. He inhaled, shrugged and moved on.

Shifting uncomfortably, he knocked twice on the wooden door.

No answer.

After thirty seconds, he knocked again.

Mrs Limar did tell him six thirty was fine. Stan hoped she hadn't changed her mind.

Baffled, he knocked twice again, but this time harder.

Nothing.

Then he heard footsteps coming down the hallway. He adjusted his tie yellow and straightened up. Right now, he could have done with a glass of water. His mouth felt like cardboard. His nerves were a wreck.

During his twenty-five years in the force, he had visited hundred of victims' families. The hardest part was meeting them for the first time. Now matter how many times he went through the process, Stan still felt butterflies in his stomach. He feared the moment when someone opened the door to greet him for the first time. He felt the grief of the family members in his soul. One question which nagged him for years was where did they find the strength to carry on.

But they always did.

Stan learned people were stronger than they thought themselves to be.

The door finally opened.

Mrs Limar was in her mid-thirties, brown short hair, blue eyes, average figure, but the loveliest smile Stan had ever seen. How she could smile so genuinely two days after her husband's death was beyond him. But her puffy eyes gave away she was all cried out.

'Detective Stan Moore?' she asked, her voice disembodied.

Stan raised his shield. 'My condolences,' He said, avoiding eye contact.

Mrs Limar didn't even look at the shield. 'Come in, detective.'

Stan followed Mrs Limar down the foyer and to the living room.

He circled the room with his eyes. Twin black leather sofas, an oak coffee table, a hi-fi system, a large television.

Stan stood next to the television.

'Would you like something to drink?' Mrs Limar said.

'I won't take much of your time, Mrs Limar,' Stan said, his voice expressing embarrassment 'I'd just like to ask you a few things about your husband.'

'His study is upstairs.'

'He had a study?'

'Well, sort of. It more like a studio. He was fascinated with audio visual equipment.'

'You don't mind showing me where he worked?'

'Come this way.'

Stan Moore followed Mrs Limar down the hallway and upstairs to Henry's study. 'I've already spoken to the police,' she said when they reached the room.

'I know. I've read the report. But sometimes questions come up days after the initial investigation.'

Mrs Limar opened the door to the study. It was a rather large room filled with all kinds of video and audio equipment

'I didn't realize you were black on the phone,' Mrs Limar said suddenly, surprising both herself and the detective.

Stan frowned.

'Oh, I'm sorry,' she said, grabbing him by the arm. 'I hope it didn't come out wrong. I've got nothing against black people. It's just everyone must give you such a hard time being a cop and black as well.'

Stan could see her embarrassment from the red on her cheeks. He grinned and said, 'It has its days. But nothing we can't handle.'

A quick glance to the left, and he noticed a video editing desk similar to one he had seen at CableNews.

'Everything is as he left it,' Mrs Limar said. There was a strain in her tone.

'Thank you. You don't mind if I look around?'

'Go ahead. I'll be downstairs if you need me. I can't stay in this room for to long. It makes me feel nauseous.'

'I understand. Thank you for your co-operation, Mrs Limar.'

Mrs Limar left the room, closing the door behind.

Stan circled the room, sketching and noting anything he saw in in his notebook.

Videocassettes were piled up next to one of the two video display units. Stan picked a couple and scanned the titles. They were marked by date and code. What the codes meant, Stan didn't have a clue. It was a combination of letters and numbers. One was labeled *GTR7865*.

He selected the videocassettes labeled with the most recent dates and tucked them under his arm.

He picked up a book and riffled through the pages. A incomprehensible technical manual on video editing.

Then he checked the drawers.

Nothing grabbed his interest. Pen, blank pads, rubbers, thumb pins, a black Stanley stapler, self-adhesive video labels, a pair of scissors and two large markers.

No guns.

No ammunition

Nothing out of the ordinary.

Stan scribbled a few more notes in his notebook. He flicked to a fresh page and drew a clumsy sketch of the content of the drawer. Right now this type of information might have seemed irrelevant, but from experience, Stan knew everything was important. Sometimes the smallest details came back to mind during the investigation, something which provided him with a major breakthrough in solving a crime.

And this is when he noticed the silver waste basket

Carefully, he emptied the content of the bin on the green wool carpet. Mostly papers and empty envelops. He checked everything carefully.

Then he came across a crumbled piece of paper, slightly creamy in color Carefully, he unfolded the ball of paper, uncovering a page from a desk calendar. The date was a Friday, just the day before Henry killed himself.

But it wasn't what intrigued Stan.

The handwriting with the name Gavin White, his address and a telephone number under it made his Adam apple quiver like a sparrow.

Hell! Could this suicide be connected to the death of Senator Garry?

Stan folded the piece of paper neatly and placed it in his wallet.

He has suspected foul play all along.

But the connection with Senator Trevor Garry never crossed his mind.

Now he had something substantial to go on with.

CHAPTER 71

Amanda Ryan tried to sneak into her office.

'Amanda!'

Amanda recognized the voice of Tracy Hamilton.

'Yes?'

'Hugh wants to see you in his office immediately'

Damn it! Amanda could tell by the secretary's tone of voice it wasn't good news. 'Tell him I be there in a minute.'

'He said immediately'

Amanda felt perspiration running down the small of her back. A look crossed her face as she approached Tracy Hamilton's desk.

'What does he want?'

'Go in,' Tracy Hamilton snapped. 'He's expecting you.'

As soon as Amanda opened the door, Hugh screamed, 'And where the hell have you been for the last two days?'

Amanda swallowed 'Working.'

'Working? Don't you carry your cell phone around any more? How am I supposed to contact you in case of an emergency?'

'I forgot it on my desk.'

'Close the door and sit,' he muttered darkly.

Amanda didn't like the way Hugh was talking to her. She felt like telling him where to go, but he seemed so worked-up, she had to hear him out first.

'What is the meaning of this?' she asked, refusing to take a seat at the desk.

'I want to know what you've being doing for the last two days.'

'I told you I was working.'

'On what?'

'On the Senator's story.'

'What Senator's story? That was finished weeks ago.'

'I just felt—'

'—You just felt what? Let me remind you who you're working for. You do not go around chasing up stories without my permission. At $80,000 a year, you're a luxury around here. And seeing how you're wasting time, I don't know if you're worth it.'

A chill rippled down Amanda's back. She had never seen Hugh Gawler so uptight. His lower lip was quivering. He blinked rapidly, his arms crossed over his chest. This was not the Hugh Gawler she thought she knew.

Hugh walked to the bar-fridge, filled a short glass of Southern Comfort and drank it in one go. He filled another glass. 'I asked you where you were?'

'Just doing some more interviews-'

'Where about?'

'Some family members of the Senator.'

'You lying bitch!' he shrieked.

Feeling her temper snapping, Amanda took on step forward. 'I don't have to take this.' She wanted to cry, but kept her composure.

'Sit down!' Hugh screamed, pointing his finger to the chair.

Like someone's pet, Amanda took her seat. 'Really, Sir-'

'I'll give you *Sir*. Do you know who I had on the phone less than an hour ago?'

Amanda gave Hugh a blank look.

'Justin Smith. I think you too have already met.'

Amanda's blank look froze on her face.

'What were you doing interviewing Gavin White?'

'Something to do.'

'Who asked you to interview Gavin White?'

'I just thought I'd follow up on the Senator's story.'

'Did I ask you to follow up on the Senator's story?'

'No, but-'

'Or maybe it was Michael?' Hugh picked on the phone. 'I'll call him and ask him myself.' He begins to dial Michael's extension number.

'Michael didn't tell me anything.'

Hugh hung up the phone violently and continued as if cued, 'Then who did?'

'No one.'

'How dare do you go around doing interviews as a reporter from CableNews when I or anyone else haven't giving you authorization to do so?'

Amanda could no longer hold herself together. Hot tears cascaded down her cheeks. 'I didn't know you were going to be so upset,' she sobbed. Something about the look in his eyes frightened her. She wanted to say she was sorry, how she would never do it again.

She hung her head.

Hugh circled the room. He looked up to the ceiling a few time and scratched his head. Then he turned to Amanda and said in a dry voice, 'I want you out of this building. Pack your stuff and leave.'

Amanda was trembling. 'But, Mr Gawler, this is so unfair. I thought I was doing the right thing. I'm a journalist. I'd thought I'd show some initiative.'

'I'll tell you what's unfair. You snooping around my desk and tapping in my computer when I leave you in my office for twenty minutes.'

Shit! Tracy Hamilton probably told him.

Amanda's jaw locked.

'Leave the building immediately,' Hugh went on. 'I'll have you escorted outside. Good-bye Amanda Ryan. It was nice meeting you. You can always call me at home. I'm free after hours.'

Amanda stood from her chair, her face puffed up from crying. 'You bastard!'

Before Hugh had time to react, she ran out of the office and slammed the door behind her.

CHAPTER 72

Furious, Hugh unlocked the third drawer of his desk and took a Combat Commander.38 automatic in his hand.

He had enough of Amanda Ryan. This whole thing had been a mistake from the beginning. He should have never taken her on board.

And now she had the nerve to slam the door at his face.

Hugh checked the weapon was loaded. His hands were clammy. Beads of perspiration appeared on his forehead. He knew it was a crazy idea, but he didn't give himself much time to think. Right at this moment, he was mad as hell.

The bitch was playing with his head. He wanted to make love to her, but he also wanted to kill her. *God damn woman!* Why couldn't she just let herself be controlled?

He thought for a few seconds and raced after Amanda.

CHAPTER 73

LAPD: Tuesday, 7.28 p.m.

Sitting behind his desk, Detective Stan Moore looked at the note he found in Henry Limar's home. GAVIN WHITE. He pondered for a few seconds and dialed the telephone number under the name.

'San Quentin State Prison,' the male voice said at the end of the line.

Stan hung up. When he saw the 415 area code, he knew it was an interstate number. And because Gavin White lived in Los Angeles, it couldn't have been his home number.

An empty cup of coffee was sitting on his desk. The FBI-Hugh Gawler file opened on his desk, Stan Moore flicked through the content. He puzzled over the meaning of his finding.

Why did Henry write down the telephone number of San Quentin State Prison where Gavin White was staying? Did he actually get in touch with Gavin White? And if so, why? Henry Limar was a videocassette editor, not a journalist.

The Detective had never linked the death of Senator Garry to Limar's suicide. But now, there seemed to be some kind of connection. The link so far was Gavin White. Did Limar and Senator Garry get killed by the same person? Or people? Okay, Limar's death was officially a murder. But Stan Moore didn't want to bet on it.

As he continued flicking through the FBI file, Stan wondered how this whole thing was connected to Hugh Gawler, if it was connected at all. The man intrigued him. He wanted to know why. Something wasn't right about his clean criminal record for the past twenty years. It didn't match the FBI reports he had in front of his

199

eyes right now.

Time for a hypothesis, Stan decided. Lets say Hugh was involved in the deaths of Senator Garry and Henry Limar. It would be silly to assume a logical reason at this stage. There was no evidence whatsoever to link Hugh with the deaths.

But Stan didn't need any evidence. After twenty-five years in the force, he knew experience was as good as evidence. And his experience told him Hugh was the man who held the key to the mystery of the deaths of Henry Limar and Senator Trevor Garry.

The only thing he needed now was a motive. Why would Hugh Gawler want the men dead? Was it some kind of political foul play? If so, how the hell was Limar involved in all this?

Okay, what if the two deaths had nothing to do with one another?

Tired, Stan Moore lit a cigarette and sucked on it slowly.

The talk with Mrs Limar that evening didn't amount to anything. After he had finished searching through Henry's room, he went downstairs to question her.

'Did you notice anything strange about his behavior lately?'

'No. He was always quiet. Always working. I don't think I knew him well.'

'Did you know your husband had a gun?'

'No.'

'Do you have any idea where he might have bought it from?'

'I don't know detective.'

'How close were you to your husband?'

'I told you. He was always working in his room. Sometimes he came back from work very late.'

'What about the night he killed himself? That was a Sunday morning. Did you worry your husband was not home by one o'clock in the morning?'

'He often went out. He said it was for work. You now, journalists have irregular hours.'

'I though he was a news editor, not a journalist.'

'Whatever. He often stayed behind at the office and worked odd hours.'

The rest of the conversation drifted nowhere. A few things about Henry Limar's habits, what he ate for breakfast, and other irrelevant bits and pieces.

Stan blew the smoke from his cigarette into a perfect circle. The next step seemed clear. Stan would have to go and visit Gavin White in jail.

Since Henry Limar was dead, then the only person who could help him now was Gavin White.

Of course he could always interrogate Hugh Gawler, but he

knew it was pointless. He needed something more concrete before moving forward. If Hugh Gawler was as clever and manipulative as those FBI files told him, then Stan had to calculate his every move. He couldn't just jump on Gawler and make wild accusations.

He folded the piece of paper neatly and tucked it back inside his wallet.

He would get some sleep on the flight to San Francisco.

CHAPTER 74

CableNews: same day, 6.02 p.m.

Amanda Ryan stormed into Michael Hall's office.

'What's going on?' Michael asked, infusing his tone with confusion.

'Just got fired,' Amanda said, her eyes filled with tears.

'Fired? Why?'

'Hugh. I can't explain right now. It's too complicated. Something to do with an interview he didn't want me to conduct.'

Michael jumped from his chair. 'I'll talk to him. He can't let you go for just one mistake.'

Just then, Hugh walked into Michael's office. In a swift move, Hugh tucked the Combat Commander .38 between his belt and the small of his back.

Amanda noticed the move but wasn't sure about what had just happened.

'What's going on?' Michael said when he saw Hugh looking flushed.

'Michael, I'd like you to escort Amanda out of the building. She's no longer working for us.' Hugh stood erect, obviously trying to hide his anger.

'Why?'

'Ask her. She'll tell you. And I want her out now!'

Without saying another word, Hugh left the office.

Michael shut the door behind him. He frowned as he wrapped his arms around Amanda. 'What's going on? You're going to tell me?'

'No,' Amanda cried. 'Not right now. I just want to go home. Can you take me home?'

'Sure.' Michael passed one hand over her wet cheek. He picked up his blazer and his briefcase. 'I'll take you home.'

'Thanks,' she said. 'Give me a few minutes to get my things together.' She straightened her jacket and lifted her chin up. No one was going to take her pride away.

'I'll wait for you at reception.' Michael said, wiping her tears with the back of his hand. He gave her a bear-hug. 'Everything is going to be all right.'

'I'll live through it,' Amanda said, now more in control of her churning emotions.

Amanda walked into her office, closed the door and froze. She looked around the room. She realized how little she had time to enjoy the luxurious environment of her office.

Slowly, she circled the room, her head filled with confusing thoughts. Since she was no longer working for CableNews, what was she going to do? Go back to Globe Network? What about Gavin White? What about Henry Limar? She couldn't just pretend nothing ever happened. What if she was the only one who knew about the connection?

She knew she was on to something. Why in the world did Hugh Gawler get so upset?

As she emptied the contents of her drawers, she didn't think Hugh had acted logically. Journalists were expected to get out of their way to pursue a story. What she did was not out of character whatsoever. Such realization made her even more angry. She was sick and tired of being made inferior and vulnerable. All she was trying to do was better herself. Maybe she had been too weak. Maybe she'd let other people walk over her too easily.

As she finished filling a plastic crate with her belongings, she knew things would have to change.

When Amanda came back from her office, she seemed refreshed. Her eyes were still puffed, but she was no longer crying. Her hair was brushed back and tied in a ponytail. She even smiled when Michael's eyes met hers.

'Feeling better?' Michael asked, standing up from the reception couch.

'I'm fine.'

She didn't take the time to say good-bye to any of the staff. And under the circumstances, Michael couldn't really blame her.

They took the elevator to the underground car park.

Neither said a word.

Amanda stared at the stainless steel door, wondering what she was going to tell Michael. She knew eventually she would have to tell him the truth. The realization paralyzed her thoughts. She could see Michael looking at her from the corner of one eye. He was being patient. Amanda admired his integrity He obviously knew better than probing her with questions right now.

Amanda looked up to the floor numbers flashing at the top of the elevator. The elevator stopped at UG.

When the stainless steel door of the elevator opened, Michael said, 'I'll have a talk to Hugh when I get back here.'

'Don't bother,' Amanda snapped.

'Why?'

'There's nothing you can do.'

'You're going to tell me what this is all about?'

A chill rippled down her back. She had hoped he wouldn't ask until they got home. All this time Michael thought she was a honest-to-good employee. Now she had to tell him she was a spy. What was the alternative? That he found out from Hugh Gawler?

Restless, Amanda raced to Michael's BMW.

'I'll tell you what this is all about,' she said, 'but you're not going to like it.'

Amanda waited for Michael to unlock the car.

Michael inserted the key in the driver's side of the BMW. Half a turn clockwise activated the central locking and unlocked the four doors of the luxury vehicle.

They climbed in the car.

Michael turned the ignition on and locked the gears on reverse. 'I'll live through it.'

Determined to get it over and done with, Amanda explained, 'Hugh caught me snooping around his office.'

'When?'

'Actually, it was Tracy Hamilton who saw me. I was looking through his drawers and computer files.' Amanda felt a knot in her throat. She was relieved to have told the truth, but she knew the truth made her look like an idiot.

'Why?' Michael asked, his look confused.

'You're not going to believe me if I tell you.'

'Oh, for Christ's sake, Amanda. We're both grown-ups here. What is it? You work for the CIA or something?'

'Almost.'

As the car pulled out of the car park, Michael gave her an inquisitive stare.

'I was spying for Globe Network,' Amanda said, her tone lacking confidence. She closed her eyes as if a bomb was about to explode.

Michael didn't answer.

She opened her eyes. He was staring at the road in front of him. Movement in his jaw indicated he was grinding his teeth.

'I was a spy,' Amanda repeated.

'A spy? Spying for what?' His voice was dull.

'Eight months ago, our ratings have been at their lowest level. We lost millions of dollars in advertising contracts. CableNews seemed to be at the right place whenever something happens. We didn't know what was going on. We couldn't understand how you people managed to get all the footage and the best stories. Globe Network had been in the business for more than two decades, and suddenly Hugh Gawler and his team come out of nowhere and undersells us.'

Amanda moved uncomfortably on the seat. She looked at Michael, but he was still staring at the road. He blinked rapidly.

'I was a spy Michael. They've sent me here to find out how you guys did things.'

There was a full minute silence before he snapped, 'Why did you do it, Amanda? What's the point? Do you think we're criminals or something? Do you realize you could go to jail?'

Amanda swallowed 'I know it was a mistake. I've never done something so wrong in my life. It's just that I needed to prove myself. No one would give me a chance. I had to show them what I was worth. If I could take it back, I would. I don't know what to say.'

'This is so wrong, Amanda.'

'I know.' She thought for a few seconds. 'But you know, after everything that's been happening, maybe it wasn't really the wrong thing to do. Maybe there is a reason why all this has happened. Maybe it was fate. You used to believe in fate at university.'

'So?'

'Remember when I saw Henry trying to kill himself in the editing room?'

Michael nodded.

'Well,' Amanda said, 'I have a feeling Hugh's got something to do with this.' Amanda explained how she found Gavin White's name in Hugh's computer. She told him about the meeting she had with Gavin White and how angry Hugh had been when he found out. 'And him being so angry doesn't make much sense.'

'Maybe it does. Maybe he found out you were spying around in his office. I don't know Amanda, I would have been angry too if I knew you'd been snooping in my office.'

Amanda hesitated, but finally said, 'There's more to it. Hugh has come on to me a few times.'

'He what?'

'He told me I was naive if I thought he employed me because I was a good journalist. In several ways, he implied I was only here because he wanted to fuck me.'

Color rose on Michael's cheeks. He turned to Amanda. 'Why didn't you tell me all this before?'

'Because I was afraid of how you were going to react.'

'Wow! This is just great. What other surprises have you got for me?' He slammed the palm of his hand on the steering wheel.

Amanda was upset but happy Michael knew the truth at last. She didn't know how this was going to affect their relationship. But if Michael wanted to end it, she would understand. Not that she would get over it quickly, but she would understand. If someone had lied to her the way she had lied to Michael, she didn't know if she would still talk to them.

Amanda wiped a tear from her eye as Michael pulled up in her driveway. 'You don't hate me, do you?' Amanda asked, grabbing his hand.

Michael turned to face her. He placed one hand behind her neck and looked into her eyes. 'How could I hate you. You're a fool. Look at the mess you got yourself into. I'm upset. Of course, I'm upset. What did you expect? I was going to say, *great you're a spy, let's have some champagne*? I'm a founding director of the company, for Christ's sake.'

Amanda hesitated. 'I'm so sure there is much more to all this than what I've just told you.'

Michael removed his hand from behind her neck. 'I'm sure it's a fascinating story. But I don't know if I have the heart to hear it right now. I need some time to think things over.'

Amanda opened the door of the BMW. 'I'm really sorry, Michael. You're the last person I wanted to hurt. But I didn't know you worked for CableNews when I decided to spy. If I had known, I would have never taken the job.'

'You better go now,' Michael said. 'I'll call you tomorrow to see how you are.'

'Sure.' She kissed him on the cheek.

He didn't respond.

Amanda stepped out of the BMW.

Michael reversed the car out of the driveway. He flashed the high beams a couple of times and disappeared down the street.

Amanda stood alone in the dark, wondering if everything had just been one long nightmare.

Sometimes, when life seemed to be against her, she just wanted to be back home to Australia. She missed her parents. Four years of University. Seven months of work. She realized the years were going faster than she had anticipated. And now she was far away from her parents, she knew how much she loved them.

Engulfed by a deep sense of hopelessness, Amanda turned around to face her home. She hoped everything would be over soon, and she would begin to live a normal life again.

But when she saw the door ajar, she realized the nightmare was only beginning.

CHAPTER 75

San Quentin State Prison: Wednesday 9.29 a.m.

Detective Stan Moore didn't bother making an appointment with Gavin White. Since he was officially investigating Limar's suicide, he felt he had the right to come in at any time and interrogate anyone he wanted in relation to the case.

Stan Moore parked his white Saturn in the visitor's car park.

He stepped out of the car and checked his shield was in his pocket.

All night he had been thinking what connection there might have been between Limar and White. One was a journalist. The other a thug. It was unlikely they've ever met. The only way Stan Moore was going to figure out what the hell was going on was to talk to Gavin White.

He approached the reception desk and flashed his shield.

'Detective Stan Moore. I'd like to see Gavin White.'

The prison officer checked his list. 'Did you have a booking, detective?'

'No. But it won't take long.'

The prison officer shook his head. 'I'm sorry, Detective. But you can't talk to Gavin White unless you have a booking.'

'Fine. I'll make a booking now.' He looked at his watch. 9.34 a.m. 'Book me in for nine forty.'

The prison guard shook his head again. 'Can't do that.'

'What do you mean can't do that?'

'Gavin White is not allowed to receive any visitors without prior arrangement with his lawyer. You must make a booking four weeks prior to a visit.'

'I'm a law enforcement officer. I don't have to book four weeks ahead of time.'

'I still can't let you in.'

'And who says?'

'His lawyer.'

Stan stood there for a few seconds. 'Do you have his lawyer's name and number.'

'Just hold on a sec.' The prison officer looked up through another list. 'His name is Justin Smith.'

Stan flipped his notebook open and wrote the name down.

The prison officer gave him Smith's mobile telephone number.

'Is there a phone I can use around here?' Stan said.

'Right at your back.' The prison officer pointed to a public phone behind Stan.

Stan turned around, picked up the phone, threw in a quarter and dialed Justin Smith's number. The line rang three times before it was answered.

'Justin Smith,' the voice said.

'Detective Stan Moore.'

'Yes?'

'I'm at San Quentin. I'd like to talk to Gavin White, but apparently I have to check with you first.'

'My client's got nothing to say to the police without my presence. We've already made a statement regarding the Senator's death anyway. What did you say you name was?'

'Detective Stan Moore, LAPD.'

'I didn't know you were handling the Senator's murder, Detective More.'

'I'm not.'

'So why do you want to see my client?'

'Another crime.'

There was a laughter on the phone. 'You can't be serious. Do you think my client is going to talk to you about another crime while he's in jail for one already.'

'This will not incriminate your client in any way.'

'Sure, it's exactly what the cops said. I'm sorry. No deal. Good-bye detective.' The line went dead.

'Shit,' Stan Moore mumbled, slamming the handset. *Damn it!* He would have to do it the hard way. Get a summons for a hearing as soon as possible. But it will take another three to seven days. A waste of time. He thought for a moment and picked up the phone. He threw in a quarter and dialed San Quentin State Prison's number.

The telephone behind his back rang twice.

The prison officer at the reception answered the call. 'San Quentin State Prison.'

'This is Justin Smith,' Stan said, imitating Smith's voice the best way he could. 'I've just received a call from Detective Stan Moore regarding my client Gavin White.'

The prison guard looked over the glass. He saw Stan on the public telephone. 'Detective Stan Moore is still here. Did you want to talk to him?'

'No. Just tell him it's fine. He can visit Gavin White.'

'Are you sure, Mr Smith?' the prison officer said, his tone expressing concern. 'I thought after this young journalist came to see Mr White, you didn't want any more visitors.'

'Just let him through. I'll take full responsibility.'

'As you wish, Mr Smith.'

Stan Moore stayed on the line another thirty seconds after the prison officer hanged up.

The prison officer tapped on the glass.

Stan told him to wait with a gesture of his hand. He said good-bye to the dead line and turned to the prison officer. 'Yes?'

'Your nine-forty booking is two minutes late.'

Detective Stan Moore smiled.

CHAPTER 76

Santa Monica: Tuesday, 7.15 p.m.

Amanda Ryan froze in front of the open door. She didn't want to go in. Someone might still be in the house. She took two steps back.

No sound from inside the house.

Amanda turned around and ran down the driveway and unto the street. She looked out for Michael's car. It had just turned the corner.

She looked back towards the house.

The lights were turned off.

Carefully she removed her cell phone from her briefcase. She though of dialing 911, but then changed her mind. She dialed Michael's number instead.

'Michael Hall.'

'It's me. Come back straight away.'

'What's wrong?'

'Someone broke into my house. I don't want to go in by myself.'

'Hell! Just hold on. I'll be here in a minute.'

Amanda pressed the END button and threw her cell phone in the briefcase.

She could feel her knees shaking. It was the last thing she needed after a day like this. What else could go wrong?

Michael's BMW raced around the corner, tires screeching.

Amanda moved from the driveway when the BMW arrived at sixty miles per hour.

Michael killed the engine and got out of the car. 'Is anyone in there?' he asked, looking towards the house.

'I don't know,' Amanda said. 'I haven't been inside.'

'Did you call the police?'

'No.'

'Why not?'

'I thought I call you first. You were closer'

Carefully, Michael walked to the door. 'All right. Just stay behind me.' He pushed the door with his foot. 'Where's the light switch?'

'Just on your left,' Amanda said, holding on to Michael's arm.

He flicked the light on. The hallway was empty. He slowed to a creeping pace, hugging the wall. He then turned into the living room and reached for the light switch.

The contents of the room had been turned upside down.

'My God!' Amanda said, coming just behind Michael. 'What the hell happened in here.'

All of Amanda's books had been thrown on the floor. The sofa had been slit open, the rug pulled to one side of the room, the pictures taken off the walls, the tube of the television cracked.

Michael didn't say anything. He circled the room.

Not a word was spoken for a full minute.

The shock of what had just happened was sinking in slowly.

Finally, Michael's gaze shifted to Amanda. 'Is anything missing?' he asked.

'I don't know. I don't think so.' Amanda continued to looked around, trying to figure out if anything was missing. But her mind was confused. Everything was there, either misplaced or broken. It didn't look like an ordinary burglary. It seemed clear whoever had broken into Amanda's house was looking for something.

'There must have been more than one of them to make such a mess,' Michael said, hands on his hips.

Amanda didn't know if she wanted to cry or scream. She looked around carefully. She took two steps forward and muttered, 'I'm going to check the kitchen.'

Amanda crossed the room to the kitchen. The contents of cupboards were open and emptied on the floor. Every plastic container had been emptied, every bag slashed, every item turned inside out.

Amanda walked carefully around the mixture of flour, rice, coffee, tin fruits and breakfast cereals. Even the content of the fridge had been emptied on the kitchen floor. She nearly stepped on a box of broken eggs. The sour and sweet smell of the mixture made her nauseous.

The garbage bag was split open, revealing what Amanda ate for the past week.

Amanda put her head in her hands and groaned, 'Who could have done such a thing?'

Suddenly, she felt Michael's presence behind her. 'Do you have any idea what they were looking for?' he asked, his eyes circling the room. He stepped in front of Amanda, carefully avoiding the mess on the floor.

'I bet you it has something to do with Gavin White or Harry Limar.' She stopped for a few seconds and went on, 'God, Michael, someone is watching me!' Her eyes opened in astonishment.

'What do you mean?'

'If someone broke into my house to find something connected to Henry Limar or Gavin White, then this person must have known she had been in touch with the two men.'

But Michael didn't seem surprised. His hand were locked behind his back. 'Do you think someone killed Henry Limar? Michael asked.

'If they did, it's because he had something they wanted. And now that he's dead, maybe they think I've got it.'

'What else did Henry tell you?'

'Nothing. I told you everything. But Gavin White did mention something about some videocassette Probably a videocassette Henry had in his possession.'

Michael finished for her, 'And now someone thinks you have the videocassette. It's the reason why they've turned your home inside out.'

'And that's why I'm so convinced that there was something suspicious about Henry's death. Since Hugh has been acting strangely over this, he probably has something to do with this.'

Michael took one deep breath and gestured, 'Why do you insist on pinning everything on Hugh Gawler?

'Because he gives me the creeps.'

'Well, there's a reason. Call the police. You've got enough evidence,' Michael said statistically

Amanda gave him a cold stare.

'You should. If you think this has something to do with the death of Henry, you should call the police.'

Amanda was lost in thoughts. Maybe Michael was right. But the idea of having the police around didn't comfort her. Probably because she was spying at CableNews. She realized her fear was inappropriate. Her spying at CableNews didn't seem really connected to the break-in. And spying was not illegal, not that she thought it was, anyway. 'All right, let's call the police.'

Michael grabbed the handset from the yellow phone attached to the kitchen wall, next to the fridge.

He dialed 911.

CHAPTER 77

CableNews: same day, 8.16 p.m.

Hugh Gawler crossed the office to the bar fridge and back to his desk. *What the hell is going on?* The waiting was driving him crazy. He rubbed his hands together to get rid of the perspiration. The muscles in his shoulders were tense. They felt as hard as wood. With one hand, he massaged the back of his neck.

The beginning of a migraine.

The phone rang.

His heart thundered.

He picked up the receiver and said, 'Yes?'

'There was nothing at her place.'

'Are you sure?'

'We looked everywhere. The bedroom, the kitchen, even the toilet.'

'Damn! What about her car?'

'We checked the car as well. Nothing.'

There was a pause for a few seconds.

'What do you want to do?' the voice at the end of the line said.

'Get rid of her.' Hugh hung up and felt dryness in his throat. Now he knew he was never going to make love to Amanda. But he didn't care. She was just another piece of meat like all the others. All he knew is she was getting in the way. It should have never happened. It was his fault.

And this realization made it worse.

Hugh crossed to the bar and poured himself a Southern Comfort in a short glass filled with ice. He drank it slowly, enjoying the bitter-sweet medicated taste at the back of his throat.

God, he hated when things got out of control. He should have seen this one coming. He should have listened. His obsession for the woman was stronger than his reasoning. But it didn't have to be

214

this way.

Hugh had self-control.

Dignity.

Power.

Drive.

Ambition.

Amanda Ryan had to go.

CHAPTER 78

San Quentin State Prison: 9.45 a.m.

Detective Stan Moore was sitting in the small room, face to face with Gavin White. The two black men felt immediately connected because of the pigmentation of their skin.

The two white guards stood in each corner of the room.

A security mesh separated the two black men.

'Did you know Henry Limar?' Stan asked.

'No, I didn't, man. Why you become a cop, anyway?'

'Tell you some other time.'

'Cops are assholes, man. Why you wanna be a cop for? Let them white scum asses be cops.'

'I don't have much time. I'm just trying to figure out where you fit in with Henry Limar's suicide.'

'Fuck you, man. I don't know shit about no shit. You think I'm going to sit there and talk to some motherfucker pig. You guys got me in this shit-hole in the first place.'

Stan Moore's eyes narrowed. He moved his head up to the security mesh and whispered, 'You're pissing up the wrong tree. I'm here to help you. You tell me what you know, and maybe you won't have to go the gas chamber.'

Gavin White tilted his head sideways. 'Fuck you, Mr Tough-fuckin-guy. I'm telling you I know nothing about a Henry Limar.'

'He had your name on his desk calendar with the phone number for this place. You tell me what he told you, and I'll see what I can do for you.'

Gavin White locked his eyes in Stan Moore's.

Stan didn't twitch a bit. He went on, 'If you don't tell me what's going on, I'm out of here in the next thirty seconds. I'm your last chance.'

Gavin kept his eyes locked into Stan's, obviously trying to figure out if he was for real. After a short pause, he tilted his head like a pendulums 'All right. He rang me here the day before he died.'

A relieved look crossed Stan's face. 'What did he want?'

'To tell me I wasn't guilty of the Senator's death. Fuck, I knew that. It wasn't me he had to try to convince.'

'Did he say how he knew?'

'No. But he reckoned he had proof.'

'Did you tell anyone else about this?'

'Nope.' Two seconds hesitation. 'Yes, actually, I did.'

'Who?'

'My fuckin lawyer. Also a journalist who came the other day. A lady. Nice looking white bitch.' Gavin winked at Stan Moore. 'If you know what I mean.'

'Did she say where she was from?'

'Gave me her business card.' Gavin reached inside his pocket. He removed a white business card and passed it under the security mesh.

Stan Moore grabbed the card and read.

AMANDA RYAN. CABLENEWS CORPORATION.

He couldn't place a face to the name. In fact, he didn't recall anyone mentioning anything about her when he was at CableNews the other day.

'She got kicked out half way through our conversation by my lawyer.'

'I wonder why,' Stan said laughing to himself. He thought for a few seconds. 'You said Henry Limar had proof you were innocent. Did he said what kind of proof?'

'He said he was going to send it to me.'

'Did he?'

'No.'

'What did you lawyer say when you told him?'

'He would look into it.'

'Has he?'

'Don't know. He seems to think I'm guilty. Doesn't help. You need a defense lawyer, and they give you some fuckin smart-mouth jerk who thinks you're guilty as hell.'

Stan Moore hated the legal system in this country. It seemed only the rich were capable of getting a decent lawyer. Gavin White was represented by a court-appointed attorney. The attorney probably didn't care. He wouldn't make more than a thousand dollars out of the case. And with all the evidence stacked up against Gavin White, he would have no chance to win the case anyway.

Lawyers like Justin Smith were already up to their necks defending lesser crimes. At the most, they didn't spend more than an hour per client. It paid his rent. The easiest and fastest way out was to get the client to plead guilty and wrap up the case. Public defense was seen by many people as representing the enemy. And who could blame them.

But the Senator's murder was big publicity. Justin Smith didn't mind spending ten hours in all. The money would be useless, but the publicity good. Any type of media exposure was free advertising. He wouldn't win, but he didn't care. People wanted to see Gavin White prosecuted. He would make sure they were going to get what they wanted. Detective Stan Moore knew all that, but there was nothing he could do.

'So, that proof,' Stan Moore said. 'What was it?'

'A tape. A video tape, I think.'

'Of what?'

'Don't know. He didn't really say.'

'And you told Amanda Ryan about the videocassette?'

'Yeah, I did. I felt if more people knew about it, the more chance I had to get out of this mess.'

Stan Moore made a mental note of calling Amanda Ryan as soon as possible. 'Look, Gavin, I don't know whether you did it or not. But something doesn't ring right in here. I'm really trying to investigate the death of Henry Limar. You're sure you've never met him before?'

'I'm telling you, man, I don't know this man. Never seen him, never heard of him. He rang me up out of the blue.'

Stan Moore knew Gavin White was telling the truth. There would be no point in lying.

'Do you think you can find who killed the Senator?' Gavin asked, a look of despair crossing his face.

'I'm not assigned to your case, Gavin. But I promise if I find anything which proves your innocence, I'll pass on the information to your lawyer. What we really need to do right now is to get our hands on the videocassette'

'I really appreciate it, man. Hey, brother, maybe not all cops are assholes after all.' He stood from his chair.

The two guards at the door approached him.

Stan Moore closed his notebook.

Gavin gave Stan Moore a vulnerable smile.

In return, Stan gave him a blank look. His jaw dropped. He looked past Gavin and to the small glass window from the door.

Justin Smith's blood shoot eyes glared into his.

218

CHAPTER 79

Santa Monica: Tuesday, 9.28 p.m.

Amanda decided to stay over at Michael's apartment. They hadn't figured out who broke into her home. Both Michael and her agreed it wasn't a safe place to stay at for the time being.

Amanda picked up a few clothes from her bedroom and packed them into a suitcase. While packing, she became horrified at the thought of what could have happened to her if she had been home during the break-in. According to the police, there were at least two people who would have conducted the burglary. Various sets of footprints had been found around the premises.

Los Angeles didn't feel like a good place to live any longer. Amanda wondered why the media always glorified the city in spite of all its violence. Maybe it was part of the thrill. The excitement of not knowing where life was taking you from one day to the next.

Amanda decided to leave her SUV behind. She didn't want to drive alone on the way to Michael's apartment. She would catch a cab and pick up her car the next day.

The morning after Amanda moved into Michael's apartment, she learned about the Oklahoma bombing. Like the rest of America, she was disgusted by the act of terrorism. But being physically detached from Oklahoma, the incident felt distant, as if it had happened in another world, a world of violence and anger. And yet, it had been a little over a week since Senator Trevor Garry had been butchered.

Amanda realized how living in a society were violence was a part of everyday life desensitized the human soul. All these horrible things were happening around her, but she was powerless to stop them. The only thing to do was to get used to them. She had to find her own peace.

But Amanda's life was not in any way peaceful. With her own problems to take care of, she didn't give the Oklahoma bombing much thought.

She quickly learned how CableNews managed to get a crew at the scene minutes after the explosion. The speed and efficiency in which Hugh Gawler had organized a news team to Oklahoma was incredible. An insider's gossip claimed CableNews was the first team at the scene. This was surprising since Oklahoma State had its own cable news network and commercial stations efficiently covering Oklahoma City.

But Amanda hadn't been long enough at Cable News to find out how its news team always managed to get first at the scene of the crime.

And she wasn't certain she wanted to know. She knew she might just become another six o'clock news statistic.

Michael told Amanda he was convinced if someone was so desperate to get something from her, they would probably be willing to hurt her. And since Amanda had no one to turn to but him, he knew he had to help. In spite of his disappointment of finding out she was a spy for his rival, Michael didn't want to give up on her just yet.

At least that's what he told her.

On the second night, Michael and Amanda sat in the living room, discussing for hours the possible identities of the people who broke into Amanda's home.

The police came shortly after the break-in. They looked around the house.

Amanda made a statement. She was asked to come to the LAPD the next morning to talk to a detective. It was clear to the police the break-in wasn't just another burglary. Whoever had broken into the house was looking for something. Burglars don't normally slit pillows and sofas, unless they're looking for something in particular.

Like Amanda and Michael, the police were anxious to find out what the break-in was all about.

Amanda was still trying to come to terms with the way everything had happened so fast.

She was sitting with Michael in the kitchen of his apartment, over a cup of coffee. The needles on the clock above the fridge showed 10.32 p.m.

'I wish you would have told me everything earlier,' Micheal said, his voice showing disappointment.

Amanda tilted her head and said, 'I couldn't. Why can't you

understand. I didn't tell you because I love you, not because I wanted to hide something from you.' She didn't have another way of explaining herself. She tried to be as honest as she could. *If he loves enough, he will understand.*

Maybe it was too early to expect forgiveness.

It didn't matter right now. She was just happy to be with him. Staying at home by herself would have been too horrible and lonely. Surely, he understood how much she needed him.

Michael went on, 'I could have helped you before things got blown out of proportion. I don't know who we are dealing with. Looking at the state of your home, it's clear these people are serious. I'm scared something is going to happen to you. Why don't you stay a few weeks here, just to see how things turn out?'

'I was hoping you were going to ask. You're sure it's not going to be any trouble? After all the hassles I've already caused you.'

Michael moved his head close to Amanda and crushed his lips against hers. 'I love you. Nothing is too much. You are the only person who matters to me.'

Amanda closed her eyes and believed for a moment life could be safe again.

CHAPTER 80

East Los Angeles: Wednesday, 12.32 a.m.

Oranlis Avenue was peaceful at the time of the morning. The night was warm, but the air heavy.

Detective Stan Moore realized he should have gone to bed by now. But his mind was preoccupied with Gavin White and Henry Limar.

When Justin Smith walked into the visiting room at San Quentin State Prison the previous day, Stan Moore shrank in his chair. Justin Smith was yelling abuse and talking about suing LAPD for tempering with his client. The lawyer couldn't understand how the detective managed to talk to Gavin White. His instructions had been clear. No one was to talk to his client without his approval.

But Stan Moore didn't care. He managed to get what he wanted out of Gavin White. *Lawyers are vermin.* They always managed to use loopholes in the legal system to their advantage. Criminals given light sentences, bail was approved on ridiculous amounts, and police officers' hands were tied with a legal system devised to help criminals.

When Stan Moore left San Quentin State Prison, he could hear Justin Smith yelling at the prison officer behind the reception desk. Stan heard something about suing the prison as well as the police.

The flight from San Francisco to Los Angeles had been pleasant. The detective managed to get some hard-earned sleep.

As soon as he landed at Los Angeles International Airport, Stan called CableNews and asked to speak to Amanda Ryan. He was informed Amanda Ryan no longer worked for the company.

He decided to call Amanda Ryan at her home. He found her number in the telephone directory. When he called, the line was dead. He grabbed a cup of instant coffee from a cake shop near-by and after five minutes tried calling again. This went on for the next half hour. Anxious, he called the operator to see if he could get connected.

'I'm sorry,' the operator said, 'but I can't get to the number either. The phone is probably off the hook.'

What the hell was going on? Maybe she was having someone over at her place and decided to take the phone off the hook. Or she was having a long conversation. Or she was in some kind of trouble.

He left the airport and went home.

For two hours, Stan Moore watched the videocassettes he took from Henry Limar's home. The contents of the videocassettes were nothing but news footage of the last few months. Most of the work was uncut and unedited. None of them gave him a clue as to why Henry Limar killed himself.

Stan sighed as he slouched on the black imitation-leather couch. It would take days to view all the videocassettes The detective didn't have time to waste. But he knew it was vital to watch all the videocassettes He contemplated assigning a young detective to do the watching and report anything suspicious.

His eyes growing heavier by the minute, he decided to hit the sack.

He lay in bed, a crime novel in his hand, but his thoughts kept drifting back to the case. If Henry Limar had committed suicide out of fear, whoever was after him must have been powerful. Powerful enough to drive a man to end his life.

And who was this Amanda Ryan? How come no one mentioned her when he visited CableNews the other day? She was a journalist, Stan Moore knew that much. He also knew it was her business to stick her nose in other people's business.

He threw the paperback on the floor and turned the light off.

Journalists really rubbed him the wrong way. He didn't like people who got paid for being a pain in the ass. Somehow the press was always a step ahead of the police. Like when Senator Trevor Garry got killed. A news van got to the Senator's home before the first police car arrived at the scene of the crime. Fair enough, the killer had called the news station first, but still, this was rather annoying.

And now this Amanda Ryan was one step ahead of him. She had already visited Gavin White. It was possible she had made the link between the death of Senator Trevor Garry and the suicide of Henry Limar.

Stan tossed to the other side of the bed.

He needed to talk to Amanda Ryan, to hear what she had to say. Maybe she had located the videocassette If she did, she could be in

223

danger. And the chance of getting his hands on the videocassette was pretty slim. Journalists were vultures. But he desperately needed a good lead.

At 3.02 a.m., Stan Moore knew he would never get to sleep. Soon the sun would rise, and people would start making their two-hour journey in peak-hour traffic.

But he had something else in mind.

Instead of driving straight to the office this morning, he would go to Santa Monica where Amanda Ryan lived.

At 4.12 a.m., he showered and shaved in less than twenty minutes.

While making a cup of brewed coffee and two toasts, he turned the television on with the remote control.

His eyes staring at the coffee machine, Stan Moore was not really paying attention to the what was coming out of the tube. For years, he got into the habit of turning the television on first thing in the morning. It made him feel as if there was someone else in the house. It helped to ease the loneliness.

Six years ago, Stan Moore married a nurse from St Vincent's Hospital. He met her when a bullet landed in his right shoulder.

Marriage had been a mistake.

His job didn't give him time to take care of someone else. And he knew it sounded like the oldest cop cliche in the world, but it was true. Cops don't make good husbands. They're always working odd hours, always wondering if he's going to make it home tonight, always thinking about early retirement.

But it never happens.

And then, it's the wife who's sick of waiting, sick of sleepless nights, sick of not having sex any more.

When Stan Moore wanted to patch his failed marriage, it was too late. She had already made up her mind. She never wanted a cop as a husband. It just happened she'd fallen in love with one. Like many nurses, she dreamed of marrying a wealthy doctor and live a life of luxury. And when she realized her dreams were never going to come true, she filed for divorce.

Stan should have taken the bottle up. He should have drunk himself to the grave. But he didn't. Instead he worked harder to keep himself level-headed. He didn't want to become another rundown police officer. He didn't want to become a cliche from a b-grade detective novel.

He wasn't going to deny it.

Stan Moore loved his job.

The voice on the television interrupted his fascination with the coffee percolator. He heard the name GAVIN WHITE a few times. Living the percolator to do its business, Stan rushed to the living room. With the remote control, he increased the volume.

'...at around one o'clock this morning. Prison officials say Gavin White used the sheets from his bed to hang himself. With the death of the prime suspect of the murder of Senator Trevor Garry, it looks as if the case will never be solved.'

Stan shook his head in disbelief. How could Gavin White kill himself? A few hours ago Stan was talking to him face to face. Gavin White seemed so willing to live on to prove his innocence. He certainly didn't look like the type of guy who would cloak himself.

Bewildered, Stan turned off the television and grabbed his car keys.

There was only one person who could help him now.

CHAPTER 81

Santa Monica: same day, 5.12 a.m.

When Stan Moore parked his white Saturn in front of Amanda Ryan's townhouse, he knew something was wrong. The front door of the house was sealed with yellow police tape.

Stan returned to his car and radioed LAPD. He inquired as to why the townhouse had been sealed off.

'Yeah, we got a call for a 460,' the dispatching officer said.

Stan knew he meant a burglary. 'And?'

'Nothing was taken.'

'Who's in charge?'

'Hold on a sec.' A pause. 'Detective Strauss.'

'Any victims?'

'Negative. The owner rolled up after the burglary.'

'Okay. I'm coming over to check the report.'

In less than thirty minutes, Stan was inside the LAPD building.

He asked to look at the initial crime report from the two officers who were at Amanda Ryan's the previous day.

He was told Detective John Strauss had the report. He was supposed to meet Amanda today for an informal interrogation.

Stan Moore walked straight to John's desk.

John was thirty-five, white, a long nose, and more work than he could handle. 'What's up,' he said, his head in his paperwork.

'You don't mind if I handle the break-in from last night,' Stan asked.

'Why?' John said in a dull voice as if he didn't care one way or another. His mustache was colored pink from the strawberry iced doughnut he'd just consumed. Stan knew John was overworked with numerous break-ins and other minor felonies. He had bags

226

under his eyes. His hair neatly combed on one side and his yellow tie gave him an almost nerdy look.

'I'm investigating the Limar suicide. Limar worked at CableNews. Amanda Ryan worked at CableNews as well. I have a feeling these two cases are related.'

John took a sip of second-grade vending machine coffee. He looked up for the first time, glaring into the black man's eyes. 'Be my guest,' he said and looked down again. He grabbed a manila folder from somewhere under mountains of paperwork and jabbed it in the air without saying a word.

'Thanks.' Stan grabbed the manila folder. He walked to his desk.

All he had to do now was sit tight and wait for Amanda Ryan to walk through the door. Somehow he got lucky. He didn't have to waste time chasing her around.

He read through the report:

Initial Crime Report

Los Angeles Police Department
Case number: 95-04-0234

Offense: Burglary
Victim: Amanda Ryan
DOB: 7-4-73
Location: 62a Greenfield Crescent, Santa Monica, household
Date: Tuesday April 25, 1995
Means: Forced entry through bathroom window
Weapons: n/a
Details:
Call was received for a 460 at 62a Greenfield Crescent, Santa Monica, at 2040 hrs. Complainant Amanda Ryan was waiting outside her home with friend, Michael Hall. I, reporting officer Mike Wallish, entered the house. Everything in the house was in a chaotic state. Outside investigation revealed various footprints around the perimeter of the house. Footprints were of different shoe sizes, probably hiking or Military boots. Complainant said nothing was missing from the house. Fingerprint tests conducted were negative. It is believed the intruders were wearing gloves. Because of the state of the house, area was sealed off for further collection of evidence.
Complainant said she had already looked through the house before calling the police. Complainant volunteered to talk to a detective the following

227

day.
    Detective John Strauss arrived at the scene half
an hour later. Case was turned over to Detective
John Strauss for further investigation.

    Mike Wallish, PH.

_____

The report stated nothing had gone missing from the house. It looked more like an act of vandalism than a burglary.

But Detective Stan Moore knew it wasn't vandalism.

Someone wanted to get their hands on the videocassette Gavin White mentioned.

Amanda Ryan was the most likely person to be in possession of the videocassette She was the last person, apart from the detective himself, who had a chance to speak to Gavin White.

And now he was dead.

The detective pinched the bridge of his nose with his thumb and forefinger. He needed to track down the videocassette quickly.

Amanda Ryan's life was on the line.

CHAPTER 82

'Damn!' Amanda gasped, staring in disbelief at the television screen. She had just learned of Gavin White's suicide. She was having breakfast in Michael's living room. Only two days ago, she was talking face to face with Gavin White. Now he was gone. He was the last person who could have shed some light into the death of Henry Limar.

Michael paced up and down the living room, between a short coffee table and a bookshelf cramped with works on criminology.

Amanda looked up to him.

He didn't say a word.

Amanda was nervous. The death of Gavin White had taken her by surprise. She was shocked by the pace at which events had unfolded within a week. Now, she found it difficult to understand everything around her.

'Do you seriously think Gavin's death is a coincidence?' Amanda said, standing up from the sofa.

Michael had a blank look on his face. His mind seemed to be miles away. 'I don't know. I really don't know any more. Maybe it is, maybe it isn't.' He looked into Amanda's eyes. 'I think you're in deep trouble, it's what I think. Someone's coming for you.'

'I'm going to find out what's going on,' Amanda said. 'I can't stay here and wait until they get me.'

Amanda was scared. She wasn't going to deny it. But she was also tired of running away. She had to take some action. She had to find out what was going on.

Her life was ticking away like a time bomb.

First the death Senator Trevor Garry.

Then the suicide of Henry Limar.

229

Now the death of Gavin White.

And who broke into my apartment?

'I'm going to the police this morning,' Amanda said, recalling her appointment. 'They're expecting me. I'm going to cooperate. I'm going to tell them everything I know. This whole thing is driving me crazy. I need to know it's all going to be all right.'

Michael didn't react. He stood there, a cup of coffee in his hand. He seemed particularly disturbed by Gavin White's death. 'Sure, do whatever you want,' he finally said, his voice disembodied.

At last, Amanda felt she was taking her fate into her own hands.

Maybe it was her fault she got involved with all this spying business in the first place. She's the one who suggested the plan to Steve Thorn and his team. She was willing to take full responsibility for the situation she had put herself into.

But she was no longer going to let everyone walk all over her. After *they* had broken into her apartment, she knew it was only a matter of time before she would get killed.

Just like Senator Trevor Garry.

And Henry Limar.

And Gavin White.

Maybe the police wouldn't be able to do much. But still, she would feel safer knowing they were on her side.

'So, what do you think?' Amanda asked, standing directly in front of Michael.

Michael took a sip from his mug. 'It's a wise decision. Talk to the police. I don't understand why you waited so long to speak to them.'

Amanda snapped, 'What was I going to tell them? When I spoke to you about Henry's death, you thought I was a nutcase. If you didn't believe me then, what makes you think the police would have?'

'It's not that I didn't believe you-'

'I know. From where you were standing, I could have imagined things.'

'But you know I believe you now.' Michael locked his eyes into hers. 'You know I do, don't you?'

'Sure I do. And it's the reason why I'm going to talk to the police.'

Michael looked at his watch. 'I've got to get to work. Do you want me to drop you at the police station?'

'I'm going home first to get my SUV. You go ahead. I'll catch a cab.'

'Okay.' He grabbed his car key. 'You be careful out there.'

'I'll be fine.' Amanda switch off the television with the remote control.

She hoped to God nothing else was going to go wrong.

CHAPTER 83

Santa Monica: same day, 8.15 a.m.

The cab driver dropped Amanda in front of her home. The temperature was in the high fifties. The smell of the ocean filled the cab as soon as Amanda opened the passenger door. A gentle breeze played with her blond hair.

She glanced towards her home. The front door of the townhouse was still sealed off by yellow police tape. She hoped everything would be over by the weekend. All she wanted was to get on with her life.

'Keep the change,' Amanda said as she stepped out of the cab.

'Thank you, miss.' The Indian-looking taxi driver had no trace of an accent. Amanda thought he might have been a second-generation migrant.

The driver reversed the cab out of the driveway. He gave Amanda a quick hand gesture and vanished down the street.

Amanda stood for a full minute in the front yard. She breathed in the fresh air. It was good to be home. But she realized how this place might never really feel like home again. How could she ever feel safe in a place which had been torn apart by complete strangers? How could she be certain the same people wouldn't come back when she'd be asleep? How could she ever close her eyes without wondering if she would ever wake up?

A chill rippled down her back.

She knew if she had been in the house at the time of the break-in, chances were she would be dead by now.

Her attention strayed to her blue SUV at the end of the driveway. She circled the car while removing the keys from her handbag. She tried to insert a key in the driver's door keyhole.

The key wouldn't go in.

She looked at the key. It was long, silver and edged on both sides.

It was the right key.

She tried again.

The key wouldn't go in the keyhole.

God, dammit! What's going on?

On close inspection, she noticed someone had tampered with the lock. There were scratches on the paint work, just under the keyhole.

Nervous, she peeked through the side window. The glove box was open. Its contents was thrown on the floor and on the front seats.

Instinctively, she looked around, feeling she was being watched. But she knew there was no one around.

Whoever had broken into her home had also broken into her car. It would have happened on the same night. *They* hadn't found what *they* looking for in the house, so *they* looked for it in the car.

Shaken, Amanda circled the SUV again and tried the passenger door.

It was open.

Bastards must have gone through the door when they realized they couldn't get through the other one!

She climbed over the gear stick and to the driver's seat. At least no one had smashed any of the windows.

She cleaned up the mess on the passenger seat. Everything seemed to be there. A torch, a GeoCenter Los Angeles city map, a blue and red Biro, and a small Spirax notebook.

After closing the glove box, she fastened her seat belt.

She turned the key once and pressed on the gas.

The engine roared.

She cracked the gears and reversed the SUV out the driveway.

It was full daylight when she disappeared at the end of the street.

Her head lost in thoughts, she didn't notice the white Toyota Hi-Ace parked on the other side of the street.

As soon as she passed the first intersection, the driver of the Toyota Hi-Ace turned on the ignition.

CHAPTER 84

CableNews: same day, 8.16 a.m.

When Michael Hall arrived at the office, Hugh Gawler wasn't in sight. He walked up to Hugh's office and knocked on the door.

No answer.

Now was the perfect time.

Michael crossed the hallway to the editing room. He looked around, making sure no one was watching him.

He stepped inside the room and closed the door gently.

Slowly, he circled the room with his eyes. Next to one of the video recorders, he found a box filled with videocassettes Someone should have taken those videocassettes down to the basement by now. But since Henry died, no one had bothered clearing the editing room.

Michael took one of the videocassettes and inserted it in VIDEO ONE. He pressed the PLAY button and began to fast forward footage of news.

He had seen a lot of the footage before. Nothing but news footage of the past six months.

For more than two hours, he watched the videocassettes There was nothing suspicious, not to his eyes anyway. He didn't know exactly what he was looking for.

With his right hand, he massaged the back of his neck. His eyes stung from sitting at close range in front of the video monitors.

All he needed was a lead of some sort. Anything at all. Something which would explain why Henry Limar committed suicide.

He realized watching every videocassette would take forever. He was already bored beyond belief.

He checked the time: 10.21 a.m.

Hugh Gawler was probably in his office at this very minute.

Michael didn't need a head-to-head collision with Hugh right now. Michael knew Hugh had faith in him. He wanted to keep it this way.

And for all Michael knew, he might just be wasting time with those videocassettes If Hugh caught Michael in the editing room, he would get suspicious. He would ask questions. Michael would have to improvise some unlikely story.

And since Michael *knew* Hugh Gawler was carrying out a dangerous, illegitimate business practice, he had to be extremely careful.

Hugh Gawler was a dangerous man.

He would kill Michael if he had too.

Michael took the box of videos downstairs to the car park. He decided it was better to take the videocassettes home. He wouldn't have to worry about Hugh coming up behind him without prior warning.

Michael crossed the car park, the box of videocassettes in his arms. He threw the box in the trunk of his car.

Just as he was about to walk to the driver's door, Hugh's BMW came roaring down the center lane of the car park.

Michael turned around, feeling the redness on his cheeks.

CHAPTER 85

LAPD: same day, 9.15 a.m.

Detective Stan Moore sucked nervously on a cigarette when Amanda Ryan walked into his office.

'Take a seat,' Stan Moore said, his tone almost apologetic. Gavin White had been right about the journalist being somewhat attractive. Stan had seen many beautiful women in his life, but never someone more dazzling than Amanda Ryan. Sure, he enjoyed pictures of gorgeous women in girlie magazines, but they were made-up by professional make-up artists, sat at the right angle, photographed under the right light.

Not the young woman in front of him.

Amanda Ryan possessed stunning natural beauty. She wasn't exactly *Vogue* cover material.

She was better.

Translucent hazel eyes and winter-wheat colored hair.

Amanda Ryan captured an innocent girl-next-door quality which supermodels lacked.

Amanda sat on the green plastic chair, frowning at the concentrating smell of cigarette smoke.

Stan Moore offered his hand. 'So, you're Amanda Ryan. I've been anxious to meet you.'

'I can't deny I'm happy to be here.'

'Why?'

'I think I'm in great danger,' she whispered to him intimately.

Stan read the fear in her eyes. He picked up the break-in report from his desk. 'Any idea why someone would want to break into your home?'

'It's a long story. I don't know where to start. I don't know if you'll believe me.'

236

'It's why I'm here. But before we get into it, just a few things I have to make clear. You understand you're not under suspicion at this stage?'

'Suspicion for what?'

'You're only here as a witness. I just have to point this out to you. Because you're not a suspect, you don't need a lawyer.'

Amanda knitted her brows. 'What's going on here?'

'Nothing. I just have to tell you of your rights. You can end this interrogation anytime you want. Do you have any objection in testifying in court?'

'Isn't it a bit premature to ask me if I'm going to testify in court?'

'Okay, okay, I'm sorry. let's get on with it then.'

'I don't know where to start.'

The detective took a drag from his cigarette. 'Maybe I can help you. Do you think the break-in had anything to do with Henry Limar or Gavin White? Or even the death of Senator Trevor Garry?'

Amanda seemed surprised. Her eyes were wide open. 'Well, you know much more than I do.'

Stan Moore smiled. 'Not really. It's the reason why I wanted to see you. I'm interested in Hugh Gawler and how he fits into all this. But first of all, tell me why you think someone broke into your home?'

'They want something I don't have.'

'Like what?'

'A videocassette of some sort.'

'It's what I heard too. Have you got the videocassette?'

'Never seen it.'

'Are you sure?'

'Yes, I'm sure.'

'Then why would someone think you had a videocassette?'

'Because I spoke to Gavin White. Because I spoke to Henry Limar. Because I work for Hugh Gawler. Because I'm in the middle of a bloody mess!' Amanda was losing her cool.

Stan scratched the back of his neck. So far, the young woman seemed to be telling the truth. But he wasn't convinced she didn't have the videocassette After all, she was a journalist. Depending on the contents of the videocassette, she could be lying to protect herself. 'Do you have an idea what's on the videocassette? What did Henry say?'

'Henry never mentioned a videocassette It was Gavin White who told me.'

'Okay, Amanda, I think I believe everything you're telling me.

But I still don't understand how you fit into all this? Why you?'

'I don't know, detective. I guess I'm just in the wrong place at the wrong time.'

'And it's all there is to it?'

Amanda looked down. She fidgeted with a button on her dress.

'Take your time,' the detective said. The young woman was in a difficult situation. Stan Moore knew it was better to let her talk at her own pace. From past experience, he knew it wasn't good to extract information from people by force. If Amanda had something important to tell him, she would tell him in due course. She had to trust him. 'I know this is difficult for you, Ms Ryan. But I can't help you unless you tell me the truth. What am I supposed to do?'

'It's just so complicated.'

'Sometimes things seem much worse than they really are. I'm sure it's not so bad. We can keep this confidential. Off the record. Do you want to tell me what's really going on?'

The young woman hesitated for a few seconds. She looked into the detective's eyes.

Stan Moore smiled in return. He had to get her to trust him. It was the only way to get her to talk. 'How about it?'

'Alright,' Amanda finally said. She explained how she was spying for Globe Network.

'You what?' His tone was filled with surprise.

'Globe Network sent me over to see how CableNews was working.'

Stan shook his head. 'And you went for it?'

'It was actually my idea.'

The detective had a grin on his face. He sympathized with Amanda. She really got herself in hot water. 'Looks like you've jump-started your career. Does Hugh Gawler know about you spying in his company?'

'He never mentioned anything. But his secretary caught me looking through his desk. I got thrown out of the building yesterday.'

Stan Moore crushed his last cigarette in a glass ashtray. He removed a fresh one from his shirt. Obviously, Amanda Ryan had no idea who Hugh Gawler was. 'Well, Ms Ryan, no wonders you're in such a mess. I'm willing to help you, but you've got to be ready to help me. From now on we've got to be totally honest with each other. Is there anything you didn't tell me?'

Amanda puzzled over his question for a few seconds. 'Michael Hall and I are seeing each other. He's one of the company directors.'

'Now, there's a surprise. I thought you only began working for CableNews a month ago.'

'I have.'

'But this Michael guy? It didn't take you long to size him up.'

'I knew Michael before I joined CableNews.'

'And he knows about all this, I assume.'

'I've told him everything.'

Stan looked at his watch. He really wanted to get all this information in writing. 'You're not in a hurry, are you?'

'I'm out of a job at the moment. I've got all day.'

'Good. I'd like to spend more time talking to you. I think we've got a lot of ground to cover. Are you free at lunchtime?'

'Sure.'

'Perfect. I've got a few things to take care of. In the meantime, I'd like you to write down everything you remember since you began working for CableNews. You think you can do that?'

Amanda gave him a sour look. 'I've told you everything I know.'

'It's true,' the detective said, 'but sometimes small details crop up. I don't want to find you dead somewhere because you forgot to tell me something relevant.'

Amanda nodded.

'You do understand you're in danger?'

'It's why I'm here, detective. Are you always so patronizing?'

'I'm sorry. I deal with a lot of different people during the day. It's hard to see inside someone's head. I guess you're a pretty smart woman, eh?'

'I don't know about smart. I just want to get on with life.'

'Good. Let's see if we can get the bastards before they get to you.'

CHAPTER 86

Amanda was seated by herself in a room at the LAPD building.

She read her statement once more. Everything she knew was in there. Even her relationship with Michael Hall. After all she had been through, she wanted to trust Stan Moore.

She had to trust him.

No one else could help her.

She stood from her chair and looked at her watch. 10.37 a.m. It would be another hour and twenty minutes before she would have to meet Detective Stan Moore back at his office. There was nothing more she could add to her statement. She exhausted all her memory. If some thing came up later, something she forgot to mention in the statement, she would tell the detective anyway. She had nothing to hide anymore.

She circled the room a few times, her head filled with confusion.

And suddenly, she felt caved in. She had to get some fresh air. She placed one hand on her chest and felt her pulse racing.

Frantically, she pulled open the door of the room.

I think I'm going to die in here!

CHAPTER 87

The man in the Toyota Hi-Ace had been waiting outside the LAPD building for more than an hour.

The air was hot and humid.

He undid his tie and threw it on the passenger seat. He wore his dark hair neatly clipped around the ears, highlighting the roundness of his face. There was nothing attractive or repulsive about him. His nose was small and straight. His eyes expressed no emotion. He could have been anybody's next door neighbor The one person you never notice on the street. The one who blends in with the crowd. The one no one cares about.

And it was the way he wanted it.

It's was better for the career he had chosen.

Contract killer.

It was a terrible job, but the pay was good. With the twenty thousand dollars, he thought of changing cars. Something sportier.

He felt the SIG-Sauer P226 9mm semiautomatic against his ribs. It was fully loaded and ready to use.

So far, he hadn't had a chance to come close to Amanda Ryan.

But he knew if he followed her long enough, opportunity would strike.

His instructions were clear.

Shot to kill.

Disappear.

It has to look like just another murder.

People were killed everyday in Los Angeles for all kind of reasons.

Sometimes for no reason at all.

But the killer knew it wouldn't look so simple.

Now that Amanda Ryan had spoken to a police, it would be hard for anyone to see her death as random killing.

The killer felt a dash of hunger. Just as he was about to grab a tomato and cheese sandwich from his briefcase, he saw Amanda Ryan leaving the LAPD building. He muttered to himself and shut the briefcase.

He turned the engine on, but killed it straight away when he saw Amanda Ryan walk pass her SUV.

He couldn't follow her with the car.

She would notice him.

He would follow her on foot instead.

Now could be the right time to do the job. If she happened to venture in a quiet street, then the whole job would be over and done quickly.

Before he lost sight of his target, the killer stepped out of the Toyota. He locked the doors and crossed the street.

He was careful to keep a distance of at least fifty feet behind.

A few people were in the street, but not enough to worry about.

Think fast for an opening line.

An idea came.

'Miss Ryan,' he yelled, pacing towards her.

Amanda turned around, a worried look on her face.

'Miss Ryan,' the man repeated, reaching inside his sports jacket. 'Detective Lou Brigman.' He removed an ID and flashed it for a few seconds in front of her face. 'I need to ask you a few questions about the burglary at your home.'

Amanda looked relieved. She smiled and said, 'I was going to come back. I just needed some fresh air.'

The killer smiled back. 'If you'd just like to come with me.'

'Sure.' She studied his expression.

She was looking at death in the face.

CHAPTER 88

CableNews: meanwhile.

'What are you doing here?' Hugh asked, a blank look on his face. He held on tightly to a black briefcase.

Michael noticed the gold combination lock on the briefcase. Immediately he knew he had never seen the briefcase before. 'I'm just on my way out,' he said, infusing his tone with assertion. 'Got an interview to wrap up for the evening news.'

'Sure, whatever.' Hugh gestured with his hand for Michael to carry on. He raced across the car park to the elevator. He looked to the left and the right, checking if anyone was looking at him.

Michael, slightly surprised by Hugh's indifference, stepped inside the BMW. *What is he up to now? And what's in the briefcase?* He knew Hugh Gawler was up to one of his tricks again. But he didn't care right now.

He had his own puzzle to solve.

Half an hour later Michael was sitting comfortably in a black leather lounge chair with the video remote control in one hand and the television channel selector in the other. The strong smell of black coffee filled the room.

Michael never watched television at home in the morning. He felt kind of weird, out of place, as if he was on holidays or in another world.

The vertical blinds were closed, leaving the room in almost complete darkness. It was hard to tell if it was daytime or evening.

Next to the couch was the cardboard box filled with videocassettes Michael took from the editing room.

Michael watched the videocassettes one after the other non-stop. News events from the last few weeks. Some of them had never gone on-air. Too many things came in, and time was limited. Only the news which seemed to hold the interest of most staff members at CableNews had a chance to make it into a news program of one kind or another.

Michael Hall was responsible for assigning news stories to various freelance journalists and organizations. An in-house team took care of the most important news.

After watching the small screen for two hours, Michael's eyelids grew heavy. He still didn't know what he was looking for. But his instinct told him to persist.

Just before lunch, he decided to give himself a break.

He refilled his cup with black coffee and made himself a cheese sandwich.

There was a lot of work waiting for him back at the office. If he disappeared for too long, Hugh would notice his absence.

And the way Hugh Gawler had been carrying on lately, it wouldn't have been a good idea to draw any suspicion on himself.

He knew Hugh Gawler was a murderer.

CHAPTER 89

Hollywood: same day, 11.36 a.m.

Steve Thorn ran through a red light, two streets from CableNews headquarters.

He was mad.

Globe Network was losing every advertising contract. The company would have to close its doors within two months.

But it wasn't why Steve Thorn was angry.

Hugh Gawler had ignored him.

He never returned Steve's phone calls or carried out any of his suggestions. If it hadn't been for Steve, Hugh Gawler would have never managed to get CableNews off the ground.

Now Hugh had to keep his part of the deal.

The deal had been straight forward. At Globe Network, Steve Thorn had little control as to where the company was heading. He didn't own Globe Network. He always wanted to set up his own news network. But without the capital required, it was an impossible dream.

Then one day, a stranger named Hugh Gawler wanted to talk to him urgently. He wanted to negotiate with Steve a business deal which was going to make both men rich beyond their wildest dreams.

The strategy was simple. Steve Thorn gave Hugh Gawler all of Globe Network's contacts to get CableNews off the ground. In exchange, Hugh Gawler's injected his own personal money into the newly-formed news company. After the collapse of Globe Network, Steve Thorn would become a joint partner at CableNews.

At the time of the deal, both men saw a dream they could share. But as CableNews turned into a mufti-million dollar machine, greed began to take place.

Steve wanted to know when and how.

But Hugh made him wait.

And wait.

And now Steve Thorn was losing patience. Globe Network was on the edge of bankruptcy, and Hugh Gawler was leaving him in the cold.

Well, damn Hugh Gawler!

Steve Thorn parked the green Ford Falcon in a no-standing zone in front of the cream-colored CableNews building.

He stormed out of the car.

He was going to give Hugh Gawler a piece of his mind.

CHAPTER 90

CableNews: meanwhile.

Hugh Gawler had just got in the office, counting the contents of his briefcase.

He was up to $82,600 when the door of the office flew wide open. In came a red-faced Steve Thorn, slamming the door behind his back.

'Why the fuck aren't you returning my calls?' Steve screamed as he approached Hugh's desk.

Confused, Hugh froze with hundreds of dollar notes still in his hand. He managed to close the briefcase.

But it was too late.

Steve had seen the money.

'What do you want?' Hugh said, his voice lacking authority.

'What's all this?' Steve asked, pointing to the briefcase with the gold combination lock.

'Don't you believe in knocking before waltzing into someone's office?'

'And why should I? Don't tell me about manner when you don't return my calls. And what the fuck is all this money?'

'None of your business.'

'Like hell! I haven't seen a dollar since we set up CableNews. Isn't it about time I got something?'

Hugh Gawler reached for the .38 in the top drawer. He didn't need this right now. Steve Thorn was a nuisance and wanted everything done his way. Hugh had honestly believed he would make Steve Thorn a partner in the company. But with time Steve became a burden more than anything else. Everyday he was on the phone telling Hugh how to conduct his business, wanting to know all financial details of the company, insisting on being given a date when he could move into CableNews.

'What are you going to do?' Steve continued, his lower lip trembling nervously. 'Shoot me? Is this how you conduct business?'

One hand on the drawer, Hugh looked straight into Steve's eyes. 'What do you want from me?'

Steve moved two steps forward. 'What I want is what I deserve. We had a deal. I helped you through, but so far I haven't seen anything in return.'

Hesitating, Hugh lifted his hand off the drawer. Something would have to be done about Steve. But not now. It was the wrong place and the wrong time. One thing was certain: Hugh would never be able to work hand in hand with Steve Thorn.

Steve had to go.

And then there was another problem. If Hugh decided not to make Steve Thorn a partner, Steve could always tell his story to the press. This would mean the end of Hugh Gawler and his media empire.

Reflecting on his thoughts, Hugh moved to the bar fridge. 'You know, Steve, I'm sure we can work something out,' he said, injecting warmth in his tone.

'What? Later? Another day maybe. No way. I want a solution now.' Steve forehead was covered with perspiration beads.

Hugh poured two glasses of Southern Comfort. 'Okay. I make a deal now.'

'No more deals. I want results now.'

Hugh placed both glasses on the corner of his desk. He opened the briefcase and counted the money.

Speechless, Steve Thorn watch Hugh stack piles of one hundred dollar notes on the desk. His lips parted as if he was about to say something. But no words came out of his mouth.

Calm and collected, Hugh emptied half the content of the briefcase on the desk. He lifted his eyes and looked straight at Steve. A broad smile on his face, he explained, 'I give you $50,000 now as down payment. Actually, make it a gift. This is just to show you I'm serious.'

Steve looked at the money and then at Hugh. He shook his head from left to right. 'No deal I said. Especially something as pathetic as this.' He jabbed his fat finger in front of Hugh's face. 'I haven't insulted you, Mr Gawler. So, don't insult me by offering to buy me off with $50,000.'

'I'm not buying you off.' Hugh emptied the rest of the money on the desk. 'Take it all, $100,000. This is just so we understand we're on the same side.'

Steve looked at the money on the desk. Okay, so $50,000 could be sneezed at, but $100,000 was more in line with what Steve probably expected. His menacing finger turned into a cordial handshake.

Hugh grabbed Steve's hand and gave it a good shake. He had to restore confidence in Steve even if it was for a little while.

And the $100,000, he could always get it back later. The Texan Militia would be paid with Hugh's own funds.

'Okay, you've got a deal,' Steve said, obviously concealing his excitement. 'But don't think it means you've got the right to treat me like shit.'

'Let me shuffle some paper work, and by next week you'll have your own office in this building,' Hugh lied. 'My lawyer is working on our partnership contracts right this minute. You'll see, everything is going to be exactly the way we planned it.'

Steve began to fill up the briefcase with the one hundred dollar notes. 'You don't mind if I take the briefcase with me?' he said, his hands shaking with excitement

'Be my guest.'

Hugh liked this briefcase.

But it didn't matter.

It was only a matter of time now.

A week at the most.

When Steve finished filling the briefcase with the hundred dollar notes, he slammed the top down and turned to Hugh: 'Nice doing business with you, partner.' He tapped Hugh on the shoulder and went on, 'And keep in touch.'

'I will.'

All smiles, Steve walked himself out of Hugh's office, holding on tightly to the briefcase.

Hugh watched him vanish.

Stupid bastard!

He picked up the telephone handset and punched some numbers on the keypad.

The phone rang twice.

'Yeah?'

'It's me,' Hugh said.

'What's up?'

'I've got the rest of your money.'

'Great.'

'I've also got a little job for you.' Hugh Gawler told him about Steve Thorn. 'And make it look like an accident, will you?'

CHAPTER 91

'I've already spoken to Detective Stan Moore,' Amanda said to the hitman standing in front of her.

The hitman felt the bulge of the SIG-Sauer P226 9mm semiautomatic at the small of his back. 'I know you have,' he murmured, controlling his fear, 'but I still have to ask you a few questions.'

The young woman scanned her surroundings. A few people were coming up and down the street.

The hitman was about to retrieve the semiautomatic from the back of his jacket, but he suddenly froze.

'Sure, why not,' Amanda Ryan said, walking towards the main entrance of the LAPD building.

Dammit!

'Let's go and talk in my car,' the hitman said, his tone lacking authority. He turned to the white Toyota Hi-Ace parked on the other side of the street.

'Why? Can't we just talk in the office?' Her ankles were locked. She wasn't moving an inch. The hitman knew she was sensing something was wrong.

'We'll have more privacy in the car.'

Amanda Ryan moved one step back.

He was losing her. Asking her to get in his car had been a mistake.

But it was too late.

He made the mistake.

He had to find a way to correct it.

'What did you say your name was?' Amanda asked, her tone now filled with intrigue.

Suddenly, the hitman turned around and took two giant steps in Amanda's direction. He clamped his fingers around her left arm and withdrew the SIG-Sauer P226 9mm semiautomatic from his leather belt and the small of his back. He pushed the gun into Amanda's ribs. 'Get in the car and shut up.'

Her eyes opened in fear. 'What are you doing?' she said in a suffocated voice.

'Shut up and get in the car.' The hitman didn't have time to listen to her protests. He had to move fast, even if there was hardly anyone in the street. 'If you say anything, I'll kill you right now.'

'You're not a cop, are you?'

'No, I'm not. Now move on.'

The hitman pushed Amanda towards the Toyota Hi-Ace, keeping a tight grip around her arm.

So far, so good.

They crossed the road, watching out for oncoming traffic.

We're nearly there.

When they reached the Toyota Hi-Ace, the hitman dragged Amanda to the passenger door.

One hand tightly gripped around the semiautomatic, he forced her inside the Toyota Hi-Ace. 'Get in, you bitch!'.

'Ouch! You're hurting me,' Amanda shrieked, trying to put on a useless fight.

A couple looked towards the white van. The hitman smiled back at them, rolling his eyes all at the same time. They had to think it was a lover's spat.

And they did.

The couple walked away smiling.

The hitman ran quickly down the other side of the car, concealing his weapon between his belt and the small of his back.

By the time he opened the door on the driver's side, the young woman was already out of the Toyota Hi-Ace, running towards the entrance of the LAPD building.

Furious, he slammed the driver's door. There were a few people in the streets, but he didn't have a choice. He pulled the SIG-Sauer P226 from the small of his back and aimed at Amanda.

Hurrying up the stairs of the LAPD building, the girl looked back one more time before he pressed the trigger. She tripped and fell on the stairs, covering her face with her hands.

The bullet hit the side of the door, missing Amanda by a few inches.

He pressed the trigger three times more, each time missing his target.

Someone screamed, 'he's got a gun!'

The hitman was devastated He was never going to get an opportunity like this one again. He didn't have time for another shot. Everyone was looking in his direction. He had to get back to the van.

'Hold it right there,' a plain-clothed detective ordered, just outside the LAPD building entrance. He aimed his weapon at the hitman.

The hitman ignored the order and ran to the driver's side of the Toyota Hi-Ace.

'Hold it right there,' the detective repeated.

Angry, the hitman turned on the ignition and pressed his foot flat on the accelerator.

Amanda Ryan had survived.

His life was on the line. The main man would never accept his failure.

Dammit!

He would have to try again. But he would never get the same chance. He had her right there on target, and he missed.

The detective fired twice at the Toyota Hi-Ace.

Fuck you, Mr fuckin' cop—fuck you and fuck that bitch!

Amanda was still on the steps of the LAPD building, wondering if she had been hit. She was too weak to stand up on her feet. Her mind was running frantically between flashes of her past and the present time. She could still hear the gunshots echoing inside her skull.

Maybe the killer was still shooting.

She opened her mouth, but no sound came out. His hands were clammy. She felt dampness on her back from perspiration. She gasped for air as if it would be her last breath.

A man dressed in a gray two-piece suit grabbed her by the arm.

'He's gone now,' he said. 'Why don't you come with me?'

Amanda looked up to the detective.

She couldn't believe she was still alive. She looked up and down the front of her body, searching frantically for some type of wound, for her own blood.

But there was nothing.

She couldn't believe the hitman had missed her. As she slowly regained her composure, she realized how closely she had brushed with death.

With difficulty, she managed to get back on her feet.

The detective was holding on to her arm.

She looked behind her back, searching for the killer in the white van.

But he was gone.

For the time being, anyway.

CHAPTER 92

When Steve Thorn got back to the office, his hands were clammy and the back of his shirt drenched with perspiration.

He threw the black briefcase on his desk, fantasizing of all the things he could buy with of $100,000. He knew it wasn't an enormous amount of money, not in terms of what he had been expecting from Hugh Gawler. But when it appeared out of nowhere in less than an hour, it felt like a fortune.

First, he would pay off the damn holiday house in Santa Monica. The second mortgage was killing his cash flow. He hardly used the place anyway.

With the rest of the money, he would get a new set of wheels. The old green Ford Falcon was on its last leg.

Slouching his fat body on the executive leather chair, Steve Thorn didn't know what to make of Hugh Gawler. First Hugh ignored him for weeks. Suddenly he gave him a $100,000 just to keep things smooth. Sure, Steve didn't have much to argue about, but the whole thing was making him nervous.

And what happened to Amanda Ryan? Too obsessed with his own greed, he forgot to ask Hugh Gawler. As he shook a cigarette out of its pack, he made a mental note of giving her a call later in the evening.

He lit the cigarette and sucked on it obsessively.

Right now his mind was set on how CableNews was going to make him rich beyond belief. Once appointed on the board of directors, he would get rid of Hugh Gawler. How, he wasn't sure yet. But he knew it was important to make the first move.

He blew a ring of smoke, watching it grow and eventually disappear into thin air.

If he didn't make the first move, Hugh Gawler wouldn't miss
the opportunity.

CHAPTER 93

Detective Stan Moore offered Amanda Ryan around the clock police protection.

But she refused.

'Why,' the detective asked, passing one hand over his black cranium.

'Because it's not a necessity.'

'Not a necessity? You nearly got killed a few minutes ago!'

What was Amanda going to say? Well, you have to understand detective, at the moment I've got some ideas of my own. I intend to follow this thing through myself. I want to find out who killed Senator Trevor Garry, Henry Limar and Gavin White. Of course, in the meantime I'd like some police protection, but not twenty-four hours a day. Just when I say so.

She looked at the detective and smiled. Injecting her tone with self-assurance, she explained, 'I'm here because I need some help, you're right. But I'm getting so close to the truth—'

Stan Moore finished her sentence, '—you want to be a hero.' He crossed his fingers behind his head and stretched his legs under the desk. 'Look, I understand your thirst for fame and glory. Every journalist wants the big story, the one which is going to change their life, their career. The one which is going to win them a Pulitzer prize. It's the same everywhere. But if you get killed, there won't be any story. Not one with your by-line. You're name will be the headline instead.'

Amanda knew the detective was right. But he wasn't the one who had spent four years at university, endless hours slaving over books instead of having fun like other undergraduates. And risk her entire career spying for Globe Network.

The detective's only interest was to protect the innocent and punish the bad. And hopefully get a medal of honor in the process.

Amanda stood from her chair. 'I want to go home. It's been a long day.'

The detective offered his hand and said, 'you give me a call anytime you want.' He slipped a business card between the handshake. 'Anytime at all. My after hours number is on this card.'

'Thanks for the offer.'

Amanda placed the card in her bag.

She left the office, feeling the weight of the detective's stare.

When she took the first step down the building, she had the urge to run back inside. In her mind's eyes, she saw the killer standing at the corner of the street, pointing a gun in her direction.

She froze in front of the door for a few seconds.

Maybe she should have taken up the detective's offer of twenty-four police protection.

As she walked to her SUV, she began to realize the seriousness of what she had got herself into. She had little choice left in what had to be done. Who was after her? Whoever it was, she knew they would try to find her again. There was no reason to believe the danger was over. Even more than before, she was left with very little choices.

She had to find out about the mysterious videocassette

About Trevor Garry and Gavin White's killer's identity.

About her killer's identity.

CHAPTER 94

Washington D.C.: Tuesday, 5:09 a.m.

It took Sam Willicon twenty-one hours and thirty minutes to get to Washington D.C. from Houston, Texas. He chose driving because he liked privacy. The FBI had a harder time following his moves if he made no booking or reservations. He used cash for all his gas, food and odd expenses. He knew how easy it was for the government to prove where someone has been just by checking their credit card records.

Sam Willicon knew the FBI didn't have anything to pin on him. But being the leader of the Texan Militia meant he had to watch his back at all times. Someone out there was trying to monitor his every move. Especially after the successful Oklahoma mission.

The modified black Ford pick-up truck left Texas on the I10, switched to I65 in Alabama, took the exit at I85 past Montgomery and made it straight to the District of Columbia. The last exit onto I95 took Sam Willicon five minutes from Washington D.C.

Already in the early hours of the morning, the city was busy with traffic. Nothing to be compared with the morning rush which would appear at about the same time as sunrise.

The black pick-up truck was parked at an Exxon gas station, just out of I95. As Sam Willicon sipped into a paper cup filled with coffee-flavored hot water, his thoughts returned to Tom Davidson, the young new recruit who blew the Alfred P. Murray building in Oklahoma. The mission had been a success. The bombing made worldwide headlines.

Sam Willicon denied his and the Militia's involvement in the incident when he was probed by the media and the police.

The day of the Oklahoma bombing, young Tom Davidson got pulled over for speeding a few miles out of Oklahoma. After the police searched his car, Tom Davidson was arrested for carrying unregistered firearms. He was thrown in the local jail.

It took another two days for the local sheriff to realize Tom Davidson was the man who made it to the top of the FBI's most wanted list. Tom Davidson, clean-cut American baby face, made the papers and television stations everywhere around the world. Speculations were running high when someone suggested the young redneck belonged to the Texan Militia. Sam Willicon strongly denied the allegations, insisting he had never met Tom Davidson in his life.

Of course, Sam Willicon knew the winner in all of this had to be Hugh Gawler. After all, Hugh funded the Texan Militia. CableNews was guaranteed exclusive live footage. The footage was later sold to other television stations in America and around the globe for millions of dollars.

Initially, a camera crew was to be at the sight of the Alfred P. Murray building when the bombing occurred, but Hugh Gawler decided against it. The coincidence would have been too remarkable.

Instead, CableNews settled for being the first news team at the scene minutes after the explosion.

As Sam Willicon blistered the top of his pallet with the hot brew, he was more or less satisfied with the Oklahoma bombing. The exercise proved nothing was impossible. It had paved the way for the Texan Militia to carry out the ultimate act of terrorism.

Only Sam Willicon wasn't satisfied in keeping quiet forever. It was due time for Texan Militia to assume responsibility for its action. It was time to show the world Sam Willicon and his men were ready to fight the source of all evil, the US Government.

Maybe Americans around the country would open their eyes. They would begin to see the truth, how the present government was no longer serving its people like it was meant to do, but using them as instruments for its own greed and corruption.

The end of the second millennium was around the corner. Sam Willicon believed the world needed a drastic change. He believed the way Americans lived their lives, they were doomed for chaos and extermination.

But the Texan Militia would not let it happen. Members of the militia would fight for the rights of the constitution, the rights their fathers and grand-fathers had fought and died for.

Sam Willicon looked at his watch, surprised at how fast time had gone.

7.14 a.m.

For the first time since he took off from Texas, he begun to grow tired. The twenty-one hour trip from Houston felt like a two-hour trip. On the road, Sam Willicon remained alert and in control. He knew he could have gone right around the country in his pickup truck without any sleep.

It was only now, at the end of the trip, that his mind and body felt the need to recuperate.

But there was no time now.

Soon Sam Willicon would get together with the Washington members of the militia to discuss their new act of terrorism.

An act which would shatter the United States and the rest of the world.

The bombing of the White House.

CHAPTER 95

Meanwhile...

Hugh Gawler was on flight 680 from Los Angeles to Washington D.C. The bombing of the White House was going to be the most important event of his life. And probably of every Americans' lives.

The timing was perfect.

Since the Oklahoma bombing, the country was on red alert. Even though a young man had been accused of the bombing, everyone was still puzzled by the event. Who was responsible for the atrocious act of terrorism? Surely, this wasn't the work of a single person? But the young redneck denied everything. So far the government was unable to point the finger at anyone with certainty.

Hugh felt the contents of his stomach move. He always suffered from air sickness, and as a result, avoided flying whenever possible. But this time he didn't have a choice. Washington D.C. was too far from L.A. to justify a rail or road trip. It would have taken him forever. And time was not something he had plenty of at the moment.

As he looked through the porthole of the Boeing 747, he thought about the two people he had ordered to be killed back in L.A. Steve Thorn and Amanda Ryan. Being in Washington D.C. during the killings would put him too far from the scene of the crime. His plane ticket would be his alibi.

By the time Hugh would get back from Washington D.C., Steve Thorn and Amanda Ryan would be dead, the White House no longer exist, and CableNews would possess the most astonishing footage of the century. This would undoubtedly make him a very wealthy man, wealthier than he already was. He was ready to fight with Rupert Murdoch for the number one spot.

Then later, maybe, he would consider retirement. The war would have been won. He would have build himself from rags to riches twice in a lifetime. It was more than the average man could ever achieve.

A metallic voice coming through the intercom interrupted his line of thoughts, 'Ladies and gentlemen. This is your captain speaking. We'll be landing in Washington D.C. in three minutes.'

Soon, Hugh Gawler would meet Sam Willicon. It would be the first time he would come face to face with the leader of the Texan Militia. Up to now, all deals had been done by scrambled telephone conversations or through the medium of another person. He was excited in a way. Meeting the other person who would change the course of America's history. Someone who might even one day be proclaimed a hero, a savior, an angel who had the vision of keeping America pure and free.

As the Boeing 747 landed at the Ronald Reagan Washington National Airport, Hugh Gawler realized how much he loved America. It was still a great country. People could make it here, no matter where they came from. He certainly had proven it could be done. Only in America could a boy from the Bronx become a billionaire and control a large chunk of the country's media. Only in America could someone speak his mind openly. Only in America could a man expand his mind and power to greater heights.

Free speech and justice for all.

Only in America.

CHAPTER 96

Los Angeles: Wednesday, 5.46 p.m.

Burning red lights and causing near-collisions, Michael couldn't believe someone wanted Amanda dead. Sure, she might have got herself involved in things which were none of her business, but as far as he knew she didn't know anything anyway.

Or maybe she did, but she kept it secret from him.

He made himself sick all the way to his apartment in Downtown L.A.

Fifteen minutes ago, Amanda called him in the office and told about the shooting outside the LAPD headquarters.

Michael parked the BMW in the driveway, just next to Amanda's SUV. He stepped out of the car and ran up the stairs to the front door of his apartment.

This time Hugh Gawler had gone too far.

When he opened the front door, an aroma of grilled capsicums filled his nostrils. He went straight for the kitchen where Amanda was preparing dinner.

Michael came behind her and wrapped his arms around her tiny waist.

'Are you all right?' he asked, injecting his tone with concern.

Amanda turned around. 'I'm fine,' she said, but the look in her eyes showed the fear.

'Who could it be? Why you?' Michael had to pretend he didn't know anything.

'I've told you something was going on. I told you I was in danger. But you thought I was just imagining things. This has something to do with the death of Senator Trevor Garry, Henry Limar and Gavin White. And I'm sure Hugh Gawler is right in the middle of this mess.'

Michael took two steps backwards. God, what was he going to tell her? 'Assuming you're right, why would Hugh Gawler want you dead?'

'Because he thinks I've got the videocassette'

'You mean the videocassette Gavin White has been talking about?'

'Yes. What other videocassette did you think I was talking about?'

'Have you?'

Amanda's eyes widened. 'Have I what? Have I got the videocassette?'

'Well, have you?'

'If I had the videocassette I wouldn't be standing in your home trying to convince you I hadn't. What kind of a question is this anyway?'

Michael had to be sure. He didn't know what to believe any more. What the hell was this tape anyway? How the hell did this come into the game? 'I just thought maybe you were not telling me everything.'

'Thanks a lot.' Amanda turned her back on him and went on slicing tomatoes for a Greek salad.

'Don't look so surprised. You've never been forward with me. I didn't know you worked as a spy. You only told me because you didn't have the choice. Anything is possible. And now you tell me Hugh Gawler is surely responsible for the death of the Senator, Henry Limar and Gavin White? What am I supposed to believe? Someone wants you dead? What does it mean? Why shouldn't I assume you know more than you're telling?'

Amanda inserted the butcher's knife in the wooden chopping board. 'I'm going home. I don't need this right now. I thought you were my friend.'

Hell! what have I done? Michael followed her down the hallway. 'I'm sorry. I've been worried sick since you've called me. I don't know what I'm saying. Do you think it's easy for me?'

Amanda turned around and snapped, 'Not easy for you? Well, excuse me, but I'm the one who nearly got my head blown up this afternoon. I'm the one they nearly killed, not you.'

Michael lost his cool. 'Sure, but if you didn't stick your nose in what's clearly none of your business, maybe none of this would have happened.' He felt a lump in his throat.

Amanda locked her eyes into his for a few seconds. He could feel the anger in her.

She picked up her coat and bag from the sofa and rushed to the front door. 'You won't have to worry about me any more. I can take care of myself. University days are over, Mr Hall.'

Before Michael had time to say a word, she slammed the door to his face.

Speechless, Michael stood in the hallway, wondering if he should go after her. But his mind remained numb, unable to reach a decision.

Only one thing was certain.

He wanted to put an end to this mess and get on with his life. He wanted to love Amanda more than anyone in the world. But she was standing in the way. She was making things too complicated and too dangerous. She could end up jeopardizing his grand plan. She wasn't a risk he was ready to take.

Michael turned around and headed back for the kitchen.

He had to keep his mind on the big picture.

Even if it meant losing Amanda.

CHAPTER 97

Globe Network: same day, 8.35 p.m.

Steve Thorn finished work for the day. He lay back on the brown leather executive chair of his office in Downtown Los Angeles, his hands clasped behind his head.

The clutter on his desk was piling up. That same morning he swore he would have his desk clear before he went home. But one thing led to another, and now there was more mess than when he came to work.

His eyes were circled from lack of sleep. The only thing he wanted to do was go home to a nice meal and fall asleep in front of the television. He didn't have some fancy hobby or a family to go home to. He never claimed to be any different from the rest of the world. He wasn't a gym freak, something obvious according to his waist line. His life consisted of going to work and coming home.

God, he hated what he had become.

Steve spent so much time trying to make his career work. He neglected the present. And the years went by too fast, much too fast. All he got for in return for his effort was a monotonous desk job. He took up journalism because he loved the printed word. He loved writing. He wasn't even writing anymore.

But everything would change soon. He would begin work at CableNews. The money would be fantastic. All the places he wanted to see, he would see them. Paris, London, Melbourne, Hong Kong. In the meantime, he would just have to be patient and hang on a bit longer.

He looked around the office. His eyes stopped at the black briefcase next to the gray metallic filing cabinet. *One hundred thousand dollars.* He smiled to himself. This was the beginning of something big. This was going to change his life and make everything worthwhile again.

The car park was dark when he left the building and walked to his '77 green Ford Falcon. People often wondered why the producer of a news network drove a beaten up Ford. No one knew Steve Thorn had a gambling problem. Money which went in his pocket soon vanished into the casino's black hole of poverty. So when Hugh Gawler gave him $100,000, it was too good to refuse. Back then, he would have even taken $50,000, but he knew by playing hard to get, Hugh would have given him more.

And he did.

Steve walked across the badly lit car park. He noticed three other cars parked on the east side. A blue Camero, a Mercedes-Benz 420E and a Saturn coupe.

Nothing unusual from the other nights. *I'm the only one driving a crap car.*

Yawning to the point of nearly dislocating his jaw, Steve stepped inside the car.

He took the night air into his lung. It was cold, but there was no point turning the heater on. It didn't work. It hadn't worked for six years. And Steve never had the heart or the money to fix it.

He rubbed his hands together, realizing he would have to drive home freezing to death.

He was wrong.

As soon as he fastened his seat belt and turned the key a quarter turn, the car exploded into a ball of fire.

Steve Thorn didn't get a split second to wonder what had happened.

One minute, all is normal.

Then, *boom!*

The sound of the explosion could be heard in a three-mile radius.

The flames jumped twelve feet high. The door of the Ford Falcon on the driver's side flew fifty feet over the parking lot, crashing on the bonnet of the black 450SE Mercedes Benz.

In the darkness of the night, nobody heard the cries of agony coming from the inflamed vehicle.

Nobody.

CHAPTER 98

Washington D.C.: Thursday, 8.02 a.m.

Hugh Gawler met Sam Willicon in a deli-bar.

It was time for both man to put together the final agreement of the bombing that would shatter the nation.

The coffee shop was empty, apart from the bald owner sitting behind the bar, watching a re-run of *The Odd Couple*. An aroma of espresso and toast filled the room.

In another hour, the place would be crowded with early commuters who didn't want to get caught in peak-hour traffic, or others who had finished their night shift and wanted something to fill in their stomachs before going home to bed with a set of ear-plugs and eye-mask.

Hugh Gawler sat at one of the sixties dinners table at the far end of the deli-bar, over a cup of coffee and eggs on toasts. He placed a black briefcase with a gold combination lock beside the steel legs of his chair.

The bacon in his plate was burned on the edges. Hugh didn't have the energy to ask the owner to cook fresh rashes. He was too hungry to wait any longer

And the smell of cooked bacon and brewed coffee in the morning was a pleasure in itself.

Two minutes after Hugh sat at the table, scoffing his eggs on toasts, Sam Willicon walked into the empty deli-bar.

Hugh wasn't surprised by Sam Willicon's appearance. The man looked like anybody's next door neighbor. A sweatshirt with a shooter's rights logo, a pair of faded no-name jeans and a red baseball cap with the name of some university league embroidered

When Sam Willicon sat at Hugh's table, the contrast between the two men's dress sense was like fire and water.

Hugh Gawler wore an Italian tailored black three-piece suite, a Pierre Cardin 100% cotton shirt and a polka dot Givanchi tie. His salt-and-pepper hair was perfectly slicked back on his tanned cranium. The media executive looked more like someone from the Godfather than a business man.

Both men greeted each other without any fuss or compassion. This was a business meeting.

Feelings played no part in it.

Less than an hour ago, Hugh had looked forward to meet the leader of the Texan Militia. Now he was no longer excited. Sam Willicon didn't look like the type of man he could have a decent conversation with. And frankly, the way the leader of the Militia dressed was an embarrassment in itself.

Hugh knew they were both leaders.

Both above the law.

But this was where the similarities ended.

Hugh Gawler dressed and talked like a lawyer.

Sam Willicon sounded like an army recruit in its fifth week of training.

Hugh Gawler sipped his espresso, avoiding eye contact with Sam. 'How's the schedule?' he said, his voice disembodied.

'Okay,' Sam answered, trying to make eye contact with the chiseled-faced man who deliberately looked down at his eggs on toasts.

'Is there anything else I need to know? Do you need help in any way?'

'Have you got the money?'

Hugh looked up for the first time into the man's eyes. He looked down again and took another sip from his espresso 'It's in the case,' he said, slamming the briefcase next to his chair with the palm of one hand.

'What about the Oklahoma bombing? When do we see the money?'

'Give me a month or so?'

'A month? What kind of bullshit is this? I deliver on time. You guys always take ages to fork the dough. I need the money sooner, man. The job is done.'

'Checks take time to clear.'

'It's bullshit, man. With what money am I going to fund the bombing of the White House?'

Hugh Gawler ignored his plea. The man would have to wait his turn. After all, he could always have someone else to get the job done. Maybe not as fast as he wanted it, but if Sam Willicon was going to give him trouble, he would always consider it. In the meantime, the Militia self-proclaimed hero would have to be patient.

'Just hang in there a while longer I'll keep you posted.'

Sam Willicon removed his red cap and shook his head. 'The militia is not a fuckin' credit agency. It costs me a mint to finance a bombing of this scale. Especially the White House. Security personal has to be bribed, police paid off, politicians threatened and blackmailed, security technicians hired. It not just a matter of let's go and blow the White House.' He was now jabbing his finger in front of Hugh's face. 'To you it might have seem like a piece of cake, but you're only behind the camera. You're only come when the shit is over. You never soak one toe in it. I'm doing all the planning and shit. I can't proceed unless I get more funding.'

Hugh scratched the back of his neck and looked up to Sam. The man was really pissing him off. 'There's a hundred thousand dollars in the briefcase. How much more do you need?'

'Five hundred thousand as a pay-down.'

'Five hundred thousand?' he said, injecting shock in his tone. He looked down at his plate, playing with the bacon and muttering to himself.

'What do you expect? You people think we can just waltz inside the White House and blow it up without any preparation? You think I'm going to put my butt on the line with no down-payment? Fuck you, man. I don't have time for this crap. You pay, or I'm out of here.'

Hugh looked up to the man and gave him a hard stare. Damn! He didn't need trouble right now. 'I'll sign you a check for two hundred thousand now,' Hugh said, removing a rigged check book from the inside pocket of his jacket. 'Who do I make it to?'

Sam Willicon shook his head slowly. 'No way man. I'm not doing shit for less than half a million dollars.'

'Can you spell it for me?'

Sam stood up from his chair, letting it fall to the floor. 'Fuck you. Go and find someone else.'

The bald owner of the deli-bar turned around and stared.

Hugh grabbed Sam by the arm and forced him down to his seat. 'Don't walk out on me. And watch your mouth while we're in public'.

Sam gave a deadly look at the bald man behind the counter. The owner turned his back and continued to watch his television show.

'What the fuck, man,' Sam said, turning his attention back to

Hugh. 'What do you expect? You guys are going to make millions out of this. This is the White House we're bombing. THE WHITE HOUSE. Not some damn government building in Oklahoma. I'm going to the death chamber if this thing fucks-up.'

Hugh Gawler wanted to put a bullet in Sam's head right now. But he knew better. Although he felt like getting someone else to do the job, there would be no time. It would take month to find someone trustworthy and reliable. And yet he didn't want to give in to this army-styled turkey who thought he was doing America some huge favor.

Sam retrieved his arm from Hugh's grip. 'Let go of me. My turf, my terms, or there's no deal.'

Hugh locked his eyes into Sam's.

Thirty seconds of silence.

Both men hated to be challenged.

But Hugh Gawler knew there was more at stake here than just pride. Both men's integrity was at stake. Who ever gave in would show weakness. And Hugh Gawler never showed weakness. In every past occasion he had encountered, it would have been a fatal error.

But this time it was different.

Hugh took his eyes of Sam and wrote a check for five hundred thousand dollars.

CHAPTER 99

East Los Angeles: same day, 11.22 p.m.

Jacqueline Chambers watched the videocassette for the second time that evening. News footage from somewhere. News she had seen before on television. Maybe not the same angles, but the same stories.

Jacqueline Chambers sat cross-legged on the green-felt couch, a cigarette hanging from her mouth. At the age of thirty-two, she could have easily been ten years older. Lack of sleep, too much drinking, too much doing nothing. Her floral gown was open in the front, revealing a faded bra and stained underwear. Her blond hair was long and greasy, almost hiding her dark little eyes. She was extremely bony, bordering on anorexia. She took one mouthful of bourbon and focused her eyes on the screen.

The videocassette came in a yellow envelope with no receiver's or sender's name. Just her home address. It arrived last Tuesday via standard U.S. Mail. She watched it as soon as it arrived, but nothing in it grabbed her interest.

A week had gone, and now Jacqueline Chambers wondered if she had missed something in the videocassette

The reports were obviously unedited because of the sometimes-weird camera angles and the cut-let's-try-again interruptions.

After a while, Jacqueline Chambers became lost in her own thoughts. The bourbon and lack of sleep were taking their toll.

The television was flashing images, but no one was watching.

Jacqueline Chambers had seen the entire tape three times already. She also watched the news every day on CableNews. Nothing in the videocassette was new to her. The videocassette didn't intrigue her as much as the unknown identity of the sender.

Jacqueline Chambers dozed off for a while, losing track of time. Her mind was drifting into another world, a world more pleasant than the one she was experiencing when awake.

She woke up a few seconds before the last images appeared on the screen. A footage of an interview with the basketball star Michael Jordan.

When the video footage turned into static snow, Jacqueline Chambers pressed the EJECT button on the remote control. She took the videocassette our of the video recorder and threw it in the television cabinet with tens of other videocassettes

The time on the video recorder was 1.03 a.m.

Jacqueline Chambers yawed and emptied her glass of bourbon.

Time for bed.

She dragged herself to the bedroom, her thoughts confused. She didn't know what the videocassette meant or where it came from. If it was someone trying to play a joke on her, she didn't get it.

Maybe one day it would become clear.

But for the time being, the videocassette would be re-cycled to record next week's episode of the X-Files.

CHAPTER 100

Santa Monica: Wednesday, 9.34 p.m.

It had been an awfully long day when Amanda Ryan sat in front of the television that evening. At least whoever broke into her home didn't smash the television.

That same morning she nearly got shot.

One hour ago, she was arguing with Michael Hall.

And now she almost wished the hitman didn't miss his shot. The agony of living in fear, of knowing nobody out there could really protect her, made her want to end everything.

The thought sent a chill rippling down her spine. Has she past a point where she believed life wasn't worth living? *Don't be a fool! There's still so much you can do.*

Maybe the easy way out was to take the first plane back to Australia.

But she knew it was an impossible option.

If she left with no warning, it would be the second time she would break Michael's heart. And right now, it was the last thing she wanted to do.

Staring blankly at the television screen, she never dreamed her life would turned into such chaos. Six months ago, when she began working at CableNews, she had the world at her feet. Now she was unemployed and running for her life.

Everything she had worked for was crumbling.

Her journalism career was permanently on hold.

One day she will be found in a dark alley with a bullet lodged in her head.

Just like Henry Limar.

They would make it look like a suicide.

They would make sure she would never find the truth about the death of Senator Garry.

And they knew she was getting damn close to the truth.

Is this why they tried to kill me this morning?

Amanda couldn't find any answers. But she knew one thing was certain. As much as she felt self-destructive impulses, she could never find the strength to end her life. She was willing to fight like hell to find out who tried to kill her and why.

She let her head rest against the arm of the couch. Her frown turned into a smile.

As of tomorrow, nothing was going to stand in her way. Even Michael wasn't strong or committed enough to protect her.

There was no one she could rely on.

For the first time in her life, she realized how fragile she was. Never before had she felt so insecure, so much in need of love and help.

And never before had she ever felt so alone and vulnerable instead.

But as the television screen kept flashing electronic images which didn't register in her mind, Amanda knew she had very little choice left. If she wanted to stay alive, she had to find the answers behind the death of Senator Trevor Garry, Henry Limar and Gavin White.

And only one person could get those answers.

She stood from the couch, flicked the television off and went to the bathroom.

As she stood in front of the bathroom mirror, she knew who she was.

She locked her eyes into hers.

Amanda Ryan.

CHAPTER 101

East Los Angeles: Thursday, 5.45 a.m.

Detective Stan Moore spent another sleepless night. The shooting outside the LAPD building was going around in his mind. He was certain the people who shot at Amanda Ryan were serious about killing her. It took a hell of a nerve to shot someone outside the police building.

Stan also knew the next time they wouldn't miss their target.

And now Amanda has refused police protection, he felt personally responsible for her safety. Why, he wasn't sure. Maybe it was because he had spoken to the young woman the day before someone tried to gun her down. Maybe he was dumb and infatuated by like other men.

He stepped out of bed, feeling a massive headache coming on. He passed water and went to the kitchen.

He placed a clean filter in the percolator and added four scoops of ground coffee. His eyes were bloodshot from lack of sleep. But still, he loved his job. It gave him a reason for existing.

Everything in this case had been mystery and intrigue. He knew it was all connected to Hugh Gawler, but he didn't know how. And, of course, he couldn't move in on Hugh unless he had enough evidence accumulated. But even if he did, what would he be looking for?

Stan Moore gulped his black coffee and headed for the bathroom.

After removing his pajamas, he stepped in the shower. He puzzled over how to convince Amanda Ryan to accept police protection. The young woman was strong-minded and confident. She wanted to handle everything herself. Why in the world she agreed to work as a spy was beyond him. She was bright, intelligent, beautiful and courageous. Now her life seemed totally wasted.

276

Feeling the weight of the sleepless night throbbing in his head, Stan Moore stepped out of the shower. He dried himself ferociously with a large white bath towel. With the palm of his hand, he wiped the steam from the mirror and applied shaving foam to his face.

As the single blade glided smoothly against his dark skin, his mind raced at a hundred miles per hour.

The videocassette

There was still something about *the* videocassette which wasn't clear. He had viewed Henry's videocassettes in the last few days, but found nothing suspicious in them. So what videocassette was Henry Limar talking about? What videocassette did he send to Gavin White? And why did Gavin White never got the videocassette?

Stan Moore dropped the orange Bic single-blade shaver in the green hand sink.

Why didn't Gavin White get the videocassette?

If Gavin White never got the videocassette, maybe it was because it never got to his place. And if it never got to his place, then where did it go? Who had the videocassette? What was on the videocassette which was so vital to Gavin White?

Stan Moore raced to the bedroom.

He emptied the content of his wallet and looked desperately for the little piece of paper with Gavin White's address which he found in Henry Limar's office.

The crumbled page from a desk calendar was tucked away between his Visa card and driver's license. The address read 6/14 Batman Avenue.

His heart beat in harmony with his throbbing headache. Stan Moore held on to the piece of paper as he crossed the bedroom, knocking his left knee with the side of the bed.

Limping to the lounge room, he reached for the telephone directory. Under W's, he ran his finger down the Whites. God, he never realized there was so many people called White.

Impatient, he threw the directory on the floor and picked-up the telephone receiver. He punched 411 for assistance.

'What name?' the operator asked.

'Gavin White.'

'Address?'

'6/14 Batman Avenue, East Los Angeles.'

A few seconds waiting.

'I've got no listing for a Gavin White at 6/14 Batman Avenue. I've got a listing at 14/6 Batman Avenue.'

Stan Moore thanked the operator and hung up the phone. He

crossed 6/14 from the piece of paper and wrote 14/6 instead.

He stepped back in the bedroom and began to get dressed.

It was now obvious why Gavin White never got the videocassette Henry Limar sent him.

Henry Limar sent it to the wrong address.

CHAPTER 102

Los Angeles: same day, 7.32 a.m.

The hitman sat in the hotel room by himself. The cream-colored drapes were closed and the air conditioning turned on. Outside the temperature had already reached seventy degrees.

The hitman lay on the single bed, trying to catch up on some sleep. He'd been out all night in the Viper Room, a room in the nightclub where actor River Phoenix fried his brain with some cheap crack.

The main man would be pissed when he learned Amanda Ryan was still alive.

But he doesn't have to know, does he?

Hugh Gawler was in Washington D.C. doing some business. This suited the hitman perfectly since he didn't want to tell Hugh he missed killing Amanda. On the other hand, he was proud of the job he had done with Steve Thorn.

There was no way anyone could have come out alive from the bombed vehicle. Steve Thorn never knew what happened. It only took a split second for the bomb to explode after he turned on the ignition.

Boom!

Showtime!

A job well done.

But the hitman knew he wouldn't get paid until he finished both assignments

Back to assignment one.

Killing Amanda Ryan.

And this time he couldn't afford to muck it up. Hugh Gawler would have his head instead.

The hitman removed the SIG-Sauer P226 9mm semiautomatic

from the drawer next to the bed. He looked at it, aimed at the color television, and pretended to be shooting. *Bang, bang, you're dead. Couldn't we just make love instead?* The tune from one of English singer George Michael's song ran through his head. *And I've had such a hard day.* A hard fuckin' day, he thought.

The hitman loved hand guns. They gave him such a sense of power. Knowing he could destroy a life just by a light pressure of the index excited him. It was like being a God. The power to choose and decide.

He threw the gun back in the draw.

And I've had such a hard day.

Except he wasn't the one who decided who had to die.

He wasn't really God.

Hugh *fuckin* Gawler was God.

CHAPTER 103

The preparation for the bombing of the White House was no easy task.

Sam Willicon spent months working with the men from the Texan Militia. A lot of money and bribery took place to get a blueprint of the White House.

The blueprint was now lying flat on a desk in front of Sam Willicon. It showed the full electrical and alarm wiring system of the White House. With the blueprint came a list of the President's schedule during the next two weeks. Based on this information, the bombing would take place at an exact moment when the President would be attending the White House. And when security would be the most lax.

Of course, Sam Willicon knew when the President was in the White House, there was no such a thing as lax security. But taking advantage of the security guards shift changes meant some slackness in the security system.

And this was when the bomb would be placed.

Hugh Gawler would later give his go-ahead for the countdown.

For weeks now Sam Willicon had spent hours in libraries, devouring clips on the President of the United States and his entourage. He had to know everything about the man. In fact, Sam Willicon was so convinced of his knowledge of the President, he would have bet with anyone on his ability to write an unauthorized bibliography. Another bestseller by *Anonymous*.

Sam Willicon took the planning of his assignment as the most important thing in his life.

If Hugh Gawler could have seen the preparation Sam had put into the bombing of the White House, he wouldn't have hesitated when Sam requested a $500,000 advance. As far as Sam was

281

concerned, the advance was chicken feed in comparison to the risk he was taking.

But bombing the White House had never been about money.

It was about destroying the root of all evil.

The Government of the United States of America.

The President.

It was about giving Americans back their rights to the constitution, their rights to freedom, their rights to choose their way of life without having big brother looking over their shoulders all the time. Their rights to not be harassed on minor charges. Or having their every move monitored as if every citizen was a criminal.

Sam Willicon and the Texan Militia would bring peace and justice back to America, the way it was meant to be since his forefathers had landed on the soil of this great country.

Hugh Gawler's task in comparison to Sam Willicon's was easy. All he had to do was arrange for his news team to be present.

CableNews camera crews would be ready to jump in just before the massive explosion. They would capture the entire incident on camera. The bombing would not take place if there were other television or cable station news teams in front of the White House.

CableNews would be the only footage provider of the bombing of the White House.

And as a result, the only one which would make millions of dollars from the venture.

Sam Willicon knew it.

And he would get his share.

CHAPTER 104

Downtown Los Angeles: Friday, 6.36 a.m.

Steve Thorn lay in bed. His body was covered in moist, sterile dressing soaked with normal saline of sodium bicarbonate. For the last twenty-four hours, he had been given intravenous infusions of plasma. He also consumed plenty of hot sweet drinks to combat shock.

When the car exploded, it didn't kill him on impact. The green Ford Falcon had had a metal plate attached by the previous owner under the driver's seat to combat corrosion.

Steve Thorn was projected through the front windscreen. If he ever lived through the ordeal, it wouldn't be something he was looking forward to. His face had been severely cut from the shattered glass. He nearly lost his left eye when a splinter lodged itself above his eyelid. It took a surgeon two hours to removed the piece of glass without damaging the iris and the retina.

Earlier on, a doctor making his rounds was explaining to a young medical student what had happened to Steve.

Although Steve had one eye closed and the other bandaged, he wasn't asleep.

'This man has third degree burns to seventy five percent of his body. Do you know what third degree burns are?'

'His top skin has been destroyed.'

'Correct. Only the layer of true skin has been affected, exposing the papillae with nerve-ending. When nerve-endings are left exposed, the patient experiences unbearable pain which causes considerable shock. Constitutional upset is the hardest thing to deal with. Third degree burns in themselves do not need skin-grafting; sufficient skin-cells survive this type of burns to ensure healing by natural multiplication of cells.'

'What are his changes of recovery?'

'Pretty good if he makes it through psychologically. He will be left with

scarring which may produce contractures and deformity. Some burnt victims become delirious as a result. They can't cope with the amount of pain all at once. When this patient first came to us, we had to make sure his circulatory system wouldn't collapse because of the severity of the extent of the burns. Although they are only three degree burns, they extend to most parts of the body.'

Steve Thorn wanted to smile, but the pain on his face forced him to remain still. He didn't want to smile because he knew he would survive. He wanted to smile because of how naive he had been. How could he have believed for a second Hugh Gawler was going to let him go without any fuss? He saw and heard the way Hugh Gawler dealt with his enemies. And although Steve Thorn never considered himself to be Hugh's enemy, now he wondered why he had made such assumption.

Steve Thorn feared the man since the day he walked into his office, proposing some fairy tale about setting up the biggest news cable network in the States.

But he fell for it.

He fell for it like others before him. He fell for Hugh's charm and good looks. He fell for it because of his own greed and thirst for power. Success wasn't enough. Steve Thorn had to have more and more. For years he tried to fulfill his life, but nothing ever did it. So Steve continued to search for more power, more money.

He opened his right eye and felt nauseous.

He closed it again.

The face of Amanda Ryan crossed his mind.

What was going to happen to the poor girl?

Only now that he was in a near-death situation, Steve realized what a fool he had been. The young woman had no chance in the world to live through this. He should have never let her go to work for Hugh Gawler. It didn't matter what everyone else at Globe Network felt. He was the boss. He should have remained firm on his decision.

But he failed.

Even when he had been given a second chance to get Amanda back on his side, he turned her down. When she came back begging for her job the other day, he could have swallowed his pride and save her life.

But no.

Steve Thorn was very much like Hugh Gawler. Too proud to slow down, to know when to stop. It was easy to blame the girl now for where she was. It was easy to say now how she paved her own destiny.

Amanda Ryan wasn't the bad player in all this.

Steve Thorn was.

He had known all along.

He blinked with his right eye, letting a warm tear roll down the white bandage on his face.

Steve Thorn wished he died when the car exploded. The pain from the burning was unbearable. Every inch of his body felt like it was being pricked with thousands of small needless. He wanted to scream, but couldn't find the energy to open his mouth.

Laying in pain, Steve Thorn knew who had done the deed. He should have known better than to trust Hugh Gawler. He should have figured out when he confronted Hugh things wouldn't be going down so easily.

But now, it was too late.

Hugh Gawler had won once more.

As Steve closed his weary eye, he knew only one thing could revenge what Hugh Gawler had done to him.

The truth.

The world had to know what was going on. Someone had to speak up and expose Hugh Gawler and his corrupt empire.

And Steve knew who this someone was.

CHAPTER 105

East Los Angeles: same day, 9.34 a.m.

'What's on the videocassette?' detective Stan Moore asked Jacqueline Chambers.

The housewife freaked out when the detective first appeared at the door, shoving his LAPD badge in front of her face. Her eyes widened with fear as if she had something to hide. The detective knew straight away he was dealing with someone who was going to give him trouble. The woman had a cigarette hanging from her lower lip, and her hair was in a shamble. Although the detective didn't want to come to any hasty conclusion, in this case, he really believed in *what you see is what you get.*

'Have you got a warrant?' she snapped, after letting the detective through the front door.

'A warrant for what? Do you want me to search your house?'

'Good, then I don't have to tell you anything.'

'All I want to know is what's on the videocassette sent to your place by accident.'

'News reports, I told you,' she said, injecting her tone with authority.

Stan Moore had been in the house ten minutes. No matter how many times he asked Jacqueline Chambers to cooperate, she refused to hand the videocassette over.

'Why can't you just give me the tape?' he asked, his hands clammy and his knees locked together. If it had been a man standing in front of him, he probably would have hit him. He had never hit a woman to get some answers, no matter how frustrated he was. Once more he would have to be patient and play it by the book.

'It was sent to me, not to you. It's my videocassette You don't have a warrant and no right to harass me in my home.'

'What are you going to with it anyway? What good is it to you?'

'You must think I'm stupid or something. I could sell this videocassette for a lot of money. Why should I just hand it over to you? What's in it for me?' Jacqueline Chambers was obviously aware of how much magazines and television stations were ready to pay for a good story. 'What about this guy in England last year who got $100,000 for pictures of Princess Diana doing a workout? How much are you willing to pay for the tape?'

Stan Moore shook his head in disbelief. The woman had to be joking. What was it with the bored housewife? She'd spent to much time watching television, waiting for something to happen in her life. He couldn't believe the nerve of the woman. But by the same token it didn't really surprise him. The bloody media always portray police as ruthless and bloodsucking. The result was no one trusted cops. So, instead of being faced with law-abiding citizens who were willing to help police in their investigation, Stan Moore had to listen to all kind of nonsense.

'I'm going to come back with a warrant and turn this house upside down. Is this what you want?'

'Get lost.'

'I'm going to mess up this place so badly, you'll remember this day for the rest of your life. And if I find any illegal substance, I'm going to push for prosecution.' The illegal substance was a stab in the dark. She just looked like the type of person who would use some stuff.

'Is this a threat?'

'No, it's not a threat. I'm giving you an easy and a hard way to do things. And you're choosing the hard way. It's your game.' The detective shook his head and walked to the front door. 'I'll be back before lunch.' He waved goodbye without looking behind.

Before he crossed the front door, Jacqueline Chambers said, 'Hold on a sec.'

The detective turned around.

Jacqueline Chambers reached underneath the television cabinet, next to the video recorder, and grabbed a videocassette

She handed the videocassette to the detective.

Stan Moore felt relieved. 'Thank you,' he said, a broad smile on his face. 'You're doing the right thing.'

'You've got the damn thing, so get out of my house.' Her tone of voice had turned nasty.

Sam grabbed the videocassette, thanked her again, and left the house.

Jacqueline Chambers stood at door, smiling as the car reversed from the driveway.

Stupid bastard!

The detective might have got the videocassette, but he wouldn't win the battle.

CHAPTER 106

Santa Monica: same day, 10.32 a.m.

When Amanda Ryan woke up from a deep sleep, she was surprised of how late it was. With the stress of the past week, she somehow managed to sleep ten hours straight without any disturbance.

This morning, as the sunlight gently filtered itself across the bedroom, caressing the pink cotton sheets of her bed, Amanda felt a surge of energy coming from within. She remembered the promise she made to herself last night. Today was a new day, a new chance. She would find the people who tried to kill her. She would find the truth about the death of Gavin White, Henry Limar and Senator Trevor Garry.

The traffic outside made her think of when she use to work. Right now she didn't miss getting up at 5.00 a.m. and rushing to the office. Being out of the rat race was kind of nice. Maybe it would be what she'd choose to do when this whole thing would be over.

The window of the bedroom had been left ajar, letting the fresh sea smell of the ocean enter the house.

Amanda sat on the bed, smiling to herself. The room was warm, just like the inside of a cocoon. Nothing seemed impossible.

If no-one else was willing to help her, she would find a way. If she didn't, *they* would get to her first.

Amanda passed one hand through her blond hair. She didn't want to die just yet. She still dreamed of becoming a successful journalist and seeing her parents again one day.

Memories of her childhood in Perth came back to mind. She remembered the fun times she had with her family. Afternoons sun-baking at the beach or strolling down the yacht club. Evenings at home playing Uno or Monopoly, sharing jokes together, or reading a good book.

Determined to see her home again, Amanda knew she had to get a grip on herself and follow her dreams.

And until she had achieved just this, she would never be satisfied.

CHAPTER 107

The White House, Washington D.C.; Tuesday 11.03 a.m.

President Gerald Standford sat behind his wide antique desk, preparing himself for the eleven o'clock meeting with the National Security Council.

No one else was in the Oval Office of the White House, the sanctuary of the most powerful ruler in the country.

The French windows were open, letting a smell of freshly cut grass whip through the room previously occupied by every past American Presidents.

President Gerald Standford was staring pensively at the classical marble fireplace in the north wall.

His face, which usually bore a broad smile in newspapers and television shows, was creased with concern. His hair had turned gray in the last two years. But he didn't mind. It gave him the look of someone wiser than he really was. Deep down, Gerald Standford knew he was just another man. His nose was straight, and his eyes sat closely together. His thin lips were slightly parted, exposing a perfectly symmetric row of white teeth. His eyes blinked nervously.

President Gerald Standford was angry.

The Oklahoma bombing had hit America in the heart of what it stood for. Freedom. Innocent lives had been destroyed. Lives of decent citizens who where working for *his* departments. It was *his* people who had been killed.

Gerald Standford wasn't going to let the culpable get away with it. The bombing was obviously revenge against the raid of the Branch Davidian compound in Waco, Texas by the FBI and the army. At least, it was what the national security adviser suggested.

But President Standford took the attack more personally. It was an attack against him and everything he believed in.

The Oklahoma bombing took place one year to the day after the

Waco federal assault. The raid of the Branch Davidian compound had been a mistake. The President had agreed to it upon advise from this defense counsel. He thought he was doing the right thing at the time. But the incident had caused more harm than good.

And now revenge bounced back in the form of the Oklahoma bombing.

Jesus, when will it stop?

What angered President Standford was how innocent people had to lose their lives over a war which didn't really exist. The government had enough trouble with outsiders. The didn't need extra pressure from the inside.

The Texan Militia had denied responsibility for the Oklahoma bombing.

The President had read the press release by Sam Willicon, leader of the Texan Militia, and didn't believe a word of it. He knew the militia was involved in the bombing. He knew it was a direct attack against him and the government of the United States of America.

But he wasn't afraid.

At 11.30 a.m. he would consider a plan of action put together by the National Security Council. The plan code-named *The eagle had landed* would outlined specific strategies to bring down militia groups which were considered a real threat to America's national security. The President had already consented to use any force necessary to overcome the enemy.

Because it's what those Militia groups were.

The enemy.

If it had been entirely up to the Gerald Standford, he would have already declared a private war with the militia groups. But the constitutional rights of the groups made it difficult for him to take further action until considerable threats were being made against the people of America.

In the meantime, all he could do was hope his defense team was clever enough to unveil some of the militia's secrets, especially the Texan Militia. Something that would prove they were acting as a security risk to Americans.

This nonsense had to stop.

The militia was giving people bad ideas about the government.

And although President Standford knew some of his departments often walked a thin line, in general he was satisfied with the way things were being handled.

He had enough problems trying to establish a likable public image without having some militia undermining everything his government did.

Every move the President made had to be carefully planned. One step in the wrong direction, one mistake which would upset the public, and his chance for re-election would dissolve into nothingness.

And since most militia groups claimed to be the voice of the oppressed and the disenchanted, it wasn't an easy task to plan a head-to-head attack without using bulling tactics. Americans wouldn't tolerate bulling tactics.

The Waco attack raid had been heavily criticized by the media and various freedom groups in the country. Gerald Standford knew this type of action was not to be favored because of the damage it did to the government's public relations credibility.

Lost in his thoughts, the President straightened on his chair when someone knocked at the door.

Captain Clifton Millar swung the door open and aimed his stare at the south wall of the Oval Office where the President remained seated. 'Mr President, the chairman of the National Security Council and the Secretary of State are ready for briefing.' The captain's gray hair was cropped with a number two behind his ear and above his collar. His green uniform was as stiff as cardboard from the excess usage of starch. His decorations looked like rows of M&Ms glued to his chest.

Captain Clifton Millar was adviser to the President on military strategies.

The President dismissed Captain Clifton Millar with a gesture of his hand. 'Tell them I'm on my way. You go ahead.'

Captain Clifton Millar nodded and left the room, closing the door behind him.

The President gathered various papers and documents from his desk and placed them inside a folder with the President of the United States of America official seal and the words 'Top Secret' stamped in red ink.

He stood from his personalized, made-to-measure, black leather-bound executive chair.

His brow furrowed.

It's time to put an end to this god-damn nonsense!

CHAPTER 108

West Executive Drive, Washington D.C; 11.30 a.m.

A black Ford van stopped at the blue-canopied guard-house of the White House.

The driver, clean-shaven with a white shirt and brown slacks, felt a bit anxious when the guard approached the van. He straightened the identity card clipped to the pocket of his shirt.

Although it wasn't the first time the driver had passed the gates of the White House, today he did so for an entirely different reason.

For the past six months, he had driven in and our of the White House's ground to maintain the electronic security system. The thirty-something driver was a familiar face around the White House. What no one knew was he had been bought by the Texan Militia to sabotage the electronic time security device and place the necessary explosive to blow up the White House.

It was a risky move.

The driver knew was aware of the danger.

But the $200,000 the militia had offered him wasn't an offer he could refuse. Hell, he still had to put his kids through university. He never got himself a tertiary education. In this day and age a tertiary education was not a luxury, but a must. Gone long were the days when one could just jump from one job to another with no qualification and little experience. Gone were the days when a man didn't have to worry about where his next piece of bread was coming from.

This was the nineties.

And the nineties motto was *look after number one!*

So as far as the driver was concerned, the President could go to hell and back as long as he got his kids through university.

The security officer approached the van on the driver's side.

The driver opened the window.

'How you going?' the security officer asked.

'Not bad,' the driver said.

'You know the routine.'

'Sure do.'

The security officer walked to the back of the van and opened the back doors.

It didn't matter whether someone walked through the doors of the White House a hundred times a day. Routine checks were indispensable, especially when that someone was an outsider.

The driver was aware his life was no secret to anyone in the White House.

The security officer more than likely knew the driver had no prior criminal record, no involvement with any protest group of any kind, in fact nothing made him a threat of any kind to the President. His background had been checked and double-checked by every possible mean.

But still, the security's instructions were clear. He had to check every vehicle which went past the gate, no matter how reliable he felt the driver of the vehicle was.

The driver was nervous, but he had no reason to be. After all, there was nothing in the van which would arouse any suspicion. The only thing the driver had to carry with him in the White House was the instructions he had in his brain. He had spent days memorizing every details given to him by Sam Willicon. The plan was straight-forward.

The bombing device would be disguised as a fuse box in the central alarm cabinet, just under the Oval Office. The trigger would be set by an outside microwave pulse emitted from a ordinary cellular phone.

The President would return to his office, no idea of what was waiting for him.

On signal, Sam Willicon would punch the 9-digit secret number on the cellular phone.

And boom!

The beginning of a new era.

CHAPTER 109

L.A.: Tuesday 10.33 p.m.

Michael Hall was working on his computer when someone opened the front door.

He jumped on his seat, wondering for a second if it was a break-in. But then he heard her voice.

'Michael,' Amanda said, 'are you there?'

Michael stood from his seat, his heart racing at the thought of seeing her again. For the last twenty-four hours, he hadn't been able to get any sleep. When Amanda left his apartment after the argument, he couldn't stop feeling he was at fault. He knew already Amanda was in danger of being killed, but contributing to the problem didn't help. Sure, it takes two to have an argument, but he could hardly blame Amanda for being on edge. He wasn't the one who was going to get his head blasted any minute.

'Are you there?' Amanda repeated, placing the spare key Michael gave her in her handbag.

Michael stood from his chair. 'In the study,' he said, realizing how much he had missed Amanda in the little time they had parted from one another.

Nervous, Amanda approached the study, wondering if she had made the right choice by coming back to Michael's apartment. She decided she was going to find out the truth about all this death with or without the help of Michael. But she wanted to give him at least the chance to decide whether he was going to help her or not.

And she couldn't wait to make love to him.

Michael came out of the study, his hair out of place, looking like he had just recovered from a hangover. He never expected Amanda to turn up that night. Quickly, he tossed his fringe up his cranium when he saw Amanda appearing at the end of the hallway.

'I'm here,' Michael said, now mesmerized by the sight of his lover.

Amanda walked straight to him without a word. When she came face to face to Michael, she pressed her lips against his.

He took her kiss in his mouth, feeling the electricity passing between the two bodies.

It took only a kiss for Amanda to realize how much she needed Michael to be with her. Did she seriously think she could have carried on by herself without Michael on her side? Yesterday, she was sure she could have handled it. But now, with Michael so close to her, feeling loved and wanted, she wasn't sure she had the strength to carry on all by herself. She would have to win Michael over.

She unzipped his shirt and made love to him.

When they finished, Amanda buttoned up her skirt, still feeling the surge of the love she had made with Michael. Now she knew she could never live without him.

'Why don't you help me to find the killer of the Senator?' Amanda said. 'You know I can't go on living on the run forever.'

Michael adjusted his tie. 'You could always go back to Australia,' Michael said. 'No one would ever find you there.'

Surprised by Michael's comment, Amanda couldn't understand his abruptness. They had just finished making love, and he was telling her she could leave the country forever.

'But I love you,' Amanda said. 'I couldn't just leave you behind. You know how much you mean to me.'

Michael knew she was right. But when he told her she could go back to Australia, he didn't mean he wanted her to leave him. His mind was filled with confusion. He knew he wanted Amanda to be with him forever, but having her around was also a hazard.

Wrapping his arms around Amanda's waist, Michael looked her in the eyes. 'No matter where you go,' he said, 'I'll never leave you this time. I made the mistake once, but you're not getting rid of me so easily.' He meant every word he said at the time, but he knew tomorrow might make him see things in a different light.

'Oh, Michael,' Amanda said, her knees knocking.

For the first time in her life, she really believed everything would turn out fine. Somehow, in the mist of all this chaos, Michael and she would find a place in the world where they belonged. There would be no more running around in search of an identity, trying to be the people they were expected to be.

As Amanda held Michael in her arms, for the first time in her life, she realized maybe the only thing which mattered was the ability to just be who you were.

She let a sigh of relief when Alan pressed his lips against hers.

CHAPTER 110

Detective Stan Moore inserted the cassette in the video recorder and sat comfortably on the couch.

With the remote control, the detective pressed the PLAY button. Anticipating some revelation to all the mysterious murders of the last few weeks, he found it hard to settle on his seat. He moved like a cat trying to find the right spot.

The television screen began showing snow and soon images appeared on the screen.

Instantly, the detective recognized the person on the screen. It wasn't someone he knew personally, but the face was awfully familiar

What the hell?!

The detective pressed the FWD button and watched the images speed up on the screen.

When the title came up, he froze the frame.

'The X-Files'.

God Damn it!

Jacqueline Chambers had taped the television series over the original videocassette

Or she gave him the wrong videocassette

One thing was certain, this damn videocassette wasn't going to be any good.

Angry, the detective stood from the couch, grabbed his car keys and walked to the front.

The videocassette was still playing when his car vanished at the end of the street.

CHAPTER 111

Michael and Amanda were seated at the kitchen table of Michael's apartment. It was 6.56 a.m., and both of them had found it hard to get some sleep.

'Where do we start?' Michael asked, pouring hot water into two mugs of instant coffee.

'From the beginning,' Amanda said. 'I've been rushing through everything. Nothing makes much sense. We have to go backwards and find the source.'

'Sure, sounds good in theory. What exactly did you have in mind?'

'Well, the first thing we know went wrong was the murder of the Senator. Therefore we should concentrate on that.'

'But I thought you already covered the case.'

'I did, but Hugh Gawler seemed awfully agitated when I went to visit Gavin White in prison. Something was upsetting him. And I know it wasn't just because I didn't listen to his orders.'

'So what's going on?'

'He knew something about Senator Trevor Garry's death before it happened. He knew the Senator was going to get killed.'

'How do you know?'

'I don't, but then Henry got killed. And why do you think Henry got killed?'

'Because he knew something he wasn't supposed to tell.'

'Correct. And what if this had something to do with the death of the Senator?'

'Possible.'

'Right. So Henry knew something about the death of the Senator and Hugh assumed he told me. So the next thing you know, Henry

299

gets killed and now they're after me. They think I know the truth when in fact I know nothing at all.'

Michael took a sip from his coffee cup. Amanda's version of events made sense. But she had no proof of any sort. 'Assuming Hugh Gawler knew the Senator was going to get killed, why would he hide it? What was in it for him?'

'I don't know,' Amanda said, trying to think of a reason. 'Why would he say nothing? Maybe he organized the killing?'

'But why?'

'For money, I don't know.'

'Something doesn't make sense. How would Hugh make money from killing someone?'

Amanda's eyes opened wide. How could she have been so blind? It had been so obvious. It had been in front of her all the time. CableNews began to gain ratings only when they had exclusive footage of news events. In the second quarter of the year, CableNews had banked $30M dollars in comparison to a loss of $15M in the same quarter the previous year. With so much money at stake, it was easy to understand what was happening. The reason why the Senator got killed was for CableNews to increase its ratings. The Oklahoma bombing ensured CableNews would remain at the top spot for at least another year. And since CableNews was always first at the scene of the crime, then it made even more sense. Amanda frowned, shaking her head.

'Are you okay?' Michael asked, wondering what was running through Amanda's mind.

'He got the Senator killed for the ratings!'

'What?'

'Hugh Gawler got the Senator killed so he could get exclusive footage for CableNews.'

'Not very likely.'

'Of course he did.'

'How do you know?'

'How do I know? What about the Oklahoma bombing? How come CableNews got the first footage? What about when they found Gavin White? Why was it CableNews was the first team at his apartment? And when Gavin died? How come CableNews was also in the prison before anyone else? How is it that in less than a year CableNews manages exclusive and first footage on every major news event?'

'Because they got there first?'

Amanda shook her head. 'No, no, no. The only reason why they got there first is because they knew about the crimes before they happened. And they knew about the crimes because they organized them!'

Michael stood from his chair. 'Whoa, it seems very unlikely.'

'What's so unlikely? It's the only theory which fits the picture.'

As much as he didn't like to admit it, Michael knew Amanda was right. She got close to the truth, and it frightened him. How much more was she going to unveil? Everything major CableNews had covered over the past few months had been a chance, a tip-off, someone there at the right time and the right place. And the odds were something of that nature couldn't happen. After working a few years for CableNews, Michael knew luck played a large part in getting first exclusive footage. But no one could have been as lucky as CableNews had been in the past year. Michael was certain. But he had to play the game. He had to make Amanda believe he knew nothing at all.

'Let's say everything you've told me is correct,' Michael said, giving himself no chance at making a mistake. 'What's all the story with the videocassette?'

'Obviously the videocassette Henry was suppose to have given Gavin White showed something no one was supposed to know?'

'Like what?'

'Like proof of who really killed the Senator.'

Not fully convinced, Michael stroked his chin. 'Okay, so we have some proof of some sort on videocassette, but we don't know where the videocassette is or how to get our hands on it. Even if everything you said was right, what do we do now?'

'Trace back the scene of the crime. Try to pick up clues or any leads which would get us closer.'

'We could be going around in circles.'

'I know. So I was thinking, since you still work for CableNews, you might be able to find something back at the office.'

'You want me look for what?'

'Get into Hugh's office and go through his paper work, his computer, everything you can get your hands on.'

Michael shook his head nervously. 'I don't know. This is very risky.'

'We need to find the truth, Michael. Someone's out there ready to kill me.'

'What if you're wrong. What happens if Hugh Gawler has nothing to do with all this? What if I get caught going through his stuff? I could loose my job over this.'

For a moment there, Amanda felt she was losing Michael. How could he think of his job when she was about to be killed? This was insane. All she was asking him to do was to get in the room and look for some evidence of some sort.

Amanda emptied her cup of coffee in the sink. 'Fine,' she said, 'you want to keep your job, then keep your damn job. I'll take care of this by myself.'

'Come on, Amanda. You know what you're asking me here. I could lose my job if we're wrong. I'm a company director. I can't just act on blind speculations. We have to be more certain if I'm going to go through Hugh's paper.'

'You're all the same,' Amanda screamed in anger. God damn it, if no one was going to help her, then she'll do it by herself. 'I thought you were on my side. I thought you were willing to help me. Thanks a lot.'

Michael felt fear taking over him. It was true. He did tell Amanda he would help her no matter what. And he also promised himself he would have nothing stand in the way of his job. Or in the way of his love for Amanda. But now both his job and his love for Amanda were standing in each other's way, Michael was confused. He had worked so hard to get to where he was. And he loved Amanda so much. He didn't want to throw it all away. He wanted everything. The girl, the job and the truth. But he knew life wasn't like that. Everything was always a compromise of one sort or another.

Amanda was down the hallway, disappointed and hurt. Michael was the last person she could count on, but now she was on her own again.

'Wait a minute,' Michael said as he raced to the hallway.

'The hell with you,' Amanda responded as she closed the door to his face.

If Michael wasn't willing to break into Hugh's office, then she would have to do it herself.

CHAPTER 112

Steve Thorn tried to call Amanda several times, but her phone was off the hook.

His condition was now stable, but still critical. Laying on the hospital bed, he pressed the nurse call button.

A few seconds later, a blond nurse with hazel eyes walked in the room.

'Something wrong, Mr Thorn?'

'I'd like to try that number again.'

'Mr Thorn, I'd like to help you, but I can't spend all my time with you dialing a phone number which is not connected. There are other patients in the ward.' The nurse re-adjusted Steve's pillow. 'Why don't you rest a bit. We'll try later.'

Steve grimaced. 'Sure, whatever.' He didn't feel like arguing with the nurse.

But time was running out.

He had to get in touch with Amanda.

She would be the only one who would believe him.

The home of detective Stan Moore on Oranlis Avenue, East Los Angeles, was unoccupied.

Since the detective had left the house a couple of hours ago, the videocassette in the video recorder had been playing.

When the episode of the 'X-Files' ended, the screen turned to snow and within a few seconds to news footage. The same news footage Jacqueline Chambers had seen.

Nothing to raise suspicion.

And then the footage ended.

The screen was covered in snow once more.

Apart from the light of the television tube, the room was dark, giving it an eerie atmosphere.

Minutes went by, with no noise in the apartment but the grizzling sound of the television set.

And suddenly pictures began to appear on the television screen once more. But this time they were not news footage from the CableNews Studio.

It was an angled shot from one corner of a room showing two man exchanging hundred dollar notes.

'Have you got the money,' the first man asked.

The other man placed a briefcase on the conference table in the middle of the room.

'One hundred thousand,' the man said. 'It's all in there.'

The first man began switching the money to his briefcase.

'Are you sure it's safe here?' the other man asked.

'I've asked not to be disturbed. You don't have to worry about a thing. Let's just get this over and done with.'

'What if someone finds out we killed Trevor Garry?'

'No one's going to find out as long as you keep your mouth shut.'

The second man grabbed the briefcase full of money and said: 'I'll get in touch with you regarding the talk show.'

After greeting each other, both men walked out of the room, passing the camera by only a few inches.

The pale skin, thin lips and thick glasses identified clearly the first person to be Senator Terence Maxwell.

Not Senator Terence Maxwell or Hugh Gawler, the other man in the shot, knew the transaction had been video-taped.

The recording turned to snow again.

Within a few seconds the videocassette reached its end, and the video recorder set itself to rewind automatically.

CHAPTER 113

Washington D.C., Tuesday 3.15 a.m.

Laying on the bed of his hotel room, Hugh Gawler had too much on his mind. No matter how hard he tried, he just couldn't get to sleep. He tossed and turned, his head heavy from the one-too-many glasses of Southern Comfort he had before going to bed.

The drink was meant to help him find sleep.

Instead it kept his level of Gamma-Amino Butyric Acid at a high-level for the first couple of hours, giving him the impression he would get to sleep. And now the alcohol began to dissipate in his blood stream, and Hugh Gawler found himself as agitated as before he began to drink.

For months he tried to keep himself under control over the bombing of the White House. Even a man of his status, he acknowledged, wasn't invincible to fear, anxiety and uncertainty. But he knew he would get through it all one way or another.

It wasn't the first time he had risked his life to get to the top.

However, he was conscious of the seriousness of bombing the White House. This was no drug-scam operation like his hey-days in New York, or getting rid of a Senator. The bombing of the White House was the ultimate crime.

Hugh Gawler was thinking about retirement.

It was a shame about Amanda Ryan.

For a while, he though he was going to retire with her by his side. He really liked the girl.

His mind still numbed by the hangover and his need to sleep, he saw the young woman's face in his mind's eyes.

She was the cornerstone of perfection.

Apart from her determination to get her nose into other people's business, he couldn't think of any one better to spend the rest of his life with.

And now she was dead.

Shame.

They could have been so good for one another.

Hugh Gawler liked young women. He always had. It was easy for older women to go on about how men value youth too much. They didn't understand. They didn't have any appreciation of what true beauty was. They didn't have any respect for the beauty of youth. Only men like Hugh Gawler could understand. Only men had sex on their mind constantly. Women never understood it was part of the male physical and psychological make-up. Men who were not afraid of saying what was on their mind. Men who loved young flesh for what it was and nothing more.

In the haze of his drunkenness, Hugh fantasized what his life could have been if Amanda Ryan had been his wife. Different in a way. Maybe he wouldn't have taken all the risks he had. Maybe they would have had a child or two, and he would have given up his old bachelor habits; the womanizing and drinking. But what would have happened when she got older. Would he have found the strength to love her irrespective of her age? Would it have made a difference if in twenty years she would no longer have the figure she has today? Would he have gone out to look for another young woman? Could he have remained faithful to Amanda after living like a bachelor for most of his life?

As Hugh tossed to the left side of the bed, he knew he couldn't have wished for anyone else.

It was the truth.

His head hurting with confusion and lust, he knew he could have loved Amanda forever.

What he couldn't have accepted was the idea Amanda didn't love him, she just stayed around him for his money, his power, his prestige. Or as a career move. He didn't have much respect for women who used sex as a career-accelerating tool. He loved women for their womanhood, and he wanted to be loved for his manhood.

But all these thoughts of love and belonging did nothing but continue to keep him awake until the early hours of the morning.

And then other thoughts crept inside his head.

The White House.

The bombing.

Sam Willicon.

Steve Thorn.

His mind was like a pressure cooker. Soon everything would come to an end. After this, he would retire to some foreign coast, away from Los Angeles and its hectic lifestyle. He would pace himself one day at the time. He would find the tranquility and peace he had been searching for so long. He'll have everything he ever wanted.

And if he was lucky, maybe even love.

CHAPTER 114

Los Angeles: Long Beach Memorial Medical Center, 6.32 a.m.

Steve Thorn was not expected to leave hospital for another two weeks. Then he would be flown over to the Grossman Burn Center for further treatment. There it would take him at least another five years to begin a normal life. But Steve knew even if the physical scars disappeared, the mental agony would go on forever.

As he lay alone in room 224, he wondered if he would have been better off dead.

Then maybe not.

If he had died in the car, Hugh Gawler would have got away with it. This way, Steve Thorn still had a chance for revenge.

He looked towards the only window on the east side of the room, wondering why he had made all the wrong choices in life. Why he had always denied authority to the little voice inside his head. Why he had always taken the easiest way out, and too often the wrong way.

But in this moment of mental agony, he couldn't come up with answers. He reasoned most people were just as confused as he was. Life was nothing more than humans gathered together in mass confusion.

If there was an after-life, Steve thought, maybe he would be able to look back and laugh at the stupidity of it all. Maybe he would even be able to laugh at himself.

But alone in this hospital bed, it was hard to see the funny side of things.

And if God was laughing right now, then he had a sick sense of humor, Steve thought.

As soon as breakfast would arrive, which happened to be seven-thirty on the dot, he would request another phone call to Amanda

Ryan. And the nurse would probably tell him she was too busy, and he would have to try again later.

This would go on all day, like the day before.

So today, Steve thought he better come up with another idea, because he wasn't going to lay there and feel sorry for himself, and let Hugh Gawler get away with it.

Even though his burns made it difficult to fight on, he was determined to get in touch with Amanda Ryan. She would be the only one who would believe him. She was also the only one determined enough to find the truth. After all, it was her idea to spy for CableNews in the first place.

Damn it! Steve Thorn wasn't even sure he could make it another week. The doctors said he would live, but he didn't know whether he wanted to. What kind of life would he live after coming out of this mess? Just trying to think where he would be in a year's time made him cringe. Probably on a wheelchair in some under funded government refuge housing for invalids and the likes.

Slowly, he looked around the room for his clothes. The nurse probably put them in the wardrobe next to the bed.

Since he couldn't get Amanda Ryan on the telephone, he would have to see her face to face.

Even if it meant crawling out of this damn hospital.

CHAPTER 115

At 11.24 p.m. Amanda parked her SUV two blocks from the CableNews building. There was no point parking in the underground car park. Her SUV would arouse suspicions, especially at that time of the night there weren't many cars around, apart from the security night watchman's gray Toyota sedan.

She walked straight down the main street and turned left to the main entrance of the CableNews building. She swiped her photo access employer's card and punched in her personal identification number. She cringed for a few seconds, wondering if Hugh had already invalidated her access card. But the light on the security monitor went from red to green. She moved forward and the door opened automatically.

Once in the building, she would go straight to Hugh's office. The night watchman's office was on the ground floor.

As Amanda walked up the stairs of the entrance of the building, trying to remain confident so as do not attract any unwarranted attention, she thought maybe the reason Hugh never asked her for the access card was because he was going to get her killed anyway. Or maybe he just had plainly forgotten.

She shivered at the thought, remembering how close she had been to death near the entrance of the LAPD headquarters only a few days ago.

Looking self-assured, Amanda placed her access card in the pocket of her jacket. She pushed the main glass door, glancing behind to see if anyone was following her. She passed the security cameras quickly. She knew night watchman were useless anyway. Most of them sat behind their monitors, reading a novel or flicking through a pornographic magazine. If the alarm didn't wake them up from their day-dreaming, they never bothered looking at the video monitors.

Casually, Amanda walked up to the elevator. She moved her index forward, ready to push the UP button, but decided against it.

Taking the back stairs would attract less attention.

Apart from the night watchman, the building was empty at that time of the night. Still, the sound of the lift might arouse suspicion. She didn't like the idea of having to explain what she was doing at 11.30 p.m. in the CableNews building. She was in clear breach of trespassing, and right now she couldn't think of one good story to tell the night watchman if he caught her.

She opened the door leading to the stairway. The stairway was well lit, but without windows it felt like a prison cell. The enclosed atmosphere made her shiver. She closed the door carefully, making sure not to slam it.

Carefully, she climbed the stairs one at the time. If Hugh Gawler had locked his office, as he tended to do, Amanda would have to find a way to get in. She didn't know anything about lock picking, but she would figure a way once she gets to the door.

Within five minutes, she reached the ninth floor. Breathless, she stopped for a short while.

Suddenly, as she was about to open the door which led to the office, she heard a noise coming from down the staircase.

Bang!

One of the doors from the other floor was slammed.

She stopped moving, feeling the pounding of her heart beat.

Who could it be?

She listened while slowly sliding to the wall.

At first, she didn't know if it was her imagination, but as it became louder, she realized the noise coming from the stairway were footsteps.

And the footsteps was getting closer.

Amanda slowly reached for the door knob. As she opened the door, the hinges made a dreadful creaking noise.

The footsteps stopped.

Whoever was down the stairs must have heard the hinges creaking.

Her hand still on the door knob, Amanda froze.

She listened.

The footsteps started again, but this time at a slower pace.

Amanda knew she would have to move fast. She couldn't wait until whoever was downstairs would come up and see her in the building. What if it was a security guard? Maybe it was better if she just faced up to the person and showed her access card. The guard would think she was still an employee. After all, it had been less than a week since she had stopped working for CableNews. But who was to know, especially when she still had her employee's identification card with her.

Gently she closed the door and moved towards the staircase, looking over the railing. She couldn't see anyone, only the spiral effect of the staircase which made her feel somewhat nauseous.

The footsteps were getting closer.

'Who is it?' Amanda said, listening to the echo of her own voice bouncing from one end of the staircase to the other.

The footsteps stopped.

No answers.

'Is anyone there?' Amanda asked.

No answer.

She knew she made a mistake by speaking up. If the person downstairs was a security guard, he would have said something by now.

Quickly, Amanda opened the door leading to the office and ran into the corridor.

Before the door closed itself, she heard the footsteps pacing up the staircase.

Amanda never realized how frightening an empty office could be at night time.

She stood for a few seconds.

There was no time to waste. She had to think fast. Whoever was coming up the stairs would be there any minute.

Quickly, she rushed to her office. She turned the knob, but the door was locked. She looked for her keys, but panic-stricken, she was unable to find them.

Damn it!

The walls around seemed to be caving in on her.

Almost delirious, she paced to Michael's office.

It was locked as well.

Suddenly, she heard the creaking hinges of the ninth floor staircase door.

She froze.

Quietly, she sneaked to the reception and knelt under the desk.

The floor was covered in red plush carpet. She listened, but she could no longer hear the footsteps.

Like an animal trapped in a cage, waiting to be put to sleep, Amanda felt the fear closing in on her. She couldn't explain it, but she smelled death only minutes away.

She had to think fast.

Amanda reached for the drawer on the right side of the desk.

Locked.

She couldn't hear the other person, but she could feel his presence. It was a male—she knew it. A man's presence felt different to a woman's. He was very close to her now. She could almost hear his heart beat.

Trapped between the reception desk and the chair, she looked up to the wall for a sign.

Her eyes almost bulged out when she saw the shadow of a man holding a gun in his right hand.

Frightened, she stood up, knocking her head on the desk.

The shadow froze.

Amanda opened her mouth, her jaw locking up, no sound coming out.

The shadow moved in, pointing the gun towards the reception desk.

'I found you, bitch,' the shadow said.

The last thing Amanda saw before closing her eyes was the barrel of the .38 pointing at her head.

CHAPTER 116

Los Angeles: Long Beach Memorial Medical Center, 7.37 a.m.

Steve Thorn managed to leave hospital before breakfast. No one noticed he left the building because he took the back door.

Getting dressed hadn't been easy, especially with all the burns. His flesh felt raw. He couldn't believe how painful burns were, and furthermore, he couldn't comprehend where he found the tolerance to sustain so much pain.

Outside, the air was cool, but Steve couldn't feel it. He tried to keep a straight face. He didn't know how much longer he would be able to stand on his feet. Everything around him felt artificial, as if he was having a bad dream. He wondered if he made a mistake by leaving the hospital.

Soon, he reached a bus stop and waited with a group of young people, equipped with back bags, obviously taking the first step towards a trip or an excursion.

Stan felt the stares of the young people, but he pretended not to notice. He didn't care. He knew he would have to get used to it if he decided to live through the ordeal.

The only subject on his mind, apart from the pain and agony of the burns, was Amanda Ryan.

Where would he find her? If she didn't answer her telephone at home, this meant she wasn't there. Or maybe something had happened to her. Maybe Hugh Gawler got to her first.

Oh, God, don't let it be so!

Steve knew he would never be able to live with himself if Amanda had been killed. If he had insisted for her to stay at CableNews, nothing would have happened to her. He wasn't even sure why he felt so much for her right now. It was only a few weeks back when he didn't care one way or another what happened to her. But now that he had brushed shoulders with death, he knew how precious life was.

At first, he had seen Amanda Ryan was nothing more than a sexual fantasy. Only now he realized what a fool he had been. Blinded by his lust, he never saw Amanda as a person like everyone else. The feelings he had for her now was quiet strange. He never had a child, but he felt this father figure empowering him. Maybe it was because he was so close to death. Maybe he could see the whole picture. He had to tell Amanda the truth. She was still young and so determined to succeed in journalism. If she exposed the entire scam, her career as a journalist would skyrocket.

But this was only a secondary concern to Steve. The most important thing was to make sure she was safe from Hugh Gawler.

The bus stopped adjacent to the bus stop, and the young people jumped in first.

Steve took his time. The burns were excruciating. He could only move slowly.

The driver gave him a strange look as if to say 'what the hell are you waiting for?'

Steve bought his ticket and sat at the back of the bus.

He had thought about how he was going to find Amanda. The obvious was to try her place, but he knew she wasn't there because she didn't answer the phone. If she didn't answer the phone, it could mean only two things. Either she was dead, or she had moved somewhere else. If she was dead, the police would know about it. But if she moved to another place it would be harder to trace her.

The bus stopped near the Southern Plaza building.

The young students got out of the bus, yelling and carrying on.

Steve Thorn looked at them with an air of regret. There were so many things he had missed out on. He always put work ahead of everything, and now he couldn't remember if his years at university were happy ones. In fact, life only seemed to be an endless stream of deceptions and disappointments.

And then Steve laughed out loud.

The driver and the few passengers tried their best to ignore him

But he laughed until tears came to his eyes.

Laughing made everything much easier.

Not better, but easier.

The driver of the bus shut the doors and took off.

Life was so cruel, Steve thought, and yet so just. When he heard years ago everything in life had a way of coming back, he laughed it off. But now, he knew it was true. His greed for money, his carelessness with people and his gambling problems had paved his way.

Alone in the bus, Steve Thorn realized he had gotten where he was because of his own deeds. And it hurt. Not only did he have to deal with the pain, but also with the realization he was a fool.

And he laughed.

CHAPTER 117

Detective Stan Moore was in his office at the LAPD headquarters at 100 West 1st Street.

He was shouting into the phone receiver.

'I don't care if he's in or not!,' Stan Moore yelled. 'I want a warrant to search the place now...and yes, for the five hundredth time, I do have enough evidence to justify an application for a warrant. Have the damn thing on my desk by two o'clock.'

The detective slammed the receiver and looked at his watch: 12.46 p.m. That gave him over an hour to organize a search team.

And then he was going to turn the offices of CableNews upside down.

When he spoke to Amanda that morning, she told him about Henry's suicide attempt at CableNews. She also told him how Hugh took the gun from him, and somehow, the gun get back into Henry's possession. With Amanda's report, he had enough power to obtain a search warrant.

And it was what he was going to do.

CHAPTER 118

The hitman took a step back.

'You can get out from under there,' he said, still pointing the gun to Amanda's head. 'And no silly moves like the last time.'

Shaking, Amanda dislodged herself from under the reception desk. Even in the dark, she recognized the face of the man who tried to kill her in front of the LAPD building.

'What do you want?' she said.

'Never mind,' he said, grabbing her under the arm. 'This time, you're not going to run away from me.'

Amanda stood up, her knees shaking. She felt the barrel of the gun pressing hard against her temple.

'You're hurting me,' she said, jerking her head to the side.

'You don't have to worry for much longer. Because where you're going, you won't feel a thing.'

The hitman pushed her towards the staircase. 'Let's go the same way we came,' he said. 'We don't want to alert anyone.'

'How did you get in the building?' Amanda asked.

'I just followed you.'

'But I had an access card.'

'And I didn't. Now move.'

Amanda thought if she could only distract him by asking questions, she might have a chance to escape. But with the gun stuck to her head, escaping for the killer's grip seemed impossible.

'Where are you taking me?'

The hitman didn't answer.

'Who sent you to kill me?'

'Just keep moving,' the hitman said, pushing Amanda past the door of the staircase.

'You going to kill me, aren't you?'

'Correct.'

'At least you could tell me who paid you. I'm going to be dead anyway.'

The hitman was annoyed. He didn't have time to play mind games with his victim. She had already fooled him the last time he tried to kill her. And now she was going on and on with her questions. 'If you don't shut up,' he said, 'I'm going to do you here and now.'

Amanda swallowed her saliva. She sure in hell didn't know how she was going to get out of this one. Maybe this was really the end. After all this search and running around, she was going to be found in a dark street somewhere in L.A., just like Henry Limar. And after a few days no one would care. She would be just another statistic.

The gun pointed to the back of her head, Amanda walked down the stairs, unable to see the hitman. She never expected her life to end this way. Maybe she should have just gone back to Australia as soon as trouble started brewing instead of playing private detective. She realized how naive and irresponsible she had been. Especially when Detective Stan Moore had offered protection after she nearly got killed in front of the LAPD building. But no, she wanted to take the matter into her own hands, thinking she knew better, believing she was clever enough to unveil the mystery behind the deaths of Senator Trevor Garry, Henry Limar and Gavin White. And the mystery was probably behind her back right now, in the form of a man pointing a gun at the back of her head.

But even now as she was certain she was going to die, she still wanted to find out the truth. Something in her had to find out.

'You know I'm going to die,' she said to the hitman without looking behind, 'so you may as well tell me who you work for.'

'No chance, honey,' the hitman said, pushing the barrel further against Amanda's skull. 'Keep moving.'

Amanda stopped. 'I'm not moving another step until you tell me what's going on.' She couldn't believe what she had done. She closed her eyes, expecting a bullet to blow her brains.

The hitman froze in disbelief. The girl had to be joking. If he wanted to, he could kill her right here. But it was impossible. Too many questions would be asked if the police found her body in the CableNews building. It had to be somewhere else.

'Get your arse moving,' the hitman said, forcing the gun into her head.

'I'm not going anywhere until you tell me what's going on.'

Hell! Where in the world did she come from?

'I'm tired of this nonsense. Get down the stairs now or I'm going to blow your fuckin' brains.'

Amanda hesitated. She could do as he told her, and she would die anyway. Or she could continue to probe her killer, and she would die anyway. But if she didn't ask anything, she would never know the truth. And since she was going to die, wasn't she better off dead knowing the truth than not knowing it? Did it really matter one way or the other?

There was only one thing Amanda was certain about.

She didn't want to die.

CHAPTER 119

Detective Stan Moore was at his desk, looking over a ballistic report from Homicide when Steve Thorn walked into his office.

'Detective Moore?' Steve asked.

The detective looked up, surprised to see the overweight blistered man walking into his office.

'What the hell happened to you?' Stan Moore asked.

'My car blew up.'

And then the detective remembered. The car which blew up in a car park a few days ago.

'You name was?' Steve said.

'Steve Thorn.'

'Sure, I know who you are. The guy who runs CableNews.' Steve offered him a seat. 'You're out of hospital already?'

'I'm not supposed to be. I had to see you.'

The detective raised one eyebrow. He couldn't wait to hear what the burned man had to say.

'What's on your mind?' Steve asked.

'I'm looking for Amanda Ryan.'

'Ah, yes. Well, it seems a lot of people are looking for Miss Ryan these days.'

'I know.'

'What exactly do you know about young Miss Ryan?'

'She's in grave danger.'

The detective sat straight on his chair. 'Well, Mr Thorn, that much we know too. What about all this spying business? Did you have anything to do with it?'

'It was her idea.'

'So you say. Why are you looking for her?'

'I need to talk to her.'

'About?'

'The person who tried to kill her.'

'And you know who this person is?'

'I might.'

The detective scribbled on his notepad. 'You're looking very uncomfortable, Mr Thorn. Are you sure you're going to be okay?'

'I'm fine.'

'Can I get you a glass of water or something?'

'Water would be nice.'

The detective stepped from behind his desk. 'Won't be a minute.'

Steve Thorn was left by himself in the office. He looked around, wondering how someone could work in such a mess. His office was always tidy in comparison to this one. In movies they always showed cops' offices as messy. And now Steve Thorn knew it was real.

Sixty seconds later, the detective came back with a paper cup filled with cold water.

'Here you are,' Stan Moore said, passing the paper cup to the burned man. 'You sure look like you should be in hospital.'

'I know. But I have to find Amanda Ryan.'

Stan Moore took his seat back behind the desk.

'Is there anything you'd like to tell me about who tried to kill Miss Ryan?'

'I need to find her.'

'I understand, Mr Thorn. But you're coming to my office claiming you know who tried to kill her, so you must understand why I'm a little nosy.'

Steve Thorn looked at the detective straight in the eyes. The cop was right of course. What did Steve expect? A chauffeur ride to wherever Amanda was? But he knew he could tell anything to the detective. Not just yet.

'I really have to talk to her.'

Stan Moore shook his head. 'I know you're trying to do good. But can't you see if we work with you on this, we'll have a better chance to save Miss Ryan?'

Steve Thorn stood from his chair. 'Thanks for your help, detective,' he said. 'I think I can handle it from here on.'

The detective rolled his eyes. Steve Thorn was obviously determined not to reveal anything he knew. If he walked out the door, nothing would have changed. Amanda Ryan was still in danger. Steve Thorn would probably be running around in circles trying to find her. And the detective would just drive himself crazy wondering what was going on.

Stan Moore stood from behind his desk. 'Hold on a minute,' he said. 'We're on the same side. We can work on this together.'

Steve Thorn glanced back at the detective. 'It's not so easy,' Steve said. 'You cops think everything is black and white. You think once I tell what I know you can just fix the whole problem with the click of a finger. Believe me, it's not so easy.'

'But if you don't at least give me a try, what chance do I have to help you?'

Steve Thorn stared at Stan Moore for a few seconds. What was he supposed to do? Of course he wanted to save Amanda. Of course he wanted Hugh to pay for his crimes. And of course he didn't want the White House to go up in flames. But who would believe him? Well, detective, it's like this. Hugh Gawler, Executive President and owner of CableNews Corporation, is in fact a terrorist. In a few days, he's going to blow up the White House. How do I know this? I knew about the death of the Senator before it happened. I knew about the death of Gavin White. I knew about every other crime he committed. And I know he tried to kill me because I knew too much, and he probably felt it was too dangerous to have someone around who knew so much. So there you have it detective. How can you help me?

'Why don't you just help me to find Amanda,' Steve Thorn said, 'and then I'll keep you informed about everything else I know.'

'By then it might be too late,' Stan Moore said.

'It's a chance you're going to have to take. Easy you help me find Amanda, or we're going separate ways.'

The detective didn't take much persuasion. The burned man obviously knew a lot about what was going on. What the detective had to do know is get the man to trust him. And the only way to do this was to give him a reason to trust him.

'Okay,' the detective said. 'I'll help you find Miss Ryan.'

CHAPTER 120

Amanda Ryan felt the gun digging into her ribs.

The hitman pushed her down the stairs. 'If you don't hurry up, I'm going to hurt you.'

Amanda lost balance and almost tripped down the stairs. She turned around to face her killer.

'Why are you doing this?' she yelled, 'You want to kill me? Then go ahead, shoot!' Enraged she pointed to her face. 'Shoot me now and get it over with. I'm sick and tired of all this crap. You want to shoot me, then do it now.'

The killer was losing patience. Stupid bitch! he thought. You want to die, then die. He pointed the gun towards her. 'That's the way you want to end it, fine with me.'

Seeing the barrel of the gun in front of her face, Amanda no longer felt brave and crazy. But she maintained her composure. 'Go ahead, I dare you to shoot.'

The gun shot echoed up and down the stairway.

CHAPTER 121

LAX: Monday, 2.02 a.m.

Hugh Gawler was tired from the 4.5-hour trip from Washington D.C. His meeting with Sam Willicon hadn't gone as well as expected. The Militia leader would go ahead with the bombing of the White House, but it would be the last time Hugh Gawler wanted to deal with the man or his Militia.

It had always been Hugh Gawler's number one rule to be in control. And when he met Sam Willicon at a coffee shop that morning, Hugh didn't feel in full control. That was bad news. Sam Willicon wanted more money. The next time he would ask for even more. And then he might even black mail Hugh Gawler for anything else he wants.

Hugh Gawler didn't want to find himself in a situation where he would have to kill Sam Willicon to guarantee his own safety. The last thing he needed was an entire Militia group on his back. It was bad enough he had been watched by the FBI on his back since his drug days in New York.

When Hugh Gawler left the airport, the air was cool. He pulled his collar and hailed for a cab.

'Where to?' the cab driver said.

Hugh gave him his home address. 'On second thoughts,' Hugh said, 'take me to the CableNews building.'

The driver nodded.

It was the middle of the night, but Hugh felt like being in his office. He needed to ground himself again after the trip to Washington. And he also wanted to check for any messages while he was away. He also needed to know if he had got rid of Amanda for good.

Glancing in the rear mirror, the driver smiled to himself when he saw his passenger sipping alcohol from a small silver bottle.

CHAPTER 122

The sound of the shot rang in Amanda's head. She didn't feel a thing. So that's how a bullet in the brain feels, Amanda thought.

That's when she realized she was thinking. And if she was thinking, how could she be thinking if her head had been blown away?

'Amanda,' the voice said.

Her eyes still closed, Amanda couldn't believe she was still breathing. Slowly she took one deep breath. Yes, she was still alive. She raised her hands to her face and felt it. The nose was still there. Her flesh was whole. Her eyes, her hair were here too.

And that voice.

'Amanda,' the voice said, 'are you okay?'

Amanda opened her eyes.

In front of her lay the body of the hitman in a pool of blood. He had been shot in the temple.

Quickly, Amanda turned around.

Michael looked like a ghost who had seen a ghost. In his right hand, he held a silver .38 semi-automatic.

Still shaken, Michael climbed the stairs.

'What are you doing here?' Amanda said, unable to comprehend what happened.

'He was going to shot you.'

Amanda looked at the dead hitman once more and then back at Michael.

'You shot him?'

'I shot him. He was going to kill you.'

'He was going to kill me?' Amanda was still in shock. She had lost sense of time and place. She looked at Michael, barely recognizing him.

'That's right, he was going to kill you. I was just on my way up, and he said he was going to kill you. And you said go ahead shot.'

326

'I did?'

'You did. And why did you tell him to shot? Jesus, Amanda, if I hadn't been here, you would be dead by now.'

Shaken, Amanda sat on the stairs.

Michael walked up to her, took his jacket off and placed it on her shoulders. 'We don't want to hang around here for too long,' Michael said, fearing someone might have heard the gun shot.

Amanda sobbed.

Michael gave her a hug. It was good to feel her next to him. It was good to know she was still alive. When she left him after they had the argument, he couldn't help feeling guilty. He knew if Amanda got in trouble, he would have blamed himself for the rest of his life. So he went after her. But he never knew he was going to get there just when she was about to get killed.

Having Michael so close to her made Amanda feel secure. She began to understand what had happened only a few minutes ago. And now she was angry someone had come after her.

'I'm so sorry,' Michael said.

'Sorry for what?' Amanda said, her voice sounding more confident than it did when Michael came and sat next to her.

'Sorry I didn't come with you in the first place. I didn't know it would be so dangerous for you. If I had known, I wouldn't have left you all by yourself.'

'You were not to know. And what are you complaining about anyway. I'm here, aren't I?'

That much was true.

Michael would have gone completely insane if Amanda had been shot. The whole incident happened too fast. He had never shot anyone before. He hated guns in the first place. He only kept the .38 because it was a gift from his father. But this time, he didn't give himself a chance to think. When he saw the killer with the gun, Michael had to shot. It was the killer or Amanda.

Amanda managed to get on her feet. 'We better leave this place.'

'Do you know who this guy was?' Michael asked, while helping Amanda to stand up.

'The same jerk who tried to kill me in front of the LAPD building.'

Amanda told Michael how she was being followed in the building, and how the killer dragged her from under the reception desk.

'How long had he been following you for?' Michael asked.

'I don't know. I didn't notice I was being followed.'

'What about the security cameras in the building? And how did

327

he get in the building?'

Michael and Amanda looked at each other.

'The security guard!' Amanda gulped.

'Hell!' Michael said.

They raced down stairs to the security room

When they arrived in front of the room, the door was half open.

'Stay there,' Michael said, blocking the way to Amanda.

Michael pushed the door.

The security guard was laying on the floor with a gunshot to the head.

'What's going on?' Amanda, peering through the door way. When she saw the guard on the floor, she tried to say something, but no words came out of her mouth.

'Hell!' Michael said. 'What are we going to do now?'

Amanda took Michael by the hand and out the room. 'We have to get out of here.'

'What about the security guard?' Michael said. 'We have to call the police.'

'If you call the police, they're going to charge you with murder.'

'That was self-defense. I was only trying to save your life.'

Amanda thought for a few seconds. Michael was right, but with everything gone wrong lately, she wasn't sure she wanted the cops involved. The last time she got in touch with the police, she nearly got gunned down.

'I'll take my chances,' Amanda said. 'But I don't see how the police are going to help us.'

'My God, Amanda. They're going to think we killed both the guard and the idiot upstairs.'

'Nobody knows anything about us.'

Michael knew they couldn't stay in the building forever. Sooner or later they would have to decide whether to call the police or not. If they did call the police, at least he wouldn't feel in such danger. It would make things easier. But what if they did arrest him and charge him with murder. How long would he be in jail before a trial? There was no way Michael wanted to go to jail. He heard many stories about jails, and finding himself in one was his worse nightmare.

Amanda shook Michael by the arm. 'We're going or what?' she said, wanting desperately to leave the building.

'All right,' Michael said.

Amanda closed the door of the security room.

'I left my bag on the ninth floor,' Amanda said. 'I must have dropped it behind the reception desk.'

'Okay,' Michael, 'let's hurry up, get the bag, and get the hell out of this place.'

They took the elevator to the ninth floor.

Amanda found her bag behind the reception desk as she had anticipated.

As they turned around, ready to leave the building, the engine of the elevator turned itself on.

Michael and Amanda looked at each other puzzled.

They ran quickly to the elevator.

The light stopped in the building's underground car park.

'Somebody's here,' Amanda said. 'Let's go.'

'God damn it!' Michael said.

'What now?'

'I parked my BMW in the underground car park.'

CHAPTER 123

When Hugh Gawler stepped out of the cab in the underground car park of the CableNews building, he didn't notice Michael's BMW straight away. He paid the cab driver and told him all he had to do to leave the car park was to press the red EXIT button on his way out.

'You sure have strange working hours,' the cab driver said.

Hugh Gawler didn't answer. How ironic, he thought, a cab driver doing night shift commented on his hours of work.

Just before he reached the elevator, Hugh saw the front of the BMW sticking from behind a concrete stump.

He looked at his watch.

2.45 a.m.

Who could be in the building so early in the morning? At first, Hugh thought it might have been the security guard. But when he got closer to the car, he recognized the model of the car. As far as he knew, security guards did not go around driving BMWs.

On close inspection, the BMW looked like Michael Hall's car.

Hugh Gawler walked around the vehicle, looking for anything suspicious. The driver's door was unlocked and the alarm was not activated. Hugh tried to reason how at three in the morning in a secured private car park, there was little reason to switch a car alarm on.

But still, Hugh knew something was wrong. There was absolutely no reason for Michael Hall to be in the building so early.

Hugh's thoughts raced to Amanda Ryan.

She was dead.

At least, he thought she was dead.

And Michael was having an affair with her. Hugh Gawler was certain of it.

Did Michael knew Amanda got killed?

Hugh retrieved his .38 semi-automatic from his briefcase. He checked it was loaded. The handgun was capable of holding eight rounds. Satisfied, Hugh hid the handgun behind the small of his back and headed for the elevator.

After swiping his access card and punching in his PIN number, Hugh pressed the UP button and waited anxiously.

If Michael was upstairs, then it would have something to do with Amanda. There was no other reason why Michael would be in the building.

The elevator opened. Hugh stepped in.

Hugh had worked with Michael Hall since the formation of CableNews. He took Michael on board because Michael was straight out of university and eager to make his mark. The young rookie was still wet behind the ears, ready to believe in anything. But Hugh didn't want to corrupt Michael at the beginning of his career. Michael was the type of man who lived and breathed ethics. It would have taken him another two or three years before he could have confided in Michael.

But now, it seemed Michael could have double crossed him. Of course, Hugh wasn't sure, but the stakes were high, so Hugh didn't want to take a chance.

If Michael got in the way Hugh would do what he had to do.

Kill him.

CHAPTER 124

'Let's go through the front door,' Amanda said.

Michael watched the elevator lights climbing towards the ninth floor. 'But my car is underground,' Michael said.

'I know, but we don't need your car. I've got mine parked a few streets from here.'

'What about the bodies?

Amanda raised her eyebrows as if to say so what?

'My car's in the building. Two men are dead. Who do you think is going to be the main suspect?'

Amanda looked at the light from the elevator getting closer to the ninth floor. She grabbed Michael by the hand. 'Come on, let's take the stairs.'

They ran past the elevator and towards the staircase.

Just when Amanda closed the door of the staircase, the door of the elevator came open.

CHAPTER 125

Hugh Gawler walked into the corridor.

The door of the elevator shut itself behind his back.

The .38 semi-automatic in his hand, Hugh Gawler walked slowly around the hallway, his back to the wall.

'Michael?' he said, almost in a whisper.

No answer.

Hugh moved closer to Michael's office.

'Michael? Are you there?' Hugh said.

No answer.

When he got to Michael's office, he turned the knob.

The door was locked.

Where is he?

Hugh walked to the reception desk, and then to his office.

The door of his office was locked. It didn't look as if anyone had been there. Then why was Michael's car parked downstairs? Maybe he left it there overnight for a particular reason.

No matter how many ways Hugh tried to convince himself there was a simple explanation, his gut feeling told him otherwise.

Hugh opened his office door and walked in the room.

He closed the door and turned the lights on. Everything seemed in place. No one had been in his office while he was away for two days.

Feeling the tiredness wearing him down, he sat behind his desk and flicked the computer on.

Just then, in the quietness of the night, he heard the roller door from the underground car park. At least it's what he thought he heard.

Hugh stood from his chair and walked to the window.

He did hear the roller door from the underground car park.

His eyes followed Michael's BMW until it reached the corner of the street.

Damn it!

Michael had been in the building after all.

Hugh knew he would have to move fast.

Very fast.

CHAPTER 126

Stan Moore's Saturn stopped in the driveway of Amanda Ryan's home. The yellow police tape had been removed. Crime scene had ended twenty-four hours ago. Stan Moore thought Amanda had decided to go back home. After all, where else would she go?

The detective killed the engine and stepped out of the car.

A few seconds later, Steve Thorn, opened the passenger door and joined Stan Moore at the front door of Amanda's home.

The detective knocked twice.

'She won't be in,' Steve Thorn said. 'I told you I've rang a hundred times since yesterday, and she hasn't answered the phone.'

The detective rang again. 'Maybe she doesn't want to answer the phone.'

After sixty seconds, no one came to the door.

Stan Moore thought quickly and said: 'I'm going in.'

The burnt man didn't want to argue. He knew Amanda wasn't in the house. The detective was wasting his time.

Stan Moore pushed the door which was unlocked.

Both men looked at each other.

Stan Moore walked in first, his gun in his hand.

'Amanda Ryan?' he said. 'Are you in there?'

The detective listened for an answer or a noise.

No one answered.

Steve Thorn flicked the light on, blinding both men for a split second.

'God damn it!' Stan Moore said. 'Thanks for the warning.' The detective rubbed his eyes, trying to adjust his sight to the sudden brightness.

'You're wasting our time,' Steve Thorn. 'It's obvious she's not in the house.'

Stan Moore was getting irritated. 'If you know so much,' he said, 'then why do you need me to find her?'

335

Steve Thorn swallowed his saliva. He didn't like to be patronized, but he needed the damn cop to find Amanda.

'Look,' Steve said, 'I'm just trying to save us some time here. And you should know time is not something we have plenty of.'

'Thanks for the lecture. If you didn't keep everything bottled up inside, maybe I would have a better idea of where I could find Miss Ryan.'

The detective went walked carefully to the living room.

'I'm sorry,' Steve said, wondering why in the world he was apologizing. 'I'm pissed with this as much as you are.'

'Amanda?' the detective said, raising his voice. After a few seconds, he turned to the burnt man. 'All right, she's not here. So where the hell could she be?'

'Hell, don't look at me. I came to you.'

'You were her boss, right?'

'So?'

'You knew her well?'

'She'd only been with us for six months.'

'And what about the spying business. Did you put her up to it?'

'It's really none of your business.'

'None of my business? Well, I'm telling you now that it's god-damn my business.' Stan Moore moved up close to Steve Thorn. He shouted : 'I don't care whether you got fried like a piece of bacon. If you don't cooperate with me, I'm going to have you arrested for interfering in a homicide investigation.'

Steve Thorn looked up to the sky. 'Fuck!' he said, 'Great. You're going to arrest me when I'm trying to help you find the killer.'

'You're not helping one damn bit here. You said you knew who the killer was—'

Steve interrupted: 'I said no such thing. I said I might know who the killer was. And if you continue to talk to me in a accusative tone, I'm going to get a lawyer and not say another word until I get counsel.'

Still angry, the detective moved back a couple of steps. He knew he shouldn't have lost his temper the way he did. Steve Thorn was supposed to trust him and then confide in him. But by yelling at him, nothing was going to happen.

'Hey, look,' Stan Moore said. 'I was out of line. You've got to understand it's hard for us too. I just want to make sure the girl doesn't get killed.'

'It's what I want to,' Steve Thorn said. 'We're on the same side.'

The detective slipped a cigarette between his lips. 'So how well did you know Mrs Ryan?'

'Like an employer to his employee.'

'Details?'

Steve Thorn rubbed his chin with his hand. 'She was intelligent. Maybe too intelligent for her own good.'

'What else?'

'She was determined. The whole spying thing was her idea. She wanted to find out why our ratings were screwing up while CableNews had gained so much ground in so little time.'

'And?'

'And, and... and what?'

'Did she have any friends? Family?'

'All her family is in Australia. Friends? Don't think so. Never seen her with anyone during the entire time she worked with us.'

'No boyfriend?'

'Nope.'

'What about this Michael Hall?'

'Who?'

'Michael Hall. The guy who works for CableNews.'

'Young rookie?'

'Yeah, him. Do you know him.'

'Nope.'

'Was she seeing him?'

'Don't know.' Steve Thorn could see no point with all the questioning. 'I don't know why you're asking me all these questions. I don't know a damn thing about her, all right?'

'Then why do you want to see her so badly?'

'Save her life.'

'What is it you know that could save her life?'

'I've already told you I wasn't going to discuss anything with you until I find her.'

'Okay, fine with me.' Stan Moore walked towards the front. 'If she didn't know anyone, and if she has no family in L.A., then where the hell could she be?'

'It's what I hope you were going to tell me,' Steve said, now wondering why the hell he ever bothered going to the police for help.

The two men returned to the Saturn.

'So you got no idea where she could be staying,' Stan Moore asked, desperate to get a lead of some sort.

'If I had an idea, I wouldn't be here with you talking riddles.'

Stan Moore started the engine and reversed the car from the driveway.

Even if it took all night, Stan Moore was determined to find Amanda Ryan.

CHAPTER 127

Amanda and Michael arrived at his apartment in shock.

'My God,' Michael said, 'I've killed someone. What am I going to do? What the hell am I going to do now?'

Amanda grabbed him by the arm. 'Get a hold of yourself. Everything is going to be all right.'

'How do you know? So far, everything has been going from bad to worse. I don't know if I can take much more of this.'

Amanda was surprised Michael had less strength than she did. But then he had much more on the line. If the cops found the body in the CableNews building, it would take them little time to find the the bullet in the hitman's head matched Michael's gun.

'What do we do now? Jesus, what do we do now?' Michael said. He was becoming hysterical.

Amanda ran to the living room. 'Let me get you something to drink. You need to lay down and relax.'

'Relax? Are you nuts? It was your idea to break into the building.'

'Sure, but that man was going to kill me either way. It just happened to be in the building.'

Amanda filled a glass of bourbon and gave it to Michael. He drank it almost in one go.

'You have to get a grip on yourself,' Amanda said. 'If we want to win this game, you have to focus.'

'Game? I don't know, but this surely doesn't feel like a game to me. Is this what it feels like to you? A game?'

'You're being unreasonable. It was only a figure of speech.'

Michael gave her his empty glass. 'Give me another one of those.'

Amanda walked to the bar and filled the glass again. What was she going to do with Michael? Let him sleep it off, and then she would take care of the rest. But what would she do next? So far she had learned nothing. The only thing she was certain about was someone wanted her dead. And it didn't take much to guess this someone had something to do with Hugh Gawler. Who was the man who tried to kill her? Who did he work for? Did Hugh pay him to get rid of her? If so, why?

Amanda had already figured out in the past it probably had something to do with the videocassette Gavin White was supposed to have received.

As she poured the glass of bourbon, she realized what she had to do.

Find the damn videocassette

But where would it be? Did Henry Limar send it to the prison? To Gavin's place? To another address? And if the videocassette had been sent to Gavin's place, then how come it hadn't turned up anywhere yet?

Taking the drink to Michael, she knew what her next step was.

'Thanks,' Michael said as he took the glass of bourbon from Amanda. This time Michael drank the second glass slowly. The effect of the first glass was showing. Michael felt more relaxed.

'Why don't you stay here and rest,' Amanda said. 'I'm going to go and get something to eat.'

'Are you crazy? They're out there to get you!' Michael said.

'No one's out there.'

'You nearly got killed tonight. If it wasn't for me-'

'The guy is dead. He was the only one who tried to kill me. And what do you want me to do anyway? Stay around here to see what happens next. If there is someone after me, then I better keep moving. Maybe the next time they won't miss me.'

'Oh, God!' Michael said as he fell back on the couch. 'Do what ever you want.' He rubbed the back of his head. 'I'm getting a damn headache.'

'I won't be long. I promise,' Amanda said, grabbing her handbag from the coffee table.

'Sure. Makes me feel a whole lot better.'

Amanda ignored his last comment and went straight to the front door. She had to get to Gavin White's apartment. Maybe the videocassette was still there. Maybe the cops hadn't looked carefully.

As she climbed into Michael's BMW, she knew this was her last chance.

CHAPTER 128

Hugh Gawler grabbed the phone and dialed the number on his electronic diary. The phone kept ringing, but there was no answer.

What the hell is he doing? Hugh asked himself, banging the oak table with his fist.

The hitman hired by Hugh Gawler in conjunction with the Texan Militia was suppose to carry his cell phone at all times. And now Hugh couldn't get in touch with him. Damn it! It was really important Hugh found out whether Amanda had been killed or not. Only then would he be able to assume why Michael Hall was in the office in the early hours of the morning.

Hugh placed the receiver back in its cradle.

He looked at his watch.

3.32 a.m.

By now he should have gone home to get some sleep, but his thoughts kept him agitated. If Michael's car was parked in the underground car park, and he left after Hugh had gone up by the elevator, then how did he get down? There was only one elevator. Maybe he was already in the car park. Or...

The staircase!

Hugh rose to his feet.

The damn staircase. Michael must have ran down the staircase when he saw the elevator going up. Why didn't he just wait for the elevator to reach its destination and take him back down? Obviously, he must have had something to hide.

Hugh checked the .38 semi-automatic was still attached to his belt before blazing out of the office.

He sure as hell wasn't going to get double-crossed.

CHAPTER 129

Amanda Ryan parked her SUV in front of Gavin White's apartment. Or what used to be Gavin White's apartment.

Gavin's letter box was filled with junk mail. Amanda wondered why no one bothered cleaning up the letter box. A cramped letter box only told potential burglars no one had been in the apartment for a while.

Under a street light, she emptied the letter box. She placed the contents on the edge of the brick veneer fence. Quite a lot of the mail was advertising material. There were a few letters with a window at the front. Bills which hadn't been paid and never will. Amanda scanned the names on the letters. All of them were addressed to Gavin White.

All but one.

Amanda held the cream envelope to the street light.

```
Jacqueline Chambers
6/14 Batman Avenue
```

Amanda was intrigued. She didn't know Gavin White lived with a woman. In fact, she knew Gavin White didn't live with a woman. His life story had been in the papers for days. She had read everything about him. Gavin White was a bachelor and had been all his life.

Jacqueline Chambers.

Looking around to see if anyone saw her, Amanda wondered if she should open the letter.

Hell, why not.

She ripped the top of the letter by sliding the nail of her index finger along the edge.

The paper inside the envelope was the same cream color as the envelope.

She held the letter close to the light:

```
Dear Jacqueline,

It's been a while since we've heard from you.
We're having a get together at my place on Saturday.
Why don't you come and join us. Who knows, you might
meet someone you fancy. Give us a call soon so I
know if I have to count you in. Take care.

Love,
Rachel.
```

Amanda read the letter again. Maybe it got into the wrong letter box. At that thought, she grabbed the envelope. The address said 6/14 Batman Avenue. She grabbed the rest of Gavin White's mail. The addresses on the other letters said 14/6 Batman Avenue.

Amanda smiled.

Obviously the postman made a mistake. The cream letter was suppose to have gone to Jacqueline Chambers.

As she was tossing the letters back in the letter box, the cream-colored letter sent to the wrong place sparked an idea. If the postman made a mistake by mailing a letter at 6/14 instead of 14/6, then maybe the same postman made another error and delivered Henry Limar's videocassette to the wrong address.

Of course! Amanda almost jumped with excitement. This would explain why nobody knew where the videocassette was.

Amanda looked at her watch.

4.27 a.m.

Too early to go and knock on some stranger's door.

Annoyed, Amanda looked up to Gavin's apartment. Although she felt like going home for a sleep, she decided to use the few hours left to see what she could find at Gavin White's apartment.

Her head heavy, Amanda climbed the stairs of the hallway, wondering how much longer the chase would take. She grew tired of the cat and mouse game. But she knew she couldn't stop just yet. If she gave up, they would find her.

And kill her.

CHAPTER 130

Washington D.C., 6.23 a.m.

Sam Willicon woke up with a headache. The phone kept on ringing, and he didn't know whether it was ringing in his dream or in the outside world.

He sat on the edge of the bed and realized the ringing came from the living room.

Damn! Who could it be so early in the morning?

He stood naked on the wooden floor and ran for the phone in the other room.

'Yeah?' he said, half sleepy, when he picked up the receiver.

Hugh Gawler was at the end of the line. He told Sam he found the body in the staircase.

'Who killed him,' Sam said, now fully awake.

'It looks like one of my employees.'

'Christ, he was my best hitman!'

'And you told me he would kill Amanda. This guy is dead, and I don't even know if Amanda Ryan is still parading around, sticking her nose in my business or talking to the cops.'

Sam Willicon pulled the receiver away from his ear. He just lost his best man. The last thing he needed was some stuck-up yuppie from Los Angeles giving him a lecture on business ethics.

'He was the best, okay,' Sam said. 'I want to know who the fuck killed him. I'm going to get the sonofabitch!'

'Your guys are bloody useless. Don't think I'm going to pay for this one. You stuffed up.'

'I didn't stuff up, all right. He did. I can send another man. We'll find Amanda Ryan and get rid of her for good.'

'Thanks for the offer, but I'll take care of the problem myself. You get this White House bombing on the way.'

344

'Fine with me.'

Sam hung up and walked back to the bedroom.

He hated doing business with Hugh Gawler. The man was a pain in the arse, and Sam Willicon didn't need this right now. There were enough of those in the government and police departments.

He slipped back between the sheets and tried to go back to sleep.

But he couldn't.

His best hitman was dead.

The White House bombing was only hours away.

Hugh Gawler was giving him a hard time.

And, God damn it, he wasn't sure he wanted to live this lifestyle any more!

CHAPTER 131

6.31 a.m.

Amanda Ryan looked everywhere in Gavin White's apartment. The police had taken all the evidence. The only things left in the room were furniture. The place was still sealed with yellow police tape, but now Gavin White was dead, it wouldn't be long before the apartment would be put up for lease.

Disappointed she hadn't found anything, Amanda walked back down the stairs and removed the cream-colored envelope from her pocket. She looked at it:

```
Jacqueline Chambers
6/14 Batman Avenue   .
```

The address indicated it was only a few blocks away. A walking distance, Amanda thought. She decided to leave the SUV in front of the apartment.

She checked her watch and realized it was only 6.40 a.m.

Was it too early to get a stranger out of bed?

What the hell! This is important.

She walked passed a house and a block of flats. Aware someone might be watching her, she looked over her shoulder a few times. No one was in the streets so early in the morning. She thought she would have at least met a few early morning joggers or someone walking the dog. But the street was dead quiet and eerie.

When Amanda arrived in front of 14 Batman Avenue, she stood there to regain her composure. What was she going to say to the woman? Excuse me, have you got a videocassette which doesn't belong to you?

Amanda wondered why she was being so self-conscious, especially when she had done so many cold-calls when interviewing for the murder of Senator Garry and his family.

Her chin up, she walked the courtyard of the flats until she reached door number 6.

She stood in front of the door, took a deep breath, and gave three hard knocks on the wooden door.

Her knees shaking, she looked at her watch.

6.45 a.m.

God damn it! It is early.

CHAPTER 132

Hugh Gawler hung up the phone.

He was angry Sam Willicon's hitman hadn't been able to do his job properly. Who in the world can you trust these days to get a proper job done? Amanda was probably still at large. And soon the office staff would be coming to work.

Hugh knew he would have to call the police soon. The body of the hitman was in the trunk of his car. He would have to get rid of it later. Nobody had to know the hitman got killed in the building. But the security guard was dead. And Hugh had no choice but to call the police. If he didn't, the whole thing would fall back on his head.

He removed a card business card from his pocket and dialed the LAPD number.

'Detective Stan Moore?' he said when someone picked up the phone at the other end.

CHAPTER 133

Steve Thorn was too tired to go on.

'Why don't you drop me back at the hospital,' Steve said to Stan Moore.

Both men were sitting in the Saturn in front of a Seven-Eleven store.

Stan Moore was chewing nervously on a yellow-iced doughnut and washed down with a cup of black coffee, no sugar, no milk.

'Yeah, yeah,' Stan said, his mind wondering everywhere but the present time. 'Where could she be?'

Before Stan had time to finish his coffee, his cell phone rang.

'Detective Moore,' Stan said, a mouthful of coffee.

'There's been a murder at the CableNews building,' the dispatcher said.

'Who? What?' Stan sat straight on his seat.

Steve Thorn tried to listen.

'A security guard got shot overnight,' the dispatcher said. 'We got a call just a few minutes ago.'

The dispatcher told Stan Moore it was Hugh Gawler who asked for him.

'I'll be there in a minute,' Stan said and pressed the END button of his cell phone.

Stan Moore turned to Steve Thorn and said: 'I'm taking you back to hospital. I've got an emergency to attend.'

CHAPTER 134

Michael Hall woke up with a headache. He had too much to drink. It took him a few minutes to recall the events at the CableNews building.

God, damn it!

Everything in his mind was chaotic.

Soon he would have to make a choice. There was no way he could have everything, and he knew it.

Amanda or his future.

CHAPTER 135

Jacqueline Chambers was still in bed when someone knocked on the door. Heavy banging.

The cops!

It was the first thought which came to her mind. She got out of bed and walked slowly to the window.

It had to be the stupid cop and his videocassette He probably found out she gave him the wrong videocassette, and now he was coming back to give her trouble.

For a second, Jacqueline thought about the marijuana plantation in the bathroom. Two small plants. Hardly a plantation.

Two knocks, this time louder.

Jacqueline peered through the window.

It wasn't the cop. It was some young woman dressed *à la* executive. Maybe she was another cop. At least it was better than talking to the other arrogant cop.

Jacqueline put on a bathrobe and walked to the front door.

Play it cool. Act normal. Just be yourself, and she will go away.

She turned the key of the deadlock and opened the door.

CHAPTER 136

When the door opened, Amanda stared at the woman in front of her, unable to say a word. Her hair was messy. She wore a dirty bathrobe with stains around the collar. A cigarette was hanging from her mouth.

'What do you want?' Jacqueline said.

'Jacqueline Chambers?'

'Who wants to know?'

'I'm a journalist.'

Jacqueline Chambers twitched. A journalist? It was better than a cop.

'What can I do you for?'

Amanda told her about the videocassette

'And what makes you think I've got the videocassette?' Jacqueline Chambers said, crossing her arms.

'I don't know whether you have it or not. I'm just asking.'

'I don't have the videocassette any more.'

Amanda glanced quickly behind her. No one was in the street.

'You don't mind if I come in? I feel a bit awkward standing out there.'

Jacqueline Chambers glanced at her from head to two.

'Yeah, sure. Come in,' Jacqueline said. 'You've got a nerve to bang at someone's door so early in the morning.'

'I'm really sorry,' Amanda said as she stepped in the hallway.

Amanda followed Jacqueline to the kitchen. Dishes were piled up on the sink, and cigarettes filled two ashtrays on the kitchen table.

'Would you like a coffee?' Jacqueline said, already removing to mugs from the sink and rinsing them under water.

'It would be nice,' Amanda said, wondering why she agreed. She feared catching some kind of disease from the dirty mugs.

'So,' Jacqueline said, 'as I said, I already gave the videocassette to

352

someone else.'

'Who?'

'Some cop who came around the other day.'

'What cop?'

'Hold on a sec.' Jacqueline reached on top of the fridge. 'There.' She handed Amanda a business card. 'Detective Stan Moore, an arrogant little shit.'

Amanda took the card. So the detective had the damn videocassette

'When did you give him the videocassette?'

'Yesterday. Or was it the day before?' Jacqueline said as she reached for a cigarette inside her bathroom robe.

'Did you watch the videocassette?'

'Yeah.'

'What was on it?'

'News footage. Nothing special. Just news stuff.' Jacqueline stood in front of the kitchen bench. 'How do you have it.'

'Eh?' Amanda was still looking at the business card.

'Your coffee.'

'Regular.'

Amanda wondered why the detective hadn't contacted her yet. If the videocassette showed something then he would have tried to contact her. At least it's what she thought they had agreed on. Or didn't they?'

'You don't mind if I use the bathroom?' Amanda said.

'First left at the end of the hallway,' Jacqueline said. And then she remembered the marijuana. 'I smoke a bit of pot. Don't mind the two plants in the bathroom. Don't go and tell anyone.'

Amanda smile. 'It's really none of my business.'

Jacqueline Chambers turned her back on her and continued to make the coffee.

Amanda closed the door of the bathroom. She looked at herself in the mirror. She realized she looked more tired than she thought. The colors she wore on her face a few weeks back had turned white. Bags under her eyes showed the little amount of sleep she has had. She peered into her eyes and saw nothing. Not fear or joy. Nothing. She wondered if she had lost the zest to live. And if she did, was it obvious to other people.

Then she glanced around the bathroom and saw the two marijuana plants near the window. She found it funny she had never tried drugs, not even soft drugs like marijuana. And it wasn't like there wasn't enough to be found. During her school years, there was always a kid whose parents grew some of the stuff in the backyard. Drugs was freely available to anyone who wanted them. Amanda never gave much thought about them. All she knew was she didn't feel the need for them. It frightened her more than anything else. She could not stand the idea of casual drug usage becoming an addiction.

She walked to the hand sink and rinsed her face under cold water. When she pulled her head up, she thought about the videocassette What was all this chasing around with the videocassette if there was nothing on it but news footage? Now she feared she might be on the wrong track. If there was nothing on the videocassette, she was just going around in circles. And then, whoever had sent someone to kill her might send someone again.

She closed her eyes and saw the hitman aiming a gun at her face and the gun going off. The image of the previous night would be engraved in her mind for a long time. She knew it would take years before she would be able to think of a gun without feeling nauseous.

A knock on the door.

'Are you all right in there?' said Jacqueline Chambers from the other side of the door.

Amanda opened her eyes, wondering for a few seconds where she was.

'I'm coming,' Amanda said, conscious she has been in the bathroom for more than ten minutes.

She fixed her hair, smiles quickly at the mirror, and opened the door of the bathroom.

CHAPTER 137

When Detective Stan Moore arrived at the CableNews headquarters, three police cars were already at the scene. There seemed to be more media vans than any other vehicle.

A young male journalist had a microphone stuck under Hugh Gawler's nose.

'Did they take anything?'

'Nothing is missing from the premises,' Hugh Gawler said, standing straight and looking very much in control of the situation. In fact Stan Moore felt than Hugh Gawler was actually enjoying the experience.

The detective pushed his way amongst the reporters, flashing his badge, yelling: 'Police. Move to the side'.

Hugh Gawler noticed Detective Stan Moore pushing his way towards the top of the stairs.

'And here's my good friend Detective Stan Moore,' Hugh Gawler said into the microphone of the reporter.

The reporters turned to the detective.

'Any comments on the murder took place this morning,' one of the reporters said.

'No comments.'

'Do you think this has anything to do with the suicide of Henry Limar?'

'No comments.'

'Detective, this is the second employee of this company who has died in less than a month. Any connections between the two deaths?'

Stan Moore kept his lips sealed, wondering how so many reporters got here so fast. One thing was certain. Hugh Gawler didn't seem publicity shy. In fact he was willing to bet Hugh Gawler had organized the media conference.

When Stan Moore reached the top step where Hugh Gawler was

standing, Hugh grabbed him by the arm.

'Ladies and gentlemen,' Hugh said, 'this is Detective Stan Moore. He's been looking into the death of Henry Limar. I'm sure he will be able to answer any questions you have.'

Stan turned to Hugh and gave him a dirty look. But before he had time to let a word out, Hugh continued his speech.

'This incident is a shock to all of us here at CableNews. We will work hand in hand with the Los Angeles Police Department to find who is responsible for the crimes committed in this building.'

The detective turned to Hugh and whispered in his ear: 'Do you mind?' Then he turned to the crowd of reporters and smiled. Back to Hugh: 'Can I see you in your office?'

Hugh Gawler turned to the crowd. 'We'll have to leave it for the time being. Detective Stan Moore and I have some matters to discuss.'

The cameras continued to roll as both men entered the building.

Once inside the foyer, Stand Moore could no longer suppress his anger.

'How dare do you organize a press conference and tell everyone we're working together,' the detective said, almost screaming in Hugh's ear. 'This building is now sealed off from the press and the public as of now!'

Hugh Gawler smiled. 'Excuse me, but I didn't mean to offend you. I thought it would clear any confusions of the public knew straight away where CableNews stood.'

'For your information, CableNews is not another branch of the Los Angeles Police Department. You have no right to talk on my behalf or to assume I'm going to be working hand-in-hand with you to solve anything.'

Hugh turned to face Stan Moore. 'Have you got a problem, detective?'

'Yes, I do.'

'What's bothering you?'

'You are. Don't think I don't know about your past. Playing high class media executive. I know where you come from. I know you dealt in drug trafficking. I know you got charged.'

'All those charges were dismissed. Never proven. As far as the law is concerned I'm a perfectly innocent man.'

'You certainly play the game well.'

'I don't have to take this arrogance.' Hugh pressed the button of the elevator. 'Why don't you escort yourself out of the building?'

'I haven't finished here, and I haven't finished with you.'

'Well you have to excuse me. But I've got some work to do, so this time I won't be by your side while you're making a nuisance of yourself on my premises.'

The elevator door opened. Hugh Gawler stepped in. He pressed the ninth floor button.

'Now if you don't mind, detective, I've got some urgent matters to attend.'

Stan Moore lodged his foot between the two closing doors of the elevator. The doors came open again.

'What are you doing?' Hugh Gawler said, his white face reddening.

'Don't patronize me, Mr Gawler. You are in no position to talk to me this way.'

'And why not?'

'Because right now you're my number one murder suspect for the death of Henry Limar, Senator Trevor Garry and Gavin White.'

Hugh Gawler swallowed his saliva. 'You're crazy,' he said and pressed the number nine button of the elevator. 'I want you out of this building as soon as you're finished investigating the death of my security guard.'

The detective let the door of the elevator close itself.

He knew he was losing the battle.

CHAPTER 138

Washington: Wednesday, 9.06 p.m.

Sam Willicon hung up the phone and smiled.

Everything was going like clockwork.

The bomb hidden in the White House and set to explode at exactly 9.00 p.m. The following day. Almost twenty-four hours from now.

Satisfied by his performance, Sam Willicon grabbed a can of beer from the fridge. He pulled the ring and gulped half the contents of the can in one go. He closed his eyes and two seconds later burped his heart's content.

When all this bombing business would be over, Sam Willicon would seriously consider retirement. He had enough money to live on for the rest of his life. And since he couldn't stand the political system in America, he was thinking about spending the rest of his days on a beach somewhere in Mexico. Down there no-one knew who he was. No-one would hassle him when some other Militia group decides to blow up a government building.

He knew the government was targeting the Texan Militia, especially after the Oklahoma bombing. FBI agents were always snooping around the training center It would only be a matter of time before an agent would infiltrate the system from the inside. Every move the Militia makes would be monitored by the FBI. And then, when the Militia would least expect it, the FBI would raid the training center

Sam was waiting for the Wacko incident to repeat itself.

But he would get to the government first.

Soon the White House would be no more.

CHAPTER 139

The President of the United States of America rushed down the corridor and into his office.

He had canceled his two-thirty appointment with Foreign Minister John Taylor.

Flushed, he sat behind his desk and picked up the phone.

'I put you through now,' said the voice at the end of the line.

The President waited a few seconds.

'Mr President?' said Bill Major, Special FBI Agent in charge of the Bureau's Washington Division.

'Yes, Mr Major,' the President said, his lower lip shaking nervously.

'We have inside information a major bombing will take place in the next twenty-four hours.'

'Really?'

'Similar to the Oklahoma bombing.'

'Where? What? God damn it! Don't make me guess.'

'We have someone on the inside of the Texan Militia right now. The bombing is going to take place right here in Washington D.C.'

The President rattled his throat. 'Who's your source?'

'Not one of our men.'

'And how do you know he's telling the truth?'

'We've paid him a lot of money.'

'What building are we talking about?'

'He won't say.'

'Make him say it.'

'We've tried everything, Mr President, and he's agreed to disclose the information on one condition.'

'Which is?'

'Complete immunity in writing and $10 million dollars into a bank account of his choice.'

The President banged his fist on the oak table.

'I want you to get this clown and make him speak.'

'I'm afraid it's impossible, Sir.'

'Why not?'

'We don't know the identity of the informant. The only thing we're certain about is he's from Los Angeles. We've traced back the telephone calls to L.A. The informant always uses a telephone booth when contacting us.'

'Twenty-four hours?'

'It's what he said, Mr President.'

'What are the chances of evacuating every government building in Washington within the next twenty-four hours?'

'Impossible unless you want to create mass hysteria.'

The President grabbed his silver pen and tried to chew it. What if the informant was bluffing? What if there was no bombing? But the Oklahoma bombing was damn real. It happened. There was a good chance this bombing would take place as well.

'Mr President?' John Taylor said. 'Are you still there?'

'Yes, I'm here.'

'What do you want us to do?'

'I want you to keep an eye on the Texan Militia's activities and try to track down this informant.'

'Sir, we've only got twenty-four hours if he's telling the truth.'

'Report to me in twelve hours.'

The President hung up.

Someone in Los Angeles was playing a dirty game. Someone wanted to get paid on both sides.

The President placed the palms his of his hands against both sides of his head, ready for a mental combat with the opposite sides of his brain.

Should he just authorize the $10 million payment to avoid the bombing? What if the informant was bluffing? The President didn't like to be taken for rides. If the bombing was a bluff, and disclosure of the government paying $10 million for blackmail was leaked to the media, there would be no chance of re-election.

Gerald Standford removed his hands from his head.

Hell, he had no choice.

This time it was war.

CHAPTER 140

Amanda Ryan left Jacqueline Chambers's apartment confused. Now she knew Detective Stan Moore had the videocassette, but she couldn't understand why he hadn't told her.

Her next step was to get in touch with him.

She walked back to the SUV parked in front of Gavin White's apartment. The traffic was moderate. People were starting to make their one-way morning journey to work. Amanda would have been doing the same thing if she hadn't started this whole spying business with CableNews. But she no longer wished things were different. She knew something was wrong, and she felt an obligation to make it right.

Climbing inside the SUV, she glanced quickly in her rear mirror. Her eyes were puffed from tiredness. But the need to find out the truth kept her going.

She turned the engine on and crunched on the manual gear-box. She turned off Batman Avenue.

The traffic was much heavier on the highway.

Anxious, she wondered what story the detective would come up with. Could he be involved in this whole scheme? Was he covering up something? Amanda shook her head from left to right, not worried about what other drivers thought. She couldn't believe the detective had anything to do with the murders. He seemed so dedicated to help her. And yet, every time someone seemed dedicated to help her, they turned out to be someone different from what she expected.

From the next two miles, she thought about Michael Hall. Her emotions were now in turmoil, and she wondered what she felt for him. Was it love? At times she was certain she loved Michael more than anyone in the world. But when Michael acted irrational, she didn't know what to make of him. She was still young, not really her fault. There would be many men walking in and out of her life. And if she felt Michael wasn't the right person, she didn't have to force

361

herself to live with him for the rest of her life. They made no promises to one another. In fact, marriage had never been a topic of conversation.

Amanda suddenly realized how much she missed belonging somewhere, how much she needed a home. It was the reason why she thought of Michael as a prospective husband.

If I love him enough, she thought.

Thirty minutes later she parked the SUV in front of the Los Angeles Police Department.

She stepped out of the SUV and looked towards the stairs were the hitman tried to shoot her. As she walked to the stairs she realized how desperate the hitman must have been to shot at her in front of a police station. What she wanted to find out was who paid him to kill her? Obviously someone who wanted the videocassette badly. Someone who was featured in the videocassette And she was sure as hell it couldn't be the detective. Only one name echoed in her head.

Hugh Gawler.

CHAPTER 141

Steve Thorn lay on the hospital bed. He was exhausted, but couldn't get to sleep. Daylight kept him awake. He always found it hard to sleep during the day.

When he arrived back at the hospital with the Detective Stan Moore, the nurse in charge wasn't happy. Even though the detective explained he was the one who asked Stan Moore to come and see him, she didn't seemed pleased by the explanation. As far as she was concerned, she had a responsibility to keep on eye on every patient in the hospital. If anything happened to them while they were under her supervision, she would be held liable.

The detective left in a hurry, and Stan Moore had to endure another half hour of verbal abuse. Hell, if he hadn't been in such a bad shape, he would have taken his belongings and left the hospital. But all he wanted was to lay in bed and forget about life for a while.

However, he knew he would never find peace of mind.

Not until he had found Amanda Ryan.

CHAPTER 142

Hugh Gawler was pacing up and down his office.

He tried to hide his fear every time the telephone rang or someone walked into his office.

But the body in the boot of his car made him nervous.

What if the police decided to check the cars downstairs? And since Detective Stan Moore now told him he was the number one suspect, the chances were high. Even if the cops wouldn't check the other cars, they might check his for the sake of it.

The reality of what might happen started to make him lose patience. He couldn't live with the idea of having to go through another major court case and have his face plastered all over the papers. No matter which way he turned the story in his head, he couldn't figure out what he would say if the police found the body of the hitman in the trunk of his car. He had to get rid of the body as soon as possible.

Hugh walked to the bar fridge and poured himself a glass of Southern Comfort.

He had to focus now.

Trembling, he swallowed the content of the short glass in one go. Better. He didn't feel as nervous any more.

He poured himself another glass.

God damn it! He couldn't figure out what the hitman was doing in the staircase in the first place. Was he after Michael Hall? But he never told the hitman to kill Michael Hall?. He was only supposed to get rid of Amanda Ryan and Steve Thorn.

He swallowed the contents of the second glass of Southern Comfort.

Now he felt more in control.

Focus.

So, if the hitman was in the staircase while Michael was in the building, and he wanted to kill Amanda, then it could only mean one thing.

Hugh managed to walk a straight line to his desk. His body had become accustomed to the alcohol. It would take far more than two glasses to get him dizzy. The only thing the two glasses had done was put him in a relaxed state of mind. And it's exactly where he wanted to be. He needed to think fast and clearly.

Now, if the hitman wanted Amanda Ryan, then she must have been with Michael Hall. And the both of them were in the building at around two in the morning. When they saw Hugh arrive, they fled. Did they meet the hitman on the way to the car park?

What does it matter? Hugh thought. The point was Amanda was probably still walking around like a time bomb. She was too clever for her own good, Hugh had often told himself.

He grabbed his car keys from the office desk.

It didn't matter if the cops were still in the building. He had to get rid of the body.

And then of Amanda Ryan.

CHAPTER 143

'Detective Stan Moore?' Amanda asked at the inquiry desk of the Los Angeles Police Department.

'Just a sec,' the receptionist said.

Amanda waited while the receptionist dialed the detective in his office.

A few seconds later, the receptionist turned to Amanda: 'I'm afraid Detective Stan Moore is not in his office. Can anyone else help you?'

'Do you know where he is?'

'He's been out all night. He's probably gone home.'

'It's really important I get in touch with him.'

'You're sure another officer can't help you.'

'I have to see Detective Stan Moore.'

'Hold on a sec,' the receptionist said and returned to her telephone.

Amanda waited impatiently. The Detective had been out all night. Doing what? And then she realized maybe he had been looking for her. In the last twenty-four hours she had been hiding from one place to another. It would have been impossible for anyone to find her.

'Detective Stan Moore,' said the receptionist, 'is on a call right now.'

'Any chances of finding out where?'

'He's attending a murder at the CableNews headquarters building.'

Amanda felt a surge of electricity running through her body. A murder? At once she thought Michael Hall had got killed. But, no, he couldn't have. He had been with her all the time. She left him back at his apartment.

'Who got killed? Amanda said, redness on her face.

'I don't have such information,' the receptionist said. 'I can give you the detective's mobile number?'

Amanda felt her whole body tremble. She couldn't wait any more. 'It's okay. I'll just go straight to CableNews.'

Frantic, Amanda rushed out of the building and to her SUV. Then her logic returned. How silly of her. Of course the dead body must have been hitman's.

Or the security guard's.

Or both.

CHAPTER 144

Detective Stan Moore was in the security room of the CableNews building when a uniformed officer approached him.

'Detective, I thought you'd like to know Mr Gawler is leaving the building.'

The detective lifted his head. 'When? What?'

'Just now, sir. I saw him taking the elevator to the underground car park.'

'Damn!'

Stan Moore left everything behind him and rushed to the elevator of the building.

Maybe Hugh Gawler was running away from the scene of the crime. He was probably scared Steve Thorn was going to find something, some kind of link which would put Hugh Gawler, and then maybe he was just attending a business call.

The elevator took ages to come.

The detective looked patiently at the numbers ascending on top of the doors.

Hugh Gawler was guilty as hell, and he knew it. How? The detective wasn't sure. Why? It was another mystery in itself.

The doors of the elevator finally opened and the detective stepped in. He pressed the button of the underground car park.

God, he wished he could solve this case and go back to living a normal life. He was getting too old for running around like a madman. This kind of lifestyle had already cost him his marriage, and now it was costing him his health. He made a quick mental calculation and realized he hadn't slept for at least thirty hours in a row. Not a healthy habit for a man of his age.

When the door of the elevator opened, the detective saw Hugh Gawler walking towards his car.

'Hold it right there,' Stan Moore yelled.

Hugh Gawler turned around, losing the color from his face.

CHAPTER 145

Michael Hall was relaxed. At least he convinced himself he was in spite of the bumper-to-bumper traffic on Route 66.

It would take him another twenty minutes or so to make it to the CableNews building.

As he patiently cruised behind a white Dodge, he wondered if someone had found the bodies of the hitman and the security man yet. They must have. He was running late, and he knew some come company employees were already running frantic, trying to empty the bulk of their in-trays before lunch.

As the BMW made a right turn, Michael wondered who had been in the building at two in the morning, just after he and Amanda found the dead security guard. Maybe it was another hitman. Maybe the killer had an accomplice. And maybe the accomplice wondered why the hitman took so long to kill Amanda, so he decided to check for himself.

But all these thoughts didn't get him any closer to the truth. Who wanted Amanda dead and why? Amanda was convinced it was Hugh Gawler, but Michael Hall didn't want to jump to any conclusions. He had known Hugh Gawler since the formation of CableNews, and although he didn't always approve of Hugh's methodology, he couldn't see why his boss would want to kill anyone.

Especially Amanda Ryan.

Michael pressed his foot flat on the accelerator and overtook the white Dodge.

CHAPTER 146

Amanda Ryan parked her SUV in a no-standing zone, apposite the CableNews building.

Across the street, she saw five police cars parked awkwardly between the pedestrian walk and the road.

She stepped out of the SUV and crossed the road, zigzagging between the peak-hour traffic.

If she was lucky, Detective Stan Moore would still be in the building.

Anxious, she rushed to the front of the building.

A police officer placed one hand on her shoulder.

'You can't go in there.'

'I have to see Detective Stan Moore.'

'I'm sorry, but Detective Stan Moore is busy right now. Why don't you see him back at the office.'

'It's urgent.'

The police officer looked at her from head to toe. 'What did you say your name was?'

'Amanda Ryan. He knows who I am.'

'Just wait here.'

The police officer went inside the building.

Amanda looked around and decided to go through the underground car park. She ran to the corner of the building and entered through the main entrance of the underground car park.

The security guard stepped out of his booth.

'Can I help you,' he said.

'I need to see Detective Stan Moore.'

'I'm sorry, but I've got orders to let no-one enter the building.'

Amanda searched in her bag for her ID card.

'I work here. I have the right to enter the building.'

The security guard approached her and took the ID card she was presenting.

'Miss Ryan?' He looked at the ID photograph and then at her face. 'You're the new journalist who started a few months back.'

'It's right. Now can I get through?'

The security guard didn't like the way Amanda looked nervous. He could smell something was wrong. But then with a dead body in the building, it might have been normal every one looked a bit out of place.

'Why didn't you take the front door?' the security guard asked, now determined not to let her in the building.

'Because they wouldn't let me go in.'

'I'm sorry. But I have instructions to only let senior personnel enter the building.'

God damn it!

Amanda snatched her ID back from the security guard. 'Have it your way,' she yelled as she walked back to the exit.

Just then, a car drove quickly into the building, nearly running her over.

'Why don't you watch where you're going? Jerk!' Amanda screamed.

The black BMW stopped beside her.

'Amanda,' Michael said, his hands gripped on the steering wheel. 'What are you doing here?'

Amanda looked towards the security guard, smiled and stepped inside the BMW.

'Let's go. Detective Stan Moore is in the building and he's got the videocassette'

The BMW raced towards the security guard.

CHAPTER 147

As Hugh Gawler got closer to his car, he heard the voice again.

'Hold it right there,' Detective Stan Moore said.

Hugh Gawler turned around, forcing himself to smile. He stood there not saying a word. What did the detective want now? Hugh Gawler thought about the body in the boot of the car. I hope he's not going to search the car. He remained calm on the outside, but on the inside he was ready to burst with fear and anger.

'What is it detective?' he finally said, hoping to terminate any suspicions the detective might have had. 'Have you found the killer?'

Detective Stan Moore walked faster towards Hugh Gawler. Hugh was getting on Stan's nerve.

'Where do you think you're going?' Stan said.

'I beg your pardon?' Hugh said, raising his chin up in the air.

'You're not to leave this place until I say so.' Stan Moore stopped in front of the Hugh Gawler.

'You've got a damn nerve, detective,' Hugh said. 'I ring you up to let you know what's going on, and you treat me like a five year old kid.'

'You're under suspicion of murder. You're not to leave this building until I have finished with the scene of crime investigation.'

Hugh moved closer to the detective. 'Excuse me, detective. But is this something personal?'

'It could be if you insist on making an idiot of yourself.'

'Have I insulted you?'

'You—'

'I haven't insulted you, detective,' Hugh screamed. 'You're walking a very thin line, and you know it. I'm getting my lawyer on this and pressing charges against you and the Los Angeles Police Department for harassment.'

'Go ahead, you low-life scumbag.'

372

Hugh Gawler turned his back on the detective. 'I'm very impressed by the extent of your vocabulary.' Hugh reached the door of his car.

'You're not going anywhere,' Stan Moore said, removing his .38 semi-automatic from his holster. He aimed the gun at Hugh Gawler. 'Put your hands up where I can see them.'

Hugh turned around, his jaw wide-open. 'You've got to be joking.' He left his hands alongside his body.

'Raise your hands above your head.'

Hugh Gawler hesitated.

'Now,' the detective shouted.

'I'm going to get you for this,' Hugh said, his blood boiling through everyone of his veins.

Stan Moore moved closer to the detective and ran his hand under his jacket.

Hugh Gawler's lips were sealed.

The detective removed the .38 gun from under Hugh's jacket. 'Well, what have we here?'

'A licensed weapon,' Hugh said and smiled,' and a licensed shooter.'

'We'll see about that. And why would you be carrying a concealed weapon at work?'

'It might have something to do with how unsafe this city is becoming.'

'Cut the bullshit,' the detective said as he removed a pair of handcuffs from under his jacket. 'You're under arrest for carrying a concealed weapon.'

Hugh exploded: 'I'm telling you it's licensed!'

'I can't take your word for it. So I'll have to arrest you until I can check it out.'

Just when the detective grabbed Hugh by the arm, a black BMW came racing down the middle lane of the car park, screeching its tires, nearly running the detective over.

Avoiding the car, the detective dived on the concrete floor, feeling the full weight of his body.

When he looked up again, Hugh Gawler was reversing his car.

A stunned Michael and Amanda looked from the inside of the BMW.

The detective stood on his feet and pointed his gun towards Hugh's car.

'Stop it right there,' the detective said.

Suddenly Amanda jumped from the BMW and ran towards the detective. 'Detective Stan Moore,' she yelled, blocking the way of the detective.

'Get out of the way, God damn it,' Stan Moore said, unable to get a clear view of Hugh's car.

By the time Amanda realized what was going on, Hugh's car vanished into the next corner of the car park.

'What the hell do you think you're doing?' Stan Moore said to Amanda as he rubbed his bruised elbow.

'Detective, I have to see you.'

'Well, I'm here, aren't I?' He placed the gun back in his holster, and for the first time realized it was Amanda who was standing in front of him. 'What are you doing here anyway. I've been up all night trying to track you down.'

'The videocassette,' Amanda said.

'What?'

'The videocassette You've got the videocassette Why didn't you tell me?'

Stan looked puzzled for a few seconds. 'Oh, the videocassette Well, there was nothing on it. It was a hoax.'

Amanda looked disappointed. 'Nothing on it?'

'Just news footage.'

'And what's with him,' she said, pointing towards the direction where Hugh's car had just vanished.

'I was about to arrest him when you nearly ran me over.' Michael Hall was now standing next to Amanda. He looked at Michael in anger: 'And where did you learn to drive like an idiot?'

Amanda, Michael and Stan walked to the elevator.

'We need to talk,' Amanda said.

'Steve Thorn wanted to see you badly,' Stan said, trying to make eye contact with Amanda.

'About what?'

'You didn't know about the explosion?'

'What explosion?'

'Steve got blown up in his car.'

'When?' Amanda looked at Stan, shaking her head. 'Who did this?'

'He wouldn't say, but he wanted to see you badly.'

'Did he say why?'

'He claims to know who tried to get you killed.'

'Who?'

'Wouldn't say.'

They stood in front of the elevator.

'So where are we going now?' Michael asked, almost surprised to hear the sound of his own voice.

'To your office,' Stan said.

CHAPTER 148

Hugh Gawler looked nervously in the rear mirror. No one was following him. When he took a left turn at the next intersection, he heard the corpse in the boot of the car moving. He had to find a place and get rid of it quickly. But since it was daylight already, he would have to be careful.

He worried about what was going to happen now. For sure Detective Stan Moore would alert officers to be on the look out for him. Hugh had to be careful.

His heart beat increasing, Hugh kept on eye out for police patrols.

Quickly, he ran in his mind all the places where he could get rid of the body. He knew of a park two miles from his home, where people jogged early in the morning. This would do the trick. Not many people there at other times.

Hugh pressed his foot on the accelerator.

He played back in his mind the scene in the underground car park. He was sure it was Amanda he saw running out of the black BMW which nearly ran over the detective. So, she was alive after all. And now that she was with detective Stan Moore, things would only get worse.

Hugh had to think fast. There was very little time left. But he didn't care because he knew no matter what Stan Moore and his friends did, they would never be on time to stop the bombing of the White House.

CHAPTER 149

Amanda was looking nervously at Michael.

Detective Stan Moore sat in the chair behind the desk at Michael's office.

'I don't know what's happened here last night,' Stan said, looking at Amanda and then at Michael, 'but one security guard is dead, and we found blood in the staircase.'

Both Amanda and Michael kept their thoughts to themselves.

The detective expected them to make a comment, but when the two of them remained silent, he knew something was wrong.

Amanda looked up towards the windows overlooking the building across the road.

'Do you two know something I don't,' Stan said.

Looking confused, Amanda and Michael looked at each other.

'Such as?' Michael asked, turning his attention to the detective.

Stan Moore didn't answer straight away. He gave a hard stare to Michael. He looked at him straight in the eye, trying to see what was happening inside his head. And he could see fear. Michael Hall was scared and hiding something.

Michael gazed down to the floor.

The detective then looked at Amanda.

She gave him an awkward smile.

'Well, Miss Ryan,' Stan said, 'anything you'd like to share with me?'

'You've got the videocassette,' Amanda said. 'You're the one who's hiding something.'

Stan stood from his chair, slamming his hands on the desk. 'I've got something to hide? You guys never told me you knew each other. You've kept everything quiet all along. How much are you really telling me? Why is it Steve Thorn wants to see you so badly?'

'Why don't we go and find out,' Amanda said, 'instead of arguing like a bunch of idiots.'

'Let's do it,' Stan said, walking towards the door.

Michael looked around the room.

'Are you coming,' the detective said.

'I've got some work to catch up with. I think I'll give it a miss.'

'What?' Amanda said, not believing what Michael was saying. Was he going to leave her all by herself with the detective?

'I'll stay around the office. I've had enough of running around.'

'Suit yourself,' Stan said. He then turned to Amanda, 'Let's go.'

Amanda followed the detective. She looked at Michael one more time before leaving the room.

Michael gave her a quick smile.

Confused, Amanda didn't understand what he was doing, or why he had decided to stay behind at the office.

But when the detective and Amanda left the room, Michael sat comfortably behind his desk and punched a few numbers on the telephone pad.

CHAPTER 150

Hugh Gawler covered the body with leaves and stepped back inside his car.

Without giving it more thought, he put on his seat belt and took off.

His next stop was at the hospital. He hated the smell of hospitals, but today was a special trip.

He hadn't seen his friend Steve Thorn for a while.

CHAPTER 151

Steven Thorn was fast asleep when Hugh Gawler walked in the room.

'Hey,' Hugh said, probing Steve with his .38 semi-automatic. 'You're awake big boy?'

Steve opened his eyes. The voice of Hugh send a shiver up and down his spine.

'What are you doing here?' Steve screamed.

Hugh gave him a blow on the shoulder with the gun. 'Shut up! You're trying to wake the other patients up?'

His eyes filled with terror, Steve looked at him and said, 'What do you want?'

'Looks like you've got yourself a nasty burn.'

'Bastard.' Steve felt the rage building up inside him.

'Not nice. After all we've been through together.'

'Why don't you leave me alone.'

'Oh I will. In fact I intended to do then much earlier on, but things didn't exactly work out the way I planned.'

Steve understood Hugh had just admitted he tried to kill him. And now he had Hugh's gun probing inside his shoulder, he knew Hugh was not here for a friendly chat.

'You're a fool,' Steve said. 'You think no-one knows about you.'

'The only person who's giving me a real headache right now is you. And your little friend, Amanda Ryan.'

'Fancied her, didn't you?'

Hugh smiled. 'There was a time when I probably did. But you know what it's like. Women, they're all the same. You can't trust them. I thought once I got to know her, she would eventually begin to respect me. But no, she was too hung up with the likes of you.'

Steve shook his head. 'You don't know what you're talking about. The girl wanted out. She came to see me at the office. She said you tried to come on to her but she could not stand you. You made her want to puke.'

Hugh grimaced. 'You haven't changed a bit, have you? Always the competitive spirit. Just don't know when to stop, do you?' He pressed the barrel of the gun into Steve's temple.

Steve felt the burns on his face stretch, giving the impression his mind was going to explode.

'You're sick,' Steve said between his breath. 'You're not going to get away with this.'

'Good-bye, Steve. It was nice knowing you.'

Hugh pressed the trigger of the .38 semi-automatic.

Steve closed his eyes, waiting for the bullet to explode in his brain.

Just then the door of the room was swung open.

The nurse who had just walked in saw the gun pointed at Steve's head. 'What are you doing,' she said almost in a whisper, like if she was apologizing for disturbing the two men.

Hugh turned around. His eyes locked themselves into those of the nurse. He raised his gun. 'Get out of my way,' he said, pushing the nurse aside.

Steve lay still with his eyes closed. He was so sure he was going to die, he didn't hear what was happening around him.

The nurse fell to the ground as Hugh made his way down the corridor.

'Help!' the nurse screamed. She managed to grab the side of the bed and get back on her feet.

She saw Steve with his eyes closed, perspiration running down his face. She realized if she had walked in the room a few seconds later, Steve Thorn would have been dead.

She collapsed on top of Steve.

CHAPTER 152

Hugh Gawler ran down the hospital corridor. He looked behind, but no-one was following him. He realized he would create more attention by running, so he slowed down.

A patient wearing a blue bathrobe came from the opposite direction. The patient saw the gun in Hugh's hands. He said nothing.

Hugh noticed the patient saw his gun. As if nothing had happened, Hugh smiled at the patient and place the gun under his jacket. He had to get out of the hospital as soon as possible. In fact he had to get out of this town at all cost.

Just as he approached the main doors of the hospital, he saw Amanda Ryan and Detective Stan Moore walking up the stairs.

Hell!

He turned around hoping they hadn't seen him.

But as he walked back down the corridor, he saw   the patient with the blue bathrobe talking to a security guard. The patient was pointing to Hugh.

The security guard place his hand on his holster. He paced up towards Hugh.

Hugh turned around again and saw Amanda Ryan and Detective Stan Moore at the top of the stairs, looking as if they were arguing with one another.

He turned back to where the guard was.

'Hey, you,' the guard yelled, removing the .38 from his holster. 'Stay where you are.'

Hugh was trapped. He only had a split second to think. Confront the armed guard or come face to face with Amanda Ryan and the detective?

He removed the gun from under his jacket.

CHAPTER 153

Washington DC

Special Agent Bill Major picked up the phone on the second ring.

'Agent Major.'

'Have we got a deal?'

Agent Bill Major recognized the voice of the informant. He had to act smoothly. With twelve hours to go, the risk of messing up was to great.

'We got a deal.'

'Ten million dollars. Right?'

'I've talked to the President, and you know, ten million dollars is a lot of money.'

'No shit.'

'We're willing to give you five million.'

Silence.

'You're there?'

'I'm there.'

'Five million? It's still good money.'

'Listen to me, Agent Major: the government can waste a spare ten million dollars. They do it all the time.'

'Oh, really?'

'You're kidding me? All these assholes like you who get paid for doing nothing. Now I bet if we cut the FBI's work force in half, we'd save at least ten million dollars. And what about all these stupid space projects. Billions of dollars thrown in space for no reason. How dare you try to bargain me down for a tiny five million dollars? Do you realize when the explosion will be over the cost of repair would have exceeded those ten million dollars by a large margin?'

'You're being unreasonable.'

'Hey, look pal, I don't have the time or the patience for this. And frankly, neither do you. You guys are a bunch of morons. The world is just filled with morons. If I don't receive ten million dollars in the next twelve hours then boom!'

Agent Bill Major placed one hand on the receiver. He rubbed the bridge of his nose with two fingers. He didn't want to bargain anything any more. He had spoken at length with the informant, and he knew there would be no two ways about the deal.

Bill Major removed his hand from the receiver: 'Ten million it is.'

'I knew you'd come to your senses.'

The informant gave Special Agent Bill Major the banking details and the time where the money had to be transferred to a secret Swiss bank account.

'When we will get this information?' Bill Major said.

'When I get the money.'

Bill Major looked at his watch.

Two hours should be enough.

'Okay,' Major said, 'we can meet the deadline.'

'And remember: if the ten million dollars are not in the bank account on time, you'll have a lot of deaths on your conscious.'

The phone went dead.

Agent Bill Major kept the receiver to his ear for another thirty seconds. He wished he could get his hands on the informant and beat his face into a pulp. Major didn't like to take orders from anyone who was not a superior. Especially from spies and informants. When this whole thing would be over, he would make it his life mission to find the sonofabitch who dared to make him look like a fool in front of the President of the United States of America.

Special Agent Bill Major slammed the receiver in its cradle.

Two hours later, the FBI deposited $10 million dollars in an account in a bank in Zurich. The President had been furious no-one managed to track down the informant. Special Agent Bill Major's career had suffered a set back. He was now seriously considering early retirement to track down the informant.

Bill Major was still in his office when the call came through.

'Bill Major,' he said, showing no emotion in his voice.

'It's me.'

Bill Major didn't have to guess who me was. 'Have you got the information?'

'What's the rush? Okay, I've checked with the bank. The money's in.'

'Don't bother with the thank-yous. Who's going to bomb what?' Bill Major wasn't in the mood. He had been waiting for weeks to get his hands on this information. His patience had passed saturation point.

'Agent Major, let me ask you a question.'

'What?'

'How can you be sure I'm going to give you any information? How can you be sure I'm for real?'

'I don't. I took you word for it.' Major had to think fast. 'I guess you sound like someone who keeps his word.'

'But how do you really know?'

Major knew the informant was only playing games. The informant was only exercising his power. Major knew all about power play. Give the bastard what he wanted.

'I gave you my word on this. You've got your money. I trust you will deliver your part of the deal. You've got the power now. There's nothing I can do. You give me the information or you don't.'

'I'm beginning to like you agent Major. You have depth of vision. You know how the mind works. You're trying to flatter me. You wouldn't have graduated with honors in psychology by any chance?'

Bill Major had enough: 'Cut the bullshit. Just give me the god-damn information and stop being a fuckin' jerk!'

There was no sound at the end of the line for the next fifteen seconds. For a moment, Bill Major believed he had made a mistake by yelling at the informant.

'All right, Major,' the informant said. 'You don't have to get upset. I'm with you.'

The informant gave the information to the Major.

'Thank you asshole,' Major said. 'I'll see you in hell.'

Bill Major slammed the phone before the informant had time to reply. He looked at his watch. Plenty of time to evacuate everyone from the White House and organize a full-scale war on the Texan Militia.

CHAPTER 154

The security guard shot at Hugh Gawler.

But Hugh had already turned into another corridor angled next to the reception desk.

The bullet of the security guard's gun landed in the glass door of the main entrance of the hospital. The glass shattered in thousand pieces.

On the other side of the door, Detective Sam Moore pushed Amanda Ryan to the ground.

'Get down,' he yelled, diving on the concrete stairs.

Not knowing what was going on, Amanda did what the detective said. The shooting in front of the Los Angeles Police Department flashed back in her mind.

Detective Stan Moore removed hi .38 from his hostler and aimed towards the shattered glass. He didn't shot, but tried to focus his eyes inside the hospital corridor. A security guard ran towards him, his gun up in the air.

'Are you okay?' the security guard said as he approached the detective and Amanda, both looking up from the floor.

Stan Moore stood on his feet and removed his LAPD badge. 'What were you shooting at?' the detective said. 'Are you nuts?'

The security guard explained how he was chasing a man who was carrying a gun.

'Steve Thorn!' Amanda said as she rose to her feet. 'Where's Steve Thorn?'

'Who?' the security guard said.

'Where's the man with the gun?' Stan Moore interrupted.

The security man pointed to the corridor adjacent to the reception desk. 'This way.'

Stan Moore ran to the corridor.

The security guard hesitated for a split second, and then followed the detective.

Amanda, still shocked by the shooting, looked at both men disappearing at the end of the corridor.

She looked around and saw a nurse at the reception, mouth half-opened, still trying to figure out what happened. Amanda approached the nurse.

'I'm looking for Steve Thorn,' Amanda said to the nurse.

The nurse had her eyes on the main entrance door, obviously still in shock from the shooting. 'What happened here?' the nurse said, not absorbing Amanda's question.

'Mr Steve Thorn. Have you got a Mr Steve Thorn staying here?' Amanda said.

'Just a minute.' The nurse tapped into a computer. 'Yes we do. He's in the burnt ward, this way.' The nurse pointed to the end of the other corridor. 'Room 243A.'

'Thanks.'

Amanda ran down the hallway. She knew whoever was carrying a gun in the hospital had been there to kill Steve Thorn. If Steve had been trying to get in touch with her for the last few days, then he must have had something important to tell her. And according to detective Stan Moore it had to do with who blew his car up.

As Amanda approached room 243A, she felt herself trembling. She didn't think she had the strength to open the door of Steve's room. She looked around, wanting to ask someone for help, but there was no one where she was. A group of people, including nurses, doctors and security staff, was standing in front of the main entrance, examining the damage done to the glass door. She wanted to yell for someone to come, but at the same time, she knew she had to open the door.

Without thinking for another second, she pushed the door of room 243A wide open.

The first thing Amanda saw was the nurse on the floor, then the burned face of Steve Thorn.

It took her a few seconds to realize Steve Thorn wasn't dead. But his burnt skin looked shocking. Amanda had never seen a burnt victim before. Nothing in her life had prepared her for this. She had always thought of herself as open-minded, ready to embrace the impossible, the inexplicable, and the cruelty of life. And it was more or less another reason why she had chosen to work as a journalist.

But now, as she stood in front of Steve Thorn's bed, she realized how little she knew about herself. She froze for a few seconds, her eyes meeting those of Steve. She could see his pain in the tears streaming down his face.

'Are you all right?' Amanda finally said.

Steve didn't answer. He just shook his head, acknowledging he wasn't hurt.

Amanda knelt down to the nurse and shook her. 'Are you all right,' Amanda said, wondering if the nurse was dead or alive.

Devastated, Amanda yelled towards the open entrance of the room: 'Somebody help! There's an injured person here.'

In less than a minute, two doctors and a nurse appeared at the door. While they were taking care of the nurse, Amanda approached Steve Thorn's bed.

'I thought he was going to kill me,' Steve said, looking into Amanda's eyes.

'Who?'

'As if you didn't know.'

'Hugh Gawler,' Amanda said. 'I knew it. I knew he was behind all this.'

Steve took Amanda's hand. 'There's still so much you don't know. It's why I wanted to see you.'

'Why me?'

'Because you deserve to know the truth. Hugh Gawler has to be stopped. CableNews has to be stopped. The Texan Militia has to be stopped. Everything you hear, everything you read is a lie.'

'A lie?'

'Television news are not what they seem. Millions of people wake up every morning and switch on their televisions. They don't ask any questions. Everything they hear, everything they see, they believe it.'

Amanda thought Steve was in shock. 'It's going to be all right now. Don't worry.'

'Oh, but I'm worried, and so should you. A long time ago, the Church controlled the world, people, morality, governments. But all this has changed, and nobody has noticed. Everyone is too busy living their own little lives to see what's going on. No one has noticed the media is the new power.'

Amanda looked at Steve intrigued. It seemed to her he was suffering for paranoia.

'You get some rest,' Amanda said. 'I'm going to arrange for a police officer to stay outside your door.'

'You're not listening to me, Amanda.'

'I am listening. The media is bad, I know. Everybody knows it's a fact.'

'No, no. There's more to it. And I want you to know the truth. You always wanted a great story, a story which was going to make headlines. I'm giving you a story. I'm giving you the truth. Every major news CableNews reports is per-fabricated'

Intrigued, Amanda remembered what she had told Michael earlier on. It's what she had worked out. But she wanted to hear it out from Steve. 'But it's what news is all about,' she said. 'It's very hard to be objective when reporting news. There's always going to be someone's interpretation, no matter how dedicated a journalist is in presenting only the real story.'

'It's not what I'm talking about. I'm talking about creating news. The death of Senator Trevor Garry, for example. He didn't get killed by some maniac.'

'You know who killed him?'

'You haven't been listening, have you. Of course I know who killed him. CableNews killed him. Hugh Gawler killed him.'

Amanda liked to believe Steve Thorn was losing his mind, but when she looked in his eyes, she knew he was sincere. 'What are you talking about,' she said. 'I've done a show on the death of the Senator. It really happened. It wasn't fabricated.'

'Hugh Gawler ordered the killing. He wanted the senator dead.'

'But why?'

'Money. After the O.J. Simpson trial, the murder of Senator Trevor Garry made more money than any other news broadcast this year.'

'How do you know all this?'

'What about the Oklahoma bombing? It wasn't a militia group who did the whole thing. Okay, it was, but it was ordered to them from somewhere above. CableNews organized the Oklahoma bombing.'

And suddenly everything made sense to Amanda. The ratings CableNews had been getting were not a coincidence, nor a product of their hard work. CableNews fabricated its own news, making sure each story would shock the public, guaranteeing millions of dollars in return.'

Steve Thorn squeezed Amanda's hand. 'You see what I'm saying. Nothing you see or read is real. Everything is corrupted. There is always a motive behind a big story.'

'But this is impossible. It's just too...big.'

'Who do you think killed Kennedy? The CIA? The Mafia? No. It was the media. The media controls the minds of the world. Whoever controls the media controls the world. People believe everything they see on television, everything they read in the papers without asking questions. Whenever you have a conversation with someone, they always say, "but I read it in the paper" or "I saw it on television". Do you see what I mean?'

Amanda stood a few seconds without saying a word. If Steve Thorn was telling the truth, then it made sense Hugh Gawler wanted her dead. Hugh obviously thought she knew something.

'You see,' Steve continued, 'in the past people believed the bible. Blind faith, call it what you want. Today, we think we know better. We think we're more intelligent, more aware, more knowledgeable. The only thing we are is more naive. Everything we read or see is gospel to us.'

'If you knew all this, why didn't you tell me before? Why did you agree to send me to CableNews?'

'Hold it there. I never wanted you to go to CableNews. You wanted to spy there. I knew it would be dangerous. I also knew Hugh Gawler was a dangerous man.'

'Why all the truth now? And how did you find out about all this?'

Steve explained his part in the CableNews agreement.

Amanda shook her head in disbelief. She removed her hand from his. 'My God, Steve, you're in this up to your neck. And you were going to go along with it if Hugh hadn't bombed your car.'

'I'm not proud of what I've done. Believe me, coming so close to death made me see things in a different light. But I was prepared. I never really trusted Hugh Gawler. I had to protect myself.'

'How?'

'I organized the videocassette everyone has been looking for.'

'Detective Stan Moore got the videocassette He said there was nothing on it.'

'Oh, yes, there is. He just hasn't looked properly. There is enough evidence in there to put Hugh Gawler and Senator Terence Maxwell in jail for life.'

'What about Henry Limar?'

'He was working with me. He never liked Hugh Gawler. I asked him to make a duplicate of the videocassette I don't know what happened to him, but he freaked out. He couldn't take the pressure and decided to send a copy of the videocassette to Gavin White. Maybe he couldn't bare the fact an innocent man was going to get the death penalty for something he didn't do.'

'Who killed Henry Limar?'

'Hugh did, of course.'

'Gavin White?'

'Hugh arranged his death in prison. Money buys everything. And media power is pure money.'

Amanda was shattered. She believed so much in journalism. She though the media was there to tell the truth, to expose wrong doings, to tell the world what was going on.

And now she knew the truth.

The truth was a lie.

CHAPTER 155

Hugh Gawler ran out the back door of the hospital. He looked behind him one more time.

No one was following.

There was no time to waste. He had to leave town as soon as possible. Steve Thorn wasn't dead and he could expose Hugh at any moment.

Hugh placed the .38 semi-automatic in his waistband. Frantically, he looked around him. People were just going about their business. His car was parked in front of the hospital. He couldn't take a chance and go back to the car park. He would have to get a cab.

This was not the way Hugh had imagined things would end. But all in all, everything wasn't over yet.

He managed a smile as an image of the White House being blown to pieces appeared in his mind.

CHAPTER 156

Washington DC

Special Agent Bill Major was in a bad mood. At this morning's meeting with the National Security Council, he had been reprimanded about the inefficiency of the FBI. By now, the informant of the White House bombing should have been found. But it never happened, and now some smart alec was $10 million richer, courtesy of the United States government.

Wacko was about to repeat itself all over again.

This FBI had surrounded the training center and headquarters of the Texan Militia. If the informant told the truth, this was the group responsible for bombing not only the Alfred P. Murray building, but the prospective bombing of the White House.

When the president learned the White House was the next target, he lost his temper.

I want every men and women of the Texan Militia to be arrested. Use any force necessary to enter the buildings. Shoot at anything or anyone who threatens you in any way. I will not tolerate this kind of behavior while serving as the President of the United States of America. These people will pay for what they've done. Let there be no doubt; justice will be served.

There was only issue troubling Special Agent Bill Major: what if the informant had bluffed? What if the Texan Militia had nothing to do with the Oklahoma bombing? What if the White House was never going to get bombed? What if the informant was just an opportunist who was looking at a fast way to get rich?

But there was no time for questions. He would have to move fast. The men of the Texan Militia had locked themselves in the buildings, not showing any signs of wanting to give in. This damn thing was going to get out of hand. Major could feel it. He wished he could talk to someone, preferably Sam Willicon, the man responsible for this army of imbeciles.

Sitting behind the wheel of his Saturn, he picked up his cell phone and dialed the number of the Texan Militia headquarters.

Before he had time to say a word, a voice at the end of the line abused him.

'Get those cars our of my fuckin' property,' Sam Willicon screamed.

'We have a warrant,' Major said, calmly.

'A warrant for what? We're allowed to carry weapons. First Amendment, remember?'

'I'm afraid it's more serious.'

'What?' The voice of Sam Willicon was filled with impatience.

'This is the FBI-'

'I know who the fuck you are,' Sam Willicon interrupted.

'This is the FBI, and you're all under arrest for advocating the violent overthrow of the United States government.'

'You're a sick motherfucker! You guys have shit for brains. Why do I even bother talking to you?'

The line went dead.

Special Agent Bill Major picked up the CB receiver.

'We're moving in,' he said to all the other FBI agents surrounding the place.

In less than thirty seconds, thirty-seven FBI vehicles with agents armed to the teeth enclosed the Texan Militia buildings. A great cloud of dirt was lifted in the hot air, giving the surroundings an impression of a mirage.

Special Agent Bill Major was going to do what he was told. No mercy. No pity. And no bullshit. If Sam Willicon wanted to play games, he had chosen the wrong man. Whatever it would take, every single person in the establishment would be dragged out of the buildings and taken to jail. If any of them threatened them in any away, then his men would shoot to kill. No half-heartiness about it. If the informant told the truth, these were the people responsible for killing one hundred and eighteen civilians and public servants in Oklahoma. These were the people who made this great country a living hell. And they were the people who had to be dealt with in the only way they understood.

A bullet in the brain.

CHAPTER 157

Sam Willicon panicked when he saw the cars moving in on him.

'What do we do?' someone yelled from the east corner of the room.

Sam didn't know what everyone else was going to do, but he was out of here.

He ran our of the building and towards the helicopter sitting in the middle of the dirt yard. He was glad he had been given the chance to learn how to fly a helicopter during his three months stint in the Gulf in the eighties.

Some of his men were coming behind him, hoping to get a ride on the helicopter. But he knew it would be impossible. He couldn't take the risk of overloading, and there was no time to wait either. The first FBI vehicle was already in sight.

He jumped in the helicopter.

As the helicopter lifted itself above the ground, he could see FBI agents storming inside the buildings. Some were firing towards the helicopter. But within thirty seconds, the FBI agents looked like ants running in circles.

Sam Willicon headed south-east to Los Angeles.

He didn't know how the FBI found out about the White House bombing, but it sure as hell wasn't from one of his men. It could only mean the information leaked from Hugh Gawler's side. It had to be. There were only two people who led the operation. Maybe Hugh Gawler didn't know who gave the information away. But it's didn't matter. The fact remained it had to be from Hugh Gawler's team. And now the militia was finished.

Looking behind him, the militia buildings vanished into the horizon. God, damn it! This is not he way he wanted it to end.

Although he had seriously considered making the White House bombing his last project, being chased by the FBI for the rest of his life wasn't in his plans. Someone had to answer questions. Someone had to pay for this cock-up.

Sam Willicon knew he would have to land somewhere soon. The FBI would send some helicopters of their own soon, probably from the army.

He could take a plane to make the rest of the trip to L.A., but he knew there would be postings everywhere for his arrest. The only way to get there would be by hiding in a truck. But it would take forever.

No. He would have to come up with something better.

As the helicopter made a ninety degree turn into white clouds, Sam Willicon felt the rage building up inside him.

Whatever it took, he would get even with whoever had double-crossed him.

CHAPTER 158

Los Angeles

Detective Stan Moore was ahead of the security guard. Stan open the emergency exit door of the hospital at the back of the building.

The gunman had vanished.

Unwilling to admit defeat, he ran down the street, looking everywhere for a suspicious character. Although he wouldn't admit it to himself, deep down he knew he was looking for Hugh Gawler. He was certain Hugh was the one who bombed Steve's car and was now coming back to finish him. So, if Hugh wanted to kill Steve, it seemed reasonable to presume Steve knew the truth about something. Very likely, it would be the truth about Henry Limar's death, Senator Trevor Garry's and Gavin White's.

Suddenly Stan noticed someone hailing a cab and quickly jumping inside it.

It had to be the gunman.

Detective Stan Moore ran the sidewalk, pushing people aside, saying 'excuse me' to anyone he knocked by accident, trying in vain to catch up the cab caught in traffic.

As he got closer to the cab, Stan removed his .38 semi-automatic from his hostler. He ran down the middle of the road, zigzagging between cars, aiming the gun towards the taxi cab.

He reached the front passenger door and knocked on the window with the barrel of his gun.

A surprised Hugh Gawler turned around, mouth half opened.

'Get our of the car,' Stan said, pointing the gun at Hugh's head.

Suddenly Hugh threw the door open, sending Stan flying across the bonnet of another car.

Hugh removed his .38 from his waistband, aimed the gun at the detective and fired six consecutive shoots.

CHAPTER 159

Michael Hall hung up the public phone.

He couldn't resist a smile.

He's done it.

In spite of all the set backs, all his dreams would now come true.

He walked along the busy street to where his BMW was parked. Everything had gone according to plan. All he had to do now was to convince Amanda to leave for Australia with him. In Perth they would be safe, far away from the insanity of Los Angeles life. There would be no need to fight to the top of the corporate ladder, trying so hard to make oneself better than before. From here on everything was going to be smooth sailing.

As Michael stepped inside the BMW, he reasoned he had done the right thing anyway. What remained to be known was if Amanda would approve of his doing.

Michael turned on the ignition, slipped the gear stick on reverse, swerved to the right and got on the road.

If Amanda couldn't accept what he had done, then he would just loose her. The girl had this crazy ideology the world was perfect. Or maybe she didn't. But somehow she saw it as her duty to fix what ever was wrong with it.

Michael had understood a long time ago you cannot change the world, but mold yourself around it. His philosophy was simple. All you had to do was to make the most of the opportunities life offered and be fast enough to grab them. Too many people were locked in cages, in roles which they had set up for themselves, living in psychological chains, unwilling to take a chance, to push themselves beyond normality. So many lives which they wished they could have lived. So many sins they had been tempted to pursue. And when it is too late, when the deeds were finished, they would realize not having lived those lives which they dreamed was worse than if they had taken a chance. There was no future in fear of going beyond what you are. Fear was a big mistake, the only mistake. And Michael had learned to control his fear years ago. In a way, Amanda had taught him how to.

Michael had loved Amanda dearly.

And he still did.

But when it came to choosing between the present and the future, Michael always had an eye on the future. He could never live with the security of the present, knowing it could break at any time. Amanda had showed him that years ago. Just when he thought he had found peace and happiness in the love they had shared, everything had been take away from him. Although he had now recovered from the shock and the pain, it had been a life-changing experience. From the time she had dumped him, he had never been able to see life the way he used to. He couldn't enjoy the present any longer, so he made plans for tomorrow and worked hard on them. At least tomorrow gave you a chance to carry on, to push yourself towards some fantasy of perfect happiness.

In the mist of all these thoughts, deep down Michael realized he wasn't different from anyone else. Everyone he knew lived for tomorrow. Work hard today, and reap the rewards tomorrow. Maybe there was no other way to be. Maybe every man and woman out there wished for a better present and hanged on to the future, hoping for a perfect world of happiness.

And maybe this happiness would never come.

Michael made a turn on Sunset Boulevard. He smiled to himself, realizing he had reached his future already. He looked at his present and for the first time in years, decided he was happy. Not the happiness he had fantasized about for so long. Not the happiness he had shared with Amanda back when they were university students. The kind of happiness they had shared could never be traded for anything. It was priceless.

Who cares? Michael shrugged as he led the BMW in the driveway of his apartment.

CHAPTER 160

When Amanda arrived at the scene of the crime, she felt like her breath had been taken away. A sharp pain in the chest cut her oxygen intake for a few seconds.

On the ground, Detective Stan Moore lay in a pool of blood. People were all around him, but nobody did anything. Stan Moore looked dead.

Someone yelled, 'Is there a doctor around here?', but no one made a move.

Just when Amanda had left Steve Thorn's room a few minutes ago, a plain-clothed woman ran down the hospital corridor, screaming, 'help, help, there's someone who's just been shot outside!'.

And straight away Amanda had known. Before she got to the scene, her sixth sense had told her it was the detective who had been shot. If Hugh had been shot, she wouldn't have felt anything.

As she knelt helpless beside the detective, she could hear him struggling to say something. She couldn't understand what he said, but she knew he wasn't dead yet.

The detective continued to mumble, but Amanda didn't understand. She moved closer, her ear almost on top of his lips.

'My house keys are in my right pocket,' Stan Moore whispered. 'The videocassette Get the videocassette before anyone else gets to it.'

He jerked, blood pouring from his mouth, and closed his eyes for the last time.

CHAPTER 161

Hugh Gawler was certain detective Stan Moore couldn't have been alive after Hugh shoot him six times. It was impossible. When he left the detective for dead, the cab driver didn't really want to cooperate. Hugh had to get the driver to get him home with a gun to his head. He stopped a block from his house, and then shot the driver. He knew he couldn't let the driver live because he would have been witness. And so far there were few witnesses. Few but Steve Thorn who would probably tell everything to the police. Before Hugh came to the hospital to kill him, Steve couldn't have been absolutely certain it was Hugh who had planted the bomb in his car. But at the hospital, Hugh told him the truth, thinking Steve was going to die. And now Hugh was in deep trouble.

He thought quickly as he fumbled with the house keys. If detective Stan Moore was dead, which Hugh was certain he was, then there was no way to link Hugh directly with the murder. The only person who could testify to anything was Steve Thorn. By the time he did, and the police got their act together, Hugh had another half hour or so to get to the airport.

Once in the house, he raced to his bedroom. From the drawer on the side of his bed, he removed a large-sized, yellow envelope. From it, he retrieved three fake pieces of identification. He knew one day they would come in handy, so he had them made.

In his kind of job, Hugh knew the bomb might have exploded at any time. There was no guarantee of safety, no guarantee of trust, no guarantee of anything. And after today's little ordeal, Hugh knew he had to start all over again. Not long ago, he thought if he had to start all over again, he would never find the strength. But now he knew it was a lie. He didn't want to go to jail. He didn't want to face a jury and spend months on trial being humiliated by the media and the public. He had to get out of the country before they found him.

Hugh went to his study upstairs, placed a briefcase on his desk and popped it open. In the various compartments of the briefcase, he place the IDs. Next, he dialed the combination from a safe underneath his desk. From the safe, he removed one million dollars in US currency and switched it to the briefcase.

He knew something might go wrong one day. That little stash was the cure. One million dollars was enough to get him going again, wherever he might decide to go.

Hugh closed the briefcase and checked his watch. He had no time to do anything else. He had to get to Los Angeles Airport – LAX - and take the first plane to Mexico. Once in Mexico, he would be able to figure out a way of getting to Europe or Australia, away from it all.

He removed the .38 semi-automatic form his waistband and thought for a minute. As much as he needed the gun, he couldn't go through the airport with it. It would be too dangerous. It was bad enough he had to risk taking one million dollars cash out of the country. The gun would trigger the metal detector at the airport. The gun had to stay behind.

Hugh slammed the .38 semi-automatic on top of his desk. Aware of the minutes flying by, he looked at his watch again.

I have to hurry. I have to get out of this place before they get me.

On his way down the stairs, he though about Amanda Ryan. Not a long thought, but one which made him angry. If she hadn't come into his life, maybe this whole thing would have never happened. Things wouldn't have cocked-up with Steve Thorn, and he wouldn't have acted like a love-sick idiot and taken so many risks. God, he hated himself so much for having been so weak. All these problems for a god-damn woman. To this world they bring us, and to hell they send us back! He should have foreseen a long time ago how his weakness for women would let him down one day. He should have seen his obsession for the flesh would cost him his dreams, his good fortune, his life. But at the back of his mind, he always told himself everything was going to be all right. Many time he played these little games with himself, telling himself his sexual obsession wasn't really an obsession at all, but just the way all men are. And how he had it all under control any way. Oh, yes, he did. Because if he didn't, he would have never been so successful at what he did.

But now, as he stepped behind the wheels of his other car, a red Porsche, he knew he fucked up. And it made him more angry than anything. He didn't know if he hated Amanda Ryan or himself more. In time he would learn to forget Amanda Ryan, but he would not be able to forgive himself because he would have to live with his mistake for the rest of his life, in some foreign country where he would rather not be.

The tires of the Porsche screeched on the pavement as he took a turn into Wilshire Avenue

He looked at his watch again.

CHAPTER 162

Amanda Ryan found the videocassette inside the recorder of the detective's home. She pressed the play and FWD button, but all she saw was a TV show.

There's nothing on this videocassette, she thought. But it could be true. How could this whole videocassette business lead to nowhere? How could they be nothing on the videocassette? She remembered something Steve Thorn had said.

There is enough evidence in there to put Hugh Gawler and Senator Terence Maxwell in jail for life.

Senator Terence Maxwell.

The opposition leader

And it was why Senator Trevor Garry had been killed.

But the videocassette. Why wasn't there anything on the damn videocassette?

Amanda played the videocassette on fast forward, looking for anything abnormal.

And then, while the videocassette was running at triple speed, she thought maybe the important part of the videocassette made have been inserted somewhere in the news footage.

She continued to watch carefully, certain she was right.

As she sat there, fist clenched, nothing unusual came on the screen.

And then the videocassette came to an end. White snow all over the screen.

Damn it!

Amanda threw the empty box of the videocassette against the television. This whole thing was useless. There was no evidence.

And then her mind fixated itself to the bloodied face of the detective taking his last breath in the middle of L.A. traffic.

Why did it have to end this way? Why did the bad people always win? Why, why, why? Wasn't there a God out there who cares about anything?

Amanda put her hands to her face and sobbed. She was frightened but angry at the same time. If only she could have done something sooner. If only she knew what was going on, then maybe she could make things right again. But her hands were tight, and she had nothing to go on with.

And then the television screen came alive again.

At first, Amanda heard whispers. She thought it was in her head, but the colors on the screen made her take her hands away from her face.

On the screen, she recognized Hugh Gawler.

And another man.

She looked carefully. She remembered what Steve Thorn said. The other man had to be Senator Terence Maxwell.

The ten minute segment unfolded in front of her eyes. Her tears dried up as she watched Hugh Gawler switch money from one briefcase to another.

'I've asked not to be disturbed. You don't have to worry about a thing. Let's gets this over and done with.'

'What if they find out? What if someone finds out? My career would be over. I would go to jail.'

'If someone finds out, take a one-way ticket to Mexico. It's what I would do.'

When the videocassette ended with a close-up of Hugh Gawler, Amanda froze the frame. She stared at the television tube.

If someone finds out, take a one-way ticket to Mexico.

She tried to understand what was going on behind the mask of the man she had once been infatuated by.

It's what I would do.

And then she stood from her seat.

She had to get to Hugh Gawler before he left the country.

Filled with anger, she grabbed the keys of her car from the coffee table. There was no way Hugh was going to get away with this.

She had to stop him.

CHAPTER 163

Michael Hall was in his apartment, packing a few belongings for his overseas trip to Zurich. He was still wondering whether he should tell anything to Amanda or not. He wanted to tell her, but he knew she might betray him just for the sake of doing the right thing.

But did he do anything wrong? As Michael closed a suitcase and opened another, he felt he didn't do anything wrong. It had been a fair trade. The cops wanted information, he gave them information for a price. It happened every day in every city around the world. Michael was only an informant and got paid for doing his job. The $10 millions were not stolen money. They were given to him in good faith to prevent another bombing by passing on the information to the authorities. The White House will probably not go up in flames. If it had, the cost of repair and death would have been more than $10 million. He had already told this fact to the FBI.

He slammed the second briefcase. Damn, if he knew he had done the right thing, why was his conscious still bothering him? And the face of Amanda Ryan coming back to mind?

He turned to the window of the bedroom, overlooking the center of Los Angeles, and recalled all the times he and Amanda made love. She had come back into his life at the wrong time. If it had been only a few years ago, there would not have been any hesitation as to what to do. But now everything was different. She thought he was still the same person she had met at university, but he wasn't. Life had changed him. After he had lost Amanda, he had lost faith in other people. The only person he could rely on was himself. And when she came back into his life, he wasn't sure if he could trust her again. He tried. He played the game of the lovesick puppy, even to point of fooling himself.

Michael turned away from the window, certain he was making the right choice. He didn't need Amanda in his life. There would be plenty of other women out there. And with all the money he now had, he would be able to pick and choose who he wanted. Money was everything. Money changed lives. With money, he could buy anyone he wanted.

A smile on his face, Michael grabbed one suitcase in each hand. His flight to Zurich was not due for another three hours, but he felt safer going to the airport early. This way he would be certain to get on the plane even if there was a traffic jam.

He knew once he disappeared out of the country, the FBI would eventually link his disappearance to the calls they've been getting about the White House bombing, especially if Hugh Gawler got caught. And the way things were going, Hugh Gawler was very close to getting caught.

But by then Michael would be far away in another place.

Another time.

CHAPTER 164

Amanda didn't know what she was going to do once she caught up with Hugh. What if he was at the airport? How was she going to tackle him?

The windows of the SUV open, Amanda was rushing at seventy miles per hour in a suburban street. She knew she was taking a hell of a risk of being pulled over, but it was a chance she was willing to take.

She could have called the police, but it would have taken too long. And they would have had to believe her in the first place. Give or take half an hour, eventually they would have sent someone at the airport just in case she was right. But a half hour could have been the difference between Hugh Gawler leaving the country or being arrested.

No.

She had to get to the airport first. She would call the police once she was at the airport.

CHAPTER 165

Sam Willicon booked a flight straight to Los Angeles International Airport. When he bought the ticket, he expected the cops to come around from the corner and jump on him. But nothing happened.

And now that his plane had landed in Los Angeles, he almost felt safe. He knew it would be a matter of time before the FBI would find him.

But it was a chance he would have to take.

He still had some business to resume.

He knew he had little chance of escaping from the authorities if he stayed in the USA. His best chance was to leave the country, to go somewhere where no one knew who he was. The obvious choice was Mexico. He never really liked Mexico, but it would have to do for the time being.

'Welcome to Los Angeles, the city of the angels,' said the captain, projecting his metallic voice around the Boeing 747. 'The weather is magnificent out there, and I hope you will enjoy your stay in Los Angeles. All the staff looks forward to seeing you again.'

CHAPTER 166

When Hugh Gawler arrived at LAX, he was nervous. He looked around him, thinking someone might jump on him at any moment.

He booked the earliest flight to Mexico.

Hugh knew he had to make himself invisible for the next hour or so. He decided to stay at an airport bar. If he sat quietly by himself, no one would notice him.

His plane ticket safely tucked in the breast pocket of his sports coat, Hugh Gawler ordered a short black and sat at a table at the fat end of the coffee shop. He unfolded a newspaper *The Los Angeles Times* and scanned trough the front page.

On page three, there was a small paragraph dedicated to the body found at the CableNews headquarters. At this stage nothing had yet been linked to Senator Trevor Garry or Gavin White. When the truth would unfold, no thanks to Steve Thorn, Hugh knew the further away he would be from Los Angeles, the better his chances of remaining free.

But it was not totally true.

Having lost everything overnight wasn't freedom. He had left behind years of his life, sleepless nights, dangerous liaisons, and as a result, never found anyone who loved him for who he was. All this mess for a lousy million dollars and a one-way ticket to Mexico.

Hugh sipped his short black and lifted his eyes above the newspaper to check the crowd.

Everyone was too busy going about their business to notice him. With thousands of people coming in and out of LAX every day, it was a really good place to hide.

He folded the newspaper and placed it on the round table. His thoughts drifted to Amanda Ryan. She was the only woman he would have loved to marry. She looked good. A perfect match for his ego. And at the same time, he hated her so much. What he couldn't figure out was why she was so much on his mind.

410

It didn't matter, anyway. It was all over now.

Hugh stood from behind the table and walked to the bar.

'Straight Southern Comfort and ice,' he told the bartender.

Back at his table, Hugh drank the Southern Comfort slowly.

And this drinking problem.

All right, he had to admit it. He had a drinking problem. He had to face the fact he had lost everything else in his life, so he might as well have admitted he had a drinking problem. Once in Mexico, he would sober up. No more scams. Lay in the sun and get drunk on Pina Collada instead.

His thoughts still lost between America and Mexico, Hugh grabbed the newspaper. Before he had time to turn the first page, he saw Amanda Ryan walking straight past the cafe.

He plunged his head in the newspaper.

He lifted his head up again.

Had he been dreaming?

Suddenly, his body froze, his mind unable to accept what he had just seen. Why would Amanda be at the airport? No, he must have dreamed it. He stared at his glass of Southern Comfort. It had to be the drink and the fact he couldn't get Amanda out of his mind.

He slammed his first on the table.

Damn! The bitch is here!

Furious, he stood from his chair. He was certain now he had seen Amanda. The way she walked, the color of her hair. This couldn't have been a coincidence. She found him. And if she found him, then the cops would find him too. Maybe the cops knew he was at the airport. Maybe they didn't. And if they didn't, then Amanda Ryan would tell them. Not unless someone shut her up.

Hugh gulped the rest of his Southern Comfort and raced out of the bar.

CHAPTER 167

Amanda looked around the shops frantically. How was she going to find Hugh Gawler in a crowd like this. For all she knew, he could already be on his way to Mexico.

And then a thought crossed her mind. If he hadn't left for Mexico yet, then all she had to do was wait at the departure lounge. He would have to walk past her. She thought it was a good idea, but then what? Would she be able to confront him in front of everyone? And even if she did, what was she going to say, or how was she going to stop him?

Amanda was angry at her inability to come up with a plan. Even if she did find Hugh Gawler, she knew her hands were tied. She needed someone to help her. But who? If she asked security guards, they would think she was crazy. And even if they believed her, they would need a good reason to stop Hugh Gawler boarding the plane.

Amanda kept on probing frantically inside the shops. But Hugh wasn't there. She was going insane. Since she came to America, her life had been nothing but a lie. And now she was paying the price. She wished she had never left Australia. She should have stayed with her parents. Maybe there she would have found the time and peace of mind to become the novelist she dreamed of becoming.

But all this dreaming and feeling sorry for herself was getting nowhere.

Swallowed by the crowd, Amanda felt trapped and useless. A sickening sensation rose from her stomach. She looked around for a bathroom. The crowd was driving her crazy. She had to find a bathroom to get away from the crowd for a while, to find some coherence in her thoughts.

Suddenly she saw the sign pointing to the women's rest room.

Desperate, she almost ran the last ten feet to the door.

The sickness in her stomach rose to her esophagus. She reached the door and pushed it open.

No one else was in the rest room.

She locked herself in a cubicle, lowered her head above the toilet bowl, and let the sickness come out of her.

CHAPTER 168

Hugh Gawler caught sight of Amanda Ryan one second before she disappeared inside the women's rest room.

He knew it was her.

Okay, he thought to himself, how am I going to handle this?

If he waited for Amanda to come out of the rest room, there would be little he could do. Now, he regretted not carrying the gun with him to the airport. He could have dumped it into a bin just before boarding.

Maybe he could convince Amanda to go with him somewhere quiet. But, would she fall for it? At the hospital, Hugh saw Amanda with the detective. She must have known it was him who killed the detective. Why else would she be at the airport?

Hugh glanced around him, making sure no one was watching him.

No one was approaching the women's rest room.

Damn! It's now or never!

He slammed open the rest room door.

CHAPTER 169

Just when Amanda pulled her head up from the toilet, she heard the door of the rest room being slammed open.

She thought her heart was going to come out of her chest. She passed one hand over her forehead to wipe the perspiration. Anxious, she listened. Whoever had walked in the room was tiptoeing across the tiled floor.

And then Amanda had this feeling something was terribly wrong. It was like being in a bad dream and aware it is a bad dream, but not able to do anything about it. Suddenly she had this sudden fear this was where her life was going to end. It had happened before. She looked at the plywood walls of the small cubicle and felt it. She knew death was near.

She could still hear the footsteps outside the cubicle. Although she had just passed her hand on her forehead, it was covered in perspiration.

She stood still, waiting for whoever was out there to enter one of the other cubicles. She hoped it was another woman who wanted to use the toilet.

But it wasn't.

And she knew it wasn't because she could feel the male presence in the room. There was no rational way for her to explain how she knew it was a man who was in the room. Female extinct, she told herself. It was this sixth sense of knowing but being unable to point it out.

Then his voice cut through her soul like a butcher's knife.

'I know you're in there, Amanda,' Hugh Gawler said.

Amanda grabbed the toilet paper holder.

My God, he's here. I was right.

'I need to talk to you, Amanda,' Hugh continued. 'This whole thing has been a mistake. Why don't you come out and we'll talk.'

Amanda didn't answer. If she came out of the cubicle, he could shot her. She knew he had a gun because he used it on the detective.

Hugh was getting agitated. No one else had come in the rest room yet. He had to hurry. But at the same time he didn't want to frighten Amanda. If she screamed, someone might come to her help.

'Amanda,' Hugh said. 'It's very embarrassing to be standing in a women's toilet. What do you think is going to happen? You think I'm going to shot you. If I wanted to kill you, I would have done it by now. After all, there are only twelve cubicles. Come on, I'll buy you a coffee outside.'

Amanda held her head with both hands. She didn't know what to do. Sure, if he wanted to shot her, he could have done it by now. Maybe he really wanted to talk. Maybe there would be just talk and it would be over. But he killed the detective. How could she trust him?

'What about Detective Stan Moore,' she said, surprised to hear her own voice echoing in the rest room.

Hugh smiled to himself. 'I didn't shot the detective. Believe me, this is all a misunderstanding.'

'Why should I believe you?'

'If you come out, we'll have a talk outside.'

'I'm not coming out until you leave the room.'

'Fine,' Hugh said, trying to control his anger. 'You know what your problem is Amanda? You never trust anyone. You always think someone is out there to get you. You live in this world of paranoia. I'm only here to help you. You came to find me at the airport, so why are you running away from me now? I'm here now, aren't I?'

Amanda knew she couldn't stay in the cubicle forever. 'I'll come out if you leave the room. Wait for me outside.'

'All right,' Hugh said, walking towards the exit door. 'Don't make me wait too long.'

Amanda listened carefully and heard the footsteps leaving the room. She waited sixty seconds, listening for any noise. But the room was completely silent. She stood on the edge of the toilet bowl and peaked around the room.

No one was there.

She stepped down off the toilet bowl.

It was time to face Hugh Gawler.

CHAPTER 170

Michael Hall arrived at LAX a bit nervous. He knew there was no way anyone could have found out he had been the one making the calls to the FBI in Washington, but his mind would not be at rest until his feet would be firmly grounded in Zurich. In the meantime anything was possible.

He parked his BMW in the long-term car park of the airport, knowing this was the last time he drove the car gave him so much pleasure. But he didn't care. It was a company car anyway. With the $10 million dollars he will be able to buy a fleet of BMWs.

He felt he would have no problem adapting to a life of luxury. After all, he had been thinking about it since he joined CableNews. It was only when Henry Limar told him the truth about Hugh Gawler that he saw an opportunity not to be missed. Hugh Gawler was a dangerous man. Michael knew it was factual, and therefore he didn't want to take part in any of his shaky deals. If anything went wrong, Michael would go down like everyone who had crossed Hugh. The best way to win was to get Hugh behind bars and get rewarded for it. And it's exactly what he was doing.

Walking past the airport lounge, Michael thought about Amanda and wondered if a real hero would have left her behind. He pictured himself the character of a major blockbuster movie. In the movie, the hero would have taken the heroine with him. But real life was far more complex than a motion picture. The risks were stacked up to high. And he didn't think he loved Amanda enough to risk everything.

Whatever he might have thought as he stood in front of the cashier, he knew it was too late to change his mind. The gentleman on the other side of the counter handed him his ticket to freedom.

'Have a good trip, Mr Hall,' the man said, his rows of teeth sparkling like in a toothpaste commercial.

Michael took his ticket and walked towards the departure

lounge. He felt the surge of excitement one has when traveling on a one-way ticket. It was like a re-birth. The rest of his life was in front of him, and this time he would be able to do whatever he wanted with it. There would be no obligation to work for someone else, to force a smile at people whom he would rather slap in the face, or to pretend he was happy with his monotonous everyday high profile job.

No.

This time Michael Hall had won the war. He carved himself a nice piece of freedom and was going to enjoy every minute of it.

And then, just when he got close to a Starbucks, he saw Hugh Gawler coming out of the women's rest room. For a few seconds, he thought his mind was playing a trick on him. He stood on the spot and stared at the man who was now looking directly at him and his briefcase.

Michael smiled at Hugh to ease the tension, but all he got in return was a stern look.

Frightened, Michael checked the side of his jacket and felt the . 38 semi-automatic. He had taken it with him just in case something went wrong at the last minute.

And something had gone wrong.

Of course, he was going to throw the gun in a bin before boarding the plane to Zurich, but until then he felt it would have been a bad idea to separate himself completely from it.

Now he knew he had been right.

Michael approached Hugh, forcing himself to smile as if everything was perfectly normal. But deep down, he was certain Hugh knew something was wrong. The dark stare Hugh gave him in return for his smile explained everything.

As Michael walked towards Hugh, questions raced in his mind.

What is he doing here? Why was he in the women's toilet? Did he know I was coming to the airport? Is he really here to get me? If he knew I was here, how did he find out? What am I going to say when I get face to face with him?

But Michael didn't have time to answer the questions.

Hugh Gawler rushed back inside the women's restroom.

CHAPTER 171

Amanda Ryan had just splashed cold water on her face when Hugh waltzed back in the room.

'You bitch!' he yelled as he grabbed her from behind, his arm around her neck.

'What are you doing?' Amanda managed to say.

'Had to get your little boyfriend on this, didn't you?' Hugh said, his face touching hers. 'Things could have been fine between the two of us. But you spoiled everything.'

'What on earth are you talking about?'

But before Hugh had time to answer, the door was swung open, and Michael Hall appeared with his .38 semi-automatic pointed towards Hugh and Amanda.

Michael tried to understand quickly what was going on.

'Let her go,' he said, when he saw Hugh tightening his grip around Amanda's neck.

'I can't breath!' Amanda said.

'Let her go, God damn it!' Michael said. 'Or I'll shot.'

'You try to shot, and you might get her by accident. What were you two trying to do? Frame me?'

'This is all a mistake,' Michael said. 'Just let her go.'

'You bet it's a mistake. You put the gun down, or I snap her neck like a sparrow.'

Amanda's eyes were wide open. She could feel Hugh's arm tightening around her neck. She grasped desperately for air. Her eyes met those of Michael.

Jesus, Michael thought, it's all I need right now.

'We make a deal,' Michael said. 'I give you the gun, and you let us go.'

'You don't have the choice, anyway,' Hugh said, confident Michael would not shot him. 'Toss the gun over.'

'All right, all right. Just take it easy. Loosen your grip a bit.

419

You're killing her.'

'Oh, my heart is broken,' Hugh said sarcastically. 'What's the matter lover boy? You're scared you won't find anyone else to suck your dick?'

Michael knelt down. 'Here's the gun. I'm placing it on the floor. Now let her go.'

'Kick it towards me with your foot.'

Michael stood up and kicked the gun towards Hugh Gawler.

The gun stopped halfway between Michael and Hugh.

'You asshole,' Hugh said. 'You did it on purpose, didn't you? You want her to die?'

'Hey,' Michael said. 'The gun is right there. Get it.' He raised his arms up. 'I'm not moving. Get the gun and let her go.'

Hugh looked at Michael straight in the eyes. 'I knew I shouldn't have trusted a young turkey straight out of uni. Fuckin' degree this, fuckin' degree that. You think a god-damn piece of paper makes you king of the fucking planet, don't you?'

'Come on, Hugh. It doesn't have to be this way. Just let Amanda go. We'll leave the room. You can do what you want.'

'Sure. As soon as I'm out the door, the whole LAPD is going to land on my arse.'

'What other choice do you have?'

Hugh moved forward, still holding Amanda in his grip. He grabbed the gun from the floor, and threw Amanda towards Michael.

'I can kill you both,' Hugh said. 'It's my other option. After all, your the only two who can get me into trouble right now.'

Hugh moved forward, the .38 semi-automatic pointed at Michael's head. 'Get to the back of the room,' he said, as he circled the room.

As Hugh moved towards the exit door, Michael and Amanda walked backwards to the cubicles.

'You two don't deserve to live,' Hugh said, angry from seeing Michael holding Amanda. 'I gave you both everything, and you've turned your backs on me.'

'It's not true,' Michael said. 'We—'

'Shut up,' Hugh interrupted.

Hugh raised the gun and aimed it at Amanda. 'You first. It's your fault everything's gone wrong.'

'But—'

'Die, bitch!'

Hugh pressed the trigger just when Michael threw himself in front of Amanda. The bullet of the .38 semi-automatic landed in

Michael's stomach.

Michael screamed in horror.

Hugh shot another two times, missing both Michael and Amanda. The plaster on the wall behind Amanda was blown into bits.

Amanda threw herself on the floor, next to Michael who was now feeling the full effect of the bullet in his stomach.

Michael never felt something so painful in his life. And he knew if he made it through this alive, he would never feel anything like it again. He had heard the most painful way to die was with a bullet in your stomach and be left to bleed for hours. It had only been a few seconds, but the pain was already excruciating. He wasn't sure if he wasn't better off dying now or waiting for a few more hours.

Hugh was angry with himself for having missed Amanda.

'I'm going to get you, bitch,' he said, pointing the gun towards Amanda. 'No one, but me, is coming out of here alive.' He walked up to Amanda and stood in front of her, the barrel of the .38 semi-automatic only a few inches from her head. 'You should have known better than to betray me.'

'You sonofabitch,' Amanda said, looking straight into Hugh's eyes. 'You think I'm scared of you? You want to shot me? Then shot.'

Hugh looked at the face of the woman he once loved. Standing there with a gun pointed to her head, he felt like forcing her to make love to him. He always wanted to make love to Amanda, but all she had done was play games with him.

Hugh pressed the trigger half way.

Amanda closed her eyes. She remembered the shooting in the stairway at CableNews, and how the hitman nearly got her. She waited for the blast of the gun, this time not thinking she was going to get away.

But the gun didn't go off.

'Don't think you're getting away with it so easily,' Hugh said. 'You're coming with me.'

CHAPTER 172

Sam Willicon looked around, certain FBI agents were going to jump on him at any minute.

But no one paid attention to him. People at the airport just went on with their own business.

And frankly, Sam Willicon just looked like one of the many travelers, not like the leader of what used to be the most powerful militia in the USA.

Dressed in a blue business shirt and brown pants, he could have been one of thousands of business travelers going from Washington D.C. to Los Angeles, away from family and colleagues, living on a nice allowance and taking advantage of the taxation loopholes.

But instead he was a man filled with rage. His life had been ruined by someone who lived in the god-damn city of Los Angeles. Before he would leave for Mexico, Sam Willicon was going to make sure the traitor was going to pay for his sins. The militia no longer existed. Everything he had worked for had vanished overnight. It wasn't a change Sam felt he was ready to accept.

Sam Willicon knew no one in Los Angeles, apart from Hugh Gawler, the man he was hunting.

He knew where Hugh lived and worked. It would be easy to track him down.

Still paranoid he might be followed by FBI agents, Sam Willicon kept his eyes around every corner of his viewing distance.

Suddenly, just has he was about to turn into Starbucks, Hugh Gawler appeared in front of him.

Hugh was about fifty feet ahead with a young woman by his side.

Hugh's eyes met those of Sam. And immediately, Hugh knew why Sam had come to Los Angeles.

Amanda saw the two men looking at each other. She didn't know what was going to happen, but the fear in Hugh's eyes told her it wasn't good.

Hugh shoved Amanda aside. His legs apart, he pointed his gun towards Sam Willicon.

Sam drew his gun from his waistline and aimed it at Hugh.

Hugh fired five shots from .38 semi-automatic, sending the crowd around him into a frenzy.

But Sam had already dived on the floor, rolling in a Military style, his gun pointing directly at Hugh.

Another shot.

Sam felt a burning sensation at the back of his head. He passed one hand behind his neck and felt wetness. Before he had time to look at his bloody hand, he fell face down on the floor.

'FBI,' yelled Special Agent Bill Major, standing behind Sam Willicon, his .38 pointing directly at Hugh Gawler. 'Throw away your gun and keep your hands behind your head.'

But instead, Hugh shot twice towards the FBI agent.

Without further warning, Special Agent Bill Major fired three consecutive shots at Hugh's head.

Amanda turned her head towards Hugh and saw him fall backwards, leaving a stream of blood hanging in mid-air before splashing on the floor.

When Hugh hit the floor, Amanda heard the crushing of his skull.

She closed her eyes and hoped to God the nightmare was over.

CHAPTER 173

Michael Hall was laying on the hospital bed.

The pain in his stomach was unbearable in spite of the pain killers the doctor had given him.

When they found him in the women's rest room at the airport, he had lost a lot of blood. He remembered Amanda being next to him, telling him everything was going to be all right. And then, on his way to the hospital, he wondered how he could have been so selfish and so blind. He wasn't sure if it was because he felt so close to death, his eyes suddenly opened themselves. Amanda had been so good to him, so genuine, giving everything in her heart. But in return, all he thought about was to leave the country with millions of dollars and make her wonder for the rest of her life where he had vanished to.

A knock on the door.

A nurse walked in.

'The doctor said he shouldn't have any visitors,' the nurse said. 'You have five minutes.'

A man in a gray flannel suit walked in the room. He carried an attaché case.

The nurse left the room.

Michael's eyes met those of Ron Fisher, his solicitor.

Ron Fisher didn't look at ease.

'You're okay?' the solicitor said.

'I've seen better days.' Michael forced a smile. 'Did you get the papers I asked you to bring?'

'It's all here,' Ron said, opening the attaché case. 'All you have to do is sign.'

Ron placed a pen in Michael's hand and the legal document positioned within Michael's reach.

In a tremendous effort, Michael managed to scribble something which looked more or less like his signature.

Ron Fisher took the document back and witnessed it with his signature.

'Is there anything else I can do for you?' the solicitor asked.

'I don't think so. You've done enough already. Just make sure you follow this through.'

'I will.'

When Ron Fisher left the room, Michael closed his eyes and thought about Amanda.

He knew he had been wrong all along.

He never stopped loving her.

And then he took his last breath.

EPILOGUE

Perth, Australia: one year later

Amanda was looking out the window of her study. It was nearly midday, but she wasn't in a hurry. Being late didn't matter anymore. She realized lateness was not a sign of weakness after all. The fear of lateness was a weakness in itself.

On her desk were the pages of the novel she had just completed. She wondered why she never began to write earlier instead of having made life so hard for herself.

It had been a year already, but it seemed like it was only yesterday since Michael died.

She had spent hours with Special Agent Bill Major and other FBI interrogators. With her help they put together the puzzle of the story. It seemed the informant to the FBI had been Hugh Gawler after all. And this was why Sam Willicon had killed him. It's what they all thought anyway.

But to the FBI, one thing remained unanswered. Where were the ten millions dollars they gave Hugh Gawler? The FBI never told Amanda about the money. If it was leaked to the press, the US government would end up looking like a bunch of idiots. It would be the FBI's problem to figure out what had happened to the money.

In the next few months which followed, public outrage had escalated to near-hysteria. People no longer knew what they had to believe. For the past two years all they have been fed was lies on television. The fabrication of news by CableNews had damaged the news industry beyond repair. It would take years before the public would be able to have faith in television news again.

But for Amanda, everything had been too much. She decided the best thing to do was to leave America and come back to her parents.

And she had done the right thing.

With her first novel finished, she was going to take it easy for the next six months. She still had so much anger in her when she came

426

back from the States, she couldn't find any peace. Writing the novel helped her to focus on something other than the catastrophe she had just lived through.

But not matter how hard she tried to forget the past, she could never forget Michael. She knew if love came only once in a life time, then in her life, it had come and gone.

Maybe one day there would a new opportunity.

A new person to share her life with.

Six months later, while Amanda was in the kitchen making some lunch, someone knocked on the door.

When she opened the front door of her apartment, a business man stood in front of her, handing her a card.

'Amanda Ryan?' the man asked.

'Yes,' Amanda said, looking at the card. Ron Fisher, Solicitor. There was a US address.

'I've got something for you.'

Amanda looked intrigued.

'You're not an easy person to find,' the man said. 'I have been looking all over America for you.'

Amanda didn't answer. She was anxious to find out what was going on.

The man removed a form from his briefcase. 'You've inherited ten million dollars.' The man gave Amanda a check and a pink form. 'If you'd like to sign here then everything will be finalized.'

Amanda looked at the US ten million dollar check with her name on it. 'Who is it from?' Amanda asked, still shocked by the eight-figure check.

'The will specifies the source remains anonymous. Just trust me, it's all legal and all genuine.'

When the man left, Amanda was left with the ten million dollar check in her hand.

And then, without anyone telling her, she knew where the money came from.

She didn't why or how. She knew.

She just knew.

He never stopped loving her.